A KING SO COLD

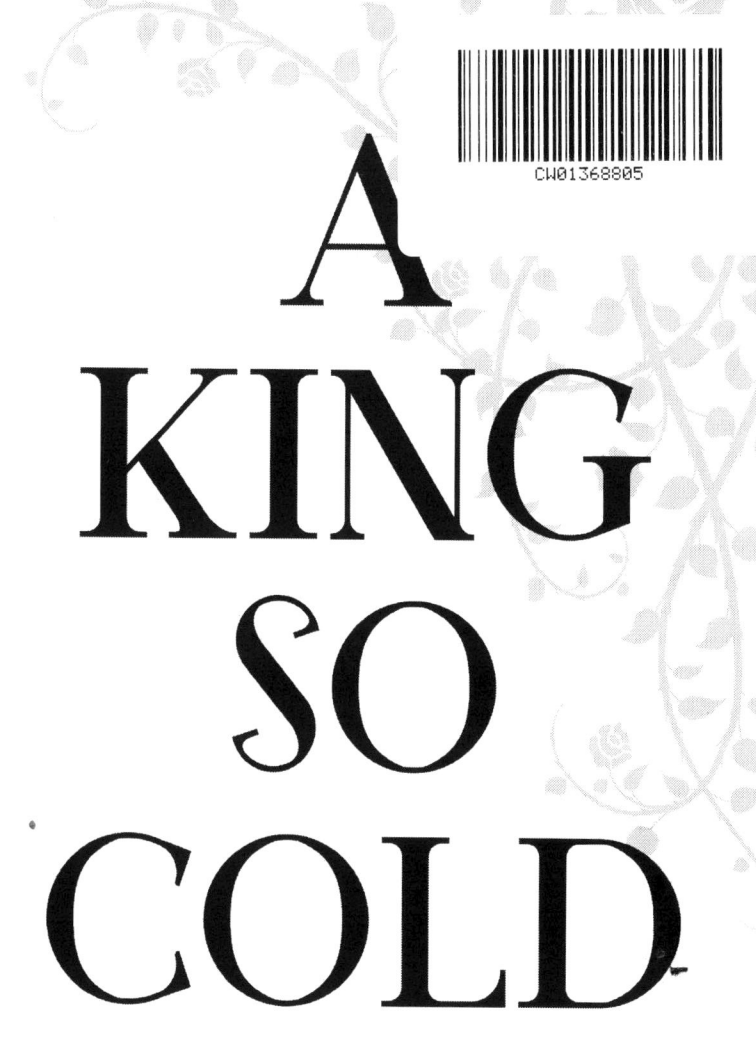

ELLA FIELDS

Copyright © 2020 by Ella Fields

All rights reserved.
No part of this book may be reproduced, copied, resold or distributed in any form, or by any electronic or mechanical means, without permission in writing from the author, except for brief quotations within a review.

This book is a work of fiction.
Names, characters, businesses, organizations, places, events and incidents are either the product of the author's imagination or used in a fictitious manner. Any resemblance to actual persons, living or dead is entirely coincidental.

Editor: Jenny Sims, Editing4Indies
Formatting: Stacey Blake, Champagne Book Design
Cover design: Sarah Hansen, Okay Creations

For me.

PART ONE

KISSING GHOSTS

ONE

Night enclosed us as I threw my head back and screamed.

Teeth scraped over my neck, and I felt Zadicus's muscles seize, the air thrumming over my skin as his seed emptied inside me.

I hissed, shoving his face away before ridding my body of him and crawling off the bed.

A sinister chuckle followed my steps to the bathing chamber. "So touchy."

"I've warned you not to do that." The door shut over my words with a boom that thundered through the rock and mortar, a charged wind catching my hair and cooling my flushed face.

After cleaning up, I washed my hands, staring with empty iridescent eyes at the pale hue to my cheeks in the mirror. A swipe of my finger over my lips and the red turned pink.

I made a mental note to eat more. Gaunt wasn't a look I favored, and my cheekbones were starting to resemble that of a corpse.

"Twenty-one summers old," Zad said, lighting a pipe he kept in the top drawer of the nightstand. "Does that mean you'll soon be through with the tantrums?"

I stalked naked to my dressing table and took a seat. "We all know you're a bore, Zad. There's no need to open your pretty mouth to inform us."

A wry smile curled his sin-shaped lips. "Why not kill me then? You seem rather taken with murder of late."

That was a question I'd asked myself a time or two before. However, Lord Zadicus had governed the east since before I was born, and he held too much power. If my father had taught me anything—and he taught me a lot—it was to squash a threat as soon as you'd assessed it.

Yet he'd never seemed bothered by Zadicus's reign of the mystical east. Perhaps giving certain threats enough room to roam and flex their muscles was enough to placate them. For now.

Besides, the lord was incredibly skilled in the bedchamber.

"Tempting." Snatching my brush, I met Zad's stare in the mirror. "But I'm not done with you yet."

His golden gaze refused to relinquish its hold, but he was no match for me. Smiling, I averted my eyes and continued brushing until the moon's reflection could be found among my waist-length sable locks.

The scent of cloves permeated the shadowed chamber, lit by only two sconces in opposite corners of the room.

Zadicus was still staring, and I was growing tired. "You're excused."

"You know," he said, unmoving from where he lay sprawled over the silver linen. His auburn hair grazed his pectorals, and the glimpse of his pearlescent canines drew away from the crook in his nose. "I don't recall our deal pertaining to slavery."

"And I don't recall you protesting not even five minutes ago."

"Sex does not make an alliance."

I hummed, deep laughter escaping my shut lips as I stood and made my way back to the bed. "More foolish words have been spoken, but I've not heard such nonsense in quite some time."

Zad's gaze narrowed as clouds of smoke drifted past his lips. He watched me tuck myself beneath the smooth sheets and lay my head down. "Marriage, Audra." His tone lost its playful edge, and out came the beast within. "The promise was your hand. A true merging for the sake of the kingdom."

Ruthless, cunning, and as previously stated, powerful, Zadicus

Allblood would make a fine king. He was a high royal by blood and worshiped among our people. Especially the women.

Fools. He hadn't given anyone so much as a second glimpse since his wife died, not even me.

It took everything I had not to swallow, knowing he would hear it. "I have not broken that promise."

"You have not fulfilled it either."

We both knew he didn't want me as his wife. He wanted the kingdom.

He wanted to ensure Allureldin didn't fall prey to Merilda. Though his desires matched my own, I knew once the Sun Kingdom was squashed, or peace had settled once more, that he would have no qualms about wresting control of my home from me.

From my family.

The Sun Kingdom had almost succeeded once, and so I'd brokered a deal with the red-haired devil of the east. I'd needed his help.

With Zadicus's presence in the kingdom, as well as his soldiers and loyal following, others were able to swallow their dislike for me and think a third time before betraying their queen.

It was that or forfeit the land the barbarians had invaded, and undoubtedly more if their disquiet grew, spreading further among my people, and formed a siege.

I'd lost too much. They would not take anything more from me.

I was queen of the Moon Kingdom, and blood would drown the entire continent before I allowed anyone to steal what was rightfully mine.

My fingers curled into my palms. I scented the copper staining the air as my nails created crescents in my skin. "I gave you my word. We will marry next—"

A rapid collection of knocks hit the chamber doors. "Majesty, there's a problem."

Zad kept quiet as I flicked a hand at the doors. One creaked open, and Mintale wasted no time hustling into the room.

A look at Zadicus had him pausing and bowing in quick succession. "Excuse me, Lord—"

"Out with it."

With a shuffle of his feet, he straightened and nodded. "We've caught a band of rogues by the border. General Rind is already having them escorted to the dungeon."

I kicked the sheets off, ignoring the wide eyes from Mintale, and headed for my dressing room. "Majesty?"

"Have them taken to the gallows." A minute later, I was draped head to toe in red feathers. I donned a black cloak, not to ward off the chill—the cold was of little concern to me—but because the velvet texture looked rather striking against the puffed and pressed feathers of my gown.

One must always look their best, especially when one was about to drain the life from traitors.

Mintale was shifting on his feet when I re-entered the room.

Zad still hadn't left. He was staring out one of the two windows in the large chamber. They granted a view of the city streets below and most of Allureldin.

His broad shoulders were taut, his cotton slacks hanging precariously from his trimmed waist. With a sigh, I tore my gaze away from his muscled form. "What, Mintale?"

"Well, it's just that a trial would be more—"

"Trials are for those who might be innocent." I grabbed my sword from its perch upon the mantel of the fireplace and clipped it on beneath the cloak, floating closer to Mintale. Using a long nail, I tipped his chin up and grinned when his throat dipped. My voice was soft but laced in warning. "Are you implying that those who choose to conspire against me, against our home, are innocent, Mintale?"

His head twitched to shake, but my nail, slowly piercing his skin, held it deathly still. "N-No, my queen."

After staring into his beady black eyes, I made a deliberate sweep of his face, taking note of the growing white fluff that peppered his chin and his lower cheeks. I plucked my finger away and stalked to the door. "And what do we do with the guilty, Mintale?"

His words were stronger, and I knew he'd found some mettle now that my back was turned to him. "We bleed them dry, my queen."

They swung in the breeze like clothing hanging from lines in the alleyways of the city streets.

Empty, soulless eyes were all that resembled who they once were.

Did they have families? Children? Spouses or linked ones? I cared not.

The winter running through my veins electrified with the need to exact more vengeance for what the cretins would have tried to take from me. For what more of their kind would try to take from me.

"Once upon a time," I sang into the dawn-painted gloom, an unmovable fragment of storm before them, "we were a land of peace and great magic. Once upon a time, we would disguise our hate with cunning smiles and goblets filled with enough wine to numb the negativity. Once upon a time, we were allies instead of foes." My boots crunched over the snow as I stepped closer. "Once upon a time, you endeavored to bring a kingdom to its knees out of spineless, toxic fear."

I reached the human female hanging in the center and tilted my head to meet her lifeless gaze. "Once upon a time, you took everything I held dear and turned it to ash. But you failed to complete the task in its entirety. I live on, and now, every single one of you will drain and be forced to walk the in-between for your mistakes, forever lost."

The wind screeched and howled, the bodies swaying like empty sacks of grain, slapping into one another.

Zadicus decided then to make his presence known. "You'll knock them down if you don't get a handle on yourself."

"And why should I care if that happens?"

The sound of his footsteps neared, then his words washed over my ear, hot steam causing my flesh to pimple. "Because you cannot make an example of husks when they are not hanging in plain sight."

I blinked, curling my fingers into my palms. The wind faded into that of a cool breeze. He was right, though we both knew I'd never admit it.

"Rage. Such an intoxicating thing," Zad murmured, his voice all breath as his hand enclosed over mine. "It manifests in ways that cut all those around you while leaving you wholly unchanged."

I removed my thawing hand from his heated one. "I have no need for your drivel, nor do I need change."

"How does it feel, brewing inside you like a storm that refuses to be tamed?"

I turned on him, gazing up into his golden eyes. My lashes fluttered, and I murmured, "Pure euphoria, the likes of which I've never encountered before."

He raised his thick brows. "That so?"

"Freedom." Grinning, I tapped his chest. "I am free to be who I am, to feel how I feel, and to act upon it should I so desire. Now that, my sneaky lord, is intoxicating."

He followed me back through the castle gates and courtyard. We walked silently, our steps slow.

Merchants and shop owners were stirring, the slumbering city coming to life with every step we took. It wouldn't be long now. My lips twitched, and I let them rise with the struggling sun.

Then came the screams.

Zad's eyes swung to me, but he wisely kept his thinned mouth shut.

Inside, the castle was aflutter with morning activity. I made my way to the dining room, opening the doors with a flick of my hand even though it remained curled around the other beneath my cloak.

Mintale bent low, and servants frantically fled, bowing swiftly without so much as a look at me along the way.

Mintale held out a chair at the head of the table. "A long night, your majesty?"

He got to work on fixing me a tea as I rearranged my layers of velvet and feathers, dampened from the creeping hours before dawn. "Long but fruitful. Send for General Rind."

Mintale set the cup and saucer down, then started fussing with buttering toast.

"Now," I snapped.

He dropped the toast and raced to the door, speaking in hushed tones with one of the guards who nodded, then disappeared from his post to deliver the message.

One couldn't run a castle without professional games of whispers.

I finished buttering the toast myself, barely tasting it as I chewed.

General Rind entered a moment later, his jet black hair and blue eyes similar to my own. "Your majesty," he said, bowing before taking his position at the other end of the table.

"Quit with the formalities, Uncle, and take a seat."

Rind was one of my grandfather's mistakes, a half breed who would forever serve the crown as a part of the guard.

Royals were created only when a royal procreated with another. Half breeds, often referred to as mixed, were created when a royal procreated with a human.

Should a mixed not born into nobility survive infancy, then they must be surrendered to the king or queen when they come of age to serve the crown.

Rind's grin threatened to make me smile, but I kept the urge at bay while he poured himself a cup of tea and snatched a piece of toast. "They sway."

I sipped my tea. "Indeed."

"Do you intend to make it so with every enemy we capture?"

I set my cup down and met his gaze. "Is that a problem?"

"Absolutely not." But his words didn't ring true. He might have been my father's half-brother, but he'd been closer to my mother. Though she had often been distant and distracted, she was not a monster like my father.

Like me.

I drank my tea as Rind explained how they'd discovered the now deceased while scouting the outer village, west of the castle.

"They'd been camping out in hollowed trees southwest of the mountains."

"Do you think they intended to travel all the way here? Or were they simply spies?"

"They did not say?" he asked.

I said nothing. Not because they didn't say anything. They'd said plenty, pleading and crying like a pack of weak trouser-wetting idiots. I just hadn't cared to ask.

"Niece," Rind began. "Might I remind you that if you insist on taking my finds from me and my men to exact revenge yourself, then you need to at least allow us time with them first."

"I'll question them next time," I said.

He sighed. "As you wish."

The sun crested the spire windows, flicking arrows of blinding light across the stone table and the gray and red tapestry hanging from the rafters and stone walls.

I tried not to flinch and pushed my chair back to escape its warmth.

The doors crashed open, and Mintale rushed in behind Truin, our spellcaster.

Truin's yellow hair, curled like a ram's horns on either side of her head, bounced around her ears, and her eyes met mine with obvious delight. "Majesty," she said, out of breath. "May I sit?"

I tapped my nails over the table, knowing I needed sleep, yet knowing I'd lay there for hours, staring at the towering granite ceiling. "If you must."

She unfurled a map, spreading it over a plate of bacon.

I frowned at it. "What is that?"

"A map."

I rolled my eyes. "I know that. What good is it to me?"

Truin bit her lips, unfazed by my temper, as per usual. About to talk, she glanced around, taking note of the guards and Mintale's presence.

"Speak," I said, out of patience.

Swallowing, she expelled a breath and nodded. "I found him." She stabbed a finger at a black blob of land on the map. "Right here, in a tiny town called Crestinburg in The Edges."

My heart kicked, then ceased beating. The drapes in the room began to flap, and the guards struggled to keep their stares fixed forward.

Closing my eyes, I drew in a deep inhale. I'd have to kill her. I'd known Truin since I was an infant, but I'd have to kill her all the same.

"Ainx," I called.

Truin laughed. "Oh, shush. Do you think I'm here only to taunt you?"

Ainx, head of my personal guard, was by my side in an instant. I waved him off, and he took three steps back.

Through gritted teeth, I hissed, "I will have your tongue, at the very least, for uttering his whereabouts."

Yanking the map from her grasp, I was about to rip it to pieces when she rushed out, "He's to be married on the eve of the next full moon." Her next words were soft with apprehension. "He's to be married tonight."

The map fell from my pinched fingertips, and the remains of my heart plummeted with it. "I beg your pardon?"

Truin nodded, then lowered her gaze. "Delon, from a neighboring coven, reported hearing of it in her sleep." Her eyes met mine, a world of pity unable to be veiled. "I knew you wouldn't want to know his whereabouts or what he was doing with his new life, but I knew you'd want to know should something dire arise, so a few of us have kept our subconscious on call."

She was right.

Darkness be damned, she was right.

It took a minute to calm my erratic heart and steady my hands. The drapes slowly quit shaking and the cutlery on the table stopped rattling as heavy silence infiltrated the cavernous room.

A moment later, three taps sounded on the door, and Zadicus glided in. With his long hair tied at his nape and dressed in all gray save for the white tunic under his vest, he bowed, his cloak folded over his arm. "I will take my leave, your majesty."

I could only nod, at a loss for words.

He was getting married. I needn't have asked to whom. Right now, the matter of who was irrelevant, but it was clear she was insane.

And it was clear I should not care.

I knew the risk I'd taken and what it would cost my heart, but I'd done it anyway.

Yet it seemed as if some naïve part of me had foolishly hoped for his return. That one day, when all this darkness had passed, he would recover his memories, and we would find one another again.

He could never return. If he did, he'd die by my own decree.

He'd betrayed me in every abominable way, but that didn't mean I'd sit on the throne I'd had every intention of sharing with him and just allow him to marry someone else.

I pushed my chair back, nodding at Truin, who was staring up at me with concern lining her milky brown eyes. "Shield your weakness, Truin. You can keep your tongue today."

I stalked past Zadicus, but I should have known not paying him any mind would have him trailing me. "May I ask what it is you're up to?"

"No, you may not." I made haste for the stairs, racing around and around each curling row until I'd reached my chambers and pushed the doors open.

Zad's presence was that of a curious cat as I changed into leather pants and a woolen thermal. The combination was hideous, but the need to blend in was paramount.

I donned my boots and cloak again, and tugged at the mustard brown chafing my stomach.

Hands gripped my upper arms, startling me from my rush. "This is about Raiden."

How he'd realized, I didn't care to know. "Remove your hands before I remove them from your body."

He didn't. If anything, his grip only tightened. "You cannot bring him back to this kingdom. He is a traitor, and our people would rather see him drained than to rule by your side."

My teeth gnashed, and I hissed through them, "And I'd rather him drain than let him swear himself to someone else."

Zad's long brown lashes swept up, and his grip loosened. "He's to marry someone."

It wasn't a question, so I said nothing else as I left him there and headed for the caves.

"We are a kingdom on the brink of war," he called. "A queen cannot abandon her people in times such as these."

"A queen can do whatever she damn well pleases." The doors shut behind me with a gust of wind so strong, the handles broke so he couldn't follow.

TWO

Surrounding the rear of the castle, looming like giant sentinels kissing the sky, were snowcapped mountains as far as the eye could see.

Clouds swallowed some of the peaks, and unless you visited them, you couldn't make out the doorways to the caves within.

Inside the two smaller mountains closest to the castle lived one of my favorite creatures.

Wen's breath plumed in the frigid air. My cloak fanned behind me, exposing me to a chill I couldn't feel. Within minutes, we'd reached the base of the mountain range.

When I neared the highest point I could take Wen, I dismounted and handed the midnight black stallion to the guard before hurrying along one of the trails that led to some of the ten cave entrances. The two gatekeepers bowed as I passed and fled inside.

Mintale was there before Vanamar's handler could even finish saddling him, demanding someone prepare his own beast.

"I do not need your reprimanding or sniveling presence right now."

Mintale clicked his fingers at the handler who was rushing to saddle his mare. "I know. I'm merely here should you need any help."

That surprised me, and I raised a brow at him. We both knew he would be useless should I need a battle companion. I knew where every spy encampment was to the west stretching toward The Edges and the gray and whispering sea. I would hide myself—probably a lot better without his presence—just fine.

Vanamar grunted, turning his horn-flecked head to the trainer to growl at him for pulling the straps too tight. "Get out."

The young male vanished, and I got to work on checking the saddle and reins before leading Van to the wider side entrance. The caves tunneled inside the peaks of the twin mountains, the scent of hay and rotting chicken carcasses staining the damp dirt within. Below them, the kingdom spread like glittering jewels hit by a ray of light, rife with energy and dazzling with hidden danger.

Furbanes were Allureldin's fastest mode of transportation. Though not just anyone got to own a beast for themselves. We bred them, but not often for it was not only difficult but also dangerous, being that the females did not care for it and would try to remove the male's horns, limbs, or even genitalia. For now, there were only eleven.

Over ten feet tall with a torso of fur that resembled that of a grizzly bear and a feathered wingspan that spread farther than that into the skies, furbanes were horned creatures both feared and envied by many.

Vanamar's folded wings twitched as we exited the cave, and he opened his mouth, releasing a roar that displayed teeth as long as my arm and shook the snow from the skies. Stuffing my hands into his fur, I hoisted myself into the saddle, then took the reins wrapped around the curled horns atop his head. "Rah."

He began to run, and within seconds, we were airborne, my stomach dipping as we soared into the harsh glow of early morning. Glancing over my shoulder, I wondered if Mintale had decided to stay behind, but then I heard his bellowed shout. Smirking, I shook my head, my knees clasped tight over Van's sides as I leaned forward, spurring him to fly faster.

Twisting cobbled streets, shopfronts, estates, and dozens of smoke-throwing chimneys soon faded into dirt roads, cottages, villages, and endless patches of green forest. Our world was a realm of beauty even though we'd done our best to tear it apart.

Smoke rose from campfires to the west, and I beckoned Van

east, toward the trade entrance of the Gray Sea. I steeled my spine, hunched down, and we flew higher into the clouds. It would be a day's journey to The Edges.

To the sole reason Rosinthe was a hostile continent on the cusp of war.

The Whispering Sea churned like a roiling serpent below, and I refrained from holding my breath as we descended and crested the darkening waves.

We'd only heard tales of what lurked beneath its waters, and I had very little desire to find out if they held any truth.

It took what seemed like the entire journey to recognize what it was that had my teeth chattering. For it wasn't the Whispering Sea, and it wasn't the cold.

The cold was my friend. Aside from the beast beneath me, perhaps my only one.

No, the emotion that caused it was better left unnamed and ignored.

"We need to leave the beasts behind," Mintale said, reaching my side, his voice barely carrying over the wind.

"No," I said. "We won't be long."

We sped forward to where the sea narrowed, then fell off a cliff to skirt between the mines. The Edges were home to those who had been exiled or owed the kingdom an unpayable debt. Beyond the minuscule stretch of farmland, tiny village streets wove in every direction toward the sea and the coal mines.

In the center of the dust-saturated land sat a church for the humans who prayed to a different deity, and I wondered, idly, what king or queen before me allowed such a building to exist.

Freedom was something Rosinthe prided itself on. We were a continent under rule, but a continent that welcomed almost anyone and their offspring. Almost anyone.

Our races mixed and were allowed to. Royal children played with human children, and should an unlikely pair link—a lifelong bond only breakable by death—or choose to pledge vows, they were welcome to.

Perhaps that was the problem. Perhaps too much freedom had dug thorn-strewn grooves into the heart of who we were, allowing room for sinister things to grow.

Spying a dock falling piece by piece into the sea, I pressed my heels into Van's flanks and leaned forward.

He dropped down, wingtips skirting the water and spraying. I nudged him again, cursing as water droplets smacked into my face.

He grunted and righted himself.

"There." I pointed at where a tiny farmhouse hid among a field of wheat.

We landed with a jolt that caused my teeth to clack. "Let's be quick," I said once we'd dismounted.

Well, once I'd dismounted.

Mintale had his foot stuck in the stirrup, and I sighed, waiting for him to get untangled. He didn't.

"Gah," he bellowed, arms pinwheeling as he fell backward to the ground. His mare turned to stare at him, then turned away and tore a large chunk of wheat from the ground.

My eyes closed momentarily, then I stomped over and yanked him up by the collar of his tunic.

"Hurry up," I said, glancing at the full moon taking shape in the sky.

No one would dare touch a furbane that belonged to the royal court, or otherwise, but in times like these, it would be wise not to draw too much attention to ourselves. Especially in a land filled with criminals and desperate souls.

A bell rang from the north, and I cursed, trudging through the field with an urgency that would have been embarrassing if I had the time to care, of which I did not.

Mintale struggled to keep up. He was five hundred and twenty years old, and it was definitely starting to show.

"How are we going to take him?"

"By force."

Mintale pondered that. "Bind his hands?"

I didn't bother answering and rechecked the flow of the sea, heading north once we'd reached the dirt road.

The day's end didn't mean much to those in this district. Eyes peeked through venetians, cracks in the rotting wooden housing, or stared blatantly from porch steps as we turned onto the main street of town and spied the ramshackle church at the opposite end.

My skin started to itch, and it took considerable effort not to rub my arms, which felt as though they'd been layered in a film of dust. I was wearing long sleeves, but I could still feel it—sticking, cloying, and suffocating. "It's so dirty here," I said between my teeth as Mintale waved like a fool at a few passersby openly ogling us.

Some dropped into a bow once their sight adjusted and they realized who was marching past them, but others were too busy gaping to react fast enough.

"It's the mines." Mintale winced. "I loathe to think what it's like inside them."

I lifted my gaze to the volcanic looking mountain to the left, then shrugged.

"Majesty!" A woman raced out in front of me with a babe pressed to her bosom. "May I please ask for your blessing?" Her lips wobbled as her soiled hand patted the babe's back. "My daughter, she be sick, coughing like that of an Ergin."

I glanced at her smudged brown face, my lip curling as my hand twitched and sent her stumbling back over the dirt. "The cursed do not bless," I said as her infant wailed.

Whimpering and muttering about the devil, she scrambled away.

We continued—thankfully uninterrupted—until we could see the closed church doors. Stopping, we studied the worn structure for a moment. The doors appeared to be locked from the inside.

"It would seem their god does not wish you to enter."

"Quiet, Mintale."

Rain began spraying the earth in soft pelts, heightening the scent of filth and grime, and casting a strange gloom across the air.

For a fleeting moment, I almost felt bad that he'd been forced to live here. Almost.

Of course, Mintale did not shut up. "They say rain on your vow day is good luck."

I skirted around a mutt chasing a tisk. "There's no such thing as luck."

Nearly stumbling over the mutt as it lunged for the insect's wings, Mintale hurried after me. "You know how humans can be. Always needing to believe in something greater than their dismal existence."

I scoffed, done with hearing such fanciful crud.

"Especially when something does not go as they'd hoped it would," Mintale continued, and by that point, I didn't want to open my mouth to tell him to shut up for fear of what I'd ingest.

We ascended the crumbling steps, and of course, he took my silence as a sign to continue rambling. "Majesty, might I ask what it is you have faith in?"

Pausing outside the flimsy wooden barriers, I curled my lips. "Me."

Then I sent a gust of wind hurtling at the doors.

THREE

WOOD SPLINTERED AND GROANED.
Screams and gasps lifted my smile as the remains of the doors crumbled in scraps to the pews and concrete floor.

I paid the attendees no mind and marched straight for the altar.

I'd expected to grab him by the neck or the hair and haul him out of there.

I'd expected not to feel anything other than the winter-crusted slice of rage that held the tattered pieces of my heart together.

What I didn't expect was for my boots to catch in a crack of concrete, twisting my ankle as he turned from his position in front of some priest and narrowed his eyes at me.

Time came to a crashing halt, rewinding and fast-forwarding all at once.

Breathe with me, silk.

He blinked, taking a slow step back.

Come undone for me, silk.

Air wheezed out of me, shallowing my lungs and electrifying the dead organ in my chest.

Hair a shade darker than soot curled around his hairline, dusting his brown cheeks. His lean form had broadened. Hardened. Muscles had grown muscles upon his shoulders and his biceps, where a tribal tattoo of a flaming sun wrapped around the taut skin.

Mintale's hand touched mine. "Majesty?"

Tugged back to the nightmare of reality, I snatched my hand away. "Seize him."

Raiden tore his green eyes from my face. Confusion swept his brows together as he looked at Mintale.

"The queen," someone gasped.

Chatter sounded from the few patrons in the pews, the aging priest nothing but a statue as his robes began to flutter around him.

"It couldn't be," said another. "Here?"

I steadied my breathing, and the breeze that'd trailed us inside the ancient structure settled.

That was, until the woman beside Raiden shrieked.

"Who in the darkness are you?" Raiden moved to stand in front of his betrothed, and the sight was enough to have the rafters creaking.

Her hair was the color of a raging fire, and her eyes that of the dark Gray Sea. She was pretty, I'd give her that much, but pretty was no match for the wrath of betrayal.

Did they think they could get away with such disrespect? Granted, Raiden would have no clue who I was, but the wide-eyed swine cowering behind him did.

Before Raiden's hands could touch her, I swept them behind his back, and he cursed. "What is the meaning of this?"

"You will come with me." I turned for the doors, my cloak billowing behind me. "Or the pretty fool dies."

"Raid," the woman said, and I spun back. One look and her mouth was sealed in ice, incapable of opening.

She should consider herself lucky that was all I did.

Mintale grabbed Raiden by the arm. "She is her majesty, the queen, and you would do well to invest more time in learning such things rather than finding a young wench to wed."

I nearly snorted at Mintale's attempt to defend my weak heart. He needn't have bothered. It was dead a long time ago.

We made it down the steps before the commotion began. "Unhand me. I've done nothing wrong!"

"You've done everything one could possibly do wrong." I couldn't look at him. I didn't trust myself to.

"No. Wait." A group of dirt-marred faces scrambled closer. "There must be some mistake."

"Believe me," I said, pushing by the stench, "the mistake was all mine."

No one helped Raiden as they saw him curse and struggle in Mintale's grasp.

Once upon a time, Raiden could've killed Mintale with but a thought. That was before Truin wiped him clean of everything he once was and left him with a bland memory of a male with a different life, a different world, and a different heart.

Stopping, I peered around at the gathered crowd, who began to slowly inch back.

"Come." I clicked my fingers at two men drinking lager in front of a tavern. They drained and dropped their tankards and stomped over the wet soil toward us. "Carry this…" I waved at Raiden. "This traitorous thing for me."

With two sloppy bows, they then hurried to wrestle the struggling six-foot-three giant from Mintale. We made it to the field before it dawned on Mintale just how difficult the journey home would be with a distressed, angry male to drag with us.

"Be gone," I told the two gents. Only when they'd scuttled back to the dirt road did I then turn my eyes to my heart's demise.

His face was a shade darker, the golden hue darkening with dust, his ire, and the growing night. I could practically smell it and tried not to let my satisfaction show. "You."

"Me," he said, nostrils flaring, pupils overgrown. "Queen or not, you must be one truly despicable creature to disrupt one's wedding ceremony. I demand you release me." His teeth slammed together as he growled, "Now."

"Or what?" I raised a brow, blinking slowly.

His bearded jaw hardened, and like fingers over a swath of silk, I remembered trailing my own over his freshly shaven skin.

His plush lips rose into a grin that once made me see red before seeing every star in the night sky within his arms—and then he was running.

Mintale sighed, coming to a stop beside me. "Shall I?"

"One moment." We watched as he made it all the way to the road before I raised a hand. A boulder rose on an invisible wind and sailed into the side of his head. He fell to the ground like a pillar of concrete. "It's fun to watch when they think they can get away."

Mintale said nothing.

"He should cause you little difficulty now." I jerked my head at the fallen traitor, and Mintale fetched the ropes and harness from his saddle while I climbed atop Van.

I was in the sky before Mintale could heave Raiden over the back of his mare.

FOUR

We made it home without too much turbulence, unless you counted that of my once flat emotions.

I did my best to squash them as Van plummeted toward a barren patch of rocks some miles away from the castle. To play in the mountain range was one thing, but to outright alert others to my presence there by riding atop a furbane during the final hours of daylight was another foolish thing entirely.

A few people marveled at the beast dipping between the clouds, and I watched, even though I didn't need to, as he circled the snow-dusted peaks behind the castle before disappearing.

Nightfall was descending once more, and I longed to soak in my tub until the trip had rid itself from every pore.

Allureldin came alive as the sun began to sink and then gradually died once the clock approached midnight. Until then, people flocked in and out of taverns, cafes, the theater, and restaurants—laughter and shouts echoing into the watery light cast from the curved necks of street sconces. Inside them lived families of fluttering beetles with glowing wings.

The expanding shadows and the hood of my cloak concealed most of my face. I wound through alleyways and slunk behind vendor carts, breathing a sigh of relief once my eyes feasted on the alabaster and onyx structure that rose high above the winding, sloping streets.

Behind wrought iron gates stood a monstrosity with three spires. The arched windows were stained red and gray with serpentine ivy crawling between them and over the stone exterior. Thorn-laden vines bound and knotted together over the curled metalwork, and when I touched the cool lock, feeling the jolt all the way to my core, the leafy whorls closest to it unknotted, slithering as a heavy click broke the still air and the gates opened.

Guards were quick to ensure they closed, and I strode through the mostly empty courtyard as Ainx left his post in front of the castle doors and approached.

"Clear out the dungeon," I said once I'd reached him.

Heavy brows dipped low over sapphire eyes. "And what do you want done with the prisoners?"

"Kill the worst, warn the rest, and let them run free. I don't particularly care."

"My queen?" he questioned with not a little alarm, keeping stride with me as we waded into the entry chamber and strode down the halls.

I glanced at the few nearby male servants, then decided I didn't much care. They were going to find out eventually. Let them try to crucify me for bringing a traitor back within our stronghold. I had greater challenges ahead of me. "Our king is coming home."

Ainx coughed, and then Azela, my second, spied us at the end of the hall and waited.

She bowed, but before she could talk, I turned back to Ainx. "Fill her in and let not a whisper of this reach the townsfolk. Then call for Truin. I'll be in my rooms."

Seemingly pale with uncertainty, Ainx's jaw shifted as he clipped, "Of course."

Ignoring the gaping castle workers, I left them to it and rounded the corner, heading down the hall lined with silver-patterned carpets and drapes for the stairs. I made it to my rooms, slammed the doors, and fell against them, my eyes closing as my heart pounded a violent, bruising rhythm.

"Will he not share your chambers?"

I'd been so distracted by feelings that I hadn't even remembered the way I'd locked Zadicus in here. I felt behind me and found no damage to the wood. He hadn't even attempted escape, and he'd had the door handles replaced.

Opening my eyes, I found him sprawled on the bed, shirtless. "I thought you were taking your leave."

A lazy sweep of my frame accompanied lazier words. "You'll need to forgive me for doubting if our agreement stands to be met after you've just flown across the continent to fetch your late husband." His bronze-flecked eyes sharpened and glowed as they leveled on mine. "I will not remain a lover."

"Many would kill to be in your position."

"And I'm sure they have." Cold aired his smooth voice. "However," he said, rising to a sitting position, pale skin stretching over taut muscle. "My pride is a problem."

"Pride is never the problem," I muttered, removing the hood from my head and then the cloak from my body. "The problem lies in how you manage it." It puddled behind me as I undressed on the way to my bathing chamber where I drew a bath, rolling my neck as Zad leaned in the doorway, watching.

"What do you plan to do with him?"

"I haven't thought that far ahead yet." It pained me to admit it, but I did owe him that much at least. The cool porcelain of the circular tub bit into my skin as I sat on the side and shook some bathing salts into the water, one to heat it and another to scent it. "I will inevitably have to kill him."

"All because you couldn't bear to see him vow to someone else."

My hand stilled, and I twisted, sliding into the scalding lavender-scented water. "The humans call it a wedding."

"All the same," Zad drawled, hands tucked in his pockets. "A pledge of commitment is a pledge of commitment."

My nose twitched. "Go bore someone else with your pointless reminders."

Zadicus chuckled, a dark, brash sound. "You know what? I actually find this situation quite... comical."

Dropping the salts on the shelf behind me, I tilted my head back to glare at him.

His eyes were on my breasts as the cool air and water pebbled them. Soft and unhurried, he murmured, "You are a beautiful fool, my queen."

"Yet you want to vow to me," I reminded him.

His eyes flashed, meeting mine. "I don't want to." His top lip curled, and my muscles stiffened. "I need to. This kingdom cannot be run by a spoiled brat with enough power in her pinky to reduce it to cinders."

A bar of butter soap flew across the bathing room, narrowly missing his head. It hit the red tiled wall, then slid to the mosaic floor in two pieces.

His lips didn't so much as twitch with humor. Hands still inside his pockets, he just raised his brows in that infuriating way before leaving me to dwell.

With a groan, I slid beneath the water.

Zadicus was gone when I drained the tub and dressed in a black silken camisole.

For untold minutes, I laid upon the bed, staring at the whorls of vines carved into the stone ceiling.

Zad was but a buzzing tisk, forever eager to annoy the shit out of me. I knew his game—he needn't remind me of it—but I wouldn't allow him to question everything I did.

An alliance was needed between our territories; for although his lands fell under my jurisdiction, his people were loyal to him. Most were not supporters of my father; therefore, I doubted they were supporters of me.

Thanks to my tyrant father and his volatile power plays, over his reign that lasted nearly five hundred years, the kingdom of Allureldin had been reduced to a cesspit of fear.

Raiden had been right to show me all the ways my father was poisoning this land.

Perhaps he had been right to kill him, too. That didn't mean I'd be the gentle princess he once hoped I'd be. Queen now, courtesy of him.

No, as cruel as he might have been, my father's blood was a heavy oil running through my veins—racing rivers of vengeance ready to upend any who dared to usurp me. It wasn't within me to cower, to fold to any males' whims, especially not that of Zadicus Allblood.

I would take him as a husband if only to aid in quelling the unrest; the dislike that fanned and feathered far beyond our territories and into the Sun Kingdom—where that dislike bloomed into blood-bright hatred.

I suppose our fathers never foresaw all the ways in which an arranged marriage, a coupling that would unite our divided kingdoms once and for all, would only make things worse. Or maybe, they did.

And they'd welcomed it with open arms.

"Enter," I said, hearing Truin's footsteps outside.

The doors creaked open and closed, and she padded over the hides of fur littering the stone floor to lean against the dark oak post of the bed. "You have him."

I didn't bother asking how she knew. "I need a spell. A tonic. A—"

"Stop," Truin said, her voice uncharacteristically harsh.

I'd have glared at her, but I was too shamed by the words that'd fled my mouth. I hadn't realized how badly I'd wanted to reinstate his memories and have him look at me like he once did, rather than with the confusion of a hostile stranger.

I hadn't acknowledged the desire at all. Until now.

"Will you not do it?" I asked, more cautious.

Truin sighed, and I felt the bed dip as she perched at the end. "You cannot do this, my queen."

"I can." If I had to kill him, then I wanted him to look me in the eye and see what he'd done to me beforehand.

"No," Truin said. "Forget the decree. I mean it's just not possible."

I sat up, my teeth gritting. "*You* cast the spell. *You* created the potion. Which means *you* can undo it."

"Audra." Her little white teeth tugged at her pink-stained lip. "There is no spell to undo something of that magnitude."

I blinked, my stomach swaying. "None?"

She shook her head, her hands curling around one another. "I told you so before we proceeded." It was probably true that she had, but I'd been barely breathing from all that had happened, from the array of pitch-black darkness that'd taken hold. Her brows knitted. "Why would you want to?"

"The why doesn't matter. If it cannot be done…" *Then he'd drain at sunrise.*

The words hung there between us, unspoken, but louder than the crack of thunder that cleaved the sky in two outside.

Truin's eyes softened, her hands unfolding in her lap to twirl her silver rings. Heirlooms said to contain magic of the souls who'd previously worn them.

Gazing at the wall where a collection of silver gilded mirrors hung in varying sizes, she lowered her voice to a whisper. "There are stories of those who have regained memories, some if not all, after periods of amnesia. It is trialed on the aging ones all the time when their years are no longer a match for their frail minds." I frowned, but she answered before I could even dare ask. "It wouldn't have worked on your father. Different feasts for different beasts."

I sneered. "I wasn't asking…" I clamped my teeth shut at the tight smile on her face. Sighing, I raked a hand through my damp hair, thinking, wondering if I wanted to know. "And what is this method?"

"You recount every memory you can remember. Mainly the ones that hold the biggest influence on him. On his mind, on his heart, and on his soul."

Lying back down, defeat crawled inside my chest cavity. "I was only nineteen summers old when we met."

Truin took a moment to answer, and I tried not to cringe at the doubt in her tone. "Then I suppose you'll just have to hope that the memories you share will be enough to coax his true self back to the surface. Or"—she lifted her shoulders—"at least glimpses of who he once was."

"Hope," I repeated, the word tasting foul on my tongue.

Truin stood, a lilt to her musical voice. "It's more powerful than it sounds, my queen."

I snorted. "That's what the common folk say to reassure themselves enough to sleep each night, I'm sure."

"I am not common."

"True. But you are a witch." I turned to stare at her, the moonlight glinting off her butter yellow hair. "Your lot believe in a lot of nonsense things."

Truin released a breath before bobbing her head and leaving me to rot in silence.

Glimpses. Would moments of clarity be enough for him to see what he'd done? There wasn't a much better alternative. I groaned, rolling my face into the bedding.

When I heard the midnight bell chime from the highest tower, I tossed the sheets away and made my way down the shadowed stairs and halls.

Ainx had retired for the night, but Azela was there, her hand on her sword until she saw me step into the candlelit swath of light floating over the entrance to the dungeon. "It stinks down here."

Excrement mingled with sweat and urine, among other lovely things, blood being the most prominent. A crow cawed at the tiny arched opening facing one of the city streets, water trickling in below its feet and down the damp rock wall.

"You killed the servants in charge of cleaning last week, and Mintale has yet to organize staff to replace them."

I frowned. "Oh."

Azela glanced behind her to where a bang sounded followed by a muttered curse. "He's still as lively as ever."

I forced my lips into some semblance of a smile, knowing she was doing her utmost to veil her displeasure over this situation, then waited for her to move out of the way. When she joined the other guards planted along the walls, I stepped forward.

My hand lifted, fingers wrapping around the cold metal of the door that led inside a ginormous chamber housing a hundred cells. He was in one of them. Close too, judging by the grunts and shaking rattle of metal.

An exhale tumbled free, burning my lips and throat when I saw a flash of his skin. His hands were around the bars, golden fingers whitening as he tugged and tugged.

If only he knew.

If only he knew that once upon a time, he had the power to melt metal and burn his way out of, or into, any structure.

Raiden was fifty years old—fifty-two now. *Too young*, my father had worried over dinner after our first meeting. He was over twice my age, but my father hadn't thought that meant he was mature enough. That he was equipped to handle me and take on the responsibility of one day running an entire continent.

Just look at us now, Raiden.

"I know you're watching me, queen."

I blinked but refrained from pulling away, knowing he couldn't actually see me. He could only feel me.

He could always feel me.

"Let me out."

That thing called hope was digging a nasty, useless pit inside my stomach.

"Let me out and I won't return to kill you in your sleep."

The guards looked at me, scowling, but I raised a hand. "He's mad. And he will die for it, but not tonight."

I strode for the stairs as Raiden's shouting chased me.

"Oh, Majesty! I do believe you've forgotten something." Sarcasm filled each drawled word, and then he deadpanned. "*Me.*"

If I could've forgotten him, then I'd have left him to rot in The Edges with his human.

The thought was so sobering that when I reached the ground floor, I stopped a guard. "Deliver a message to Mintale immediately." Didra nodded, her russet lashes unmoving. "Have him send for Raiden's betrothed before first light."

She blinked then. "My queen—"

"Go," I said, taking the stairs to my rooms. "Now."

FIVE

Three days passed before I gathered the courage to begin.

Three days consisting of meetings with the general and my guard, and ensuring new staff was scheduled to clean the dungeon on a daily basis.

Three days of my heart beating on high alert and a queasy feeling slithering throughout my body whenever I remembered the look in his eyes. I knew it would happen. I knew it, and still, I chose it. I knew he'd never look at me again, let alone look at me with love, by the way those green orbs, like that of new grass, had surveyed me as though I were brand new. Unrecognizable. Foreign.

Yet I wasn't. Not entirely.

Every night, he knew I was there—a darkness even the shadows couldn't hide.

The death threats came to an end after night two, and instead, he tried to reason with me. But a traitor with nothing had nothing to give, and he knew it.

"Anything you want. I'll do it." His hands were slippery over the bars confining him, sliding as the desperate croak within his rough voice crackled further.

I caved then, the goddesses knew why, and unlocked the door to the dungeon.

"Majesty," Azela said, reaching for me when I slipped through the following gate.

I closed it and gave her a look that dared her to worry about my safety. "Leave us."

Her head began to shake, troubled eyes watering, and still, I repeated, "Leave us." For it was time, and I refused to let anyone else listen to what I was about to retell. "All of you head upstairs to the ground floor. Now."

There was a stall, a pause of reluctance, but I waited until their footsteps could no longer be heard, then drew in a quick breath and turned around.

In the center of the dungeon, with many a cell scattered around his in a maze of rust-stained metal, Raiden stood. "Ah, so she wants something after all."

My heels clacked over stone, stone marked with years of pain and death, and I smiled. "Just your time." I lifted my nails to inspect them, if only to keep from meeting his intense gaze so soon. "Which, it seems, you have a lot of."

"Thanks to you."

My gaze snapped to him then, and he sighed, broad shoulders slumping as he laid his forehead against the bars. "What is the meaning of this? I am but a working lad from The Edges. I mine six days a week and always pay my dues." I forced my burning eyes away from his narrowed ones. "My only sin is enjoying a tankard or three of lager every other evening after work."

"Your soft side does not appeal to me." I hoisted myself up onto the torture table that sat before his cell in the center of the room, the wood crusted and worn beneath my hands. "Not now, not ever, and especially not when just yesterday, you were reciting all the ways you'd like to kill me. Slowly. I believe knives and an axe were involved." I hummed. "Creativity was never your strong suit."

He barked a harsh laugh. "You interrupted my wedding to the love of my life."

I caught myself before I flinched. "And pray tell, how exactly did that come to be?" I was curious—the painful, self-destructive type.

His green eyes washed over my face. "You wish to know of how Casilla and I met?"

"Casilla," I said, tasting the name on my tongue, imagining how it would feel to corner her with a dagger and thrust it inside her body for daring to let a king inside it.

He had no idea—none—that she was now here, rotting away in a cellar beneath a tavern outside the castle. "I suppose that is what I asked."

His lips pursed. "You are indeed a peculiar creature."

I tilted my head, flashing my teeth. "My, my. A compliment."

His brows furrowed. "But is it?"

I waved a hand, then tugged at my black gown, ensuring half my breasts were in sight—creamy globes that begged to be snatched from their restraints.

His gaze didn't waver from my face, though his throat did dip.

I pouted. "Fine. Go on then," I said with another wave of my hand. "Tell me of this fantastical romance story, and then I might just humor you with one of my own."

Silence descended for a heavy minute as we stared at one another. Me with a million memories flashing behind my blue eyes, and he with a veil of confusion and distrust burdening his.

"We are to exchange love stories?" He scoffed. "Shall I braid your hair afterward?"

I flicked my hair over my shoulder. "I prefer braids for fighting. If you must tug it, though, I encourage my lovers to grab my hair however they please."

Something shadowed his eyes, but then he shook his head and sank to the disgusting orange and brown flecked floor. "Will I be released after this little game? Or are there more to come?"

He would never be free.

Ever.

I chose to keep that to myself, though, and instead, I tipped a shoulder. "There's only one way to find out."

His knees rose, and he clasped his hands between them, dusting his thumbs over each other. They were putrid, covered in days of filth and patches of blood. The guards had given him the opportunity to bathe yesterday, but he'd refused once it'd become apparent they'd all monitor him closely.

Pride was a fickle beast.

"In all honesty, there's nothing fantastical about it. I met Casilla some months ago while I was walking home from work. I'd dropped my canteen, and she chased after me to hand it back. I wanted her instantly, and so she began warming my bed. I asked her to marry me when I found out she was carrying my babe." I sucked in a quiet breath at that. "She miscarried a couple of months ago, but I promised her we'd still wed. She…" He paused, smiling at his hands like a lunatic. "She has this warmth, you know?" He looked up at me then. "No," he laughed out. "No, I don't suppose you would know. You're one of the coldest bitches I've ever encountered."

"Mind your tongue, or I'll remove it."

Arrogance rolled off him. He might have been seated upon the floor of a soiled cage, but the way his eyes gleamed and his words rolled free of his mouth showed he was still very much the high royal. A prince. A king. And whether he had access or knowledge of his powers, he always would be. "Is it not the truth?"

Ice unfurled into heavy stones inside my stomach, yet I said nothing.

Releasing a breath, Raiden looked ahead at the opposite wall. "Casilla has this way of making you feel like you're the entire world. As though she was created to do nothing but orbit around you."

"You want a female to serve you?" That was not the prince I knew. Then again, I didn't really know this male all too well. Not as I thought I once had.

"No," he said, thinking about it. "Though there is something to be said for being loved in that way. Complete devotion. Utter surrender. Refusal to quit."

I licked my teeth, piercing my tongue with my canines. Blood infiltrated my mouth, and I smeared it over my teeth, then swallowed. "It sounds to me like you love the way she loves you." I clucked my tongue. "So selfish."

"I love her for her giving, pure heart. I love her for many reasons, but those are the most important."

It took considerable effort to keep from gagging. I wanted to grab the pail next to the table and hurl into it.

Staring at me, he grinned, displaying a row of white teeth. Like mine, the tips of his canines were sharper and slightly longer than most humans. "Your turn."

I knew he merely wanted to see what would become of him after this. There was no way this creature who was into selfless love would give a damn about a cold bitch queen's story.

But he would.

I would make him care if it was the last thing I did.

---

19 summers old

"Honestly." We rolled into a patch of wildflowers, our breaths coming heavy. "I don't know why it took me so long to work out that sex and training go together better than cheese and wine."

Berron huffed, laughing as I tucked a hand behind my head. "That'll teach you for not listening to me." After some moments, he sat up and plucked a hidden mushroom, offering it to me.

"No, I'll be a stick of jelly for hours if we rut anymore." Bluedot mushrooms heightened the senses and, in my case, made me want sex.

"I love it when you say rut."

Growling, I shoved his hand away. "When are you meeting Klaud?" Klaud was his other lover, a soldier, and didn't appreciate the trysts Berron and I so often found ourselves in. Training did make it more intense, and the release was definitely appreciated, though Klaud thought it ridiculous.

I thought he was a jealous idiot and often told him so. I had no interest in Berron's heart, much to his chagrin when we'd first began taking our training sessions to this level. My interests lay only in his sword-wielding skills. Both swords.

Apparently, when one loved another, they did not like the concept of sharing. That was Klaud's problem, not mine. And it never would be.

"I'm not sure," Berron said, words trailing away from him.

"Princess?" The weeds swished as Mintale's voice reached us. "Princess!"

I rolled my eyes at the cloud-dusted sky, then sat up and twisted my tunic back into place. "Stop it, I'm right here."

Mintale did stop, almost treading on Berron, who was munching on the mushroom with sated azure eyes. "Hello, Mintale."

Mintale scowled down at him. "This does not look like proper training etiquette."

"That's because it's most assuredly not," I said, jumping to my feet.

Mintale removed his accusing stare from Berron and swung it to me.

I waited, and he sighed. "Your presence was required at court a half hour ago. You know what day it is." At my raised brows, his jowls wobbled with his frustrated words. "Prince Raiden is already here."

A deep, dry voice sounded. "There's little need to rush, not when he is, indeed, already here."

Shocked, I stumbled back a step and turned.

Prince Raiden stood behind us, leaning against a rotted post as he squinted in Berron's direction. "If you continue fucking my future wife, I will have your head."

Berron muttered a string of curses and leaped to his feet, bowing. "Your highness."

I giggled, and the prince fixed his eyes on mine.

I think that was the first time I'd ever experienced what it was to fall while still standing.

To move when not moving at all.

To cease breathing when your lungs continued to circulate air.

Intrigue like no other gripped me by the chest, forcing my feet closer. I curtsied and held out my hand. "So we finally meet."

The prince didn't take it; he merely continued with that hard stare. After a moment, he blinked, then straightened and bent at the waist as his warm skin met my cold.

His lips were crushed rose petals, redder than unpainted lips had any right to be and softer than lips had any right to be as they landed upon my chilled skin.

Electric tension shifted every muscle inside me, pulling my spine taut and my eyes to his.

The contrast of our skin, caramel over snow, was striking, and my heart thumped like a galloping beast. He was a solid wall of charming steel, and I was but a poisonous flower.

"It is a pleasure."

"I'm sure," I said, sliding my hand from his gentle grip.

He straightened, his smile warmer than the sun soaking the tops of our heads.

Berron tripped through the brush, then chuckled. "I will take my leave, your highness."

Raiden cut his eyes at Berron, assessing his tall frame. "You eat mushrooms while training the princess?"

"That and more," I said before I could help myself.

Raiden's hands clenched at his sides, and I didn't know what he would do with that knowledge, nor did I care. He didn't get to boss me around or steal my fun just because he planned to vow to me.

He and Berron continued their stare down. Berron was the first to break it, backtracking through the tall grass with a wink my way. "Later, Princess."

It was then I realized Mintale had disappeared too, and I pursed my lips, wondering how much trouble he'd be in with my father when he returned to the palace without me.

"Take a walk with me?" It was a question, but it sounded like a command.

I tilted my head, curious. "A walk."

His grin wavered. "Well, I'm not about to ask you to frolic in the gardens with me." His expression flattened. "Not when you're probably full of that tainted seed."

My eyes widened at his crassness. Tainted was one of many less than desirable names given to the half royal, half human people.

"Are you taking a tonic?"

They widened further. "I might be only nineteen summers, but that doesn't make me stupid."

He heaved a sigh, dragging a hand over his close-cropped dark hair, muttering something I couldn't decipher.

"If you're going to say things about me, do say them at a volume I can hear. I can assure you, I've undoubtedly heard it all before, *Prince*." I hissed the title.

"If we're to take this seriously, this merger, then you need to end this dalliance. Find yourself a new trainer."

I began walking. "I'll do no such thing."

He quickly caught up, our boots crunching over dry earth. "You're as difficult as I've heard."

"And as beautiful?"

His vibrant greens filled with his smile. "More so, painfully so, but you already know that."

I did, so I kept my mouth shut, wondering what in the darkness I was going to do with this prince I'd been handed.

"So if fucking me is out of the question, what else are you good for?"

His laughter was rain and thunder combined with that of a songbird. Deep. Rough yet whimsical. "I guess you'll have to wait and see."

We'd reached the outer trail of the small mountain that sloped to meet the east end of the castle walls when he grabbed my hand. "Hold on."

I stopped, allowing him to keep hold of my hand but unsure as to why. "What?"

He turned to me and lifted a thumb to brush beneath my lower lip. "You had grass there."

"That whole time?" I plucked my hand from his. "And you didn't think to tell me?" I'd thought perhaps he was going to try to give me some pointers on how we'd walk inside the throne room. On how we'd handle my father after arriving so late, and together at that.

I thought wrong.

His top lip rose into a sneer. "It will likely take a considerable length of time to get over the way I first saw my wife. On her back." His long lashes dipped, then fanned high, almost meeting his thick brows. "With another male." Then he was jogging down the hillside, leaving me behind to wonder how much he'd seen back in that field before making his presence known.

SIX

QUIET BLANKETED THE DUNGEON.

Ghosts, the whistle of the wind through the cracks in the stone, and the beating of our hearts the only sound.

Then, finally, Raiden's jaw snapped shut, and he began circling his cell, laughter falling out of him. "You scheming royal witch."

Funny, how one was always so quick to curse a kind that was not their own. Or, at least, so he thought was not his own. "It's true, husband."

He was at the bars immediately, their clang surprising us both as they shook the stone walls and ceiling. Dust crumbled in a nearly imperceptible falling rain. "You lot are all the same. Power-hungry animals that do little more than mate and scheme for more power and then mate some more. I would never want a thing to do with the likes of you." A quick survey of my body had his teeth gnashing. "Especially you."

"Perhaps you never did." It was something that became obvious and had made me feel even more the fool, but it was all too little, too late. "Perhaps, even if you never cared, you still enjoyed playing your games. I suppose we might never know."

His brows knitted. "What in the darkness are you talking about?"

"You know." A low sound escaped me, a struggling thrum of laughter. "Deep down, you know exactly what I'm talking about."

"No," he said, sounding slightly crazed. "I really don't." He gave his head a vicious shake. "I grew up in The Edges, raised by my grandparents."

"And who told you this?" The potion forced down his throat, alongside the incantation, was meant to suppress, to give him a generic backstory formed by dreams of his own and little else.

He looked at me as if I were crazy for asking such a thing. "No one. It's just the truth."

I hummed, then slid down the table until my burgundy suede heels met the floor. Their click over the stone dragged his attention to my exposed legs as I stalked closer to his cage, my wits about me but my smile lazy. "You want to know what I think, Prince?"

His head snapped back at the word. "I'm no prince, you fucking psychotic—"

A flick of my fingers had his lips slamming closed. "As I was saying." I wrapped my hands around the bars. His nostrils flared, and his green eyes danced—wild, untamed, and filled with something I'd never seen on this male before. *Fear.* "I think you've concocted a nice little tale from nothing. All the better to help warm your bed with that almost wife of yours." My fingers neared his as he grabbed the bars, and I licked my crimson-painted upper lip. "I wonder what she'd make of it. Discovering that her betrothed was not a common worker from The Edges, but a prince." A hand met my breasts as I gasped, my lashes fluttering. "But wait, she already knew you weren't a prince. All along, she's known you were a king. *My* king." I grinned. "Naughty, naughty."

The tendons and veins in his neck bulged, and then he lunged.

His hand was steel around my wrist, but I just laughed before I sent him sailing back into the wall. His back greeted it with a booming thud, and dirt sailed through the small square space as he slumped to the floor, groaning.

"We'll resume tomorrow. Or not. The choice is yours." I left before he could answer, before he could inflict any more damage to what remained inside me.

He'd already murdered my heart, but I wouldn't put it past him to find something else to attack. My shadowed soul would surely suffice.

Upstairs in my rooms, I ran a brush through my hair, ignoring the way my hands shook as I walked circles around the gray and white Ergin hide rug. Then I braided it, something I didn't bother with unless, as I'd told Raiden, I was fighting, training, or had long days of riding.

The silken strands weaved between my fingers while I thought back to a time when I had handmaidens. I'd culled and burned the lot right before the castle walls after discovering how some had aided in my father's demise. In the attempted demise of me and this palace.

Some had probably been undeserving, innocent, but the burning inferno inside my chest hadn't cared. In any case, it was best not to take any chances.

Raised by grandparents. I scoffed and grabbed a piece of silk to tie the ends of my hair.

His parents were dead, and none of those in power had grandparents anymore.

SEVEN

UNNERVED AND FRUSTRATED, I DIDN'T RETURN TO THE dungeon for two nights.

Two nights spent staring at the cracks in the ceiling, wondering how my heart fared in comparison.

My heart had it worse than the ancient stonework.

I was better than that, and I proved it to myself. If I couldn't sleep, and if I couldn't fuck—though not for lack of trying, I just wasn't interested—then I would fight.

I dodged left, then pirouetted, arcing down and slicing through Garris's holster as he stumbled back. "Majesty," he said, out of breath, fear a shining entity in his eyes.

I swallowed, then rolled my shoulders. "Again."

Ignoring his broken holster, he took his position, raising his sword as he squared his feet.

Pinks and muted oranges gave backdrop to the square balcony, bouncing off the vines and blood red roses circling it. I dodged its rays as well as Garris's lunge and leaped backward into a roll, my stomach protesting as I found my footing.

"You need to eat," a deceptively soft voice said from behind me.

Distracted by Zad's sudden presence, Garris howled when I spun into a roundhouse kick and struck him in the ribs. He collapsed, groaning and cursing.

"When you're done whining, clean up." I sheathed my sword and left it behind. Without looking at Zad, I floated past him as I began unbraiding my hair.

"You're back," I said once he'd caught up with me.

His favored knee-high black boots scuffed over the concrete stairs, and I frowned, annoyed that I hadn't even heard his approach to the rooftop.

The sooner my king was dead, the better.

"We have things to discuss."

"Such as?"

He kept his hands clasped before him as he stared straight ahead, his profile unreadable when I chanced a quick glance. "After you've eaten."

I bit my tongue. We hit the hall, gliding past ancestors trapped in silver heavy frames, and wound down the next, and the one after that.

When concrete met woolen rugs, I caught the scent of freshly baked bread and coffee. My stomach vibrated once more, but I didn't care who heard. I pushed open the doors to the dining room and shooed the kitchen staff and servers away.

Zad prepared my coffee while I grabbed a goblet of water and drained it. I was tempted to slouch all over my chair, but I gathered some self-control and tucked my legs in, one rising to rest over the other as I reached for a piece of buttered toast.

"Things?" I prompted, taking another sip of water.

He placed a steaming cup of coffee down before me, the porcelain tiny in his large hand, then took a seat in the chair to my right. "He's not dead yet."

I coughed, tilting my head as I met his blank gaze. "And that is your concern now, is it?"

Zad sat with the stillness of a predator, his black jacket pressed to perfection, hinting at the lean yet powerful form beneath with the way it sat and draped over his muscular shoulders. A ruse, the finery, to hide what lurked beneath.

He drank some coffee, then set his cup down. "I do not pretend to know everything, but I do know one thing. I cannot vow to you when he is no longer in exile." With a coldness that threatened to engulf my skin in chills, he shifted his lips and fixed his golden eyes upon me. "He needs to die, and you're prolonging it."

"He will die, and I alone will make sure of it." I tore at a piece of buttery toast, chewing hard. If he thought he could return here and boss me around...

"You're still in love with him."

The bread seemed to expand in my throat, and I had to force it down with coffee. "Is one even capable of love when they no longer have a heart?"

Zad studied me. "Oh, you have one. It's just a little more... dead than usual."

That pulled a smile from me. "You speak the truth."

"Always." His eyes danced over my face, falling to my mouth.

I bit my lip but decided to keep things from going any further. "He will meet his end when he understands the multitude of ways he caused me to meet my own."

"Dramatic." Long, deft, thick fingers tapped a slow beat over the table.

My thighs clamped together. I knew what he was doing, so I tore my eyes away. "It is what it is, Lord. You don't like it? Leave. I'd rather not vow ever again anyway."

A caress and a threat, he crooned, "You think me so easily cast aside?"

I speared him with a raised brow and low words. "My word is my word. I will abide by it if you abide by what I've said." I leaned forward, my elbows hitting the table. "Touch him and I'll end you."

He didn't so much as blink, but he couldn't hide the instant clenching of his jaw.

I let the words hang there, then straightened and finished my toast as Mintale arrived, sputtering about court beginning at noon.

I tossed my napkin down. "It cannot be that time of the month already."

"That's what most females say," Zad muttered into his cup.

Mintale muffled his laughter behind his hair-flecked hand.

"Any word from Berron?" He along with some of our top guards were doing their best to keep control of the Sun Kingdom.

The law wouldn't hold much longer. Not with the resistance growing. I needed to devise a better way to keep order, but every idea, short of setting fire to their entire kingdom, seemed futile.

"Not yet. But I did check on the, uh, on your, ah..." At my scowl, he got to the point. "Raiden, seeing as it's been some time since you've been down there."

Of course, he had. "He doesn't need food when he's doomed anyway."

Mintale shifted on his feet, eyes downcast on the cup of tea he lifted to his lips.

"And it's only been a few days. I'm sure he's fine."

"He was hallucinating," Mintale said, lowering his tea with a tightness to his forehead that indicated he was concerned.

My hand curled, and what remained of my coffee soon decorated the floor and the broken porcelain beside my chair. "*What?*"

Cheeks wobbling, Mintale nodded. "He was mumbling incoherent things, which alerted the guards, who then alerted me."

"How long was he hallucinating for?"

Zad's eyes were stalking, unwilling to move from me.

Mintale's lips flattened. "They said most of the night. They thought he was playing another game, testing another way to appeal to someone's softer side—another attempt at freedom."

My hand met my forehead, rubbing. "So he was hallucinating—*for hours*—and no one thought to inform me until now?"

Zad's magic stirred, his discomfort and ire practically bleeding into the room to mingle with my own.

"Well, to be perfectly honest, I didn't think you'd care, my queen."

After gaping at him for untold seconds, I closed my eyes, reciting all the reasons, aside from being a fixture in our lineage for most of my father's life, Mintale was important to me. The most important being his unbreakable loyalty.

"Mintale, do not keep anything from me again. Not one single thing." My voice was gentle, a feathered wind over his face. Though he'd be stupid not to take it for the warning it was. "Now go fetch Truin to find out why this could be happening."

Mintale paled, dropping his cup and saucer to the table before bowing. "Of course."

Zadicus watched him leave, his thumb brushing over his bottom lip. "Interesting."

"I don't know what to believe." I feared heading down there, wondering if it was indeed a hoax.

Zad turned to me, leaning forward with an elbow planted on the table. "The spellcaster said she cannot undo the suppressing."

I swallowed more water, then grabbed an apple to take with me to my rooms. "No, but it is just that. A suppressing." I stood and tossed my hair over my shoulder. "I have faith that he will remember what he's done to me and to this continent before his lights go out once and for all."

I took a crunching bite from the glossy red fruit, my leather training pants creaking as I sashayed to the door.

"You? Have faith?" Zad questioned with laughter, like the obnoxious worm he was. "Wait, you're feeding him memories?"

I stopped with my back to him in the arched doorway. "Unless you know of another way, my lord, then yes, that is precisely what I'm doing."

Raiden was sitting in the corner of his cell, knees drawn tight to his chest and his head bent sideways, staring at a slice of light leaking in through a tiny gap in the stones. "You're back."

I almost faltered but kept moving forward to take my perch upon the blood-marred table, fingers digging into the wood. He didn't look at me, so I peered around his cell, taking note of the pail in the corner attracting tisks. "You've been acting a little crazy, I hear."

"Nothing for you to worry your evil head about."

I scoffed. "Don't make me laugh. That's not what I came here for."

He did look at me then, slowly, as if he was mentally preparing himself for the sight of me.

I was still wearing my training gear. The leather pants snug around my legs and hips, rising over my stomach to rest beneath the beige thermal covering my breasts and arms.

His eyes began their journey at my wolf skin boots, taking their time to roam the length of my body. When they met mine, I felt my lips part, and a small breath burst free. His skin seemed a shade paler, and his eyes, rimmed with shadows, lacked their usual translucency.

"Did our first meeting affect you, Prince?" I kept hope, that pesky bitch, in its place.

"Stomach flu," he muttered, turning away to stare back at that tiny source of light. "And I've already told you, though I'm sure it's wasted breath, that I'm no prince. And if you ask me, you're definitely no queen."

My nails scored into the wood, pieces chipping away and crumbling to the floor. "It is an act of treason to insult a queen."

"Yeah?" he said. "Well, from what I gather, I'm dead anyway. So fuck it." He turned back to face me, then did one better than that, and rose on shaking legs to grab the silver bars. "You're no better than the scum beneath our nails, the shit stuck beneath the soles of our boots, and the scorpions that try to kill us in those precious mines of yours." He spat at the ground beneath my feet, then grinned before swaying and retaking his seat in the corner of his cell. "*Queen*."

"They're your mines too." I felt the need to remind him, darkness knew why. With a thought and a flick of my wrist, the gate to his cell unlocked, and Raiden gaped as it swung open. "Now lick that filth off the floor before I send you to your grave earlier than planned."

He wore another grin as he stepped outside his cell and stopped before me. The words were low and hissed. "Fuck you."

Rage gathered my fingers. Throwing him to the floor, I watched as his hands slapped at the straw-littered concrete in time to stop his face from colliding with it.

Then I jumped down, my boot digging into his lower back as he tried to rise. "Lick it or die."

"I bet you need to say that to all the males." With clenching teeth, I waited. "I said, oh, dearest queen… fuck you."

He clearly had no concern for his own well-being.

So be it.

"How about that wife of yours, then? Oh"—I clicked my tongue—"I should say *almost wife*. Do you think she'd like to keep her pretty ring finger in order for you to dress it with a filthy piece of jewelry?"

I felt the shift in him. Felt it travel from his spine into the sole of my boot and foot, sending a shockwave of disbelief with another knife to my decaying heart.

"You took her." Not a question, but a frail murmur of fear.

"Foolish Prince." My laughter was genuine, and I sank my foot into his back, forcing him to flatten to the ground as I hunched over him and hissed, "I'm no scorpion. What I am is her worst fucking nightmare if you so much as breathe wrong in my direction again."

"Don't," he gritted out, his cheek crushed against the concrete. "Okay. Fine, okay."

I removed my foot and stepped back, folding my arms over my chest as I watched him lick his own phlegm from the stained, vermin-traveled ground.

When he was done, I kicked him in the stomach. "Now get back in your cage."

It shut with a clang after he'd hauled himself back inside, wiping at his mouth with the ratty sleeve of his white cotton tunic. The same one he'd planned to marry that scum in was now discolored from sweat and countless other wonderful things.

"Sit," I said, shaking out my arms and rolling my shoulders as I paced in slow circles around the torture table. I had half a mind to tie him to it and leave him to rot while I headed upstairs to have Zad put his mouth between my thighs. A nice way to help me forget all about the male who tortured and molested every part of me without touching me at all.

Alas, I was here, and who knew when I'd scrounge up the energy he seemed to deplete so easily to return again.

"I'm not a dog."

"I'm sorry," I said, kicking the bars with a pout. "Did you say something?"

He grimaced and then closed his eyes as his head fell back against the wall behind it.

"Are you ready for more?"

"Would you care if I said no?"

"No."

He waved a hand as I retook my seat upon the table. "Then by all means."

***

19 summers old

"Princess, please hold still." Irma yanked on my hair.

I hissed, then plucked the brush from her hand and smacked her with it before handing it to Lura to finish the job.

"Pull it out," I said, studying the crimson rouge on my lips, the shadowed kohl lining my blue eyes. "I said no updo. This is a ball, not a burial."

Irma got busy fussing over my dress in the doorway, billows of steam rising from her hands to smooth any creases. Her father was a noble who'd stepped out on his wife with a human woman, resulting in Irma—as well as all other half breeds when they came of age—being surrendered into service to the crown.

Some half breeds were born with magic—mostly elemental abilities—though those abilities often paled in comparison to the royal whom they'd inherited them from. Others were born with nothing more than greater strength, sharper senses, and a longer lifespan than the average human. Even if whatever gifts they'd stolen were of little match for a true royal, Rosinthe had thought it safer to keep those with power they shouldn't possess under the watchful eye of the crown. Doing so also ensured the high royal bloodline remained pure.

Royals could sully themselves with whomever they wished, but to procreate with a human was an embarrassment many feared. Yet, of course, there were always enough fools about who thought of little else when faced with temptation.

Why anyone would be tempted, I never wanted to know.

My gown was made from many a badger's coat, and dyed and spelled a rose red. A little black fur trim remained to line the bodice and edging, which would make even more of a statement courtesy of the crinoline beneath.

Lura heated my hair into soft waves around my face and neck, leaving it to spiral over my breasts and shoulder blades.

After helping me into my dress, I was spritzed with vanilla orchid oil and puffed with a plume of powder before being escorted out the door to the stairs and my waiting guard.

My palms grew clammy the closer we drew to the doors of the ballroom, and I frowned, pausing in the hall and demanding my guard go on ahead of me.

A few servants whistled by. Platters of smoked fish and spiced chicken scented the air of the otherwise empty, drafty hallway. From the rafters hung swaying tapestry displaying our kingdom's sigil—a full, glowing moon pressed between the horns of a furbane.

I blinked, imagining the rush of my blood slowing, and the tapestry settled, but I struggled to slow the fluttering of my heart.

He would be here. After all, this was a ball to celebrate our commitment to vow. I was supposed to meet him in the hall at the western entrance of the ballroom so we could enter together. But I'd purposely run late and told my handmaidens those plans had changed.

This is ridiculous. I was acting as if he were the first male to ever arouse interest from me.

He wasn't. Many males had taken my fancy. Berron might have been the only one I allowed inside my body—he was the only male I trusted in this kingdom—but that didn't mean I didn't take pleasure in having other hands and mouths upon me whenever the chance to sneak away arrived.

Feeling the flush in my cheeks, I decided that it was his parting words.

He'd made a scene out of my dalliance, and though I wasn't embarrassed, I didn't appreciate feeling as though I wasn't on a level battlefield.

Those parting words and the way he'd left me to stand there, then act kosher in front of our tense fathers were also the reasons I'd decided to one-up him and arrive on my own.

"I am robbed of breath."

Spinning in the direction of the whispered words, I came face to face with my betrothed.

I didn't bother with formalities and instead, took my time drinking in his towering form. Dressed in fitted black pants and a matching tunic embroidered with gold that looked as though it'd burst at his shoulders, I found my own lungs drying.

He wore a coat lined with the same rose red as my gown, and my eyes darted up to his.

He read the question in them. "Your father was so kind as to inform me of your wardrobe choices."

"Of course, he was." My tone was dry, crisp.

Raiden rolled his lips together, slowly releasing them with a lick of his tongue.

My knees quaked, and the tapestry began to stir and tremble once more.

He peered up at it, then at me, his knowing smile maddening. "If only that trainer of yours had spent more time teaching than coaxing pleasure, huh?" I scowled as he took three steps closer, his scent, apples and singed sugar, suffocating. "Maybe then you'd have a better handle on your…" His finger curled around a lock of my hair, and I shoved it away with a burst of wind. He grinned. "Reactions."

"I've been using since I was twelve." I squared my shoulders and met his grass green eyes. "And it's often drafty in here."

Technically, I'd come of age at fourteen, but I did have some nifty tricks to use on Mintale and the other staff before then.

He nodded. "I'm sure." Offering his arm, he said, "Shall we?"

I ignored the muscular limb and turned on my heel toward the ballroom. Dark laughter followed me and then warm heat wrapped around my middle.

Shocked, I growled, matching it with a blast of cold as I looked over my shoulder. "You dare try to trap me?"

He was leaning against the wall, scratching at his smooth, square chin. "You dared to walk away from me."

"I don't need an escort."

A passing server blinked at us, and I sent her tray of creamed crab flying into the wall. She cursed, then fell to her knees, scrambling to pick it all up.

And that was one of the first and only times I'd ever felt what it was like to be disappointed in myself. Not because of what I'd done. I'd done a galaxy's worse than that.

But because of him, the prince, and the way he looked at me.

Raiden stared with an intensity that seemed to probe and dig around inside every atom of my body, feeling and searching for things long buried.

I looked away, and he strode over to assist the server, who gushed her gratitude, her plump cheeks the color of my dress. Lifting my chin, I swallowed down the slime infesting my chest and pushed open the doors to the ballroom.

Golden light swathed every patron inside, and three thrones sat upon a dais. One for my father, one for Phane, Raiden's father, and another for his mother, Solnia.

My father was wearing his usual kaleidoscope of colors. Blue trousers, yellow cotton button-down, and a cape made of rich silvers and blacks that shimmered every time he breathed.

His midnight hair was combed back from his face, revealing dark eyes and a clean-shaven jaw.

He winked at me, and I sucked in a breath, forcing a smile

before walking forward to greet him. But a hand curled around mine as I wound through the crowd, ignoring the greetings and compliments.

I sneered at Raiden, and he leaned down, murmuring in my ear as we neared the dais. "Behave, silk."

"Silk?" I questioned. If it was his plan to dumbfound me into losing my ire, it worked.

"Your skin, your hair, and I bet…" His eyes found my lips. "Your mouth too. The finest silk known to our kind."

"Sweet talk will get you nowhere," I retorted, but I was all breath and heaving breasts.

His hand stayed steadfast around mine, gently squeezing, then he tugged me forward.

His parents stood, stepping down to greet us with forehead kisses and arm rubs.

"Perfect," his mother crooned, adjusting the lapels of her son's coat with adoring cinnamon eyes and shoulder-length curls to match. Her smile glimmered beneath the floating lights as her fingers danced through my hair, and she chattered on about what our children might look like.

The mere thought of breeding with the arrogant male who carried an alarmingly wonderful scent was the last thing I wanted floating into my rioting mind.

Still, I smiled, my cheeks aching as I kept it fastened, and then turned to my father who finally decided to grace us with his presence.

His arm was heavy around my shoulders, as well as the lager on his breath, when he lowered his head, and said, "Your bosom is catching too many eyes, daughter."

I swallowed, not daring to look or touch my gown. Not in public. "I shall adjust it when I get a moment."

"Do that," he said with a tap on my shoulder. "You're a committed female now. Act the part." Then he moved to Raiden, wrapping him in a hug that had my stomach clenching as Raiden's entire form stiffened. He was a head taller than my father. As I peered at him, I found his lips had flattened.

Interesting. But not interesting enough to hold my attention once I caught sight of a passing tray of wine. I snatched one, then began circling the room, searching for Berron and Truin.

I found the latter by the outer wall, standing with one of her coven friends.

Truin smiled, lifting her glass as I approached. "Stunning as always, my princess."

"Quit with the niceties." I took a huge swig of wine, swallowing. "Let's start devising a plan to get out of here."

Truin frowned. "Well, it's your party. You can't…" She stopped talking, and I needn't have asked why. I felt him approach this time, inhaled that scent of his clouding the air around us.

Truin blushed, then curtsied. "Congratulations, Prince Evington."

"Raiden," the man himself said, stepping forward to take Truin's hand.

My face and shoulders became granite as I watched his lips descend upon her skin. As if sensing it, Raiden didn't let them meet and graciously released her hand.

Truin raised a brow at me, and I felt my skin begin to warm. I drained my wine and set the goblet down on a marble topped statue of a furbane.

"Excuse us," Raiden said, taking me by the arm and leading me to the dance floor.

"You really need to quit manhandling me," I said through a fake smile.

In answer, Raiden pulled me close, aligning my stomach with that of his crotch.

His very hard crotch.

"If you think that was manhandling, that trainer of yours has a lot to learn."

Reluctantly, I looped my arms around his neck when his circled my back, and he began rocking us between the other dancing couples. "Berron bothers you that much." Not a question.

Raiden huffed, his hands roaming my back as if he were studying the curve of my hips and spine through the material while his eyes wandered the room. "I merely find it concerning that you've been left in the hands of a pup who only wants to mount you instead of teach you."

I murmured low, "Oh, but he has taught me a lot."

Raiden's gaze snapped to mine, eyes ablaze. I fluttered my lashes, and he smirked.

"Evidently. Though we do need to work on those reactions of yours. Or else when I have you in my bed, I'm afraid you'll send every piece of furniture flying about the room."

I wouldn't take shit from him. For a female of only nineteen summers, I knew I had a remarkable hold on my powers. "There's no need to worry your pretty face about such matters."

"No?" he asked, spinning me around and then pulling me back to his chest.

My stomach leaped. "No, it's never going to happen."

His head fell back, and his loud bursts of laughter caught most eyes in the room. Including my father, who squinted at us.

I hissed at Raiden, "You can shut your filthy mouth any moment now. Everyone is looking."

He did, though the amusement never left his eyes. I had a feeling that was common for this prince. "I have an idea."

"I don't care." I made to remove myself from his hold, not liking the way his skin felt against mine. The way it felt familiar and new all at once.

He squeezed my hips. "A dare?"

"I may be young, but I don't often play." I stepped back, and he chuckled.

"Fine." Reaching for me, he cupped my chin and whispered into my ear, "If you change your mind, I'll be down in the cellars, getting drunk on my own, or maybe not…" His hands skated to my shoulders, down my arms, then skimmed my wrists and palms as he released me. "I guess it's up to you who'll join me. You?" He swung his eyes around the room. "Or someone else."

I watched him leave and didn't move even after I lost sight of him.

"Princess."

I blinked, wondering how long the lord of the east had been standing beside me, and reluctantly turned to him.

"You look…" His gaze slowly swept up my body, his fiery eyes warm as they met mine. "Beautiful," he finished, and the way it rolled off his tongue, soft and intimate, felt like a thousand compliments in one word.

Peering up at him, I realized just how finely hewn his features were. High, sharp cheeks, thin yet plush lips, a square-cut jaw, and lashes a shade or two darker than his auburn hair. If it weren't for the bump in the bridge of his otherwise straight nose, one would think he were forged from magic stone by the goddesses themselves.

"It is customary to say thank you after a compliment," Zad said, waking me from my trance.

Someone must have laced the wine.

"And it is customary to leave those who do not desire your company alone." His brows lowered, and I gathered my gown, smiling tight as I made to leave. "Apologies, my lord, but you'll need to find yourself another princess to read to from now on."

Unamused, Zad nodded once. "Insults aside, we should talk."

"Talk about what?"

His eyes flicked behind me. "Not here."

I laughed at his audacity. "Not anywhere, Zad." Before I could leave, he snatched my wrist and pulled me close. "You have some nerve—"

"Listen," he said so painfully quiet into my ear, his breath tickling. "I don't know enough yet, but I still think we should—"

"Well, if it isn't my favorite lord," my father said, coming up behind us.

I wrenched free of his grip, my heart thumping as my father threw his arm around Zad's shoulders.

"I'm glad you made it. We have much to discuss." With a wink and a hard look that suggested I go play the role expected of me, my father led a seemingly reluctant Zad away.

I stared after them for a beat, worry rolling over me in the form of a shiver.

Across the room, Zad's eyes flicked to me while my father reached for two goblets from a passing tray, then fell away as he accepted the wine.

My father sipped, cringed, then tossed the goblet at the server's head, red wine spraying his white uniform and face. I didn't need to hear him to know he was berating the server for something he wasn't aware he did wrong. Zad said something that caught my enraged father's attention, and when he turned back to the lord, the terrified server raced away while he had the chance.

Zad smirked, sipping from the golden goblet, and my father threw his head back, clapping the lord as he laughed loud enough to scare the few guests nearby.

The clenching of my muscles eased, and I released a breath that shook my shoulders. Of course, the lord of the east knew how to play my father like a fiddle, or else he'd likely had lost his lands long ago.

Walking aimlessly, I found Berron and Truin outside by the fountain smoking pipes with some of the guards.

Berron glanced up, offered me a smile, and then emptied his goblet.

My breath sailed out of me, and I rushed forward to grab his chin. "What in the darkness happened to your face?"

He winced, then plucked my hand from his bruised skin. "It's fine." Purple and blue surrounded his right eye, and a gash split the middle of his lower lip. "Your betrothed apparently meant it when he warned me not to fuck you again."

"I'll rip his—"

"Where is he?" Poppy cut me off.

I barely refrained from sneering at the young guard. "Who?" We all knew who she was referring to, but it would not behoove me to act as though everything revolved around Prince Annoying.

"The Sun Prince."

"In the wine cellar," said Garris, joining us. "I saw him head down there as I was trading shifts."

The urge to ask if he was alone itched like a rash, but I suffered the torment in silence.

They chattered on, discussing who was the best and worst dressed, and who would pair off with whom.

I lasted all of ten minutes before I was excusing myself. "Ladies' room."

Berron's eyes narrowed, and Poppy nodded. Truin merely smiled as I gathered my gown and dragged it with me back inside and through the throng of lively bodies in the ballroom.

It trailed behind me as I wound down the halls and breezed past servers and cooks in the kitchens, then down the winding, dusty steps to the cellars as fury and frustration simmered in my veins.

The door clanged shut behind me, alerting Raiden that he had company and also plunging me into darkness. A flicker of light bounced from a sconce below the stairs as I rounded the last row of them and emerged to find the prince sprawled over sacks of grain.

Apparently making my arrival known didn't deter him or his companion in the slightest.

I coughed, my hands scrunching. The handmaiden giggled while Raiden laid beside her, murmuring something into her ear.

"Ennis, aren't there guest rooms you should be preparing?"

She froze, then peeked at me beneath Raiden's arm.

He kept his attention on her, said something that made her laugh again, and then he flopped over to his back, his tunic crumpled, coat on the floor, and his smile casual. "Do you mind? We're a little busy here."

Ennis giggled once more, and I couldn't stop it if I'd tried. My fingers unfurled before I could rearrange my thoughts, suctioning the air from her lungs.

Raiden cursed, eyes no longer playful but wide with shock as he hurried off the sacks of grain and raced to me. "Stop. Now."

I couldn't, and I wasn't sure why. It was blinding, this hatred. This feeling of being defied in the highest order. I was her princess. He was my betrothed. "She laughed at me."

Ennis's hands were wrapped around her throat, her eyes twin pools of bloodshot fear.

"I am her princess, your future wife, and she laughed at me."

"Audra." Raiden's hand clasped mine, warm against my cold, but I didn't let up.

I wrenched away from him and stomped closer, my fingers spreading and forcing air back inside her lungs, but not kindly. No—all at once.

Ennis coughed, sputtering and wheezing as she doubled over onto the floor.

I felt my lips curl as I then stole her oxygen again.

And then a wave of unbearable heat sent my head spinning. I teetered, careening into a hard chest. I blinked as it drifted away, dizzy and disoriented. I was draped over the very sacks of grain the two co-conspirators had laid upon, and when I pushed up on my elbows, my dress fanning around me in waves of red, I came face to face with that of Ennis.

Raiden was handing her a goblet of wine, whispering comforting words as her shaking hand lifted it to her lips. Her eyes were still stained with red, but clear. Clear but saturated with horror as she stared at me.

"It would serve you well to quit looking at me like that, or I might just end your existence."

Raiden sighed, then stood and helped Ennis to do the same.

The way he was helping her, soothing her when she'd conspired against me and insulted me encouraged the rage to climb back to the surface.

As if he knew, he hurried her to the stairs. "Return to work and speak nothing of what you saw and experienced here."

"What's it matter if she does? She's lucky I don't drain her for her actions."

Raiden watched her go, and when the clang of the door sounded up the stairs, he turned and leaned against the stone wall at the bottom. He rubbed a hand down his face and laughed low at the ground. "You almost killed her."

"She'll lose her tongue come sunrise."

Raiden shook his head, laughing once more.

"I'd love to know what you find so amusing about this, you cretin."

"You," he said, leveling me with a gaze so cold, I felt my stomach dip.

"Me?" I asked, exasperated.

He took two slow steps forward, tucking his hands inside his pant pockets. "You abuse your magic with a dramatic flair. Only"—he crouched down in front of me—"you don't mean to play like most of us. You mean to harm in extremes."

The words he didn't say lingered there, sharp and stabbing.

Just like your father.

I shook off the accusation. "If you don't squash the rebellion of insects, insects will grow enough power to squash you."

Raiden blinked, a slow dip of his lashes, then narrowed his eyes. This close, I noticed just how smooth, how striking the planes of his face were. How his lashes looked softer than feathers and the way they curled at the very tips. Shadowing formed along his jawline, the finest dusting of hair peeking through his golden skin. He might have been beautiful—most high royal males were—but beauty was a trap. I should know.

I was the deadliest trap of all.

When I realized he'd said nothing, and I was doing nothing but staring, I snapped, "Move."

"No."

I leaned forward, growling the words. "I said move."

He knelt close, his nose almost touching mine, the scent of wine fogging my lips. "And I said no."

Stuck and outraged, I stared. "We need to call off this marriage."

"Why?" he whispered, his eyes flicking to my lips before meeting mine, that peculiar spark returning to them. "It's business, Audra."

"Because I'd rather die than be miserable."

He tilted his head. "I get beneath your skin. You've met me twice"—his finger drifted down my cheek, gliding ever so slowly—"yet I've crawled beneath that ice-cold exterior, and you don't like it."

I pushed his chest, but he didn't budge.

He tutted. "Reactions, silk. We'll definitely need to work on those."

"We'll work on nothing," I said, attempting to wiggle back over the sacks of grain.

He caught my ankle, and I screeched as he dragged me to him. "Why did you come down here then?"

Remembering what he'd done to Berron's face and likely to other parts of his body had my spine snapping straight. "Berron. I saw what you did to him."

"Me?" He had the audacity to raise his brows.

"Yes." I poked him in the chest, my nail denting his tunic. "You had no right."

His expression was irritatingly void. "And what is it that I did?"

I inhaled a deep breath through my nose, begging the goddesses for patience. "Don't try to trick your way around the truth. You know what you did."

Raiden lifted a broad shoulder, then rose and walked over to where his goblet sat on the dusty floor.

He sipped, and I forced myself to stand before marching to

the crates in the back of the cellar and yanking out a bottle of wine. I cracked the top, then took a lengthy swig. "Nothing to say?"

Raiden smiled into his goblet, then swirled the vine-engraved silver. "Not a lot."

"Touch him again and I'll—"

He was in front of me in a flash. "You'll what?"

I lifted the bottle, draining as much of its contents as I could stomach as he watched, then I smiled. "I'll find someone you care about, and I'll make what happened to Ennis look like a nice little entrée to the main course."

I went to circle him, but I was stopped by his next words. "Stay."

"In case you haven't noticed, Prince, we've deserted our own party." My father would be furious if I didn't return soon. "And I find myself tiring of you already."

"Shame." He clucked his tongue. "We were just beginning to have some fun."

"Fun?" I turned, tilting my head. "If arguing is your idea of fun, you're more delusional than I presumed you to be."

Pursing his lips, he swished his wine again before finishing it. "I find you… intriguing. To say the least."

My mouth dried. I drank some more.

Raiden slumped down onto the grain, patting the sack beside him. "Come. Drink. What's the worst that could happen? We fuck down here while they party up there?" He reached for the bottle of wine he'd left open on the floor. "We're to be married. They won't care."

"I won't fuck you." His confidence, that lazy charm—it was maddening.

"Then will you at least do me the honor of sitting with me and enjoying some of the finest wine our continent has to offer?"

It was the smile that did it. That tiny curl to his full lips that set a sparkle gleaming in his glowing eyes.

"I suppose I'd rather return drunk anyway." I trudged over and sat next to him, leaving enough space between us so I didn't feel his body heat. Even then, I still felt it. Like standing too close to a fire, I had a feeling I'd feel him in varying degrees of warmth the closer we got. "Don't touch me."

He chuckled, then drank. "Whatever you desire, silk."

We sat in taut silence for minutes, drinking and staring straight ahead at the pockmarked walls.

When half the bottle was gone, I felt my stomach relax and my limbs grow heavier. Some would say it wasn't wise for a high royal to lose their wits with so many visitors from across our lands, but even with many a tense period, Rosinthe had been a continent of peace for a millennia now. Ever since the goddesses declared two of their children king and queen, deposited them on either side of this mystical land, and then disappeared inside the mists.

So although it wasn't wise, most royals did as they pleased. Which often involved drinking until they couldn't make out their linked ones from someone else's. That was entertaining to watch, so I always made sure I was just the right amount of drunk so as not to miss out on the foolery.

"Have you linked?" I wasn't sure where the urge to know came from, and I wasn't sure I wanted to analyze it either.

To link was to find what humans would call a soul mate, only with a bond far stronger. Those who happened to bond in such a permanent way had a heightened sense of awareness of their linked one—in some rare cases, glimpses of what they were feeling. Though typically, they'd need to be in the same vicinity, or close by, for the bond to work in such a way. I'd heard only matters of life or death or extreme emotional turmoil could be felt through the connection should they be in different lands.

And supposedly, sex as a linked couple was said to be indescribable—an overflow of euphoria that could never be found elsewhere.

But all magical things must have their pitfalls. Jealousy, paranoia, and obsessiveness were just some of the lovely things to look forward to when or if we linked. I'd heard of some royals ending themselves over their linked's eyes falling on someone else too long, touching them too long, and even of some ending other people.

Needless to say, there were more guards in attendance at social events and heavily populated areas for this reason.

"No," Raiden said, his bottle of wine clinking to the ground. Lying back, he stretched his arms above his head. The bags of grain groaned and shifted beneath his weight. "There'd been a time I thought I might have, but it never happened." His voice was clear, but his eyes held that sparkling sheen of intoxication.

"With whom?" I asked, leaning down on an elbow.

He smiled, quick and sweet. "Never you mind. What made you ask that?"

I struggled to form an answer, due to having none. "I was just curious." I adjusted my gown, fingers skimming over the soft layers. "Arranged marriages are a business deal. I've heard that in centuries gone past, there have been some high royals who allowed their spouses to live with their linked ones."

"Some." Raiden watched my hand as it glided over my dress, the red swimming with the shadows beneath the meager light. "You've linked? I'd have scented it, surely."

It was but a rumor, I thought, that royal males and even some mixed males could scent linked females. A sign to stay away. Females, however, could not do the same. Even if it were two females who linked. I thought it unjust that we had not been created with equal gifts such as that. Another reason I did my best to ensure I was on equal footing or, in most cases, much higher than the males around me.

My lids drooped as I reclined and curled my arm beneath my cheek. "I'm not linked to anyone, nor do I think I'd like to be."

Raiden stared up at the ceiling. "Why?"

His profile was perfect, angular slopes, his lashes more prominent. Like that of butterfly wings. "You ask a lot of questions, Prince."

He turned his head. "Only when I'm interested in knowing the answers, silk."

My nose crinkled. "I don't like that."

"Lie."

My chest rose with a harsh breath as I squinted at him. I chose to defer. "And I don't like the idea of some male bossing me around, impregnating me with babe after babe, and then getting to have all the fun."

It grew impossibly warm, and it dawned on me, as I laid awake in the earlier hours the following morning, that maybe Raiden wasn't in full control of his reactions either. At least, not around me. "We will need to have many heirs."

I swallowed, diverting my attention to the strong column of his thick throat. It wasn't that I didn't want children. We were a species obsessed with the idea of reproducing. Only one out of two royal babes made it through their infant years due to our bloodline being too much for their tiny bodies and hearts. It wasn't something we mourned for long, being that we cannot allow the weak into our lineage. When an infant survived long enough to see their second birthday, we celebrated. Only the strongest survived, which ensured we kept our lineage as powerful, pure, and prosperous as possible.

Those amongst a mixed bloodline had their own issues, such as the struggle to carry a babe to term and stillbirth. However, if their newborns survived birth, they had a much greater chance of surviving beyond that than us royals, due to less inherited magic.

"At the risk of being too presumptuous, I'm going to guess you're not exactly the nurturing type."

My eyes snapped to Raiden's. "Presumptuous is right." Though he was right. I wasn't nurturing, and should the day come, I feared I wouldn't be nurturing enough. The last thing this land needed was another tyrant steering the ship. I wouldn't admit that to him, though. "You know too little about me to assume."

He didn't argue with that. "Tell me, Princess, do you really believe our parents' plan to unite our two kingdoms is going to put our people at ease?"

There'd been talk of rebellion, of riots and spies in different parts of the land. They were the reason I was here, lying face to face with a precarious future I never saw coming. "My father has always been this way." I rolled to my back. "I don't know why they're making a fuss about it now."

His voice quietened. "Because this past decade he's grown worse. He's... unstable. Old."

No one was more aware of that than I. Still, I scoffed. "Age is but a number." I hated my father—loathed him with a vehemence unlike any other—yet no amount of hate could ever kill love entirely, no matter how small. "And do you really believe this alliance will quell the people's concerns?"

A dripping sound ventured into the room from deep within the cellars. "It's a start," he said before standing up. "What really happened to your mother?"

Shocked, I didn't answer for the longest time, and perhaps that was answer enough.

He held his hand out, and I eyed it a moment before sliding mine inside his, relishing the feel and trying to tame the loud echo of my heart.

I rose from the sacks of grain in a swift move that had my hands flying to his chest. I left them there, feeling the hot concrete pound of his own heart beneath my fingertips. "He killed her." The memory struck me, cleaved me open enough for Raiden to see it within my eyes as he lifted my chin. Leaving my tent to find her, chasing her screams, watching and screaming for her, and then being dragged away by my father... "But it matters not anymore."

His brows gathered, his thumb a steady, gentle pulse rubbing over my chin. "You were ten summers old. She'd been dancing and drinking at Inkerbine and left the bonfire with a group of males..." Inkerbine was notorious for its partner swapping, inhibition ridding wild ways. It was a celebration of our land, our existence, peace, and it took place every year after a double full moon.

I detested it.

My voice was ice. "She was raped and tortured in the woods by countless men, dead for days before anyone found her."

"That's what happened to her?" Raiden's eyes showed no pity, only vivid curiosity.

I nodded, knowing I'd said too much, and went to leave. "I said nothing. I will deny everything. And then I will feed you your own testicles should I hear that you ran away with this knowledge."

He grabbed me around the waist, and then I was being pressed into the wall. "Princess, everyone already knows."

At that, I smiled. "No, they only think they do. Rumors are but false ribbons of truth braided into patterns to suit the weaver."

He looked at the ground a moment. "I've upset you."

"You couldn't upset me if you tried." I fluttered my lashes at him. "Now, excuse—"

His rough exhale and the wild dancing within his eyes were all the warning I had before his lips were on mine, and my hands were over my head, attached to the wall by his as he pried my mouth open and set my entire world aflame.

His tongue didn't enter, but his breath did, scorching and heating my throat while he rubbed his bottom lip between my lips. I'd never been kissed like that before. I never knew such tenderness could feel so vicious, as though it might just casually stroll in and lay something vital inside you to waste.

It was ice and fire and wine and water—a world of contradictions that should never meet.

Because one taste, one mixing of what shouldn't be, and every ounce of who I was could simply cease to exist as I once did.

Music and laughter could be heard, dancing upon the stale air of the cellar, but all I could feel and taste was him. Wine, apples, and singed sugar. Damp, gentle lips and hard edges against my soft.

He released my hands to frame my face, his mouth departing mine as his forehead fell against my own. "Intoxicating."

I couldn't respond, could only breathe and feel my breasts press desperately into his body.

When I opened my eyes to find his gazing down at me, his chest heaving, I grabbed the neckline of his tunic and pressed my lips to his for one last fleeting kiss. A quick sweep of my tongue over his, velvet heat quaking my knees. A kiss distracting enough to tear myself away from him and race alone up the stairs.

With my heart beating irregularly, I hid from the prince for the duration of the night.

※

A harsh, slow clapping ensued, dragging my mind back to the present. "I just…" Raiden shook his head. "Where in the darkness did you get this shit from? I can tell it's not made-up. I'd ask who this male really was, but I don't care enough to know."

I jumped down from the bench and ran my fingers through my hair. Raiden was still sitting as he had been when I'd begun, with his eyes closed and his face angled toward the ancient ceiling.

"I forget nothing, Prince. And hopefully soon, you'll be able to remember."

"It won't work," he said when I'd reached the gate.

I turned to find him standing with his hands wrapped around the bars of his cell.

"You know it won't. Whoever I was, whatever you think I was?" His voice lacked emotion. "He's gone, Queen Audra."

The use of my name caught me off guard. Annoyance a wildfire erasing fond memories. "Then I suggest you cooperate in making sure he comes back."

He chuckled; the sound so soft, I almost missed it. "You're going to kill me anyway, probably Casilla too. What game are you playing, Queen?" He shook his head, then rattled the bars with a growl that rumbled through the deep, haunting space. "I want out. I want off the game board and into the darkness."

I took a step closer. "So you'd rather die than spend more time recounting your past with me?"

He stared for a thundering beat, his expression hard and unreadable, then nodded. "But I will play if you bring her to me."

I eyed him up and down, forcing a pout. "Darling Prince, you seem to have lost your mind after all."

He frowned, hands slipping from the metal of his cage.

"Those at the mercy of a monster do not get to bargain." I meandered through the gate, and it rolled to a close. "For when they dare try, they simply continue to bleed."

The dungeon door shut over the sound of his agonized shouts.

EIGHT

Screaming. He was screaming. For her.
He was going to die. He was going to die, and all he could think about was *her*.

Anger had never felt quite so alive to me before that moment. So crystal sharp it sliced inside flesh and imbedded within my very bones. The ache, the tension, the atrocity that was having someone who'd already betrayed you sink that knife in farther... It was almost enough to send me into a mindless pit of nothing.

I was already halfway there.

If the traitorous whore male pushed any harder, I feared myself more than I feared how it would feel to disappear inside this insidious feeling completely.

Inside my rooms, unsure of how I'd even arrived there—if I'd taken the typical corridors and quicker routes or walked for long minutes—I moved to the glass-wrapped cabinet in the sitting room, my small personal armory. Opening it, I dragged my fingers over the blades within.

I'd never named them. Some had a penchant for naming their weapons as if they were a second skin, an extension of them. I preferred not to be such a walking cliché.

The dagger would do. I tugged it from its hook inside the velvet-lined space and skimmed my finger over the sunken ruby throwing beaded light from the hilt.

"What do you plan to do with that?"

I'd been so distracted, so enmeshed in my ire, that yet again, the lord had managed to sneak up on me. But I didn't flinch. "Not that it's any of your concern, but I'm feeling..." I smiled as the blade sliced into the first layer of skin of my pointer finger. Pain. There was such an understated anticipation associated with pain. "Generous."

Zadicus blocked the doorway to my bed chamber, arms crossed and his eyes curious with his feet braced as though he thought he could stop me. "The girl? Or Raiden?"

"That thing is no girl," I spat. "It's an animal who will pay for going against the wishes of the queen."

Zad's bland expression didn't change as his eyes absorbed the blood bubbling along my finger. "You wish to torture or kill her?"

"Oh, both. So"—I shifted forward—"if you'll excuse me."

He chuckled. "How about..." He snuck an arm around my waist, mint and cloves inhabiting my nose. Warm temptation filled my ear. "You find a healthier outlet for this rage?"

I frowned, but curious, I let him pluck the blade from my hand. "What do you have in mind?"

The dagger hit the plush rug with barely a thud, and then his hand was in my hair, rough and possessive, as were his lips as they melded to mine.

Our hands began to tear at clothing, my teeth tore at his lip, and then I was against the wall, and he was inside me. There was no fuss and no preparation—not that it was needed. Bewildering, considering he was a male I so often despised.

And if I couldn't cut skin from flesh, then what I needed was this. Him. Long, thick, hot, and bruising as he entered me in one thrust. His hands around my legs as they tried to climb his wide back, and my nails dunking inside the smooth muscular divots of his shoulders as he growled into my ear. "Open your eyes."

"Why?" I stammered, already breathless.

"Because Queen," he said gruffly. "You'll not think of anyone, of anything, but me when I'm inside you."

I opened them, if only to make sure he didn't stop thrusting in and out of me with such delicious, tormenting strokes. "I hate him."

"I know," he rasped, eyes bright and fevered, breath mingling with mine.

My hands moved to his hair, and I tugged at the long thick strands. "I hate you, too."

His harsh exhale and voice were rough. "I know."

Trapping his bottom lip between my fingers, I whispered, "But I hate you the least."

Soft and stomach snatching, his tongue snaked out to lick my thumb. "I know."

"Make me forget everything but this."

Nostrils flaring, the challenge lit Zad's features with brutish beauty, and then he was stalking out of the sitting room straight to my bed. He laid me down, then grabbed my ankles, pulling me forward to meet his hungry length, and eased back inside.

My head rolled back into the sheets as he tugged me closer, impossibly close, until my legs were against his chest and he was able to lick the curve of my ankle when he turned his head.

Heat gathered and combusted, the sound of our bodies meeting numbing everything within me as pleasure rose in a tidal wave. It crashed over me within minutes, but he wasn't satisfied with that and flipped me over to enter me from behind.

A fist wrapped in my hair had my back arching, and his other hand around my breast had me mewling.

"Your cunt has never felt so wet, so hot." His words were strained—tight. "I want to stay inside you for eternity."

I panted out, "You just want me at your mercy for eternity."

He laughed, the sound stained with his ragged breaths as he slammed home and rotated his hips, teeth nipping at my ear. "Your body tells me it wouldn't mind."

I moaned as he aimed with perfect precision and set me climbing once again, my hips rocking back into him to hit that spot continuously. "Enough chitchat," I moaned. "Make me come again."

His hand left my breast, traveling down my spine until it reached the curve of my back, and then it dipped lower. It left my skin, and I heard him suck, and then I screamed as it returned and rubbed over that puckered hole.

"That's it, shake for me. Fucking drench me."

He held me to him as he pumped one last time and then stilled, roaring into the moonlit shadows.

Afterward, I laid sprawled over his stomach with his fingers in my hair, his sated eyes fixed on the swollen moon.

"What do you think of when you stare at it so intensely?"

Zad's fingers stilled, then began another sweep through my locks. "Everything and nothing."

I shifted, resting my cheek over his abdominals, the sound of his heart and the rush of his blood a quiet hum in my ear. His long copper hair shined under the glow of night, and I absorbed the way it bounced off his angular cheeks and that crooked nose. As though his skin rejected it even though he adored it.

That gave me pause, and then his smooth voice pulled my eyes up to his. "Do you remember the first time we met? When your mother introduced us?"

My entire body pulled taut at the mention of her, but his gentle fingers coaxed it to relax. "You were besotted with her. I could see it burning in your eyes." I'd been a child when I'd first been introduced to the lord of the east.

Zad huffed.

"What? You were."

"You see what you want to see." He shook his head, his lips lifting slightly. "You were supposed to marry me."

Frowning, I blinked. Then I sat up, my palm slapping against his pectorals as I glared down at him. "What?"

He smiled, and the effect of it, so rare and genuine, drew apart my lips. He cupped my cheek, his hand calloused and large—threatening and protective. "You were to vow to me before your father devised a way to try to put an end to the upheaval he'd stirred."

I didn't want to, but staring at his earnest expression, the openness of it, I found I believed him. "But you loathe me."

"Loathe is a strong word, my queen." Rough fingers traced my lips, his gaze too. "I resented that I'd have to marry a child, yes. But your mother was a friend, and she wanted you taken care of."

That had me rearing back and removing myself from the bed. Memories, so many of them, of him always drifting on the fringes. The times he'd found me when I hadn't thought I'd wanted to be found—of rescuing me when I'd never dare admit I needed it. Running a hand through my tangled hair, I snapped, "I need no such thing, *Lord*."

I traipsed into the bathing room and took my time drawing a bath.

Zadicus as my husband.

Even though it was supposed to come to pass, the idea utterly baffled me as I dipped my toes inside the steaming water. My mother had been an idiot for a lot of reasons, one of the biggest for thinking I'd vow myself to a lord such as Zadicus.

Yet the more I thought about it, watching tendrils of steam curl toward the cracks in the walls, escaping into the frigid air outside, the more it made sense.

Of course, I was to vow to someone like Zad. The silent, mysterious, often cold, well-respected high royal with lands that had belonged to him since any of us could dare remember.

So why had I never given him the time of day after the first time we'd met? Flashes of memories thundered in, and for precious minutes, I let them.

I remembered one instance of being distracted at a ball Zad had attended. I'd been searching for Berron who'd promised to fetch three bottles of wine and meet me in the fields of the lower mountains, where we'd watch the clouds drift and seek pleasure until the sun woke. Zadicus, who'd given me unreadable looks any time I saw him, had faded from view within an hour that night, and he wasn't seen again until my engagement party.

I blocked that memory of him, built a fortress of steel and ice around it, and threw away the key.

"You were married," I said, knowing he was standing in the doorway, watching me place bubbles over my arms.

"Nova had…" He paused. "She was gone when your mother and father began serious discussion over the arrangement."

"Arrangement," I repeated, sour. "Eternally cursed to become a business transaction."

Zad said nothing for a moment, then, "One could only dream of brokering such a deal."

My lips twitched. "You rarely attended court."

"I didn't like your father's antics."

I smirked at that. "I wouldn't have guessed you to be weak in the stomach."

"His brand of cruelty didn't mesh well with my own, and you can only imagine killing someone in thousands of different ways for so long before you finally snap." Footsteps drew close, and then he was lifting a sponge to my back. Seated on the edge of the tub, naked, he lifted my hair and squeezed.

Water trickled down my back, and I hummed, my eyes shutting as my teeth caught my lip.

"Why did you come?" He was so much of a mystery to me.

I knew that was my own fault for being too wrapped up in the haunting that gathered and spread thorns inside me. It was also foolish not to know the enemy, but if I thought he had plans to kill me, he would not be in my bed. He'd already be dead for the mere thought.

He didn't need to ask when or what I was referring to. "I have my reasons."

I wanted to growl at his vague response. Instead, my hand pulled at his, and he fell into the water with a splash, his long legs draped over the side of the porcelain.

I laughed at his shocked expression, the unimpressed flatness to his lips, and the careful way he blinked at me. "Oh, relax. It's not as if you were clothed."

He righted himself in the water, and I moaned when I felt his foot brush the inside of my thigh.

His throat dipped. He tugged me close, slipping his hand between us in the water to massage my swelling center with careful strokes of his thumb. His head angled. "Why all the questions?"

He had cause to be curious. I'd never cared to ask much of him before because I never cared to know. I wasn't sure if that was changing, or if I was just in need of more to block out what festered beneath my castle.

My eyelids drooped. "You're a decent distraction, is all."

Zad's grin was nothing short of feral, and my breath caught. I averted my gaze, letting it drift over the bubbles marring his scar-flecked chest. "Then by all means." His eyes filled with something wild. "Let me distract you… thoroughly." Then I was on his lap, his arms banding around me as he sank inside my body once again.

I was almost asleep, for once curled over Zad instead of kicking him to the other side of the bed, when thoughts of the scars on his chest, of the few on my own body, and those who'd put them there came flooding back in. "I've not heard from Berron in almost two weeks."

He was to send correspondence from the Sun Kingdom once a week, being that the land and its occupants were not exactly thrilled over his presence in their late ruler's palace.

Zad's body turned to granite beneath me, his rich voice deep with sleep. "You're certain?"

I scoffed. "I would not say so if I wasn't."

"We'll send another sparrow. If there's still no news…" He paused. "Then I'm afraid we'll need to go."

I yawned, agreeing.

His chest slowly deflated, but it was a long while before he fell asleep and took me with him.

※

We waited four days until I couldn't handle it any longer, and we found ourselves at the stables, preparing to leave for the three-day journey to the border.

Berron was one of the few I trusted implicitly. Hence why I'd asked him to take on such a huge responsibility in the first place.

Coward, I berated myself as we cleared a village and set up camp by a smattering of large rocks on the outskirts of the Winding Woods. I couldn't stand the thought of traveling to the kingdom and submersing myself in every facet of what was once Raiden's life without him.

With what remained of myself. The memories and the lies and the questions that didn't need answering.

And it goes without saying that I'd likely have been assassinated before my first week as ruler was through.

Zadicus eyed me from across the fire as Garris gave the thirty-some soldiers we'd brought with us their orders to either retire or stand watch. "I'm sure he's fine."

I didn't look at him. I watched the flames dance and crackle. "You don't know that. No one does."

His voice was too calm, annoyingly so. "We will know soon enough."

"Not soon enough for my liking. We should've taken the furbanes."

Zad snapped a twig in half, tossing the pieces into the fire. "Taking the aerial approach, speeding through the skies, would make it seem like an act of war." Leaves and twigs crunched beneath his boots as he shifted forward to gather more fuel for the fire. "Besides, there aren't enough furbanes for the soldiers, and splitting up could very well be suicide."

He was right, but I wasn't going to admit it when he already knew so. I'd known too, hence the horses tethered to the trees behind us, munching on the thawing grass, but I was impatient to find out what was happening.

The closer we neared the border, the more the weather morphed into autumn. Then it would be grass, the color of Raiden's eyes, for as far as the eye could see, blanketing valleys and skirting creeks. And when we reached the Sun Kingdom, that spring warmth, that promise of fresh flowers and new life, would morph into that of insect-infested, blazing-desert territory.

The Sun Kingdom's palace was an oasis in a land filled with dry, decaying things.

Even when I'd surrendered myself to their prince, the mere thought of stepping foot onto their cracked soil, should there be any, was something I'd wanted to avoid.

One of the soldiers, of whom I'd forgotten his name, bowed before the fire. "Your tent is ready, Majesty."

I glanced up at him, then at the trees looming behind us like shadowed ghouls. "I won't be sleeping." I jerked my head at Zad. "Lord Allblood will take it instead."

Creasing his brows, Zad looked from me to the soldier. "Thank you, Creig."

Creig left us and took his post by the road where several other soldiers were keeping watch.

"He doesn't look like a Creig," I muttered.

Zad grunted. "The same could be said of your ruthlessness."

I frowned. "What do you mean?"

"I mean..." He poured a cup of tea from the thermos he'd brought in his travel satchel, then handed it to me. I took it, the heat seeping into my frozen hands. "No one would look at you and expect the things you say or do."

I sipped, relishing the burn. "You sure have a way with compliments."

"If I thought you needed to hear compliments, I'd give them to you." He capped the thermos after pouring himself a tea, then picked up his cup from the grass and brought it between his bent knees. "And you're in no need of compliments right now, my queen."

I studied the sly curve to his lips, and the bright gleam to his burnished eyes. "I find your lack of affection quite puzzling." I didn't care that there were soldiers amongst us who could likely hear our conversation from their tents. Let them.

Zad's tea paused halfway to his lips, his head tilting. "I can be affectionate."

I grinned. "Lies."

His shoulders straightened, the all-too-familiar rigidness returning to his marble-hewn jaw. "If I'd have shown you affection, just like any other cretin who tried to weasel their way into your good graces, would I be sitting here now?"

"Would you be warming my bed, you mean?" I drank more tea, eyeing him over the rim of the cup. "No, I suppose not." I stopped his roguish smile in its tracks and stabbed a finger at him. "But that doesn't mean you're affectionate, Lord. You most certainly are not."

"For the right female," he insisted, then lowered his voice as his cup rose to his lips. "I am."

Heat unfurled in my stomach, and I scowled, wondering if he was referring to someone else. His late wife, perhaps.

Then I screamed, almost flailing into the fire as I felt the whoosh of something fall and land on the ground behind me and heard the *ting* of swords unsheathing.

Zadicus dived over me, taking the blithe to the ground.

I turned to find pointed ears, black teeth, bright green scales covering a too thin face and a dagger that looked to be stolen from one of our soldiers heading straight for my chest. I grabbed the hilt, threw my body down, and flipped the blithe over my back. The dagger came loose when the creature hit the dirt, and then it was imbedded in its chest, ichor oozing between my fingers and onto my palm.

I left it there so it would stay down and spun to kick another who'd appeared over top of it.

Stumbling back, I grabbed my teacup and slammed it into its face. It screeched, a sound akin to nails down a chalkboard but a thousand times louder, and scrambled toward me, four talons protruding from each of its webbed hands.

"Audra." I heard Zad from my left and glanced over briefly

to see my sword flying toward me. I unsheathed it right as a kick landed to my side.

I went down, aiming the sword up as I did, and the blithe, not the smartest of creatures, impaled itself to the hilt.

More blood sprayed, flooding over my hand and arm like a racing black river. Wincing, I shoved it away before jumping to my feet. I stomped on the body and tugged my sword free, straightening to find the last of them being cleaved in two or bleeding from their eyes, mouths, and noses, thanks to Zad.

He'd cut one down while using his magic on another, and transfixed, I couldn't tear my eyes away. It occurred to me that I'd never seen him fight before. I'd also never seen his magic in play.

Blood puddled beneath piles of blithe, evicted from their bodies with just a thought from the lord of the east.

I'd heard of it—tales of his ability—but I'd never actually seen it.

It was both horror and beauty. It was bright life one second and the darkest death the next.

Such ease in its killing blows, such harrowing power… I shivered, then blinked and pivoted, searching for more of the disgusting creatures.

But the rest were fleeing into the trees as a horrid, whining laughter echoed throughout the woods. They didn't care that their kin were dead. They were riding the thrill, and they wanted a chase, knowing if they stayed, they would surely perish.

"Did no one scout the trees?" I asked, cringing as I swiped the purple and black gore from my cheek.

Garris came forward, applying pressure to a deep gash on his arm. "Yes, my queen. We passed their homes miles back."

The blithe built homes in the trees—some of the most archaic creatures in the land besides the royals and the Fae. They were thought to be a kind of lesser faerie, stupid but deadly if they caught you unaware.

Once our neighbors, a part of our land, the Fae were now

gone. Should any remain, they did so in hiding, for during my father's reign, he ordered them all hunted and slaughtered on sight. The rage that'd leaked from him during those first weeks of the new law being implemented was enough to have me never asking why. Rarely ever had I asked him questions, knowing I'd either not like the answer, or he'd punish me for having the audacity.

Still, some of the lesser faeries, creatures unlike those that could resemble man and woman and royal, remained. For some reason I didn't know and probably would not understand, they hadn't been a priority during the faerie raids.

Unsettled, I peered around, studying the burning night, all the dead bodies on the ground. Three of our males, one female, and at least twenty blithes.

"We need to move," Zad said, refilling his satchel with the few belongings strewn about on the grass near the fading embers of the fire.

The rest of the blithe had retreated, but that wasn't exactly reassuring.

"I don't think they'll return," said one of the soldiers as he helped Didra strap her knee.

My blood was humming, pressure bubbling in every vein and pushing at every muscle. We couldn't afford to stop. We rode through, or we returned home.

"We don't stop," I declared. "We ride on with short reprieves until we reach the border. The wounded may return to the castle." I paused when I saw a young female struggling to breathe as a male worked on repacking her insides. "Or head to the nearest village to see a healer."

No one protested, not that I thought they would, aside from Zad or Garris. But they both nodded when I looked at them, and then everyone began tearing down the tents. Well, the little that was worth taking with us. Most of them were shredded or had collapsed with dead blithes and gore strewn across them.

I spied my scabbard by the fire and leaped over a dead soldier to grab it. I eyed him as I sheathed and strapped on my sword, realizing I had no idea who he was, or anything about him.

A howl from the north broke the thrum of activity, and we moved faster.

Reaching Wen, I rubbed his glossy black coat as I inspected him for injuries.

A few minutes later, we disbanded, and as I gazed back at the clearing, the pressure in my blood pressed at my skin. "We need to set it on fire."

Otherwise, we could be tracked more easily by use of personal belongings and things containing our scent.

Fire. A gift that Raiden had.

Zad's blood magic, should he unleash it, might have been able to kill any creature with one thought, but it was harder to kill multiple people in one sweep. The cost was greater on one's eternal soul and often resulted in him needing to feast on that of a pureblood in order to rebalance and recoup what he'd expended.

Such things were not permitted unless in consensual acts, lest he accidentally take too much. It was entirely too personal, required the highest amount of trust, and I'd heard it could render those with his type of magic a libidinous beast for hours until they regained control of themselves.

I'd never seen it myself, but I'd heard of it happening to Zadicus after a skirmish broke out by The Edges before I was born. He'd apparently wiped out a band of exiled who were holding a high royal hostage in order to regain entry into the Moon Kingdom.

Raiden's fire-filled palm entered, uninvited and strangling, as I watched one of the soldiers march toward the campsite and crouch down to light a fire with his sword and flint.

I blinked slowly, encouraging the breeze to build and set the campsite ablaze.

We had no fire callers amongst us, and such skills were rare to find in the Moon Kingdom. Most magic holders carried abilities born from their home's climate. There were plenty of wind changers, water wielders, and frost makers in Allureldin. But my bloodline was the only one to carry every elemental ability gifted to our land.

While we waited, my eyes swung to the dark canopy of the woods, and a shiver rolled down my spine. Once nothing of our short stay remained, I released the breeze, and the flames guttered swiftly.

Zad's eyes, full of the same questions I felt filling my own, met mine from across an empty stallion's back.

"I'd kill for a bath," I said, returning from the creek's bank and brushing water droplets from my skin. I'd washed most of the journey from my face, arms, neck, and hands, but it wasn't good enough. I could still feel the ooze bursting over my skin, burning as my cells regenerated and soothed the sting.

Zad's eyes merely skimmed me as I shucked on my jacket and collected my cloak from him. With a roll of his neck, he gave his attention back to Ainx, who was jabbing a finger at the map in his hands.

I wasn't sure how he'd managed to appear so polished after riding for days, but it irked me, to say the least.

Zad and Garris looked east, the former saying, "Let's move. We want to arrive while there's still daylight."

The sun warming my skin made the itch the burns left in their wake almost unbearable as we drew closer to the border. Sun-weathered villages sat in pockets of blazing green valleys. The dirt road stretched onward, winding through villages but not entering them. Little roads, some cobbled and some overgrown with weeds and wildflowers, veered off to greet each one. Children far off in the distance stopped to stare as we came into view while others darted away, likely to warn their parents.

I bit a chunk out of the apple I'd stolen from Zad's satchel. Our supplies were meager, but we'd have enough to last until we reached the palace, or until we bartered for more from a village who wouldn't lock itself away at the first sighting of us.

It'd happened the day before, and Zad had scowled at me, asking why I hadn't demanded someone trade or sell to us. I couldn't muster the forethought or the energy to care, and so I'd insisted we ignore them and march on.

Enemies were a precarious thing to covet, and I was beginning to think that I had more than I'd bargained for. Therefore, some inherent part of me knew I'd need to save my strength and store that anger down deep for what may lie ahead. For what we may find in the south.

"It is the winter queen," a little voice said. I peered to my left at the young girl, her frightened eyes huge as she swayed on the spot outside the connecting road to her village. A young boy, maybe her brother, raced uphill toward us with a stricken expression.

My mouth eased into a smile so practiced, I could do it while I slept and never even know. "And should you not bow to your queen?"

The little girl, twirling a golden lock of hair around her finger, blinked. Her hand fell, and she all but threw herself to the ground.

Her brother glared as I laughed, and we soon left them behind.

"You taunt," Zad said, his stallion aligning itself with mine.

I lifted a shoulder.

I could feel his eyes on my face, almost as hot as the sun that pressed harder with each mile. His voice was soft, melodic, and how I wished I could have pulled him into one of the passing forests to hear him speak against my skin. "She won't soon forget, if she ever will, her first, and perhaps only, encounter with her majesty."

"Handing me a compliment after I've berated you for not

doing so makes you transparent, Lord." I grinned, knowing it was not a compliment at all. My smile slipped as I peered down at my riding pants and my creased cotton top. "Though I do wish she'd have seen me wearing something more... formidable."

"Your most formidable form is not one most will ever see," Zad practically purred. "Unless they should be so lucky."

I laughed and dug my heels into Wen's flanks, clicking my tongue. He took off, the wind catching my hair as the sound of galloping hooves echoed across the drying landscape.

The sun was a fading orange stone in the sky, the valleys of villages but a passing dream as we kept on, covering miles of deserted land mere hours after first light.

We'd crossed the border with no interruption, though I hadn't known what I'd expected to stop us, or who. It wasn't as if any kind of rebellion could stage guards upon an invisible marker that stretched farther than any eye could see.

Wen jerked and nickered, and my stomach hollowed.

I blinked twice to be sure I wasn't seeing a mirage. The heat was an entity all on its own, breathing fire down our backs and slickening every inch of our skin. I gave up trying to keep cool, and instead, wrapped myself in every layer I had. Not to protect my skin, but my soul. Then I sent iced waves dancing over my flushed skin, cooling myself to a more bearable temperature.

It was not a mirage.

Up ahead, the palace glimmered, a sandstone structure stamped in the center of nothing but sand. Trees encircled the rear, a lush-looking rainforest providing shade in a territory hell-bent on burning you to death. It wouldn't be enough. I'd still melt at every turn and beg for snow to grace my windowpane.

Similar words had been spoken to Raiden upon our vow... A yell cleared my thoughts as a soldier was knocked from his horse.

A round of snicks pierced the air as arrows planted themselves in horses, bodies, and the sand around us. There was nowhere to hide and not enough time to see where they were coming from.

Anger bloomed and blossomed into a tidal wave, and I sent a shield of air around us, arrows bouncing off it and hanging midair as I narrowed my eyes. It was no wonder the remainder of our journey had been uneventful.

They'd been waiting.

I raised my hand and twirled my finger, sending them back in the direction they came, smiling as I heard screams and curses.

Their veil dropped, Ainx declaring, "They had a spellcaster amongst them."

"Dead now," I murmured.

Zad cursed violently, riding closer to a fallen soldier and helping him onto the back of Garris's mare. "We should retreat."

My guard dropped as I watched an arrow soar toward him. I screamed his name, and Zad dodged it. The arrow whizzed by his ear and plunged into a horse's leg. It screeched, rearing back and tossing its rider.

"Fuck," I muttered, sending a block of air around us again, and the now exposed traitors raced forward with weapons bared and battle cries filling the air.

I unsheathed my sword, about to meet them in the middle, shield be damned, when I saw him.

Berron was being dragged through the sand behind them.

My teeth gritted, and panic held me immobile. With a shake of my head, I grabbed hold of that ever-building fury, digging deep until it felt as if I'd overflow. The air buzzed, becoming suffocating even to me as I unleashed and pushed and sent all of them to their backs, pressing them into the sand.

Sweat beaded upon my forehead, but the sight of Berron being herded like a wild animal held my concentration steady. Until another wave of traitors crested the dunes, and I soon lost count of how many we faced.

"Two hundred." Zad, back in his saddle, brought his horse to a stop beside me. "At the very least."

We couldn't.

Together, we could take a lot of them out, though it would cost us. I'd be asleep for days, unable to travel or far worse. And Zadicus would likely need to be knocked out until he fed. Still, as I saw one of the rats push Berron into the sand and kick him in the stomach, I decided it'd be worth it.

"Don't," Zad warned. "We can't. You'll only kill him too."

A growl of helplessness slipped out, and I squeezed my eyes shut, my head spinning with the effort to keep the first line of soldiers down. "Garris?"

"I... Well, I say we retreat, my queen." His voice was drenched in fear but unwavering. "There are far too many for this to end well."

"They knew we were coming. They've had him," I said to Zad. "They've had him in their filthy clutches for who knows how long, and now they're using him against me."

Zad met my gaze with unflinching coldness. "You are a queen, Audra, and you bow to no creature's demands." His next words were gentler, though still resolute. "Audra, please." Something I'd not yet seen, something that looked a lot like fear entered his eyes. "You need to go. You must let him go."

"No." The word sliced through the throng of soldiers, causing shoulders to stiffen and weapons to rise.

Jaw hard, Zad faced ahead, eyes scanning. "It's impossible."

"I'm not leaving without him."

"Behind!" Garris called, but it was too late.

Three soldiers went down as a band of twenty or more warriors appeared within our bubble of air. As if they'd been hiding within the sand, somewhere deep in the ground.

Screaming and shouting ensued. "Charge!" Garris hollered.

I coughed, struggling to breathe as my magic retreated, slamming back inside me with the force of an elastic snap. We soon became cornered pieces of meat, growing more tender by the minute as two more of our soldiers met their ends via an arrow and a thrown dagger.

I pressed forward, my sword glinting beneath their precious sun, and met a soldier's sword strike for strike, pushing him back, then drawing him forward to cleave him in two as another warrior with tribal markings upon her face dived through the air with a spear.

I was ready, emptying her lungs before she even neared, and then I was off my horse, falling to the sand with a thud as pain radiated through my skull.

My hair was wrenched back, and then a fist collided with my cheek. Darkness encompassed, dragging me down with heavy hands. Screaming, I forced my way back to a knife pressed against my neck, and then it dropped with its owner as she fell to the sand, her hands wrapped around her throat.

I grinned at my other assailant, taking in her violet eyes and ruddy complexion, and licked blood from my teeth. "Are you ready to meet your end?" I tutted. "Such beautiful eyes, what a waste."

Before I could make that happen, Zad was there, separating her head from her shoulders.

I watched it roll to the sand with a frown and then backed away from the blood leaving the decapitated body.

He hauled me up. "We need to get out of here. *Now*."

A glance around told me half of us would not return. The warriors had surrounded us, and I knew it'd take a miracle to get what remained across the border.

"Squash them," I said to Zad, grappling for my sword before I jumped up and into Wen's saddle. "I'll get Berron. Shit, behind you."

Zad swung his sword above his head, bringing it down in one clean sweep to slice the male warrior in half. "Retreat," he yelled, turning his horse. "Retreat now!"

I looked over at Berron, and even with the distance between us, I found his eyes on mine. "Go," he mouthed.

I shook my head, grabbing the reins and turning Wen to gallop toward him.

Then, I watched with my long-forgotten heart tearing out my throat, as a spear entered his side, and he fell face-first into the sand.

A hand gripped Wen's bridle, turning him in the other direction. "We've cleared as much as we can. We need to go."

"But what if they've killed him?" I said, barely a whisper as frost covered my eyes, crested upon my fingertips and wrapped around my vocal cords.

Zad didn't so much as glance back at where my trainer and occasional lover—my friend—lay bleeding beneath the unforgiving sun. "They could kill us too if we don't move while we can."

They were now running, running toward us and screaming, my friend left to swallow sand behind them.

It took more than I thought I had left within me to hurl a gust of wind behind us. So strong, it created a wall out of sand. I tightened my legs, spurring Wen away from the crowd drawing closer. From the tower of sand I sent falling atop their front lines.

Screams, shouting, and crying reached us—chased us for miles. But we raced onward, sand flying beneath our horses' hooves, our dead and gravely injured left to fester or heal in a hostile land.

A land I swore to reduce to rubble.

NINE

Tiny sprays of light leaked in through cracks in the walls. Not enough to bother me, but enough to know daylight was fading.

After riding for three days with barely a reprieve until we'd crossed the border, we returned to the castle at first light. I'd left Wen with the stable hand, ignored Zad's assessing gaze, and fled via the sleet-crusted pathways straight to my rooms.

He'd let me be—they all had—as I'd collapsed on the bed and fallen into a dreamless sleep.

"Are you just going to stand there, or are you going to enter?"

Truin's light footsteps tapped over the floor. She took a seat on the lip of the tub, her deep green homespun dress billowing over the damp stone. "I heard."

"From who?"

"Mintale," she said.

The dripping of the faucet was the only sound as her probing eyes sat upon me. It took all the remaining willpower I had to keep from screaming at her to get out.

"He might not be dead, you know."

Berron, like most soldiers, was mixed, so that made him harder to kill than humans. Decapitation, draining, a blade to the heart or brain, and old age would end any of our kind. But half-blood royals—though their bodies were stronger and able to handle more—could die just like humans, through sickness and disease, and often only lived to see three hundred years.

"Might means nothing when they still have him." Her hope was futile and the last thing I needed. "When they could kill him at any moment." If they hadn't left him beneath the fire-filled sun to rot, they were probably torturing him as we breathed.

I skimmed my hand over the warm water's surface, catching the last of the lavender-scented bubbles.

"You cannot go back." Her tone, the worry within… it sounded as if she'd spoken to a certain lord. "Not without an army."

"War," I said, my hand stilling and falling to lay upon my stomach in the breast-deep pool of water.

Truin nodded. "I fear it is coming whether we start or end it."

"I'd rather not listen to your fable predictions right now." I slid deeper into the water until it crested my chin and tickled my lips.

"It is not a prediction but a fact." I said nothing, and then she sighed. "Let me heal your cheek."

"No," I said, barely feeling the dull pang in the bone, nor the cut inside my mouth.

She scooted closer, angling her head. "It looks as if it was almost crushed."

"It will heal on its own." A bruised cheek and a few bruised ribs were nothing compared to what Berron had endured, and if he wasn't lucky enough to have reached the ever, then what he was still enduring.

Truin tucked some yellow-gold hair behind her ear. "And what of the king?"

I'd scarcely thought of the parasite who'd caused this, remembering he was still layers below us, fading away in the dungeon. "He is no king."

Truin watched me for a moment but not for long. I shut my eyes and disappeared beneath the water.

When I emerged, she was gone, and I drew in long breaths before sliding back under once more. My hair curled around my face in silken ribbons, my eyes opening to view the blurred ceiling bobbing above the surface. No sound entered this space but that of my heart galloping in my ears.

Bubbles rose from my mouth as I opened it and screamed.

When the hum of the castle settled, I left my perch by the window where I'd watched snow drift over rooftops and the mountain-specked landscape and exited my rooms.

My white gossamer robe swished, the slits in its sides revealing the expanse of my legs with every step. It fluttered behind me as I wrapped the silken lace closer over my chest and descended into the gloom.

Azela's gaze fell on my cheek when she saw me round the last of the stairs and enter the dungeon. With a nod, the door and gate rattled open, their rumble enough to wake the residents two floors above. Mostly kitchen and cleaning staff.

She didn't shut them behind me, but she did move out of earshot as I traversed the stained floor and rounded the rows of cells until I'd reached the center where the torture table sat.

I climbed atop it, weary but unable to rest after sleeping most of the day and knowing what was to come.

"Your face," Raiden said, his back to me as he stroked a sliver of arcing light falling across the floor from a crack in the ceiling. "You've been busy."

"In more ways than you'd think," I said, infusing my voice suggestively.

I did not ask how he'd known I was injured when he couldn't even look at me. He'd either heard the guards talking about what'd transpired, or he'd glanced at me briefly before I'd noticed.

"The lord?" he asked.

My heart stilled. "What of him?"

"He's the one warming your bed. Your body."

Too shaken to even inhale, I forced out, "And you would know of this how?"

He turned then, his green eyes red rimmed and his growing hair curling in a thousand different directions. "He's always wanted you. I know that much at least."

"What else do you know?" I couldn't stop myself from asking if I'd tried. It was working. Somehow. This stupid idea didn't seem so stupid anymore.

"Nothing," he said too quickly before letting his gaze roam down my body, catching my exposed skin. "Except one thing."

"And what is that?" I asked, enjoying his eyes on me. A warm caress even if it was for only a moment before he tore them away and curled his lip.

"I know I would never have fallen for a soul as rotten as yours."

I could only stare, my heart's rhythm growing quieter, fainter with every beat.

He blinked, dark lashes curling toward his brows, and then he turned back to the wall.

And still, I stared at him. At his stained clothing, at the ramrod granite expanse of his back. He was losing muscle tone being cooped up down here but not enough to make him look starved.

Not yet.

I reclined over the table, if only to hide the tremor in my hands even though he wasn't looking at me. "I'd ask myself if you ever truly had countless times." I paused. "After."

"After," he repeated. "After what?"

"After you betrayed me, my kingdom, and my heart."

There was no change to his posture. No shaking. No twitching. No tensing.

He was as immovable as a dagger imbedded in the heart. For if he slipped, he might just bleed out.

Then he laughed. Slow and growing louder, the brash sound echoed through the cells.

I waited, every bone in my body aching with anger for him to shut up.

"Sorry," he said with about as much remorse as a furbane with remnants of a chicken in its maw. "But what on this goddesses' green earth would ever possess your narcissistic brain to believe someone could ever actually love someone like you?"

I took the insult, absorbed it with my next breath, and let it freeze all that'd begun to thaw in his presence. "Why, the answer to that is simple." I closed my eyes as I was taken back to a time that blinded me with dreamlike fantasies. "You."

---

19 summers old

There was no celebration like that of a king who'd turned seven hundred years old.

Had any of my brothers lived beyond infancy to see such a thing, I often found myself wondering what they'd make of it. What they'd make of him.

Moonstone fountains filled with ruby red wine gurgled throughout the courtyards. Witch hazel, hedges pruned to resemble the moon and stars, and countless rose bushes glimmered beneath hovering blinking lights. Royal fire didn't stop burning until it was told to by its owner, and it was evident the orbs of light would glow until the sun replaced them and they were no longer needed.

Gone was the elegance and finery usually expected of high royals, and in its place, male and female mingled in scraps of clothing. My father's decree. You were to pick only one item of clothing to wear to his birth celebration, or you could spend the night naked.

The copious amount of wine and ale provided would be drunk greedily by the many guests struggling to stay warm, which gave my father more reason, and endless pleasure, to toy with them when they stumbled about like idiots. Only he, the king of the coldest lands in Rosinthe, would throw a party all invited must attend and insist they wear hardly anything.

I'd had a gown made that would support my breasts and cover enough to show some semblance of modesty. I didn't much care for flashing too much skin at once, but rather, I liked to tease. We were creatures of immense power. We could do as we wished within our flimsy laws, yet I never felt like trying to fit in or please others.

To take a larger role in the power games my father insisted on playing.

Sequined silk covered me from shoulder to ankle, the ivory tone similar to that of my skin and leaving little to the imagination. My sable hair flowed in straight lines down my back to kiss the curve of my spine and drape over my breasts, meeting my navel.

"My princess," a velvet voice drawled.

Smirking, I peered over at the lord of the east and tipped my drink to him. "Good evening, Lord."

With his hands tucked in the pockets of his black pants, he stepped out of the shadows in nothing else save for his black boots.

I swallowed hard at the muscular expanse of his chest, as well as the harsh etching of his pelvic area, which had me wondering, even if just for a second, what it would feel like to trace with my fingertips.

Shaking off the thought, I tilted my head as our eyes met. His wore a look of knowing, but it was the bored set to his mouth that really knocked me out of my trance. "Do you wish to take a closer look?" he teased. "If you stare at me like that again, I might just let you touch." Those last words were weighted, low, as though what he'd wanted to say was *beg you to touch*.

I snorted, grinning. "Just observing how predictable you are, is all."

His russet brow arched. "I can assure you, the last thing I am is predictable."

I rolled my eyes, sipping the remainder of my wine. "I'm sure."

His eyes darted behind me, hardening for a brief second, and I headed that way. The lord of the east might have been fun to look at, I was coming to realize, but he was no fun to be around.

My fingers dragged over trellises teeming with roses and

flickering with fireflies, and I could have sworn I felt the lord's eyes upon me until I'd walked out of view.

"You rob me of breath."

A stuttered exhale left me as I turned to find Raiden leaning against a vine-strangled column with a goblet of wine.

His parents had departed swiftly after the celebration of our commitment to vow. He, however, had stayed behind.

When he'd cornered me in the hall outside the kitchens just two days later, I could scarcely mask my shock at seeing him. He'd invited me to ride with him. I'd said no and left him standing there as I went in search of Berron.

That was three days ago, and though I'd heard he was making himself quite at home—roaming the gardens, training with our soldiers, and undoubtedly flirting with nobility and staff alike—I hadn't seen him since.

"You opted for pants instead of a shirt." I sat, peering around at many a male wearing similar. "How boring." My palm met the cool sandstone of the garden's edge, and I crossed one leg over the other, my gown bending with my body like a fitted glove.

Raiden emptied his wine, and I watched his throat ripple as he swallowed. He then turned to the left, bending to scoop up more.

I allowed my eyes to trace every dip and solid line of his torso. Muscles moved in his abdomen and lower back as he straightened, and I noticed only a fine dusting of hair smattered his broad pectorals.

I didn't bother hiding my assessment as he swung his legs closer, his feet bare and long toes curling over the cold ground.

He extended the hand with the goblet to me, and I lowered my brows at it. "I'd rather not drink wine that's been sitting there, open for any enchantment or laced herbs."

Raiden licked his teeth, then shrugged and drained the lot himself before tossing the goblet into the garden behind me and taking a seat.

"Smart, I suppose. But tell me, silk…" He leaned closer, close enough for the hairs dusting his arm to graze my own, his voice reminiscent of gravel over skin. "Doesn't it get tedious, not allowing yourself to truly live this ever long existence of ours?"

My nails scratched at the stone as I turned my face to his. "Oh, I do plenty of living, Prince. Believe me."

His eyes narrowed on mine, thick brows scrunching. "I believe you. Though I have it on good authority that you've not sought a lover since I arrived."

I'd have to take the finger of whoever was feeding him information and ram it down their stupid throat. "Then you need to find a new source"—I bent close, my lips a hair's breadth from his—"because they're lying."

His breath retreated, then plumed hot over my mouth, smelling of the berry-flavored wine. "Of all the lies I've ever heard, yours are by far the sweetest."

I blinked, and then his hands were cupping my face and his lips caressing mine. It was a mere touch, a tease, and then he was standing and pulling me to my feet. "Walk with me."

"I have guests that I need to at least stare at."

Raiden grinned, his hand rough and smooth as he pulled me with him toward the castle gates. "They'll still be here." He glanced at the fountains, at the people dancing and loitering in groups around them. "Until the sun rises, by the looks of it."

I relented, and soon, we were drifting through the gates and into the cobblestone streets beyond.

The hill was steep, and I wasn't wearing any footwear, but Raiden thankfully slowed his pace as we passed trade stalls tucked into weed-flecked corners, darkened windows, and wound onto even darker avenues. "The heart is that way," I said, pointing down a cart-lined street toward the main street leading to the castle.

"That's nice."

I scowled at his back as he continued to drag me through alleyways.

Murmurs of, "Royal highness, Princess, and Prince," followed us at every other turn, but we didn't stop, for which I was glad. Not because I thought they were beneath me. I knew they were. But because I loathed small talk and would rather not pretend to be interested in people and creatures that did not interest me at all.

We'd reached the far west side of the city before Raiden slowed outside a dank, crumpled structure called Cursed Pints.

"I figured you'd rather not join me in the cellar again." Raiden circled me as I stood before three sagging steps. "So a tavern it is."

"We could've just had one of the—"

He stopped before me, a finger raised. "Ah, but that's custom. This"—he gestured to the building, if you could call it that—"is not. And I'm dying to see you down a pint."

"Do you mean lager?"

Raiden chuckled, and I blinked as I studied his cheeks, his perfect teeth, and his bright eyes. "That you even need to ask that means we've made the right decision by coming here."

I raised a brow, half wishing his hand was still in mine. "I'll be the judge of that." I shouldered by him and carefully carried myself up the stairs and straight inside the swinging doors.

My eyes grew as decay gave way to chandeliers and bright white countertops.

Royals and mixed mingled, dancing in the center of the room or huddled and draped over the lounge chairs and chaises that lined it. Behind a countertop that spread across the entirety of the large space, an indigo-haired male with sea green eyes dipped and winked our way while drying a glass with a pink rag.

"The look on your face," Raiden said, laughter coating every syllable, "priceless."

"Where are we?"

He lifted two fingers to the bartender. "Exactly as the sign stated, Cursed Pints."

"Is this allowed?" I threw him an accusing glare.

He frowned. "It's been here for several hundred years. Yes, it's allowed. It's a tavern, silk. Not a hidden brothel."

Brothels were permitted in the kingdom but not within the castle quarter or among the villages. They typically set up shop out of sight but usually within distance of well-traveled roads.

"Prince," one of the males on a divan by a crackling fire called. "You've returned."

I narrowed my eyes at the long-haired blond and the female next to him. They were royals.

"Adran," I said.

His bored eyes flicked to me. "Cousin."

The female next to him was a new addition, and though I was curious, I didn't let on.

Raiden slapped his hands together. "Come, sit." With a hand at my back, he encouraged me to the armchairs opposite my cousin and his companion, a tiny glass table between us.

The brunette female eyed me a moment and then ducked her head. "Honored, Princess."

"Who are you?" Well, so much for acting nonchalant.

Raiden thanked the bartender, who'd delivered two glass tankards of lager on a glinting silver tray. He bowed, then retreated.

"Still so brash," Adran tutted. "This is Amelda, my betrothed."

"Your betrothed?" I all but spat. Raiden's smirk was a tisk I wished to squash, buzzing over my profile as I glared at Adran. "Does your mother know of this?"

Adran flapped a hand, then tugged his gold shirt from his chest, canines gleaming. "Mother is too busy with lover number nine to care about much else."

Sarine was my mother's sister, but ever since her death, she chose not to appear at court unless she had to. Like many others. If she thought my father didn't notice, she was very much mistaken. Being that our family tree didn't extend far these years, it didn't exactly look good to have our few relatives absent whenever they so desired.

"Sarine needs to be careful," I warned

"A threat?" Adran took a swig of what looked to be flavored liquor. "Let us drink some more before the foreplay begins."

"You're still an idiot."

He smiled, his drink hand swinging out. "And you're still a beautiful, ice-infused bitch."

Raiden growled. "That will be enough."

All eyes darted to him, and I startled to find his teeth gnashing, his neck and jaw tight.

"How did you meet the prince?" I asked my cousin.

His betrothed answered. "He wandered in here for a drink a few nights ago when we were leaving."

I studied her golden complexion and the turquoise of her eyes. Pretty, I supposed, though Adran usually preferred his females bigger breasted. "And do you often find your males in taverns, Amelda?"

Her expression flattened, and Adran slid his arm around her shoulders. "She's of the Sun Kingdom. We met a few months ago when she was… working."

I turned to Raiden, who tipped a shoulder. "Amelda is an emissary for yours truly."

I feigned delight and leaned forward. "So you know how it feels to put his cock inside you? Do share."

Her eyes widened, and Adran tensed. "Mind your tongue, cousin."

"Or what?" I sat back, my nails tapping over the wooden edging in the velvet armrest.

Raiden sighed. Pulling some coin from his pocket, he dumped them on the table and then pulled me to my feet. "I can't take her anywhere."

I gazed up at him as he flicked a hand to the bartender, my cousin and his betrothed staring after us with mirrored looks of distaste. "You didn't deny it," I said once we broke through the doors. I wrenched my hand from his as we jumped down the worn steps to the damp street.

Raiden just laughed and kept on walking.

"What?" I followed, unsure what he found so funny about any of this.

He stopped once we reached an abandoned shoe store, its faded sign swinging in the faint breeze.

Raiden glanced up at it, then at me with a look that set my hands clenching.

Then the sign fell to the street, cracking in two.

"You're crazy. You know that?"

"It's not my fault you've whored yourself out too many times."

He spun, his bare chest illuminated beneath the slice of moonlight that crept between the shadowed shopfronts. "I've been alive for thirty summers more than you, Princess. I've stuck my cock in many a female. Pointing out whom doesn't make me a whore; it only serves in making you appear jealous, childish, and cruel."

His words slapped me, swaying me where I stood. "You could fuck her right now for all I care because I don't. You're to be my husband, not my bed partner."

Raiden stalked back to me, his every step careful and simmering with tension. "You don't care?"

"I loathe repeating myself, *Prince*."

The biting edge left his tone. "You don't kiss me like you don't care."

"I've kissed you twice." I laughed. "That means nothing. I was merely carrying out an assessment. Had I have known you'd act like some whining wolf cub, I'd have stayed behind."

"It means everything."

"Just shut up." I couldn't believe him. "Look, we fight more than we talk. We're done here. I'll see you when it's time."

"Audra, don't walk away."

I didn't so much as look at him as I kept on doing just that. "Like you can stop me."

And then he did. My speed was no match for his. A second later, I was halted by his hands wrapping around my face. "You're infuriating."

"You're the infuriating one."

He shook his head, lips twitching as his eyes danced over my face. Slowly, I felt my features relax.

"We're not done here." He kissed my forehead, then dragged me back down the street.

"Why do you do that?" I asked, ignoring a boy trying to sell us sweetcakes when we'd reached the heart.

"Do what?" Raiden stopped and gave the boy three coins, then took two frosted cakes from the gaping child and handed me one.

I sniffed it, and upon finding nothing nefarious, I took a bite. "Kiss me."

"Because I want to."

Strawberry and chocolate ignited my taste buds, and I swallowed the fluffy paradise. "That's not a reason."

"It is." He shoved the whole cake inside his mouth, his cheeks bulging.

I contained my laughter, just, and licked my thumb. "It isn't."

I'd almost finished, the frosting as sweet as it was sour, when he attempted to sway me off my feet again.

"Because you have a face that needs to be cherished. Not just for what it is, but for what it takes from inside you. You need to be kissed where you're most beautiful."

"To counteract where I'm most ugly," I finished his lingering thought.

"Audra..." He grabbed my wrist outside the empty fish market.

"It's fine. I don't need tenderly minced words, Prince." I licked the remaining frosting from my fingers. "They only serve to piss me off."

"You're not ugly inside," he said. "You're just..."

"I'm me," I said with cold finality. "I'm just me. Like it or don't, but don't you dare try to change it or say you weren't aware."

He blinked, then nodded, tucking his hands inside his pockets as we neared the stairs leading to the docks of the bay. It flowed in two directions, out to sea and under a small city bridge, where it ran downhill into catchments and waterfalls that fed the rivers in the valleys below. Patches of ice crested the banks, crawling over the moss layered rocks that pockmarked the shoreline.

I leaned over the frosted railing, gazing at the damp sand below. Idly, I wondered if the half-dressed prince of the Sun Kingdom was cold, or if his magic kept him warm.

Throwing a glimpse at Raiden, I found him staring ahead. "Look," he said, pointing at something in the distance.

I squinted at the few fishing boats and the sails of a lone ship. "What of them?"

"Not them." He tugged me close, encircling my waist with an arm. "Them," he whispered.

A splash echoed far out in the cove where the mountains, separated by a slice of water big enough for one ship to carefully sail through, almost touched.

Mermaids.

"They're back."

Raiden's hand tightened at my hip. "My parents saw them when they were here. They said there hasn't been a sighting of them in over two hundred years."

"That doesn't mean they've been gone." I'd seen them before.

"No," Raiden agreed. "Just hiding, perhaps."

In silence, we both pondered why that could be, and I felt my body lean into his. "My mother swore she saw one up close once."

Raiden hummed. "Really? What did she say of the experience?"

"They'd been swimming, and she said she dragged Sarine back to the shore and they ran for their lives."

"They would've been babes."

I tried to remember if that's what she'd said, but all I could see was the crystal blue of her eyes, and the way her heart sometimes shone in her smile. "Five and seven summers, I believe." I cleared my throat. "It's rumored they have teeth made of bones."

"And tails made of human hair," Raiden said.

"I should like to meet one, I think."

He laughed, the sound quiet as it drifted over the pier and to the city dwellers behind us. "And what would you do if you did?"

"Ask some questions, I suppose."

"What questions would you ask of her?"

"Or him," I said.

"There are no mermen. That is but a rumor told in erotic tales."

"There is. You cannot keep a species alive without reproduction."

His hand became a furnace attached to my hip, his grip iron hot. "Well, now that's true." The words were rough. "So what would you ask him or her?"

"Where they've been. What they do all day and night long. Do they eat fish or flesh? Or both? Can they have a spellcaster give them legs? Do their tails change to—" I stopped when I found Raiden smiling down at me. "What?"

"Nothing. Keep going."

I glared. "No. What's wrong?"

"Nothing, truly." He brushed a thumb by my lip, and then sucked it. "Frosting. And I… well, I didn't realize I'd enjoy hearing you talk so much."

I felt my chest inflate, and then he directed us over the pier toward the main city street.

"What else enlivens you so?"

I kept my gaze forward and away from any of the city folk who recognized us and bowed. "Chocolate, horses, furbanes, my collection of daggers, novels, roses, steak stew, scalding bubble baths…" I paused. "I could go on."

He encouraged me to as we approached the castle, fielding my lists with many of his own.

Horses, spiced chicken, sautéed mushrooms, sweetcakes, his childhood friends, wolves, training schedule, and chess.

"Wolves?" I asked, stepping around a slush pile of gunk oozing into a drain. "How in the darkness could you call a wolf a pet?"

"They're not pets." He nodded at the guards who opened the gates for us to enter. "They're friends."

"How do they fare in such a harsh climate?"

"They don't live there," he said, tugging me away from a couple who were laughing, even as they toppled to the ground, their glass goblets smashing into tiny glimmering, red-stained specks. "They live here along the border."

That snapped my attention to him as I wondered how a sun prince of the south befriended the wolves of the northeast.

"There she is."

I stilled outside the throne room doors at the sound of my father's approaching voice. "Father." I curtsied. "You're looking very fine for seven hundred summers."

His grin was dazzling, but his eyes made you pause and wonder if such bottomless depths held a soul within. Sometimes, I swore he did, but any proof was rare.

He patted my cheeks, then smacked a kiss atop my head, whispering low, "Your absence has not gone unnoticed."

I refrained from tensing and turned to Raiden, who was watching my father with a carefully blank expression. He smiled when I gestured to him. "Raiden thought to show me some of the city I'd somehow missed."

Raiden bowed. "Tyrelle."

My father's gaze sat heavy on Raiden for a moment, and then he broke into another grin and slapped him hard on the back. "Getting to know one another. Good. Ruling can be tiresome. Ruling together shall be difficult, especially if you cannot find ways to get along outside the bedroom."

"Father," I admonished.

He laughed. "Come, come." He swung his arm to the throne room. "Dance and drink and retire when the moon does."

We followed him into the throne room, where he took his seat upon the thorn-crusted gold dais that overlooked the crowds.

Bodies rocked by us—singing and dancing and lots of skin.

The orchestra sat tucked in a far crevice of the room, their instruments gleaming under the firelight, and their music eddying through the walls to entertain partygoers in every space.

Raiden took my hand in his, and I laughed as he spun me around and then swung me into his chest. My hands slapped against it, and flushed, I absorbed the heat and the smooth texture of his skin into mine as I gazed up at him beneath my lashes.

"Your touch burns," he said, so low as if he hadn't meant to say it at all.

"And yours thaws," I said, uncaring if anyone in the room heard me.

He tucked me close and hummed the haunting melody into my hair. Slowly, I pressed my cheek into his chest and hugged his lower back.

I'd never known what it was to be held before that. Never knew what it was to have someone hold you so tenderly that you feared you might just collapse into fragments of who you once were without their touch.

I looked up as the song changed, startled and confused, and let my eyes drift over the many faces in the room. "I need a drink."

"I'll get you one," Raiden said. "Wait here."

I backed up to the closest wall, staring at my father, who was rubbing his face in a female's chest. Her husband stood beside her, unable to mask his displeasure.

I tore my gaze away and tried to search for Raiden. He was over by the outside doors, taking drinks from a server. A scream had his eyes flaring and moving to where I stood.

I closed mine, drew in a long inhale, and slowly reopened them in my father's direction.

He'd bent the female over his throne, and his hand was between her legs. "If you're going to scowl, Marteen, I'll give you something worth scowling over."

Untucking himself from his pants, he then forced himself inside Marteen's wife.

No one could stop him. No one would dare. They all knew the cost would be imminent death. Or far worse.

My spine felt as though it'd crack, and I looked away as Lady Quillion's shrieks turned to moans of pleasure. Raiden's gaze found mine, but I couldn't read his. His shoulders were set, his hands whitening from his tight grip around the two goblets.

Bodies moved about, blocking my line of sight, excitement and disgust heavy in the air.

Wanting away from the static that was filling my head, I moved toward the doors that would lead to my bed chambers while searching for Raiden.

He was nowhere to be found.

"Where is Casilla?"

I didn't dare open my eyes. Too shocked, too thrown, too sickened to my very soul.

The audacity to ask about her when I'd just spilled my innards before him… I had no words.

I almost didn't answer him.

"You were not listening."

The bars of his cage clanged as he rattled them, his voice loud enough to send the guards rushing in. "If you've hurt her. If you've so much as—"

I sat up, and his words ceased with a wave of my hand. "I tire of you. So much so"—I swept a bored glance over his frame—"I wonder what I ever saw in you in the first place."

I motioned for the guards to leave as I rolled from the table, my bones feeling brittle from days of riding and magic use. My feet slapped against the ground, my nightgown flowing around and down to meet my ankles.

"If I'm here on account of your father being dead, then I wish I were the one who killed him."

I stopped, laughter bubbling deep inside before I let it roll through my body and exit my mouth. "Sleep well, *Prince*."

"Wait," he called, rattling his cage once more. "Damn it, wait!"

I stopped out of his line of sight. "Why should I?"

"When will it happen?"

I watched a rat scuttle across the floor. "I presume you mean your death?" It paused and peered back at me with tiny glowing eyes, then raced for a hole in the wall of a cell closest to the gates.

"Yes."

"You already know the answer to that." I left him and nodded at Azela. "Have someone find me should he have any more hallucinations." After what'd happened to Berron, I'd forgotten to broach the subject with Truin and made a mental note to do so next time I saw her.

As I reached the corridor to my rooms, I trailed my fingers over the row of stained glass windows, feeling the cold bite into my skin. I welcomed it, letting it seep into my pores and rejuvenate that which was weary and defeated.

The doors opened with a thought, and I entered, making them close quietly when I saw the lord of the east sprawled over the sheets on his stomach.

I wasn't in the mood to play, so I carefully slid beneath the duvet and rolled over. Watching the moon crawl across his wide back, I noticed the thick line of scars upon it ran parallel to one another, and the muscles that seemed to clench beneath them, even while he slept.

Sooner than I'd expected, thoughts of what could have been and what should never have been followed me into a restless sleep.

TEN

Tickled by the slight breeze, the engraved wooden sign squeaked on its hinges.

Cursed Pints appeared no different to the first and last time I'd entered the deceiving blackened with damp doors. I nodded to Ainx and Azela, indicating they were to stay on the rain-scented street.

The wood protested beneath my boots as I climbed the steps and crossed the thin porch, swinging the doors open. The interior was much the same, only this time, I wasn't shocked by the white armchairs and chaises, the sparkling glassware and sitting tables, or the gleaming white expanse of the bar.

The bartender and owner, who I now knew was named Eli, dipped his head when he saw me. He approached wearing high-waisted slacks and a spotted black and white shirt with suspenders. His dark hair seemed to change shades of blue beneath the globes of light hanging from chandeliers in the ceiling.

I leaned against the wall by the door, thankful the bar was empty of patrons until after noon.

"Majesty," he murmured, a careful gleam to his bright green eyes. "She is still where your guards left her in the basement, but I must ask if—"

"Has she been causing trouble?"

He shook his head. "Not exactly, but she's—"

"Has she been asking for him?"

"Yes, though it's odd," he rushed out. I angled my head, allowing him to continue. "She eats all her meals and washes when permitted, but otherwise, she doesn't really act as a prisoner should."

I let that sit inside my mind, absorbing it slowly. The urge to discover more about this woman became a burn I wanted to soothe. "Interesting," I said. "Where is the key?"

Eli's brows lifted. "You wish to free her?"

I laughed. "Oh, no." I crept closer and patted his arm. "I wish to imprison her in the darkness but not just yet."

At that, Eli's almost translucent skin paled even further. He swallowed, and I patted his arm again. "Key. Hurry it up."

He scampered off behind the bar, and I meandered over the varnished wood floor to trail my fingers over the jeweled stones that sat on display on a crisp white shelf. I'd never been one for too much jewelry, but I did covet fine things.

A jingling sound snapped my attention from a sapphire stone.

I took the key from Eli, smiling at how he struggled to meet my gaze. "Much obliged."

He nodded, backing up a step and bobbing his head. "If you need anything…"

"Where did you find the stones?"

Eli looked over at them, scratching his hairless chin. "They are from The Edges, Majesty. Would you like one? Take your pick. I can package it—"

I raised my hand. "No. That's quite all right." My interest in them sagged and died. I swept past him to the hall on the right side of the bar, shadows swallowing me until I'd reached the last door on the end.

It was made of iron, probably to better protect the gallons of wine, spirits, lager, and goddesses knew what else. I pressed the key against the hole and heard the mechanism unlatch, metal grinding over metal, and then a poof of air.

Undoubtedly heavy, I waved a hand to open it. Dust and flecks of paint powdered the air as it slammed into the wall. I moved over the small landing to the stairs and descended, tucking the key inside a hidden pocket of my emerald velvet gown.

I waited until I'd reached the bottom where a small lantern swayed before I closed the door. Barrels and baskets and crates were stacked in every corner and against every wall of the room. I moved to the center where a cage, smaller than the one her beloved was kept in, sat square.

She didn't so much as glance up as the heels of my boots struggled to clack over the dusty floor. "You finally decided to visit." Her voice was sweet. Deceptive in the way it was both gentle and fierce.

"Casilla," I said, feeling the name roll over the edge of my tongue. "Sweet, stupid *Casilla.*"

She said nothing, didn't even move as I prowled closer.

Her homespun skirts were in dirty tatters, torn around the hem. As was her peasant white blouse, its ruffles and pearl buttons brushed with brown. Her red hair was still luminous, but the roots and curls were lathered in oil.

Peering around, I motioned for an empty drum, catching and flipping it as I took a seat before her. "I'm afraid I've been busy."

Her slim shoulders stiffened, and I knew it was there, screaming to tear out of her. The question of her beloved's well-being.

My hand curled into the softness of my skirts as my elbows rested upon my knees. "How are you finding the accommodations?"

"I could use a proper bath and some new clothes, but other than that, it beats slaving away in the miner's kitchens each day."

The insolence.

I bent forward and dragged a nail down the metal enclosure. "How about when you talk to me, you do me the courtesy of looking at me?" I tapped at the cage with my nail. It rattled. The loud noise, the small display of what I could do, tipped her head up, her gray eyes flaring wide. "I am, after all, your queen."

"I serve no queen." Her eyes simmered as her pink, cracked lips tightened. "I am one of the exiled."

I laughed, low and controlled. "Darling," I tutted. "Do you not realize that those of The Edges are still under royal jurisdiction? It predominantly houses criminals who were given one last chance to show they deserve their miserable excuse for a life, and the partners and children of said criminals." I pursed my lips. "So, what are you? A criminal? Or the spawn of one?"

A small tilt to her lips, and then her eyes were sparking as they grazed my face. "Everybody knows that the only true criminal in this kingdom is you."

I stood, the drum cracking against the concrete as wind curtained my hair, billowing my skirts and swallowing Casilla within its breath-stealing grasp.

She gasped, her hands clawing at her throat. "Less chitchat, more business." I made her stand, smiling as she stumbled to her soiled bare feet. "Whatever gave you the idea you could marry an exiled king? My husband, to be precise."

I released her, and she fell like a sack of grain, hitting her head on the side of the cage.

She winced, patting the back of her head, blood coming away on her palm. "He's not your husband. He was never supposed to be *your* husband."

"Really now?" I grabbed the cage. "How curious. Please tell me why you think this." My tone oozed sugar while I tried to kill her where she stood with my gaze alone.

"He never loved you, which was made obvious before you exiled him." She stood on trembling legs, doing her best to show she wasn't in pain. "In any case, you threw him away. You can't just expect him to spend the rest of his life alone."

"I had no such notions, stupid girl. But sharing a bed with another female is one thing while vowing to them is another thing entirely. It's treason. You lot were warned to keep your distance when the guards brought him in."

"Yeah, well many of your soldiers don't have a lot of love for you either. Only fear and hatred," she spat. "You might want to do something about that."

"You little…" I slammed her into the side of the cage, keeping her suspended there with rage alone as her legs swung and kicked for purchase on the ground.

"You're crazy," she wheezed. "Why would you think he'd ever love you in the first place?"

"Oh, now you're just goading me." My lips twitched. I gathered whatever was in the pail nearest me, likely her own excrement, and sent it sailing for her face.

Her eyes and mouth shut as what looked and smelled like urine splashed over her nose and lips. I dropped her, and she fell to the hard ground with a crack, then I forced her mouth open and sent her own bodily fluids inside it.

She screamed, sputtering and coughing until I'd made sure every drop from the pail was now on a nice little journey to her stomach.

"Everyone in that dust-covered cesspit knew he was off-limits. Even you, my stupid little traitor. So tell me, or I'll end you right now. What exactly made you think you could go against me?"

She was too busy choking to answer, so I leaned against the metal bars and inspected my nails, fearing I might have chipped one when I'd tapped it against them earlier. Thankfully, it was fine. When she stopped wheezing, I began pacing in slow strides around her.

Around and around, until she eventually gave up on tracking my movements and stared up at the swaying lantern above her head, her face damp and her hair dripping. "Do you really want to know?"

"No, I'd much rather just kill you, but I like to have my reasons. It helps one to sleep better at night."

"I'm sure," she muttered.

I stopped, and she rushed out, "Love."

After staring at her with lowered brows, I laughed again, the sound crazed and dry. Then I rushed the cage and began plucking locks of her hair from her head, one tug of too much wind at a time.

She screamed, moving her hands to her scalp to try to stop it.

"Let me tell you a story about love, you piece of vermin filth." I began pacing again, the sound of her screams spurring me on. "Love is nothing but a drug that will trick your heart for access to your soul. It seeps inside and poisons you, attempts to rid you from existence."

My gut began roiling, my breaths coming faster. I forced my magic to still and drew in a deep inhale. I had to leave. I had to leave, or I would end her.

And I couldn't do that just yet.

Her quiet sobs chased me up the steps as I slowly traversed them. The door boomed to a close behind me, and without saying a word, I dumped Eli's key on the bar, then gathered my skirts in hand as I swept outside into the bitter chill.

My lids lowered when I stopped beneath the stairs and turned my face up to the skies.

Drops of ice-cold rain slapped onto my skin and slid down my cheeks, sinking inside my pores.

"Majesty?" Ainx called, concern in his tone.

But I remained standing there, the breeze and rain a comfort against the inferno threatening to engulf me.

Only fear and hatred.

When I was sure my voice wouldn't betray me, I opened my eyes, rolled my shoulders back, and continued down the street. "I need to see Truin."

"What of the female, my queen?" Azela asked.

It was then I realized I hadn't gleaned anything of much use from the traitorous bitch. "She's not a female. She's nothing but a disgusting human fool."

"Did she know of your decree regarding...?" She didn't want to say it.

A few streets downhill, we slipped back into the hustle of the heart, people parting once they realized I was in their midst.

"Enough with the questions. She knew, and she did it anyway."

Ainx snarled, and for that, I gave him a tiny smile over my shoulder.

I knew of people's less-than-stellar opinions of me. I wasn't so self-absorbed that I didn't pay attention. I just simply did not care. I was who I was, and naturally, many wouldn't like that. Regardless, it was nice to know that not everyone loathed me. Some seemed to respect me from a place that had nothing to do with fear, and everything to do with knowing me.

A monster, most certainly. But not always.

Truin lived by the waterfront in a tiny apartment sandwiched between a bakery and a blacksmith.

She was at the door before I could knock, and I again left Azela and Ainx on the street. "I had a dream," she said as she slammed the door behind me, and I moved up the narrow steps. It was a good thing I'd left Ainx outside, or else he'd need to move up them sideways like a crab because his shoulders were too broad.

A thin red door with unnecessary peepholes shaped in every phase of the moon opened to reveal a large room. Truin's bed was a straw-filled mattress, bedecked in gold and greens in its place by the window in the corner of the apartment.

A map of the continent was pinned to the wall above a curved oak desk. Scrolls, inkpots, and quills scattered over the scratched surface. Her kitchen was but a countertop with a sink and small oven. She rarely used it unless she was brewing potions and remedies. She was paid well for her service to the crown, and for her healing aids and fertility tonics.

Jars of insects, herbs, dirt, sand, and even gold sat in uneven rows upon the windowsill and over every available surface of the small countertop.

She grabbed a large round plaid cushion and moved it before the fire and then took a seat on a spotted one next to it. "You're even more troubled than when I last saw you."

I unwrapped the scarf from around my neck, sighing as I took a seat and ran it between my fingers. Crossing my legs, I stared at the small flames dancing over the bronze hearth. "She said she did it for love."

It only took Truin a moment to realize whom I was referring to. "Her name?"

"Casilla."

Truin's muddied gaze sat upon me for long moments. "You didn't kill her."

"Is my disappointment in myself that obvious?"

A small laugh tittered from her. "No, you just seem… kind of defeated."

The glossy silk weaved between my fingers, looping and unlooping.

"And what of Raiden?"

I pushed out a hard breath. "That's why I'm here." I looked over at her. "He remembered Zadicus. And not only that, but before we left for the Sun Kingdom, it's been said he had some type of episode." I waved my hand about. "Hallucinations, apparently."

"Was he physically unwell?" she asked.

I nodded.

Truin looked at the flames, firelight flickering in her narrowed eyes.

"Why would he remember Zad but not me?"

Her shoulders sank as she eyed me. "I don't mean to upset you, but he did want you dead."

My teeth gritted, the scarf coiling too tight around my fingers.

Truin continued, voice gentler. "Is it possible he remembers, at least enough, and that it doesn't make one bit of difference?"

"To him," I finished for her, rubbing my face, the silk soft over my heated skin. "Because he detested me that much?"

Truin shifted. "I don't know. I'd like to believe, as I'm sure you want to, that he never truly hated you." She paused. "Audra, what is it you hope to glean from this situation before it's over?"

The truth. Or a truth spun well enough that it would counteract the damage wrought to my heart from his actions.

I was in search of well-spun, undetectable lies.

I said none of those things as my hands slid from my face. "I want him to look at me and see what he's done. To feel it all and suffer beneath the weight of his betrayal."

"Maybe that was your plan, but really, you want him to tell you it was all a lie. A catastrophic misunderstanding."

I groaned. "Stop being so perceptive, you fucking witch."

Truin smiled, soft and knowing, when I looked at her. "It's okay, you know." She nodded. "To still love someone who destroyed you. Your father was despicable. He killed your mother, he took everything that held meaning from you if you weren't careful, and let's not even begin with the horrors he wrought, of which he made you bear witness to many of, yet deep down, you still loved him."

She was right.

He was my greatest shame and greatest foe all in one.

Truin made tea, and we sipped it while watching the fire die before she fed it a couple more logs.

"Should I even bother trying anymore?" I was beginning to worry I was becoming transparent. "I don't want to seem like some desperate imbecile."

She grasped my hand within hers, and I stared down at her small fingers, watching the way they struggled to curl around my longer ones. "You look like a queen who has been gravely wronged, so you're taking your own form of justice." I lifted my eyes to her fierce gaze. "As all true queens must do."

I could only hope that's how I would see it when it was all over.

An hour later, my boots hit the damp cobblestone, and I re-wrapped my scarf around my neck. I'd never needed protection from the cold, but I did need to look fabulous. My own rules, and I adored abiding by them.

The sun was dimmed by a group of passing clouds, and I wished for more snow, not liking the way the damp wanted to claw inside my bones and reduce me to a pile of defeated mush. We were a kingdom stuck in perpetual winter, but the temperature only got so low before it rose again, making it easier for trade to take place and ships to glide into our shores.

No one really knew why, though if you asked the many who worshipped the goddesses, they'd bore you to tears with tales of the two sisters' personalities—light and dark, fire and ice—and how their love for one another, no matter their differing opinions and traits, was so strong it forged a world for their offspring to rule over.

Though it was true the powers of the royals were born from our lands, I had a lot of doubt about the rest of that nonsense. I didn't quite know what I believed. Perhaps one day, I'd care enough to find out more about this mystical continent of mine.

Should people ever decide to quit pissing me off, of course.

"What does he have?" I asked Azela.

"Sweetcakes." She smirked at Ainx, who'd just stepped out of the bakery. "He adores them."

I let him eat two before I snatched the box and tossed them into a thawing pile of snow.

ELEVEN

I WATCHED HIM SLEEP, LISTENING TO THE INCESSANT DRIP coming from stalactites tucked within the deepest cells.

He'd always slept so easily. I'd found it odd in the days after his betrayal, as I'd recounted all the times he'd been inside me, and how easily our lovemaking had serenaded him into a peaceful slumber. Odd because he wanted my kingdom—*me*—squashed.

How could you love someone so convincingly, so painstakingly earnest in every transaction, all the while knowing you would be their demise in every crushing way?

He slept now as he had then, as though not even a rat scuttling over his hunched form could disturb him.

I contemplated waking him by removing the bars from the stone and sending the gated door down upon him.

But I chose to start talking instead. They say the comatose can hear you wherever they're lurking within their minds. Perhaps it was the same for sleeping assholes.

Either way, I didn't particularly care.

I wanted to retell this part for me. To pluck the memory from my own mind and cast it upon every breath I took. To feel the words leave my lips as I envisioned the moments that bestowed mayhem upon every facet of who I was and changed the course of our lives forever.

Most of all, I wanted to remind myself that it was real. Once upon a time, it had happened. I was there and so was the stranger curled against the wall of his cell.

19 summers old

The snow had left, and in its place fell sunshine carried upon a crisp wind.

The grass crunched beneath his boots as he approached where I'd secluded myself with Van upon the second tallest mountaintop in the kingdom.

How he'd gotten up here, I'd love to know. I'd been here for hours, trepidation over what to do with the male who wouldn't leave me alone, even when he wasn't near, troubling me into needing utter silence. The kind only found on top of a wind-strewn field of grass, grass that was trying to coax itself back to life in the absence of the brutal cold.

Wildflowers had cracked through the earth this past week. Van was making a meal out of them, the sound of his huffing and slurping and chomping, and the faint whistle of the breeze the only exceptions to the otherwise deathly quiet landscape.

As the prince drew closer, a curious smile igniting green eyes that bounced between Van and me, I half wondered if he'd brought the warmth from the Sun Kingdom with him to ward off the worst of the chill.

For once, I didn't mind. Usually, the coldest of days and nights were my favorite. The perfect time to curl up before a roaring fire and sip tea with a book or guzzle wine with a lover.

Maybe that was my issue. It had been a while since I'd found relief in the form of a suitable male. All thanks to Prince Raiden.

A snarl rippled from Van's mouth, grass and wildflowers falling free as he speared his head in Raiden's direction. An onyx eye took him in as his nostrils widened to the size of my head.

From where I was leaning against his side, I shushed him and patted his furry leg. "He's not a threat." I then eyed the prince. "Well, not entirely."

Van stared another few seconds, then harrumphed and got busy licking up the wares he'd lost from his mouth, one eye still sharp on the male taking a seat beside me.

Raiden leaned around me, his expression one of unbridled awe as he studied Van's gray coat, flecked with white and silver, the gray feathered wings, and the brown horns curling out of his head. "They're even more magnificent up close."

"And territorial," I informed, joining a wildflower stem with the rest of the chain I'd been working on. "He can sense a large variety of helpful things, especially ill intent."

"Duly noted."

We sat quietly for a long moment before curiosity got the better of me. "Pray tell, just how did you get up here?"

Raiden ran his hand over his close-cropped hair, squinting to the melting mountains nearby. "I asked around for the fastest way, and they reluctantly allowed me to borrow your stallion." He turned to me, a glow to his eyes. "Being that you're my betrothed and all."

I tensed. "Wen? Where is he?"

Raiden pointed at the incline. "Tied to a tree some clefts down. It was too steep to have him come any higher."

My shoulders sagged. "You have some nerve, Prince."

He grinned, and I wanted to slap it right off his chiseled face. "Where you're concerned, I'm constantly on my toes."

"All the more reason for you to leave me be." I adjusted my sapphire skirts over my crossed legs, the sun causing them to shimmer.

"Never."

I peered up at his earnest eyes, the hard set to his jaw, and then averted my gaze to the flowers in my lap.

"Pretty," Raiden commented after watching me weave them for a time. "What are you going to do with it when you're done? Wear it?"

I snorted. "No, it just helps to quiet the mind. I'll feed it to Van."

"That's his name?"

"Vanamar."

Raiden tilted his head, his arms wrapped tight around his bent knees. "You love him."

I frowned at him briefly, then returned my attention to my ministrations. "Of course, I do. He was a gift for my fourteenth birthday." When I came of age. "I'd been asking for years and was given the runt of the litter." I smirked down at the violet flower in my hand. "For a time, anyway. He's since outgrown his kin in every possible way." I stilled my hands, looking up at him beneath my lashes. "Do you not think me capable of such a thing as love, Prince?"

He seemed to think about it, then that arrogant smirk returned. "Everyone is capable of it." The sun haloed behind his head, illuminating his skin and eyes, the edges of his cheeks and strong jaw—stealing my next breath. "Do you need to quiet your mind often?"

I wasn't going to answer, but I figured if I was to spend the rest of my existence with him tied to me, it was probably best he knew enough about me. Maybe then he'd leave me alone, or at least know when to.

"Every now and then. There are always so many voices."

He hummed in understanding. "Nod and smile. Bear it all."

"That." I sighed. "Sometimes it's too hard to fake it, and that's when I need to escape for a while."

The blades of cold grass tickled my ankles, and Raiden observed the way my skirts fanned around me in a rippling pillow of chiffon. "Hate to break it to you, but you're not so great at faking it anyway."

I tossed a bud at him. His hand shot up, catching it. When he opened his palm, there was nothing but smoking specks. The wind swept in, curling them off his skin and into the air.

"Do you wonder if this is what you would have chosen for yourself?" he asked.

"Do you mean marrying you?" I asked. "Or being royal."

He tipped a broad shoulder. "Both."

"Yes and no," I said. "I wouldn't have chosen to vow to you. You're not my type." His brows gathered, and I smirked. "But yes, even with the incessant boredom, stresses, and annoyances that can accompany being a royal, I would still choose it."

"Why?"

The question knocked my eyes to his curious ones. "I've lived with magic running through my veins for too long to ever go without it."

"No," he said, shifting closer, his gray tunic billowing over his chest, the opening collar exposing a tantalizing glimpse of his skin. "No. The other powers that being a royal grants you."

I knew my response would probably disappoint him, hoped for it even. My smile was genuine as it sank into my cheeks. "Never. That is my favorite power of all. One I do not take for granted by wishing it away onto someone else's incapable shoulders."

Raiden swiped his thumb below his lush bottom lip, his eyes bright. "A true queen you will make." Those eyes dulled then, and he looked away, taking in the panoramic view of Allureldin. The streets and streams of water that wound their way between wood and stone structures for miles until they faded into greener grass and dirt roads.

Van turned his head, inhaling strands of my hair as he sniffed. I laughed, then handed him a wildflower, laughing again when his tongue grazed my hand. "Impatient boy." I scratched beneath his sagging chin.

"He adores you."

I gently nudged Van's head away and wiped my hand over my skirts. "He's one of my only friends."

Raiden's question sounded like more of a statement. "You don't have any others?"

I picked up my chain, running my fingers over the silken stems, then the velveteen petals. "Only a few. Father says friends are merely the enemy wrapped in a prettier disguise."

"Is that why he's had you trained for a battle that may never come?"

We may have been a continent of peace for over a millennia, but we still had warriors, trained soldiers, and armories filled with gleaming death instruments just like other kingdoms across the Gray Sea. "No, that was my mother's bidding." I cleared my throat, ignoring the bruise that throbbed in my chest cavity. "She was defenseless without her magic, and as you know, my father's is such an entity that no one really stands a chance."

"He didn't mind that you trained?" His tone was cautious.

I laughed. "Oh yes, he punished her severely for it."

Raiden's expression turned granite. "How?"

I licked my teeth, then sighed. "He had his best soldiers fight her. Twenty-eight males compelled to follow his every order, even if it went against their base instincts. Every bone in her body was broken, and she lost sight in her right eye for months."

Raiden said nothing for the longest time, and I fought the urge to fidget. "And they had to," he guessed. "Or they'd die."

That didn't need answering.

He scrubbed his hands over his face. "Please tell me you weren't forced to watch at least."

My smile was grim, my heart a weighted beast in my chest as uninvited memories tried to resurface. I smacked them down and locked the door on the darkness. "My father does nothing in half measures." I looped another stem, my fingers shaking. "It would behoove you to remember that."

His eyes pressed, but I refused to look at him. He knew it was not a threat but a warning that should he step out of line, we would both pay the consequences.

When I'd finished with the chain, I stood and brushed dirt and grass from my skirts.

Van huffed, a low grumble escaping as he yawned, exposing teeth sharp enough to shred a hand to ribbons.

In my peripheral, I saw Raiden tense and leap to his feet as I rounded the beast and took his snout in my hands.

His tail, spiked with a tuft of fur at the tip, thumped onto the ground, almost knocking Raiden off his feet. "Don't be rude."

Van's eyes zeroed in on me, bottomless and knowing. "Okay." I tapped his nose. "But you don't need to like someone to show respect." That was something my mother would tout time and time again.

Raiden chuckled, a scratchy and deep sound.

Van's gaze slipped to my wrist, his eyes almost crossing as he eyed the ten-foot-long wildflower chain. "Lie down."

With a shuffle that shook the ground, he did, and I lifted the chain of flowers above his nose for him to slurp into his mouth.

"He likes to suck on them," I explained to Raiden as we watched Van's jaw rotate and his eyes glaze over. At his silence, I turned around to find he wasn't watching the beast.

He was watching me with an intensity that eclipsed the sun and threatened to awaken the stars.

"Come here, silk." He crooked a finger, and I felt the tug of his magic coil tight around my abdomen, luring my body to sway closer.

My hands met his chest, and his arms wound around my waist, pressing my body flush to his.

His head bent down, and I rose onto my toes, unsure of how this was happening with so much ease. Without so much as a question, our mouths joined.

A caress for each lip, a nip for every lick, we crashed and we slow danced beneath the clouds drifting over our heads.

His hand fused with my cheek, his thumb ghosting over the corner of my mouth as his forehead rested upon mine. "I have vastly underestimated you in every fascinating way."

And as I gazed up into his eyes, my chest filling with bubbling air, I recognized that I might have done the same. "Types are overrated anyway."

He chuckled, and then his lips were stroking mine once more as he stepped back toward a smattering of rocks and lowered me over one that laid closest to the ground.

Van groaned softly, but otherwise stayed exactly where I'd willed him to while Raiden lifted my skirts and I tugged at his tunic, desperate to touch his hot chest again.

The rough surface meeting my back was extinguished by the gentle slide of his hands roaming up my thighs and spreading them wide. When his mouth found me, wet and ready and greedy for his tongue, I mewled, the sound drifting like a song on the wind, carried to the bordering peaks.

He groaned, his nose rubbing against me and his hands tight around my thighs. "So fucking exquisite."

My own roamed his hair, the short strands unable to be tugged but still luxurious beneath my fingers. Another rumble soaked my heated flesh, and then his finger was inside me as his tongue coaxed me to peaks higher than the mountain beneath us.

"Prince," I breathed, desperate to have him fill me, but desperate to have him stroke me one last time and render me a dazzled mess.

"Come undone for me, silk," he said with a languid drag of his tongue as his finger hooked. Then I was shattering, my moans and curses cut short by his lips as I felt him climb over me. Felt him because although my eyes were open, I failed to see anything but shimmering clouds blurring with blue skies.

He moved my leg over his back as he pressed himself to my opening. "Look at me."

I blinked a dozen times, and the beauty of his face slowly came into focus. "From this day forward, you will see nothing but me and feel nothing but me every time you come undone."

"So demanding," I said, my voice all breath as I tried to spear myself on him by rocking my hips.

His grin was sensuous sin, and I reached for his face, wanting to lick his plush lips. "You'd better get used to it."

One thrust and his head rolled back. His neck corded, muscles spasming, and his Adam's apple exposed as he bellowed curses for the entire kingdom to hear.

I laid enraptured, full and hypnotized by all he was as my heart beat furiously.

When he looked down at me, his eyes were fevered, his expression painted with both pain and pleasure. My fingers drifted all on their own, tracing the hard and soft edges of his face. When they reached his lush mouth, his eyes softened, and he kissed them. "It feels different," he said. "Being inside you feels different to any other time."

Nodding, I agreed, my head barely feeling the hard surface beneath it. "Fun. They were fun. But this is…"

"Forever," he said, lowering his lips to mine. "This feels endless."

He kissed me with a fervor that matched the dance of his hips; his thick, swelling length filling me so completely that I gasped with every thrust. Slow and coaxing, the rhythm of his mouth matched his cock, reducing my body and all that I was to a puddle of pleasure-riddled compliance.

I liked control. But I liked what Raiden did to me far better.

As though there really were a pot of magical gold at the end of a rainbow, he took me there, over and over again, blinding colors blurring as indescribable feelings coursed through me.

"One more," he said.

We were now on the grass, and I was in his lap with my legs banded behind his back and my arms around his neck, holding every part of him as close to me as possible. Our clothing hung from our limbs, my skirts torn and stained around my waist.

"We couldn't possibly," I said, yet I kept moving over him, unwilling to separate myself from his body and the sensations it evoked.

He'd already filled me with his seed, twice, after making me lose myself three times.

Our kind could recuperate fast but never had Berron been able to stay inside me, half erect, and kiss me until he was steel pushing at all my pleasure points once more.

He tugged my lip into his mouth, dragging his teeth over the swollen flesh when he released it. "You can, and you will. Breathe with me." He shifted his hands to my rear as he picked me up, keeping my hips against his to remain inside me as he laid me down on the grass some ways away from Van, who was now sleeping.

I reached for his muscular arms, that tattoo. He took my hands in his, spreading them above my head as my feet climbed his back. "I cannot leave now. You realize this, right?"

I laughed, but then he hit that spot and stars started appearing, his canines dragging across the skin of my neck. "No," I breathed. "You can't."

He grinded his hips into mine. "Feeling my seed inside you, mingling with what I've expelled from you... I have to. I need to mark you."

In answer, I moved my head back, too far gone to realize that I was allowing a male to mark me for the first time. A sign that wouldn't always be seen, but rather, it would be felt by any others who approached me. They would know I was taken and not to be touched, but it wasn't permanent. It lasted mere months before the male would need to mark again, unless he was done with that female, or she was done with him.

His teeth pierced my skin, just enough to puncture, his body, his scent, his touch, all of him—I spiraled into an abyss from which I feared I'd never return. He followed me instantly, roaring into my ear as he shook over me and filled me to the point of overflow.

I wasn't sure how I was going to look at another male again after that, let alone seek one out for pleasure after the mark had worn off.

I needn't have bothered so much as thinking it.

Two days later, Raiden was to leave Allureldin.

I'd contemplated not saying goodbye, unwilling to play the besotted female. I changed my mind at the last minute, fearing I'd be too late after he'd left me in bed that morning with only a lingering kiss to my forehead while I'd slept.

In the hallway outside my rooms, so caught up in my

desperation, I rounded the corner and slammed into a steel-infused wall. Not a wall, I realized as I rubbed my aching nose, but a chest.

Zadicus gripped my shoulders, steadying me. "Apologies, Princess."

"Darkness be damned, you asshole," I groaned out, then remembered I had to run.

But he snatched my wrist as I made to leave. "Where are you off to in such a hurry so early?"

"That's none of your business," I said, pulling my wrist. "Let go."

He wouldn't relinquish his hold. His brows lowered, nostrils flaring slightly as he sniffed.

"What are you doing here anyway?" I asked, tugging to no avail. He showed no sign of strain as I pulled with all my might.

"Business meeting with your father," he muttered, narrowed eyes burning into my neck.

I frowned, then Zad stepped closer, pushed my hair aside, and hissed, "He marked you?"

I'd almost forgotten about the mark, but I didn't care. I wanted to scream at him, stab him, kick him, *anything* just to move already. "Release me," I gritted between my teeth. "Now."

"It's…" He swallowed. "Distasteful," he finally said, venom coating the word.

"I'm to be his wife," I reminded him. "And you're really starting to piss me off."

Zad's golden eyes lifted from my neck to meet my gaze, swirling with what looked to be rage.

The air became charged, likely from my panic over potentially missing Raiden, and the hand he'd wrapped around my wrist trembled before he dropped it and stalked away.

I blinked at where he'd stood, then shook the odd encounter off with a slew of curses.

I chased the rising sun through the back hallways of the castle and exploded out onto the courtyard, crossing it to the gardens.

Accidentally knocking a groundskeeper to his rump, I growled and kept running, my breath fogging in the fading night as I came to a screeching stop before the stables and found Raiden's carriage gone from where it had been parked beside them.

My throat constricted, and I pulled at my hair, turning in a circle over the hay-dusted ground.

"I told you I was done underestimating you."

My gaze swung to where Raiden emerged from behind a stable door, his riding pants and jacket hugging his impressive physique.

I scowled, and then his words registered. I forgot about being annoyed and threw myself at him instead. He laughed as he tripped back inside the stable, and I peppered his face with kisses. "Don't play with me."

"But it's the most fun I've ever had." He was tugging up my nightgown, and then I was against the wooden wall, riding crops and saddles clanging against it as he untucked himself and slid inside my body.

"Don't forget about me," I whispered to his worshipping mouth, my hands tight on his flexing forearms.

"Never."

Time taunted with every memory, every cell inside me that no longer belonged solely to me. Raiden's absence was a sickness that threatened to take hold and tear me asunder as each moon and sun faded.

I decided I'd write him, then scrapped each letter, feeling as though my words were nothing but romantic drivel that passing messengers would likely only snicker at.

Over dinner one night, tankards and goblets gleaming beneath floating firelight, my father shared the news that our nuptials would be moved forward.

That we were due to vow in a little over a month.

The news both rocked and calmed me. I clung to it, feeling so very unlike myself as I harbored how deeply the prince had affected me in our short time together.

Truin would joke about how I looked different, all the while eyeing my neck knowingly even though she couldn't see the tiny pricks left by Raiden's canines thanks to my hair. Berron pushed me harder at training, snarling instead of laughing, yet when he saw me smile or attempt to make light of something, his own smile was real.

Three weeks before the dawn ceremony was due to arrive, I was searching for new books to read amongst the secret selection my mother and grandmother had collected from all over the continent. Tales of sweeping romance and adventure bound into worn, rich-colored covers.

My father would have them burned if he knew of their existence. Libraries were for knowledge, and reading was supposed to be a chore, not an enjoyable way to pass the time by visiting another time entirely.

It was a great risk for Yarnt, our librarian of a hundred and forty years, to undertake, but he did so without blinking an eye behind those ginormous wire-rimmed spectacles of his.

And so it was there, deep within the darkest corner of the library and hidden inside rows of mildew-scented books, that my prince returned to me.

"You rob me of breath."

The book slipped from my fingers, tumbling upside down, pages likely crumpling upon the old oak floor as I spun around, my heart clawing at my chest. "Prince."

He was leaning against the end of the shelves with an affectionate glint to his eyes and a tiny curl to his lips.

Gathering my breath back inside me, I went to him. He met me halfway, picking me up and hugging me to him so hard that I lost my ability to breathe all over again.

"Lavender," he said, inhaling deeply.

"Hmm?" I asked against his neck.

He chuckled as he scrunched a hand into my hair. "Your scent. Lavender and vanilla. I've kept some with me everywhere I go since we passed a field of it on the journey back home."

He set me down and plucked a squashed piece of lavender from his pocket.

My lips parted as I stared down at it.

He slipped it away. "I long for the day I won't need to do so." He tugged me close, a hand at my cheek as his eyes ate their fill of my face. "But I fear even when I'm with you, in those brief moments I'm not, I'll long to be."

"You're bad news, Prince," I said, though the words lacked conviction. "Such sweet words for such a sour princess."

He chuckled and lifted my chin for his lips to rest over mine. "You think yourself sour?"

I fluttered my lashes, then inched his bottom lip between my lips. "I'm probably far worse."

He hummed, a throaty sound that had my stomach clenching. His arm tightened around me, a hand raising my skirts to slip between my legs. Against my lips, he rasped, "Then why is it that every place my mouth travels, all I taste is sugar?"

I laughed, and so did he, and then we both groaned as he eased a finger inside me, and I was pressed into a row of books, his tongue stroking mine in desperate sweeps.

He had enough patience to torture me to orgasm, his eyes alight and absorbing every reaction flitting over my face, and then I was lifted and impaled.

With his hands bruising my thighs, he pounded into me, the world spinning as we struggled to keep our lips on each other's while hunger sang and climbed within our veins. It hummed and gathered, then roared in my ears as Raiden mumbled incoherent things against my mouth, and we came crashing apart.

As our breaths tumbled from us in harsh bursts, we clung together, hearts pounding in a similar thudding beat against our flushed skin.

"I cannot leave now."

"Didn't you hear?" I almost purred as his tongue laved at my neck. "The ceremony has been moved ahead."

Raiden froze. "It's what?"

A sated laugh slipped from me. I grabbed his face, brushing my fingers over his furrowed brows. "In just one full moon, we will be vowed."

He swallowed, and then slowly, a smile moved into place. "Then I shall stay here until then."

But his reaction puzzled me, and so I asked, "You weren't aware?"

He shook his head, hands moving to my rear and squeezing. "No." His lips pinched, then he rolled them, and another easy smile appeared. "But it matters not."

"My father said he'd spoken to your parents."

He nodded, looking at the rows of books beside us. "Perhaps I was already journeying here, and they couldn't deliver the message."

"Perhaps," I murmured.

A throat clearing had my head snapping to the end of the darkened aisle.

Yarnt stood there in the shadows, his expression unreadable but able to be understood all the same. Laughter snuck out as I tapped Raiden's shoulders.

He looked at Yarnt and stilled.

"Relax," I said. "He's the librarian."

He didn't relax, and instead, he moved me out of view before setting me down and righting my skirts. "I can feel you dripping down my thighs," I whispered.

He laughed. "Shhh."

I nipped at his chin when he rose and tugged my linen dress back into place. "So sticky and warm, and I'm afraid that now…" I scraped my teeth over his chin to whisper against his mouth, "I'll feel bare without so much of you inside me."

He gave a low snarl, and his hands became concrete, pressing into my hips. He scowled. "You're determined to ruin me, aren't you?"

I grinned, grabbing his hand and tugging him back through the library. "We've yet to explore the guest rooms."

His voice knocked me from better times.

Naïve, magical, life-changing times.

A voice I'd have been happy to have thrum against my skin and sink inside my ears for the rest of my nights and days.

That was then, his callous words reminded me. "You talk of this version of you, yet I cannot place her with what sits before me."

I rolled to my side and set my head in my hand, finding Raiden in the same position yet obviously awake. How long he'd been conscious for, I didn't know. At this point, I was beginning to wonder if he ever really was the prince I once knew.

"And what is it that sits before you now, Prince?" *Go on, look at me. I dare you.*

A throaty chuckle echoed, and then he turned to his back, stretching his arms above his head. Those green eyes, endless meadows and wildflower-wrapped dreams, turned to give me the coldest appraisal I'd ever experienced. "A queen so cruel she needs to create fables just to sleep at night and fool all those around her."

"You still don't believe me." I didn't know why I bothered to even say the words. He evidently did not. But Zad and then the way he'd been so sick… "You're lying."

He barked out a cold laugh, followed by a cough that rattled his chest. "Don't make me laugh, please. I have the worst headache."

"What made you remember Zadicus?"

Raiden shifted his attention to the damp ceiling. "If I knew, I'd tell you and perhaps bargain a way out of this cesspit." When I said nothing, he went on, "You cannot keep me contained forever."

"I don't plan to."

"You will have to let me out unless you plan to kill me while I'm chained like a mutt."

I contemplated that, as I had before, but at the roiling of my stomach, I pushed the macabre thoughts away. "What I choose to do with you is really of little concern."

He rolled toward me then, nostrils flaring as though he'd caught a whiff of dinner and was planning to chase it to the dining hall. "You've seen her."

I flashed my teeth in response.

He was on his feet in half a second, rattling the bars so hard and so loud, I wondered if he was remembering his own strength. "What did you…" He stopped, ducking his head and drawing in a heaving breath that shook his shoulders. "Does she live?"

I tittered, moving to sit up. "Of course, she lives." My smile waned. "For now."

A groan so pained and raw echoed through the dungeon as he sagged against the bars, his clammy palms sliding over metal. "Why are you doing this to us?"

"It's a bizarre kind of insanity, isn't it? Wondering why someone would want to be your demise and knowing there's a good chance you might never ever find out why."

"Please," he said, his voice hoarse now. "Just tell me you haven't harmed her."

My stomach became a slush pile of unpredictable waters. I jumped down from my perch and left him there, unable to look at him nor hear his turmoil for her for another second.

"Tell me!"

I didn't stop, but as my hips swayed, my skirts a dark cloud flying on a phantom wind around me, I laughed.

I laughed, and I laughed, and then I cut it off at the gates to the dungeon. "I think I've spun enough fables for one evening."

"I'll kill you," he roared, his voice charging through the closing door, that thrumming beat of magic within trying to resurface. "I swear it on the goddesses, I'll kill you for all this and more."

TWELVE

"Such lovely threats from lips you once loved."

I stopped, the dungeon door booming shut behind me. "There's plenty of salt in my wounds already." I tightened my cloak. "No need to add any more." Stalking by him, I began climbing the stairs.

Zad was at my side before my next heartbeat. "You should have his tongue for uttering such filth to you."

I inhaled that crisp clove scent of his and felt my shoulders loosen. "I have no desire to torture him. Not when he will meet his end soon enough."

Zad kept quiet until we'd reached the second floor. We passed the kitchens where staff flitted about, the clang of pots and pans and the scent of curried fish lifting my weary feet faster over the coarse fabric of the rug lining the hall.

His silence was etching on my last fraying nerve as we rounded the corner and took the stairs to the third floor.

"For darkness' sake, speak," I snapped. "I've never known you to keep words to yourself before, so no need to start being selfish now."

He laughed, the sound a deep, dark purr—like feathers brushing over skin in the shadows of night. I shook off the shiver that threatened to unfurl and breezed into the dining room.

Zad beat me to the head of the table and untucked the gilded, velvet-lined chair. I took a seat and shooed him to his own when he tried to scoot my chair in.

"Well?" I prodded again, patience waning as he unfolded a napkin and set it beside my plate.

He took his time meeting my gaze, resting his chin upon a fist as his curled lashes shifted with every pass of his eyes over my face. "You won't torture him, but you will torture the woman."

My blood nearly crystalized, but I feigned nonchalance as I asked, "Just how did you come about this information?"

He ran his tongue over his teeth, then smiled like a wolf who'd just found his supper. "Why, you just confirmed my suspicions is all, my queen."

My hand fisted around the fork, the metal threatening to bend. "You think you're so clever."

That maddening grin stayed, brightening his eyes and stirring my lower stomach. "How many times have you paid her a visit?"

Mintale's voice echoed from down the hall, traveling to the dining room. I kept an eye on the doors as I reluctantly admitted, "Just the once."

Zad huffed a low laugh. "My dear Audra, only once?" He plucked up his fork, inspecting his perfect teeth in the gleaming silver. "Though I do bet you made it count."

I grinned. "But of course."

Mintale and Ainx entered, the latter taking post by the doors as the kitchen staff poured into the room. More sconces were lit as steaming trays of meats, ripe salads, and carefully dressed fish were set before me and the lord of the east.

Zad, ever the cautious, made a point to sniff each tray, and even went so far as to dip his fingers into the dishes and taste the food.

I smiled wanly at the affronted looking cooks. "Do you think I'd keep staff who wish to poison me?"

Zad looked from me to Foelda, the head cook, and sat back in his chair at my right side, seemingly unperturbed.

I sighed, then waved a hand at her and the other three cooks. "Leave us."

Once they had, Mintale's mouth opening and closing as he stood by the moonlit window, Zad turned to me with a groove between his brows. "You need to be profiling them on a weekly basis, at the very minimum."

"My lord," Mintale cut in with a slight bow as he approached the table. "We started undertaking such measures many months ago."

I pulled the plate of stuffed chicken closer and speared a chunk from the breast, depositing it on my plate, then reached for the salad. "You take me for a distracted fool, don't you, Lord?"

His silence spoke volumes.

A full minute later, he filled my goblet with water, and I pushed the salad dish away. "It's not that at all."

Mintale's hands were gripping the varnished wood of the empty chair to my left. "Our queen is well aware of the threats to her well-being. I can assure you that we are taking every precaution."

"You're really too sweet for caring," I said, taking a sip of cool water. I eyed him over the vine-bedecked rim. "But I mostly find it insulting."

Zad smiled, a coiled serpent. "Forgive me for worrying, but with rumors spreading of peculiar activity to the west of the mountain valley's villages, I thought it necessary."

"Oh?" I set my water down. "And when were you planning to tell me of this peculiar activity?" It was undoubtedly why he was here, along with other reasons.

Mintale's face was paling. "Of what sort? More traitors? That of the Sun Kingdom?"

Zad cut into his fish. "I've not had confirmation, but I have men in the area who are keeping an eye on things." He threw a brief look at me. "Subtly, so as to not cause any suspicion."

I poked at my chicken for a minute as he and Mintale squabbled. "What of these men? Friends of yours, I presume?"

"Yes."

Interesting that he said no more than that, his eyes steadfast on his meal.

I took a bite of chicken, then another as I watched him, yet his expression remained carefully blank. "What is this peculiar activity?"

Mintale nodded. "We need to draw them out, capture them, and garner information."

Zad looked as though he wanted to roll his eyes at my advisor. "New residents in the hills, camping with the gypsies."

"Gypsies are not residents, nor do they allow others to simply join them unless initiated or born into." Gypsies roamed from one place to another every full moon, their wagons squeaking, lanterns bobbing, and crones chanting.

Zad gave me a hard look that said, *exactly*.

I huffed and speared more food, chewing agitatedly.

"Apparently, they keep to themselves until the market, where they've been asking lots of questions."

"Do you know what they're asking?"

Zadicus sipped his wine. "Enquiring about weapons, mostly." He set his wine down. "What got the townsfolk talking was the request for catapults."

My brows shot up, and I grinned. "What, they plan to storm the castle with half a dozen catapults?" I almost laughed but refrained. Just.

He leveled me with a flat look. "If they could somehow get their hands on some, then yes, I'm assuming so."

They weren't exactly easy to come by. They needed to be manufactured. One could do so themselves, but it depended on what time of winter it was as to how usable the sources would be.

"Find them. Have them brought here," I said with a glance at Mintale. "I'd rather not have their hate and whatever schemes they're planning reach more easily influenced ears."

Mintale was already scurrying off. I forced back a groan. "It can wait until you've eaten."

"It's quite all right, my queen. The sooner we act, the better," he said, then disappeared out the doors.

Zad watched him go, his arm draped over the back of the chair beside his. "Loyal to a fault."

I returned my attention to my food, but not even a minute later, the doors crashed open.

Klaud swept in, wearing half his training uniform, golden hair falling into his bloodshot brown eyes. With his fists balled at his sides, he marched straight for me.

I gestured to Ainx, and he froze, his expression reeking of displeasure as he eyed the male.

He and Zad stiffened as Klaud banged a fist on the table, causing steamed vegetables to bounce off the plate and roll over the table linen. "You sit here, eating your perfect food, in your perfect castle, and with some other male," he cut his eyes at the lord, whose top lip was peeling back over his teeth as he snarled low, then he looked back at me, growling, "while Berron rots somewhere in his own filth, likely dying."

More guards from outside stepped in, marching to the enraged mixed blood.

I raised a hand, and they halted but did not retreat.

"We traveled there," I said carefully. "You know this, surely." It took more strength than I thought it would to hold his incredulous gaze.

His face reddened further. "Yet he is not here."

I could tell by the power rolling off Zad in heavy waves that he remained silent out of respect for me and nothing else. Part of me wished he wouldn't. That he would explain all that had happened and then force him from the room with a swift kick up the ass.

That part was a nuisance I thought long dead.

I steeled my shoulders, then set my fork down. "We tried, and we lost many good soldiers in doing so."

"You tried," he repeated, tone mocking. "Would you like a pat on the back? A sweet? Because as far as I can see, many a long day and night have passed, and you've not made any plans to try again."

He had me there, and he knew it. "It's not that simple." It wasn't.

"And that's not an excuse but the truth. We were severely outnumbered, and he took a spear to his side. Truth be told, I do not even know if he lives."

"He is half royal. He is not so easily bested," he said, lips twitching. "I know it's hard for you to think anyone not of pure blood can survive such things, but we can. *He can*, and I'm certain he has." He paused, his eyes shuttering. "I would feel it had he departed for the darkness."

My chest squeezed, and I gritted my teeth against the tightness. "Klaud, we have other matters that need our attention, but believe me when I say that this is not the end."

"Oh, I know all about your other matters." He bent low, creeping farther up the table to hiss into my face. "Your precious traitorous husband is the reason he is trapped there." He spat, a glob of saliva landing on the side of my plate. "You're no queen. You're a child playing with your toys as you see fit while everyone around you suffers."

Zadicus had apparently had enough and leaped over the table in half a breath, his chair crashing to the floor. His fist crunched into Klaud's cheek as they collided with the ground, and growling and snarling sounded from behind me. I stared at the fallen chair, floating on a dark breeze, hardly breathing, hardly seeing.

Then I blinked, and the guards were escorting the cursing soldier out the doors.

"You can arrest me, trial me, Audra, but guess what? It is you who will burn for your father's mistakes if you do not grow a heart and fix them."

His words burrowed deep, sinking inside me like laced stones, plummeting and poisoning every vital organ they touched.

I was staring at the marred meal before me when Zad returned. "He's being dragged to the dungeon."

I nodded, pushing my chair back. "See to it that he's released by morning."

"Wha—"

"I'll not be requiring your company tonight."

Mintale raced back into the dining room, his beaded eyes darting back and forth between us. "What has happened?"

"Lord Allblood can fill you in." I breezed by them, cutlery and drapes rattling and rocking in my wake.

I didn't so much as try to harness the storm inside me. I let it breathe as I struggled to do the same.

Inside my rooms, I lowered myself into the filling tub, allowing it to fill my lungs as I sank into the bubbling silence.

Untold minutes later, I emerged and toweled off, then padded naked into my bedchamber.

Zad was sitting by the fire, staring into the crackling flames. "I thought I told you—"

"You'll find I care very little about what you've told me."

I tugged on an emerald silk robe, then grabbed my brush and began dragging it through my wet hair.

"Come here, Audra."

"I'm not a mutt. I do not come on command."

His wolfish smirk almost had the brush flying at his head. "But do you not?"

I sniffed, then grudgingly walked over to the opposite armchair. Before I could fall into it, his hand coiled around mine and tugged. Then he gripped me by the waist and set me on the floor before his feet.

I was too drained, too much of nothing to care about where he'd positioned me. A queen. His queen. Sitting beneath him on the floor. Not a queen at all.

You're no queen.

Gently, he pried the brush from my fingers and gathered my hair behind my head. I let my eyes shut and felt everything that had knotted inside me slowly unravel with every careful stroke of the bristles through my hair.

"You shouldn't listen to him. Returning for Berron without a considerable army is out of the question."

"War," I said. "My kingdom, my continent, would be at war."

"It's looking to be that way already." Zad's voice was gentle but firm. "The decision to march lies in your hands."

"I might be the daughter of a tyrant, and I know I'm definitely no saint, but so many would die." I swallowed. "So many unnecessary deaths."

The lord hummed, his words gruff. "You continue to surprise me."

"Did you think I would not care?"

"You do a fabulous job of pretending you don't." Those words slid over every inch of my skin, drying flesh that was still damp.

"I cannot make an example of an entire kingdom."

Zad was quiet for long moments. Flames licked at the hearth, crackling and spitting. "No, you cannot. Though I do wonder, is it because of your king's return? Or because you truly want to spare them?"

I turned and glared at him.

His eyes smiled. "There she is."

"Not everything revolves around Raiden."

Zad sat back as I stood, rubbing a hand over his chin. "How easily you say his name once again."

I snatched the brush from him. "Enough."

He grabbed my wrist, pulling me sideways onto his lap. "You can do many things to me, my queen." His hand slid over my chest and up my neck to frame the side of my face. "But don't you ever try to spin your beautiful lies on me."

"What do you want from me?" I searched his firelit eyes, not recognizing my cracking voice. "Everyone wants something from me. Everyone."

"Never just you," he surmised.

We stared as I waited. I waited, and I didn't even know why.

The reason came when he murmured to my nose, his eyelids

closing and touch slipping. "I must take my leave." The breath behind his near-silent words... I knew he wasn't just saying for a time. He was leaving, and he wasn't sure when or if he'd return.

Panic flared, burning my limbs as I gripped his cheek. "Everyone leaves."

My mother.

My cutthroat father.

My husband.

My friend.

And now my lover.

"You need only ask for someone to stay, but," he said, his next words toneless, "I'm not so sure you can." He pressed a soft kiss to my lips. "I think in time, Raiden is going to remember, if he hasn't already, and you will be forced to make some very hard decisions." That crooked smile appeared. "And I'm nobody's hard decision."

My tongue grew thick. "You wanted to vow to me."

"I do," he said, then sighed. "I did."

"You wanted to help rule this broken place." I moved off him, my robe slithering over my skin, gaping open. "What has changed?"

Clenching his jaw, he forced his eyes to the fire. "Many things." When he finally looked at me, his eyes were warm, but his voice was cold. "I no longer wish to play these games. It's..." He cracked his knuckles, sighing as though it pained him. "I just can't, Audra."

I laughed. "What a load of shit. You've wanted a bigger title since you saw me sniveling in the gardens that night, and you happily snatched the opportunity before you."

He shook his head as he rose, tugging his charcoal coat closed. "I was promised a title that was handed to someone else." The gold of his eyes darkened upon meeting mine. "Can you blame me for wanting to finally take what I thought was mine?"

"I am not a toy to be taken," I hissed, then flinched as Klaud's words vaporized my mind.

Zad said nothing else. He merely looked me up and down with a finality that rocked my feet, then strode to the doors.

"Be warned, my lord," I called, stilling my trembling hands. "If you leave, you cannot return as you see fit." The wooden brush began to creak and splinter in my grip. "If you leave, you will lose any chance you had to fulfill your desires."

His hand curled around one of the door handles, but he kept his back to me. "You speak as though there was ever a chance in the first place."

Then he was gone.

The brush sailed through the air, shredding the wood of the closing door before falling to jagged pieces on the floor.

THIRTEEN

"So," I said to Azela and Ainx the next morning in the throne room as my nails tapped against the silver whorls etched into the armrest of my seat. "Offense or defense?"

Ainx spoke first. "I say we strike. They're waiting and probably growing weary of it." Azela's lips pinched, and Ainx looked at her, his brow furrowed. "You disagree?"

Her gaze moved to me, and I nodded.

"Majesty, I think we should wait for them to come to us. It looks better for you, and it also gives us the advantage."

"But what of the innocents who will get caught in the bloodshed?"

Ainx had a point, but I waved him off. "We set up more patrols as far as the border within a half day's ride of each other." I smiled at the irritated glint in Ainx's eyes. "Ease yourself. We will not let them enter the city or the villages."

"We're spreading ourselves too thin. What if we cannot stop them should they march?"

I leaned forward. "We can, and we will."

After instructing them to inform the general of our plans and to prepare our soldiers, I dismissed them, then stared at the rays of light dancing across the throne room floor. Six guards stood at posts on either side of the room and near the doors.

I tried not to be offended, knowing the extra eyes were considered a necessary evil in times like these. Regardless of everyone's concerns, I had to wonder if everyone in the Sun Kingdom wished me dead, or if the number of those who did simply outweighed those who didn't or were indifferent.

My skirts exploded around me in a pool of black and silver as I stood and crossed the room, taking the far-left exit down the quiet halls.

Zad's absence festered more than I thought the sneaky lord capable of. Still, this long life must go on, and I was growing tired of falling into every fanciful whim that tried to weigh me down until I could no longer hold myself up.

I was young, yes. I was the daughter of a monster, yes. I was a foolish female who'd handed her heart to the wrong person, yes. But for as long as I drew breath, I was a queen.

We'd all do well to remember that.

I made it to the kitchens before I finally registered what the distant noise was.

Screaming and shouting—loud, pain-wracked bellows.

I picked up my skirts and raced down the stairs, my heels clipping as I flew around each turn until I leaped into the entrance to the dungeon and found the gate wide open.

Azela was there, talking in hushed murmurs with another guard outside Raiden's cell. A glance around showed more guards lingering, at least eight of them, who were all wearing differing looks of dismay and curiosity.

I stormed inside, and Azela turned to me. "They called me down as soon as I left the throne room, but I'm not sure what's wrong with him."

With my breath lodging in my throat, I inched closer to Raiden. "Leave us."

"But my queen..."

"I said leave us."

They did, yet I could feel Azela's reluctance heavy in the air. Air Raiden was struggling to breathe as he gasped and sputtered, muttering words that made little to no sense.

I knelt close to the bars as he groaned and paced back and forth, tearing at his hair.

"What is wrong?"

He said nothing. It was as if he couldn't even hear me. Wherever he'd journeyed in his mind, it wasn't here.

He tugged and pulled, and I sent a flare of magic around him, removing his hands from his hair and pressing them down at his sides.

That only served to enrage him further. "They're liars who never lied, but they did. They did."

Over and over, he said the same words.

"Who lied?"

"All of them," he spat. He continued pacing, then bellowed. "All of them lied to me!"

I wasn't sure what to do. What to say. Or what to even feel as I watched him curse and mutter to himself.

When he fell into another loud rage, tendons in his neck bulging as he screamed at the ceiling, I took a seat on the ground and began to talk.

---

19 summers old

My black dress had a train that draped the length of the hall behind me as we neared the entrance to the gardens.

Eight handmaidens held it above the damp, leaf-strewn ground as we traversed the courtyard and entered the gardens that ebbed for acres beyond, all the way to the foothills of the mountains.

My corset, bedecked with circling glittering silver twigs that spiraled into the air over each breast, constricted with every future setting step I took.

I never thought I'd be happy, or that genuine warmth and excitement would be coursing through me at this moment. All my life, I'd known my marriage would be arranged, and I'd duly prepared myself for it. I'd prepared my heart to remain indifferent and reminded myself it was all just a business dealing. A way to ensure our lineage stayed true, and our reign continued.

I could never have prepared for him.

Gold and silver wrapped seats were laid out upon the long stretch of glowing green grass. It was clear of snow, but tiny icicles still glimmered upon the blades beneath the dawn dark sky.

He was wearing gold.

Golden breast plates, gold trousers, and a gold wreath of dried leaves and berries upon his head. His golden coat hung around his thighs, the sun and its flames engraved in the leather and suede. But as he took my hand in his, it was his touch, a warm promise, that took my breath away.

In the weeks leading up to that moment, we'd been inseparable. I was giddy at the mere thought of his name, and too far gone to feel embarrassed or angered over it. He was mine, and I was his.

And this was happening.

My eyes were pulled to the left in time to see Zad leaving the thick crowd. I blinked, wondering what in the darkness he was doing, and then he was gone.

"You rob me of breath."

Looking back at Raiden, I flinched as something wet trickled down my cheek.

A tear.

Raiden's brow creased, and then, much to the priestess's displeasure, he stepped forward and cupped my face to catch it with his thumb. "I am honored that you would shed any emotion for me," he whispered so low, I almost didn't hear him. Likely to ensure our attending guests and my father, who was standing behind me, didn't hear. "But I don't like seeing it."

I took his hand, and then nodded at the priestess to begin.

His eyes were locked on mine as she spoke in the old language, then made us repeat after her.

"I vow thee," I said, voice unwavering. "Eternally my love."

Raiden grinned, and when it was his turn, he said loud enough for everyone, even those who were scattered throughout the farthest depths of the gardens, to hear, "I vow thee eternally my love."

His lips were bruising as he gathered me to him and ravished mine.

Applause exploded, and little bells were rung, but it all faded away under the weight of his kiss and his hands holding me impossibly tight against him.

Dancing and drinking ensued as soon as we walked down the rose-strewn aisle, stopping to wave and shake the guests' hands.

When we reached the end, Zad was there, stone-faced. A black vest covered his white dress shirt, and he came forward, his eyes steadfast on mine. "My princess, if I may have a word."

I frowned, then laughed as Raiden squeezed me to him, his lips upon my cheek as he said to the lord, "I'm afraid you may not, for we have places to be and many people to see."

But Zad's eyes remained on mine. I could not read them, and I wasn't entirely certain I wanted to.

Raiden cleared his throat, pulling away and taking me with him. "If you'll excuse us."

"Audra," Zad said, an urgency in his voice I'd not heard before.

"Ignore him," Raiden clipped. "There's little he can do now we are vowed."

Looking back over my shoulder, I stared at Zad, then turned back to the guests Raiden was directing us to. "What do you mean?"

"He's obsessed with you," Raiden said. "You cannot tell me you aren't aware."

But I wasn't, hadn't been, and I shook my head, laughing a little. "There's nothing to be aware of."

"Suit yourself, it matters not now anyway."

Breakfast rolled into lunch in a feast that spread from the castle in a snakelike train throughout the city. Tradition demanded that the daylong celebration hold enough wine and food for an entire kingdom to eat. With the help of local bakeries, the cooks had been at work all week.

Afterward, my father was to escort me to a cabin in the trees in the secluded Forest of Promise just beyond the city limits. Every newlywed royal in the kingdom spent their vow night in the cabin and did not return until the following dawn.

"I look forward to that part the most," I said to Raiden's ear as we slowly traversed the crowds in the front courtyard, and he fed me glazed strawberries and wine.

"I most definitely do, too."

"Do you do the same in the Sun Kingdom?"

I knew a lot of our traditions were archaic and therefore similar. However, I also knew that we were a continent split in two out of choice. The residents could choose to travel, stay a while, or forever call one place home should one of the two differing lifestyles suit them.

Though most didn't choose to leave their kingdom of birth for good, the freedom to do so remained, and it made me wonder why anyone stayed in the Moon Kingdom.

Comfort and blood ties were curious and often dangerous things.

Raiden came to a stop at an open stall to fill a plate with fried goat and chicken. He licked his fingers as he handed it to me. "Eat, you'll need your energy."

I took the plate from him and picked up a piece of chicken, chewing as my blood began to thaw and heat.

Beneath an awning of a small alcove that overlooked the river, we sat. Raiden's arm kept me flush with his side as he used the other hand to eat and wave at any passersby while filling me with tales of his land.

"You don't have a cabin?"

"It's a pool," he said. "A pool that stretches to the edge of a cliff, where its waters trickle down to meet the River of Snakes below."

"Where do you sleep?" I wondered how their skin would fare if they remained in the pool for twenty-four hours.

He chuckled. "Do you think they just remain in the water, fucking the whole time?"

I pursed my lips.

He squeezed me, then leaned in and licked my lips after I took a bite of chicken. I laughed and pushed his face away. "There's a canopy of trees, almost like a small hut, with chaises and beverages and enough food to see you through."

"Perhaps we could do this there too then," I suggested, ignoring my distaste for the extreme heat.

Raiden pondered that, his lips twitching as he gazed out at the water. "I think that's a good plan."

We discussed more of his customs. How after a couple had vowed, they'd then be bestowed with an array of gifts as soon as they returned, and how the males didn't like to suffer through the visits of guests. Not while the need to claim and cement the vows would continue to run hot every time their spouse was near.

"And they're always near," he said, his tone serious. "You'll not be leaving my sight if I can avoid it."

I grabbed his chin and kissed him quickly before a young girl and her parents approached to congratulate us.

As the sun began to fade, a line of onlookers stretched from the castle all the way to the edge of the city to watch us leave.

It seemed ridiculous that we had to make our way back to the castle simply to leave, but that was what we did. I was nearly breathless when we arrived, courtesy of stolen kisses either in front of everyone or tucked beside shopfronts.

The carriage, black with silver curlicue twisting over the metallic paint, was shaped like an apple. A driver opened the door, granting view of my father who was seated and waiting.

Raiden held out his hand to help me and my extravagant dress inside, before climbing in to sit beside me. The windows were open, city and country dwellers alike waving as their children raced after the carriage.

Raiden watched with a serene smile on his face while

something foreign, something that felt a lot like peace, settled within my chest.

With his hand tucked in mine, I lowered my head to his shoulder, content to let him do all the waving and smiling at the people outside as the carriage bumped and rolled downhill.

My father broke the silence with a hard look at me. "Now that that's over with, we'll need to make me an heir and make it strong." His eyes gleamed. "Can you even imagine the power?" He laughed, low and insidious. "We are a continent of fools for not thinking to combine the two sooner. Of course, you'll undoubtedly lose many a babe trying, but it will be worth it."

I heard Raiden's jaw flex.

I withheld a biting retort, unwilling to let him steal the beauty from this day with fear or an argument I wouldn't win.

His blank eyes flitted over me, and then he smirked. "Your mother looked much the same on our vow night, though not as dark. Dazzling in reds and pinks, she resembled a butterfly just waiting to have its wings plucked."

I kept my gaze on the woven silver crown atop his head. "I wish I could've seen it."

His eyes caught mine, unwilling to release them. "I'm sure she told you all about it before her…" He flicked his hand. "Untimely demise."

The way he'd uttered the words, as if he hadn't been the one to sentence her to a death crueler than many he'd sentenced before… I swallowed and forced my eyes to the window.

We'd reached the outskirts of the city, the sun cresting waving arms and smiling faces.

As Raiden's hand squeezed mine while he and my father talked about a new trade opportunity with a neighboring continent of humans, I clung to that feeling inside me.

I wouldn't let darkness seep in and steal a moment I would forever think of as my brightest.

As our brightest.

All too soon, the crowds were replaced by giant groups of rock and dirt-paved roads as we trundled closer to the woods. The sun had met the horizon, the forest dripping with enough darkness for the use of lanterns. They sparked to life outside the carriage, and in the distance, my father's guard, who rode behind us, could be seen carrying torches.

It happened with the speed of an inhale.

Raiden's hand was in mine, and then it wasn't.

The horses towing the carriage screeched and reared, and the carriage teetered, stealing all the breath from my lungs. Drivers and footmen bellowed curses, and then a round of thuds echoed as they hit the packed ground.

The door was flung open, and then soldiers wearing the Sun Kingdom's colors were hauling the prince out of the carriage.

His shock was enough to get him out but not enough to contain him. Fire lit the world ablaze as he roared and unsheathed his sword.

But it was too late. The door had slammed shut. A sword had been speared into my father's head through the window, catching him wholly off guard.

I stared at his gaping mouth and rounded eyes. I stared and I stared, and they stared back at me, emptying of life as his dark soul seeped through his burgundy blood and fled his body.

He groaned. A male of his age didn't die easily, a sword in the brain or not.

My eyes closed, and when I reopened them, reality settled in with enough violence to have a scream scrape up my throat, slither over my tongue, and knock at my teeth. Inhaling deeply through my nose, I swallowed the urge as the acrid scent of my dead father tainted every particle of air.

Smoke scorched my lungs as the carriage began to burn, and my heart pounded even as it cried. Where was he?

His fire… the carriage.

They'd pulled him out. He was their prince. They wouldn't hurt him. They wanted to hurt me. More than hurt me.

It settled bone-deep. He wasn't coming to help.

With shaking hands, I rummaged through the compartments of the carriage, cursing the fact I hadn't had the mind to wear a blade beneath the monstrosity that was my gown.

Love made fools out of all of us. It lulled you into a false sense of security, and then it left you to burn.

But there was little time to soak in my anger—I could be furious with myself when and if I survived.

And I had no intention of dying a fool.

Panic sped in as the windows were shut from the outside. Raiden was out there.

And I was seated in a burning trap.

I half wondered if he was smiling, if he felt triumphant, or if maybe, just maybe, he was riddled with enough remorse to help me.

I wouldn't dare hope for something I wouldn't give.

I dived for the locked door and screamed, yanking and pulling. I slammed my hands against the wood, my nails chipping, fingers bleeding as I hurled wind and ice and every ounce of myself at the handle.

But the door wouldn't budge.

If my magic wouldn't work against the door, then I knew it wouldn't work against the fire. Not while I was inside. Someone had hexed the carriage.

I screamed, and then coughed as fire licked the wood, and it began to groan. The sound of shouting and swords meeting resonated outside my death.

Tremors shot through my arms as I fumbled and tore at my gown. It finally ripped, and I secured the fabric around my mouth to buy me more time as I crawled across the scalding hot floor to my father.

My hands were torn, skin blistering, but I shut my eyes and wrapped them around the hilt of the sword, then pulled.

It slid from his head with little resistance, and my heart threatened to give out as I saw the insignia on the hilt.

Raiden's sword.

It didn't matter. It couldn't matter if I was dead. If they got what they wanted.

Rage funneled through me with ice-sharp clarity. Thunder boomed overhead, and I grinned, the blade sturdy within my bloodied hands. I slammed the pommel against the weakened floor of the carriage.

Flames kissed my heels, caught my dress, and I encased myself in a bubble of ice to keep it at bay for just a second—the wood splintered and cracked.

I smacked it again and again until my next breath winded me when I met the hard earth with teeth-jarring impact.

I groaned, flames sizzling as my magic squashed them. Then I stopped breathing altogether when I saw our drivers and footmen dead on the ground. Their heads laid next to their sprawled out bodies, their blood joining and forming a pool around them.

I shifted at the sound of hooves meeting the ground, and then a face appeared, pale with fear-filled eyes. "Thank fuck." Zadicus held out his hand. "Here."

I took it, and he pulled me out. "Behind you," I said, my voice too raspy to be heard.

He read my lips or eyes and turned, knocking the assailant's sword to the ground and then ending him with a thought alone. Blood dripped from the soldier's eyes, ears, and nose, and then another swiftly approached.

The smoke was blinding, but I stumbled around the carriage to find only a few remaining traitors left. The rest were nothing but shadowed specks, fleeing south over the hills.

A hand gripped my hair, and a hoarse scream left me as I was yanked back. "You should be in that carriage, burning in the darkness with your soulless father."

The blade of a sword dug into my throat, and shocked, I didn't feel the sting, only felt my blood begin to trickle. "Where's Raiden?" Funny how even after the heart had been used and abused, it still wanted to know what it needed to.

His mother laughed, an airy breathless sound of satisfaction.

"Gone. He thought you were dead. Job done. No need to stick around and smell your burning flesh."

"Audra!" Zad roared.

The carriage erupted, a wild groan cleaving the air as it crumpled in on itself.

I used the distraction to grab her sword arm, swinging her over me into the dirt. A male I didn't recognize appeared and buried his sword in Solnia's chest.

She screamed for Phane, who rounded the remains of the carriage, face dark with fury. I met his sword with his son's as he tried to imbed it in the male's back.

He struck me in the shoulder, and I screamed, then slammed a gust of wind down his throat when fire erupted from his palm.

Before he could throw it at me, Zad was behind him, his sword cleaving through his neck.

His head rolled, and gasping, I turned to watch it land near his dead wife.

The male who'd killed her flung her heart to the dirt, and it slowly changed color, from crimson to black.

With adrenaline fueling every move, I sent my eyes everywhere, stumbling away from the dirt and landing on my ass. The pommel of the sword singed. I tossed it to the grass, gripping my upper arm as black smoke filled the lightning-streaked sky, and freezing rain started to fall.

My body shaking, I watched the trees around the carriage morph into sinister-looking faces. Faces of beasts that blurred and laughed. That laughed and watched as black crept in and stole every ounce of color from my world.

※

My hand went to that place on my upper arm. It had healed long ago. There was no scar, yet the slice of sharpened metal tearing at the skin could still be felt even now.

I'd been hurt many times before, and every injury had healed and never haunted.

I suppose it was different when you were hurt in a way that reached your very core, wrapped poisonous talons around it, and refused to let go.

Raiden was silent, sitting cross-legged on the floor in front of me with the bars between us. His bloodshot eyes were fixed on my arm, and his pupils larger than usual.

"Do you remember?"

He didn't answer, only stared.

I eased forward and grabbed the bars. "Do you remember?"

"Audra." He said my name as though it was the first breath he'd taken since this came to pass over a year ago. "What's happening?" He met my eyes, then rolled over, heaving, his back spasming as he began to vomit on the floor.

With what he'd done fresher than the next pounding beat of my heart, I simply watched as he expelled what looked to be porridge onto the stones and started coughing. Coughing as if it had been his lungs drowning in smoke instead of mine.

After a minute, he swiped the back of his hand over his mouth, then rolled to sit against the wall. "I don't…" He shook his head, his cheeks billowing as he exhaled. "I didn't mean to."

I gripped the metal so hard my skin threatened to tear. "Didn't mean to *what?* Kill me and my father?" I laughed, low and without humor, slowly loosening my grip as I went to stand. "Oh, but you did. All along, that was your plan. Trick the heartless princess into believing you could love her. All the better to ruin her, right? You should consider yourself—"

I stopped breathing, stopped thinking, stopped moving as he reached inside his pocket and pulled out tiny purple crumbs.

Lavender crumbs.

He gazed up at me, confusion a heavy cloud between us.

My mouth opened and closed, and so did his. His eyes swung from the crushed remains of the purple flower to mine and back again.

Bile thundered up my throat, and I raced out of there to the sound of my name being hollered.

"Audra, wait!"

Azela was reaching for her sword, eyes wide and darting from me to the shouting king.

"Lock the gate, lock the door," I rushed out before hurtling up the stairs and throwing myself through the first exit of the castle I found.

Upon the small balcony, I gulped in breath after breath, sliding down the rough exterior of my home as the kitchen staff smoking pipes on their breaks glanced over at me curiously.

Whatever they saw on my face had them emptying their pipes and hurrying back inside.

FOURTEEN

"He's having moments of clarity," Gretelle, the head of Truin's coven, said. "And then he's confused."

I eyed the aging crone, my fingers tapping at the arm of my throne as I surveyed the listening guards. "Has he been ill again?" Since seeing the lavender pieces in his palm, I couldn't bring myself to return to the dungeon.

I had no idea what to do with that. Had he carried it with him even during his life as one of the exiled? Or was it some type of parlor trick? Perhaps he'd asked one of the guards to fetch him some to help with any nausea.

I'd asked Truin to come yesterday, and she had, but after watching him for a full five hours and only gleaning splotches of rational mind, she'd said she needed help and left.

"He's angry, then he's remorseful, then he's confused, then he's asking for you, then he's asking for Casilla." The crone narrowed an eye at me. "Who is this Casilla?"

I waved the question away, wanting to snuff the kernel of hope that kept on rising within. "His betrothed from The Edges."

Gretelle's creased face scrunched further, and I withheld a laugh. Never had I seen the woman look so perplexed. She shook her head. "Well, then. I suppose I'll return in the morning with some of my sisters and tools."

Truin cleared her throat. "I'd like to stay, Audra. To keep an eye on him."

The crone pursed her lips. "He should have someone with

him, yes." She stole a quick side glance at me. "He's in a right state and could do with some familiar faces."

I ignored the jab and bid her farewell, watching her hobble to the door where Ainx waited to escort her out.

Truin glanced at the remaining guards, then took a seat below my throne on the marble step, her patterned yellow skirts flaring around her as she set her basket down. "Are you okay?"

I sighed, slouching a little in the uncomfortable chair. "Define okay."

She smiled, reaching inside her basket to resituate some herbs and a bottle of dark green liquid. "You should go see him. It's true, you know." She peered up at me. "That he was asking for you."

"I know." He'd been asking for me for the past two days. Ever since I'd ran out of there with my brain and heart exploding.

"You're scared. Now you've gotten what you so desperately sought, you're scared of what you'll soon need to do." There was no hesitation to her words. Only gentle assumption.

My throat tightened, as did my hands around the armrests.

Ainx returned with a box in hand and his face paling. "My queen, one of the messengers just arrived."

"Evidently," I said, eyeing the box with a raised brow. "What is it?"

Ainx held it away from him as though he was afraid to sully his uniform. "It smells of decaying flesh."

My stomach dropped, and I rose, moving around Truin to descend the stairs and take the box from him.

A scream lodged in my throat when I tore off the gilded golden lid to find two long fingers tucked away on a crisp white pillow. Drops of blood stained the satin in a few places, like crimson beads over snow.

They looked as if they'd been hacked from his hand, the skin prickled and pruned where the blood had dried, bits of bone peeking out.

Truin made a retching sound behind me.

With unsteady hands, I slid the lid back on and clutched the box tight to my stomach. Relief and regret warred. "He's alive then."

Ainx nodded. "Though I loathe to think how many body parts might be severed before he's not."

I ignored the undertone to his statement. "Prepare Wen and several guards."

"Where are you going?" Truin asked.

I was already leaving the room with plans to grab a small satchel and change of clothes. "To visit an old friend."

The lord of the east lived a half day's ride from the castle, and though I'd never ventured to his estate before, I'd heard talk of it and some of my guards knew the way.

As far as I was aware, with the exception of a few staff, the lord lived alone. Ever since he'd lost his wife.

Rumor stated that she threw herself off a cliff into the falls that crashed downstream to meet with the Gray Sea some months after giving birth to a stillborn. I'd often wondered if she was the reason he'd never found someone else. If perhaps she was the reason our every exchange in our earlier days, and even now, was swathed with conflicting moments. I'd never asked.

At first it was because I didn't care to. And now, it was because I probably cared more than I should.

Though it was rare for our kind to vow more than once in our long lifetimes, it still happened. There were few ways to escape a vow. Death, pleading—so long as both parties were in agreeance—with the crown, or treason.

Zad had remained a fixture in my court in the days after Raiden had been exiled for the latter.

Word declared his manor to be a sprawling glass rectangle with gardens upon the roof that overflowed to curtain the sides of the house, giving the appearance of an oversized, inside out greenhouse.

The whispers were not wrong, though they rarely ever were.

We exited the dark foliage of the Winding Woods and emerged into a starlit valley. Hooves thundered down the incline as we hurried to get out of view. We might have been in the lord of the east's territory, but that had never stopped miscreants from doing what miscreants did before.

Dirt sprayed beneath Ainx's horse as he led the way through mounds of moon-kissed grass riddled with white flowers.

I could see stables to the far left of the gated estate; a large white wooden expanse that looked as though it'd house at least twenty horses. Idly, I wondered if he had that many, or if he kept space for guests. Then I wondered how often the broody beast even had guests.

I shook off my useless thoughts and relaxed my thighs as we wound into the valley of his home. Behind the white wrought iron fence, which I knew would be warded, was a thin forest that stretched for miles—all the way to the cliffs where his wife took her life.

We dismounted as soon as the gates opened, our legs aching and stomachs growling after stopping only long enough to relieve ourselves and refill our canteens.

I grabbed my satchel from the saddle and handed Wen's reins to Azela as a female with golden hair and matching eyes appeared and directed the guards to the stables.

On my own, I absorbed the pristine gardens filled with every type of flower imaginable, and even some that didn't seem real. They littered the lawn before Zad's glass home in small clusters, in larger groups upon the fence line, and in beds that raced along the glass exterior.

The scent of jasmine, lavender, roses, and other unnamable flora saturated the early evening air.

Drawing a slow breath, I felt my eyelids flutter.

"To what do I owe the pleasure, my queen?"

I spun around. Zad stood before the towering glass doors, his feet bare and his gray tunic loose. He swept a hand through his long hair, but it was futile. The auburn strands fell back in place to curtain his cheeks.

With leaden feet, I moved toward him, the bag hanging from my shoulder weighing much more than it should. As I dragged my eyes from the lord to his large home, I noticed that even though it was made of glass, you couldn't actually see inside. My own reflection and the star-sprinkled sky stared back at me.

"We need to talk." I glanced around, then met his curious gaze. "Inside. I received a rather alarming delivery this morning."

Zad's lips twisted. For a moment that caused my breath to quake, he just stared. Finally, he straightened from where he'd been leaning against the open door. "You needn't worry about unwelcome ears. There is no one here who'd betray me."

I snorted, sweeping past him inside when he gestured so. "What makes you so sure of yourself?"

"Besides the fact that I pay them handsomely?" He left the doors open, seemingly amused as my mouth hung open, my eyes hungry as they took in everything beyond the small foyer. "I haven't hired anyone new in years. My people and friends know it's a death sentence to betray me."

I was too busy taking in the night sky through the walls and the slanted gaps in the ceiling to be jealous—gaps between the grass, dirt, and gardens above. "This is magical," I said, moving down the hall.

"By all means, show up unannounced and just make yourself at home."

I ignored his dry tone, my boots scuffing soft on the charcoal speckled marble floor as I peeked inside as many rooms on the first floor as I could.

A sitting room decorated in whites, blacks, and grays. A study near the kitchen dressed in dark wood and leather upholstery. An entertaining area, housing two large black velvet chaises with orange and silver throw pillows, and three armchairs with black and brown fur blankets draped over them. A fire was dancing in the giant black crystal hearth. Ancient paintings of glittering landscapes and half-naked winged females lined some of the stark white walls.

Standing on the black woven rug, I turned and traipsed past Zad back down the hall, bypassing a bathing room riddled with dark tiles and red towels to the kitchen at the opposite end.

Two males were laughing as they wiped pots and pans and re-hung them above the counter. They froze when they saw me standing there, absorbing the brick and wood and wide expanse of the room.

"Majesty." Quickly, they bowed. A blond male said, "Uh, can we get you something?"

"I'm fine." I turned to leave, and my face smacked right into a hard chest. "Oof."

For a moment, I just inhaled the smell of cloves and mint.

Then Zad's hands gripped my shoulders and pulled me back. "If you're done exploring, I'd like to get to the point of this visit."

"So rude." I huffed, tearing away and heading to the dark wooden stairs. "I've yet to see upstairs."

He grabbed my hand and tugged me back down them, and I groaned as he pulled me back down the long hall to a small sitting room. I sniffed at the stiff white-on-white armchairs and tables, and the small fireplace. "The other room seems nicer."

"That room is for guests."

"Is that not what I am?" I turned to him.

"You're many things, Audra, but a guest is not one of them." Gently, he pulled my satchel from my shoulder. "What's going—" His head jerked. "Darkness be damned, what is that fucking smell?"

I would've smirked at his comical reaction if not for the contents of the satchel. Instead, I flopped into an armchair, kicked my boots off, and grinned when he scowled. They were crusted with dust and dirt, and left a nice little mark or two on the white fur rug.

"Just open the bag and look in the box," I said, then yawned, my eyes closing as I heard him open the lid. I didn't want or need to see the contents again, though it was the least I could do.

I opened my eyes. "I asked him to rule in my stead," I said, rolling my lips. "In a land filled with those who shun and hate me. I asked him to do his best, and he did, but his best wasn't good enough."

With a blank expression, Zad set the lid back on the box, then placed it down on a table farthest away from the crackling fire. "They're goading you."

I knew that. "They've tortured him. They're still torturing him."

"That is why you're here?"

I frowned. "Does my presence in your home really bother you that much?"

Zad rubbed his stubble-lined chin, sighing as he strode to the fireplace and braced his hands upon the mantel. "Audra, I'm not sure what you want me to do."

"I'm not asking you to do anything, but your friends..." I watched his back arch as he hung his head. "I know they're the reason you knew what was going to happen on my vow night." I paused, crossing a leg over the other. "It occurred to me as I was visiting my exiled husband and replaying what was almost the happiest moment of my life that your appearance was rather timely, my lord."

The silence screamed as I continued to watch his muscular back gently rise and fall.

Finally, he murmured, "I heard of it myself, not from my friends." He straightened but didn't face me. "As the weeks after your engagement carried on, something didn't feel right, but no one would talk, so no one outside of their inner circle knew anything. They were too careful. So I pretended to go against the marriage alliance. Darkness knows I had enough reason to." At his exasperated tone, I frowned but did not interrupt. "Or so Solnia and Phane believed, being that I thought I'd one day be your husband. They knew that, and after only a few meetings, they were easily misled." He turned then, expression still blank as he said, "I infiltrated their inner circle a mere week before the ceremony."

Which was why he could attest to their guilt in the days after, other than being there to witness the horrors firsthand.

"Why didn't you tell me all this?" The words were almost whispered, and I hadn't realized until I cleared my throat how much this visit was due to me wanting to look him in the eye and have him tell me what he knew for himself.

"I tried. You ignored me at every turn, and it was beginning to look suspicious, the way I was following you around, hoping for a moment where Raiden would leave your side."

But he never did, not in those final days leading up to the ceremony.

I looked down at the fur rug and my dirtied boots. "So you decided to try to thwart their plans on your own?"

Zad nodded. "I had help as you can probably recall. We cut through the woods, which was why you wouldn't have seen me at the festivities." He snorted, shaking his head. "Not that you'd have bothered to look."

I frowned and opened my mouth, but he went on, "And then we waited. They struck before you could fully enter the forest, though. That was not the plan. They must have found out at the last moment whose side I was truly on. We had to race…" He stopped, and I could've sworn there was a tremor in his hand as he cupped his mouth with it and turned back to the fire. "I didn't know if we'd make it."

Long moments ticked by as I let that night—what he'd done, and what he'd risked—close one of the tiny cracks inside me. "Thank you," I finally murmured.

He stiffened, then slowly released a breath. "So what makes you think those are even Berron's fingers?"

It took me a moment to gather the present into place, and then I flashed my teeth, laughing. "Oh, believe me. They're his."

Zad grimaced. His jaw clenched as he ran a hand through his hair, then moved for the door while muttering, "I'll show you upstairs."

After ridding the day's ride from my skin in a tub that was almost as luxurious as my own, the female who'd greeted us delivered a platter of cheese, meats, and fruit to my room.

The room was filled with white wood. A bed fit for three kings sat in the center on a raised dais and carved trees rose from the four corners to form a canopy of wreathed, woven wood.

"Your name," I'd said as she went to leave.

"Emmiline." She then dipped her head and closed the door behind her.

I stared at it for a time, wondering exactly who she was to the lord, then my hunger bested me, and I devoured most of the food on the platter.

For hours, I'd stared at the intricate canopy above the bed. Exhaustion weighed down my lids, yet I couldn't drift away.

My guards had been shown to rooms after I had been left to mine, and other than the sound of water gurgling somewhere in the large home, there was nothing but silence.

I shucked the blankets off and swung my feet to the cool marble floor. The door creaked slightly as I pulled it open and traversed the hall until I'd reached the stairs. They continued higher, presumably to the roof.

As silent as possible, I climbed them and met no resistance as I pushed the small door, a piece of cutout glass with grass on the other side, wide open.

I soon figured out why as I let it fall closed and crawled over the soft, wet rooftop, careful not to squash any flowers on my way to where two bench seats perched in the middle, hidden behind serpentine vines and sunflowers. To the left of them sat a fountain with what looked to be blue two-headed fish swimming inside. Grends.

"You needn't bother with trying to be silent," Zad said. "You're about as stealthy as a wounded horse."

Irritation prickled at my nape. Still, I climbed into the seat next to him, eyeing the wine he was nursing. "How is this possible?"

Zad licked the corner of his lips, then smiled. "Why, the same way what we can do is possible. Magic."

"But it looks real," I said, my eyes roaming the greenery and moonlit kaleidoscope of color.

"Because it is; it just needs a little more encouragement to survive."

I pondered that, then asked, "Emmiline?"

Zad nodded. "Her powers are tied to the soil, to the earth."

I blinked, then reached for his wine and took a hearty sip. He said nothing as I handed it back with a small amount remaining. A wave of his hand had it refilled.

"I need to learn that."

"There are many things you still need to learn." Unamused, he sipped his wine. "You went straight to heavy hitting without paying any mind to what the finer, less devastating things can offer."

I ignored that. He was right, in a sense, but I had better things to worry over these days. "She's royal, then."

Zad seemed to stiffen. "She is."

I eyed him. The unyielding set to his broad shoulders, the rigid lines of his hewn cheekbones, and that hardened jawline. "Your mother?"

He took another sip of wine. "You already know my mother is dead. Emmiline is my mother's sister."

I had heard that. "She bears an uncanny resemblance to you." He frowned at me. "Bone structure, and the..." I gestured to his face. "Silent intensity thing."

His frown gradually slipped, his eyes swirling over my features, and I felt myself sag as though I'd finally been handed water in the middle of the desert. "You couldn't sleep."

I shook my head, then grinned when a throw pillow and blanket materialized before me on the clear patch of grass. "I find looking at the stars can sometimes help."

"Do you find yourself up here often?" I settled over the blanket and tucked the pillow beneath my cheek.

Zad's crossed ankles shifted from side to side near my knees. "Whenever I can."

"How is it not freezing?" Granted, it wasn't as cold here as it was at the castle; the temperature thawed with every mile away from it, but the air still carried a bite. A bite that didn't bother me, but would bother most.

"The house is heated the same way your home is, only it extends to the roof as well."

I yawned. "Which is also how you're able to keep the gardens alive." We had magic users working full-time to ensure my own gardens' survival.

Zad picked up a book that lay beside him and opened it to where he'd marked the page. "Exactly." He began reading aloud from a collection of tales that were crafted long before our parents were even blips on the horizon. Stories of princes and princesses, of royals being hunted and slain by faeries, forced to find a place of their own to ensure their survival, of kings and queens and human warriors and monsters of flesh and scale.

And all too soon, the deep, melodic timbre of his voice had my heavy lids drooping, following me into a dreamless sleep.

Some hours later, as the sun sent spirals of golden light snaking through the dark, I awoke to find the lord lying next to me, gazing at the fading stars. "Have you decided what to do?"

I stretched my legs and arms, then sat up and watched the last of the shadows disappear. "I'm not sure which cumbersome matter you're referring to."

"All of them." His voice was lilted with sleep and pressed on every single place he'd ever touched. All of me.

There was little else to be done. A war was brewing whether

I, or any of my people, liked it or not. "Raiden can wait." I turned my head over my shoulder, offering a smile. "I think it's time we go to war."

"And you'd like me to join you, of course."

I said nothing but continued to smile.

Zad nodded once with a gleam in his eye that couldn't be read but filled me with warmth all the same.

FIFTEEN

I pressed a hand to Wen's muzzle, the heat from his nostrils warming my palm. "We will stop more now that we have daylight, my friend."

He huffed as though he didn't care either way.

I grinned, sliding my hand over his neck before I mounted him and clicked my tongue. Before I could get ten feet away from the stables, Zadicus stopped me.

He stood in the sunshine, his long brown leather coat flapping behind him, and his hair kissed by the sun. Wen whinnied, and Zad stroked his neck as he neared. "You were going to leave without saying goodbye."

My brow crinkled, my gloved hands creaking around the reins. "I said goodbye—"

With a crook of his finger, my head tilted down, and he grasped it within his cool, calloused hands. His eyes met mine for an instant that morphed into something more, and then our lips touched.

Rich and soft and toe-curling, his lips moved over mine in an unhurried caress that feathered everywhere.

Sooner than I'd thought I'd like, he released me. His eyes were slow to open, and when they did, they fixed on mine for a stretched moment as if waiting for something, and then he was stalking off toward the house.

Breathless, I rode to the gate, my gloved fingers rising to my mouth as my mind tried to make sense of why and how that felt different, brand new, when I'd lost count of all the times we'd kissed before.

His aunt curtsied, but her face still held that detached quality so much like her nephew.

I nodded, thanked her for the hospitality in a crisp tone, and then joined my guard.

We stopped at a glen at noon, allowing the horses to rest and hydrate as we ate the dried fruits and meats that Zad's cook had sent us off with.

Rocks surrounded the shallow stream of water, making silence hard to achieve as our boots crunched over them. We were not foolish enough to discuss battle strategy or what we knew we would soon face. One of the first things my mother taught me as a child was that the trees had ears, and the wind was the messenger.

Even before these tense times, peace for a millennia didn't mean we were not the type to play power games, seek information, and try to one-up each other in every way we could.

Certain creatures and dwellers of the forest never evolved, and they were neither friend nor foe. It was never personal. They straddled the line between, and only played games that could be of advantage to them.

With eyes on the forest looming at our backs, the northwest sprawl of the Winding Woods stretched up ahead in a curtain of darkness barely breached by sunlight, we drank and we ate and then we made haste to the city.

Ridlow, a young guard who'd only just completed his training, saw them first.

Though seeing them didn't quite matter when I felt my very blood seize and tremble, then lower to a quiet hum. It was as though someone had reached inside me and turned out all the lights, leaving me with only natural, sluggish strength.

Panic sluiced through our group as murmurs and huge eyes were cast to the towering trees that had swallowed us.

Shadows formed around us in a semi-circle. Globs of darkness that materialized the closer they came, a glowing substance within their hands.

"Run," Ainx cried, his stallion rearing as he drew his sword.

I knew he was talking to me, urging me to flee, but the shock, the anger that arose held me prisoner and refused to let me.

I unsheathed my sword and spurred Wen to the left. "Cut them down."

A hooded figure appeared before me, a stone between their cupped hands.

My veins throbbed, pounding beneath my skin. I felt something trickle from my nostril, but I pushed forward and struck them through the ribs.

A scream filled the air as she fell back, the hood falling away from cream-colored hair, revealing thinned blue eyes. The stone rolled to the grass, and she panted, staring up at me with gritted teeth as she tried to staunch the wound in her side.

I pressed the blade to her frantic pulse, Wen huffing and skittish beneath me. "Who are you?"

Blood coated her teeth as she forced a smile. "Your end."

A cry came from above, from the trees, and I fell from Wen, who galloped away, toward the fissures of light of the woods.

Groaning, I smacked at the ground for my sword as the world spun and heard Azela scream my name. I swung as a hand yanked my hair back, but whoever it was knocked my sword loose, then kicked it away.

"Now, now," a female voice urged as I reached for them to no avail. "Be a good little queen for once in your life, and maybe you'll live long enough to see another meal."

I screamed as one of those pulsing rocks was set by my head, and then I blacked out.

I woke three times before I could finally manage to keep my eyes open long enough to see I was in some type of cage, then I let blackness engulf me once more.

"Audra."

I moaned, forcing my eyes open again, but everything was too blurred, and my head felt like it was going to either catch fire or explode.

I shut them again.

"Audra, wake up." Berron's voice slithered into the dark space I'd been locked inside.

My eyes sprang wide, a silent scream left me as the pounding in my head increased, the world hazy and filled with unrecognizable shapes. Moaning, I gripped my head. "Berron?"

"Yes." A clang sounded. "It's me. Open your eyes, stay with me. It gets more bearable the longer you keep them open."

I didn't know if I believed him, but I had to see him. I had to see if I was stuck in some strange hallucination, dream, or if he was real. I groaned, my muscles spasming as I tried to twist away from where I'd been curled up on the dirt.

The sound of someone shifting encouraged me, and I gritted my teeth against the pain in my head, in every part of me, as I rolled and came face to face with one I hadn't known I'd ever see again. "You," I rasped.

Berron smiled, and I was thankful he at least still had his teeth. "Me."

"I'm to wage a war for you."

He continued to smile, a tear streaking down his dirt-covered cheek. "For me? I think you had to anyway, my queen."

"Good point, but you forced my hand." I grunted, trying to rise onto my elbow. It slid out beneath me, and I hissed as my cheek hit the ground, my teeth nicking my tongue.

"Easy," Berron whispered, his eyes on some place behind me. They returned a moment later, filled with a million fleeting thoughts. "Just lay still for now. It's better that way."

"Why? Where are we?" And then I remembered them.

The cloaked figures. The blond female. The stones. Panic closed my airways, but I dared ask, "Where are my guards?"

Berron looked down at the ground. "One is here. I know nothing of the others."

Tasting copper, I swallowed. "Who?"

"A young male."

"Ridlow," I breathed. I wasn't comforted that the rest weren't here. That could mean anything. They could be rotting corpses in the woods or left gravely injured for the beasts that roamed at nightfall.

"Are we in the woods?" I tried to look around, but from my vantage point, all I could see was dirt and rusted metal, Berron's grimy face, and a wall made of sparkling black.

"I have no idea. We could be anywhere. They have a vanisher amongst them." A boom sounded above our heads, and he hurried to say, "Listen, don't be foolish. They *will* hurt you." He lifted his hand, the one missing the last two fingers. "Or kill you. Play the game. Buy time."

I winced at the sight of his blackened stubs. "You need to have them cauterized."

"If I survive," he said with a resigned tone.

"Berron," I growled, then cursed and grabbed my head. "A vanisher?" Those were hard to come by and often coveted by those in the royal courts. With a vision of their destination, they could travel anywhere within seconds and could take up to two people with them.

"Shhh," he urged, rolling over to face the other way.

I watched his back and how his tattered, soiled tunic moved as he pretended to sleep.

I wasn't sure if I should do the same, or if I could. The throbbing in my head intensified to a point my hands were clasping it, and my ears started to screech.

A door opened, dirt falling from the ceiling as it creaked into the wall behind it. "I thought I heard some vermin." The voice was female. Both silken and rough.

A heated retort sat on the tip of my tongue. I swallowed it, but

I couldn't pretend to sleep. I listened to the footsteps crunch over the ground, each step slow and calculated, and I waited for them to come into view.

A series of lanterns came alive. Suddenly, the walls and roof were not black anymore, but every color imaginable. I flinched away from the rainbows dancing and bobbing through the small enclosure I was in and tried to slow my breathing.

"Powerful, isn't it?" she said, wonder raising her voice. "We call them Vadella."

She knew I was awake then. She was probably looking straight at me. I didn't know about the latter being that I couldn't see, and her voice sounded as if she were underwater the more she talked.

"So powerful, they're capable of sucking you dry all on their own, but with a little light?" She laughed. "Well, as I'm sure you're aware, they're paralyzing."

I coughed. "How are you standing then?" So much for strength in silence.

"She speaks." She forced a gasp. "I'm not a precious pureblood like yourself, and therefore, years of being around them in small doses doesn't affect me like it does you."

The vanisher had to be a royal, so it was safe to assume that she was not one.

All but one lantern extinguished, the relief instant, though pain still lanced through my skull. I wiped what felt like fresh and dried blood from beneath my nostrils. "Might I ask where you found such a thing?"

"You just did," she said, her tone cold as her snakeskin boots crossed the dirt, moving out of view. "But you won't get an answer."

"Pity," I said. I drew in a few slow breaths, gritting my teeth as I forced myself to sit. I moved to the bars, preferring the cool metal over the glittering black stone that made up the rear of my cage. A cage that rose no higher than a few inches above my head.

"Is she ready?" another voice called.

The female, whose gray eyes were slanted and her hair every shade of brown, smiled crookedly. "She's ready."

I didn't dare ask what for and stopped myself from looking over at Berron, who was still feigning sleep.

A male, tall and slim, entered the small rock-filled crypt and Ridlow was with him.

His eye was swollen and his lip cut, hands bound behind his back. Other than that, he seemed to be faring okay. "M-my quee—"

The male with eyes as dark as the walls around us slugged him in the gut. "Quiet."

My tongue grew thick. I held Ridlow's gaze while they removed his chest plate, cut off his tunic, and chained his hands to a hook in the ceiling before our cages.

"Now," the male said, grabbing a knife from his boot. "Let us start with why we're here." He paused, turning to the female. "Corra, has she not asked why she's here?"

Corra shook her head. "No. She was more curious about the stone."

The male's thin lips moved into his cheek as he set his bottomless eyes upon me. "But of course. Priorities, right? Power, or lack thereof, comes first."

My lip curled. He chuckled, stepping closer to the bars and crouching down. "My, you are a sight, young queen." His eyes raked over me, his tongue snaking out to wet his lips. The hilt of the blade rolled in his palms between his knees. "I should like to have my cock inside your mouth before we are through here."

I snapped my teeth at him. "I urge you to try."

His expression blanked, and then he forced a smile. "In your ass it is."

I growled, which only served in earning me another irritating chuckle.

"Enough." Corra snatched his knife and dug it straight into Ridlow's stomach.

He howled, face crumpling as his feet struggled to find purchase.

"You're supposed to ask a question before you start maiming," I said, trying to sound as bored as possible. "But whatever, carry on." It was one of my earliest tasks as I bloomed into maturity and my training became more intense.

My father had said if I were to train, I'd do it properly. He would make me watch as he tortured random people, and even went as far as killing some, for moments just like this.

I wasn't grateful to him for much of anything, but I did have him to thank for my hardened heart.

The female glared at me while the male only grinned.

I flicked my fingers. "I have a horrible fucking headache because of you assholes, so please, hurry this along so we can get to the point of negotiation and release."

Their cackles raised the hair on my nape.

"And what makes you think you'll be leaving?" the male asked over Ridlow's groans and whimpers as Corra plucked the knife from his stomach and set it behind her next to a large metal trunk. From inside it, she then selected an angry looking dagger, its blade rusted. Her finger danced across the serrated edge.

"Why? Because I have something you want, of course." I pushed tendrils of hair back from my face, doing my best to ignore the wet tangles. "You have no way of retrieving it if I'm dead."

"You should be dead," Corra growled. "You're a monster, a blight on this land, just like your father grew to be." She spat inside my cage, and though I heard it land on the dirt near my knee, I didn't remove my eyes from hers.

"So kill me." I spread my hands. "But if you do, expect wrath like you've never seen before, as well as a dead king."

I'd left documents with Mintale and Truin weeks ago, stating what was to become of the king should something happen to me. Zadicus would rule, and Raiden would be executed within seconds of the news of my death, his head to be displayed on the tallest turret of the castle. All the better for the kingdom to watch the crows pick at his flesh and eyes.

And then Zad was to take back control of the Sun Kingdom by any means necessary.

A task I should've seen to over a year ago instead of wallowing in a multitude of festering anguish and rage.

"King Raiden," the male finally said, pacing with his hands behind his back across the tiny expanse of dirt in front of me and Berron. "Where is he?"

I picked at the dirt imbedded beneath my nails. "He was exiled."

Ridlow screamed as the dagger entered the knife wound, the female twisting her hand.

I waited for his screams and sobs to die down, and for my clenching muscles to relax. "You've heard differently, I take it." I'd known they had. It was only a matter of time. Though I'd be sure to make an example of whoever had spread the news.

I tilted my head, giving our captors a more thorough inspection. "Who were you to him, anyway? Henchmen? Harem members? Staff?"

"Soldiers," Corra said, indignant. "In his royal army."

I raised my hands. "So what have you heard?"

Ridlow bellowed a slew of curses as Corra twisted the dagger out of his flesh. Blood raced from the gaping wound, running down his armored leg to pool in a puddle on the floor and over the toe of his boot.

"One of your guards sold you out for a mere five hundred coin, telling tales of a king with no memory locked in the bowels of your nightmare-infested castle."

I contained a snort. "Okay." I nodded, fixing my eyes on my hands as I thought about who that could be. "You knew he'd have no memory of his time as a prince." I lifted my head. "So why is that even important?"

"Because," the male said with a smile. "He also informed us that you were trying to make him remember."

"Only to kill him," Corra cut in, her eyes dancing with hatred.

"He was about to vow himself to some human woman," I explained matter-of-factly. "What is one supposed to do?" I looked at Corra for some sisterly understanding. "He broke my black heart."

Her brows furrowed, and she looked at her comrade.

"Regardless," the male said. "We'll be needing our king back now that his memories are restored."

I laughed, tugging at my frayed skirts. "You see, that's the problem with this game of gossip via opportunist messenger. Things are not always true or explained correctly."

The male turned for the trunk and reached inside to grab a mace.

I groaned. "Darkness' sake. Did you think he would just take a tonic and suddenly remember everything?" I tutted. "He's still alive for a reason, and that's due to him *not* remembering yet."

The male paused. "I don't believe you."

"Then why am I here?" Magic be damned, I wanted nothing more than to beat them senseless with my bare hands. I sighed. "Look, how about this… When I am done with him, I'll send his body back to your kingdom as a gift of good faith."

Corra guffawed. "How easily you separate us still. Sending your lackey to try to rule over people who would rather see you perish."

"And you would have accepted me? A young queen in mourning who could hardly tell friend from foe?"

The male squinted at me, long pale fingers rubbing at his goatee. "We accept nobody but our blood. Here's your first warning. Follow our demands or else."

They unhooked Ridlow, and he fell to the ground with a yelp.

My eyes watched as my mind drifted.

The mace came down upon his head over and over until brain matter and blood coated the male's face, my skirts, Berron, and half of the tiny wormhole in the ground.

SIXTEEN

I WOKE UP SCREAMING.
 Unbearable heat lanced through my jaw, sticking to my skin.

"Let's see how much they adore you, how much they'll refuse to take our threats seriously, when you bear our scars for all to see on your once beautiful face."

I shoved the poker away, but it tore my flesh with it.

The rainbows were back, arching across the room, and then I passed out.

I came to again when Berron shouted my name in warning, and the poker was shoved at my cheek. It slid to my mouth, where it burned with a ferocity that rivaled the worst pain I'd ever felt. I smacked it away. The male laughed, continuing to jab it at my face.

He waited there for what felt like lifetimes, but was likely hours, just begging me to pass out so he could reach me in places he thought would most affect me.

Finally, when his name was called from the cracked open door, he tossed the poker beside the small fire he'd lit and stalked away.

I added his name to memory. I'd chant it in my mind as I watched his flesh peel back from his bones.

Cid.

It felt like razor blades had been taken to the left side of my mouth every time I drew and exhaled breath. My flesh bubbled and oozed as I laid upon the dirt ground and clung to Berron's hand through the bars.

All the while Ridlow's body decayed, the ground trying to swallow it within its warm embrace with each passing hour.

"Forever, Audra. You will forever be the most beautiful creature this land has ever seen, scars or not."

For it would scar, and I was vain enough to let the horror swallow me in the knowledge's ugly embrace. They wouldn't heal so long as we were trapped beneath this stone, surrounded by it, and access to the land and the magic tied to it couldn't be sought.

It was a dry, dizzying, barren landscape. Akin to that of the desert plains of the Sun Kingdom, where walking for days would leave your mouth foaming, head pounding, and your body weakening.

"Hey, look at me." Berron squeezed my hand, his eyes urging me to stay with him and not to burrow inside my dour thoughts. "Do you think some of the guards survived?"

I blinked, my eyelids roughened with exhaustion and dirt and unshed tears. "I don't know."

I didn't know how long I'd even been here. Time was best judged by Ridlow's decaying body, and the slush they called gruel that was delivered to us once a day.

We were given little water, which I appreciated, having relieved myself only twice as close to the edge of my cell as I could. If I had to guess, I'd have said no more than three days had passed, possibly only two.

I squeezed Berron's hand back, not wanting to wonder how long they'd kept him here for, but unable to stop myself from asking. "How long have you been here?"

"It's hard to say," he said. "Weeks, maybe."

The stench rolling off him could attest to that. "Since our botched attempt at finding out what happened to you in the Sun Kingdom?"

A small smile rode his lips. "Yes, I'd say since then."

I pinched my lips together, then moaned as more skin came away, my eyes stinging.

"Look at me," Berron said. "Give me those endless blue eyes."

I did. "What happened in the Sun Kingdom?"

His breath left him, harsh and defeated. As I listened to him rehash how hostile it was when they'd arrived, how it was hard to even sleep without fear of someone coming to slit his throat, guilt gnawed deep.

I'd been so enmeshed in my own self-loathing and hatred for those who'd betrayed me, I hadn't stopped to think clearly. Not once.

Not until it was too late.

"When did they decide to overthrow you?"

Berron swallowed, and it sounded as though it hurt. "A few months ago. The whispers turned into riots, and the riots into sieges on the palace. Most of our soldiers died, and I told the others to flee right before I was taken to their dungeon."

"They didn't return," I said, feeling those words like another burn to the face.

Berron blew out a breath, his hand growing clammy in mine. "I thought perhaps that was the case."

He told me how they kept him there for weeks, scarcely feeding him, forever threatening him as they waited for me to clue in to the fact he was no longer in charge.

The question had been itching at my mind since I'd seen him on that battlefield, a spear entering his side. They must have healed him to keep him from dying beneath these stones, being that he was capable of moving around his small enclosure with relative ease.

"Who is governing them now?"

Berron's head shook. "I can't be sure. At first, I thought it was a female. One of Raiden's favored lovers." I felt my brows lower at that. "Then a male would assert his dominance. I have no idea. Maybe more than one royal."

The door groaned open, and our hands broke apart as Cid stomped over the dirt and opened Berron's cage. Berron didn't try to fight, too weak from malnourishment and the draining effect of the stones he'd spent weeks lying beneath.

Cid chained him to the ceiling as terror drilled holes inside my chest.

Corra entered. "Time is running out, my queen." She chose the jagged dagger from the trunk and sliced open Berron's arm from shoulder to elbow.

He didn't even have the energy to scream, a silent, gasping sound leaving him, the image etching upon my heart. "You can stop." I rolled and pushed my hands under me, my head spinning as I sat upright. "Let us talk."

The dagger dropped to the dirt, and Corra stalked over. "You do not even know what our demands are."

"You want your king." I raised a brow. "I'm assuming you'll only release us if I have him brought to you."

Cid crouched down, his hands wrapping around the rust-flecked bars of my cage. "The winter queen has a soft spot after all."

"Many," I purred.

His eyes flared, and Corra smacked him in the back of the head. "Get up, you animal."

He growled but did as she said.

I met Berron's eyes and nodded. It couldn't end any other way anyway. He'd been through enough. So many of us had been through enough.

"Here's what will happen," Corra said. "We will take you close enough to the city to avoid detection, and then we will wait." Corra looked at Berron. "With your friend here, as well as a considerable amount of Vadella should you think you can try to outsmart us."

Cid dragged a finger down the bars, his tongue skirting his mouth. "Then, you will sign a royal decree, stating that due to his exile, you are no longer tied by vows made before such horrors eventuated." He let that sink in.

If your spouse was exiled, you had the choice to remain vowed and go with them or break the vow and move on. Raiden and I had not yet broken our vow. Other than rare exceptions, like being exiled, both parties had to be in agreeance to terminate the sacred union. He was no longer in exile, but I was certain getting him to comply wouldn't be an issue.

"Do we have a deal?"

"You want him a free male?"

"Of course." Corra kicked a glob of blood off her boot. It hit the bars with a splat, spraying my arm. "He needs to remarry. Not only to have a more deserving female to lead beside him, but to keep the Evington bloodline pure. He cannot do that while he's tied to you."

I looked at Berron again, but his gaze was on the ground. Crimson covered his arm, snaking around his elbow and bicep, staining his torso.

I could give up my king. It would mean breaking some archaic laws and risking my own title, but I could do so. And if I were finally being honest with myself, perhaps I needed to. Perhaps this was always supposed to end this way.

He back in his court, and me on my own.

Thunderous groans and snapping sounded, dirt and rocks raining over us.

I scrambled back against the wall as another boom came from above. The entire ceiling, rocks and all, was being ripped from the ground. I flinched as that black rock cracked and collapsed into pieces, and tree roots slithered and snapped.

Four males jumped down, swords out and swinging through the air. "No," I screamed. "Don't kill them." Crawling out from my cracked cage, I got to my feet. The sight of Zad was enough to find the strength I didn't have.

The dark-haired male standing closest to Zad looked at me, then back at him.

The other two bound the female's hands behind her back and stuffed a clump of dirt inside her mouth. She spat, but it wouldn't budge.

Zad nodded to the male. "He comes too."

I fell back against the crumbling wall, my lungs emptying as the starless night bored down into our prison, exposing the tiny space for the moon to glow upon.

"What is that?" one of the males asked, his nose and lips twitching with distaste as he eyed the pieces of black stone.

"We need to leave. It absorbs magic and slowly ruins the mind," Berron said as Zad unhooked him from the ceiling, then broke open the chains.

I went to the hole, staring up and out of it, already feeling some of the pain fade from my head. Then I was swept into strong arms and a hand was pressed to the burns on my face. "They will wish they never so much as laid eyes on you," Zad said, his voice a feral rasp.

My head slumped to his shoulder as he climbed out of the ground. "I know."

Zad had one of his friends, who I thought I heard him call Landen, hold me while he mounted his horse, and then I was situated in front of him.

He fiddled with my skirts, and I smiled as he ensured they covered as much of my legs as possible. "Modesty is the least of my concerns, Lord."

"Hush and let me fuss."

Then we were off, Corra and Cid bound and forced to walk or run to keep up with Zad's friends' horses.

Berron was having his arm strapped by Azela before they joined us. Within minutes, we slowly left the chamber of stones in the ground. "We need those rocks destroyed."

Zad jerked his head, and then one of the males tossed his torch inside the crater. Too tired to look back, I wasn't sure what he did to make it explode and then extinguish within seconds.

"How did you find me?" I asked when we neared the woods we'd been ambushed in. "Azela?"

"Wen raced back to my estate like his ass was on fire," he said, voice gruff. I smiled, glad the clever beast was okay. "But yes, Azela and Ainx." He paused. "I must warn you, your captain is in pretty bad shape."

Images of Ridlow's broken body lingered upon my lashes like dust unwilling to dissipate. I drew a scathing breath, exhaling the question. "How bad?"

"They slit his throat. Somehow, Azela managed to get him back to my estate, one hand on the reins, another holding him to the back of her horse."

I closed my eyes, the disorientation and swelling inside my head retreating and resurfacing.

Then I forced them open, unwilling to be blindsided again, and kept them trained on the trees.

"Do you think he'll survive?"

Zad's chest rose and fell at my back, his steady words rustling my hair. "It's hard to say, but he's in good hands."

"You have a healer?"

"One who lives locally with her two young children. When needed, they all come to the estate, or she leaves them with her mother."

"She lost her spouse?"

"She killed him when he came home drunk one evening and punched her in the stomach, causing her to miscarry their third child."

"How did she kill him?"

"A spork to the eyeball and a dagger to his groin. Simultaneously."

My brows rose, and I gripped the roughened strands of River's mane. "I should like to meet this warrior."

I could hear his smile in his voice. "I thought you would."

A pair of owls called to one another as we trekked beyond the shadows and rode single file down the rocky glen toward the neighboring forest.

I'd hesitated long enough in asking. "The rest of my guard?"

"Dead," he said. "Though not for nothing. Those two were all who remained of their band of eight."

"Some could have fled."

The wind carried his next words. "You are a treasure no one runs from."

"You did," I reminded him, unsure why, or if it even mattered anymore.

His arm tightened around my waist. "I was being petulant. A fool."

The admission soothed and surprised. Never had I heard him admit as much before.

Moonlight rippled over the banks and dipped inside the foliage to brush over our darkened path, and with every new rock, every new tree, and the kiss of the breeze on my face, I felt myself gradually return.

Like a storm rolling in, my blood began to churn and warm, and my heartbeat found its usual rhythm. Relief swamped me, and my head flopped against Zad's chest, my eyes closing as his lips brushed my forehead.

I awoke in his arms some time later, heading for a sea of white feathered and furred bedding. "No," I croaked. "I won't touch anything until I get this filth off my skin."

We turned for the bathing chamber, the door swinging open.

He set me on the edge of a tub large enough to fit six grown males, and I watched with drooping eyes as he scattered bath salts and fussed with the temperature.

"She was lucky, you know," I said, unable to curb my tongue. "To have you."

Zad stiffened, then set the salts down in a wooden rack attached to the mosaic tiled wall. "Luck," he finally said, "and love do not mix."

I pondered that as he tied his hair back with a strip of leather, then helped me slide into the bubbling, warm water. He left me there but returned shortly after with a plate of fruit and buttered bread, setting it on the corner of the tub. He crouched down and retrieved a washcloth from a basket below the sink.

I plucked a few grapes from the plate, letting the sour-sweet taste soak my tongue as I bit into the tiny globes.

Zad had removed his coat, his cream tunic undone at the neck, displaying tiny chest hairs and a glimpse of his firm skin. He leaned over the tub, dunking the cloth into the water, and then he did something I never would've dreamed I'd allow him to, and washed me.

He started with my face, gently gliding the roughened material over it, his eyes following. When he neared my lips, he met my gaze. "Might sting."

"Not half as bad as when it happened," I whispered.

His throat dipped. He squeezed water over the burns, careful and attentive, to rid them of any dirt.

"You haven't said much of it."

"If you think a few scars will detract from your beauty, you're more delusional than you are vain."

I sent water into his face, laughing as he swiped it off. His unimpressed expression faded into a serene smile as he stared at me.

It felt good to use my magic, but it felt better to see him smile at me like that.

He continued to wash me, and I let him, surprised he'd kept it clinical, especially when he'd reached the apex of my legs.

"Eat," he said, his voice rough as he scrubbed my legs.

I tore off a chunk of bread and nibbled at it, almost choking when he started cleaning my feet and wedged the cloth between my toes.

I kicked his hands away, and he chuckled. "Relax or I'll make you."

I laughed as he moved to the other foot and shoved his hand away as soon as I thought he'd tortured it enough. As my laughter faded, I sank back against the tub, my hands gliding through the water. Most of the bubbles had gone, leaving my body exposed.

"How did you do that?" I asked. "Cleave the ground apart like that?" With such force and swiftness, considering the power-draining stones beneath it.

"That," he said, wringing out the cloth, "is a story for another day." He hung it over the faucet before standing and leaving the room.

I watched him go, then let myself sink beneath the surface, my hands moving to my hair to rid it of days of dirt, blood, and perspiration.

A scream tore from me when a hand snuck beneath the water and pulled me up. "I was just cleaning my hair," I gasped out.

Zad pushed some of it back from my face, fevered eyes searching mine. Swallowing, he stood and spread open a towel. "Come, you need to sleep."

I let him dry me, then I let him carry me into his room and lay me on his bed. The bedding had already been peeled back, and he pulled it over my naked body. "I want to see Ainx."

Zad tugged off his damp tunic and draped it over one of the silver armchairs near a black fireplace. "There's little anyone can do for him now but let him rest." He turned to me as he undid his pants, the angles of his face stark in the moonlight. "I'll take you to him as soon as you've done the same."

I raised a brow but had little desire to argue the point as exhaustion rendered me limp over the feathered mattress. "Darkness, you're bossy."

He grinned and shook his head, and I wished I wasn't so tired as I watched his perfect ass disappear inside the bathing room. I wished I could have summoned the energy to follow him and crawl atop him, have him sink inside me and fill me with enough euphoria to chase away the filth.

I was sound asleep by the time he crawled into bed behind me and pulled me flush with his warm body.

SEVENTEEN

I woke a full day later, and Ainx followed shortly after, gasping and clutching at his throat.

It had scabbed over, but I daresay the pain and the horror would remain for some time to come.

Berron was staying in a guest room beside Ainx, his arm healing while Emmiline tended to the stubs of his lost fingers. Lotions and cleansing were needed frequently to rid the infection that'd begun to spread. To ensure he wouldn't lose his hand.

Someone had retrieved my sword, for when I woke, there it was in its scabbard attached to my belt, lying across an armchair.

On the second night, I woke alone at midnight with my face throbbing, visions of Ridlow trying to talk to me through mangled lips and a dislodged jaw.

After draining a glass of water left by the bed, I dressed in a cream nightgown that seemed freshly spun and traipsed downstairs. I refused to fall back asleep until the gruesome images had faded from my mind.

"If you wake from a nightmare, awake wholly before you let yourself drift back to sleep," my mother had said, her fingers like feathers as they'd danced over my damp hairline. "It is the only way to be sure the same nightmare cannot haunt you again."

I'd swallowed over the boulder in my throat, my voice weak as I'd asked, "But what if I have a different one?"

She'd smiled, though her eyes were sad. "Then you wake and escape that one too, and try again."

A deep voice startled me from the dark corner of the kitchen. "Good evening, Queen."

I forced my heartbeat to slow and nodded as shadows faded from the white-haired male. One of Zad's friends who'd helped rescue us. "And you are?"

He bit into an apple, then set the fruit basket he'd clearly been rummaging through back in the center of the wooden island. "Dace." That was all he said. No surname given. He just stood there, chomping away as his amber eyes coasted over me.

I moved to the exit, not because I was afraid, but because I didn't care to drum up small talk with a stranger. I merely wanted to change the direction of my thoughts and head back to bed.

"He worries for you," Dace said.

I paused in the entry but didn't turn around. "Who?"

A gravel-coated laugh reached me. "Zadicus, but you already knew that."

His actions proved that to be true, but I wasn't ready to digest them too much. "Why are you telling me?"

Dace stalked by me, carrying with him the scent of something sweet and spiced. "Because queen or not, he's not a toy to be discarded." He turned on me, eyes flashing. "He cannot handle another—"

"Audra," Zad said from the opposite end of the hall.

I peeked around Dace, who'd tensed, and found Zad walking toward us with a leather-bound journal in hand. "Dace, do not attempt to rattle the queen. She'll gut you and decorate her castle with your innards."

Dace raised a brow at me. "So I've heard." With a long sweep of my frame, he thumped Zad on the shoulder and stalked upstairs.

"Your friends have high opinions of me," I said.

"The highest." Zad grinned, but then his wolfish smile drooped. "Don't tell me your reputation actually bothers you?"

I sniffed, tipping a shoulder. "Of course not." I eyed the journal. "What's that for?"

"Tell me why you're out of bed, and I might just tell you."

I gave him a flat look. "Liar."

With a hand at my back, he led me back upstairs. "You need to rest."

"I have been." I kept my voice low as we traversed the halls. Zad had told me the rooms were crafted to keep unwanted noise out, but old habits die hard.

"You had a bad dream?" he asked, closing the door behind us.

I pulled off the nightgown, then rolled my lips between my teeth. "I did." I padded over to him, my toes curling over the soft rug. "Maybe a little play will help ensure I'm so exhausted that I don't dream at all." My finger untied the neck of his tunic to trace the skin inside.

Zad's chest rose sharply, and then fell as he released a breath through his nostrils, causing them to flare. "I'm not fucking you."

Shocked, I met his eyes, searching the resolute orbs for an answer as to why. I found nothing. "Suit yourself," I said, then made a point to sway my hips as I crossed the room and climbed into bed.

With a sigh, he turned for the door.

"Will you at least stay with me?" I hated the question. Hated the way it crept out without permission. Hated the way it sounded. "It is your room, after all."

After a momentary pause that tripped something in my chest, Zad stripped out of his clothes. He tossed them to the rug, the few burning candles winking out.

The bed dipped and the bedding swished, caressing my skin to the point of torture as I felt the heat of him so close to my back. He'd held me the night before, though I wasn't sure if he'd do it again.

As though he'd been telling himself not to, he snarled softly before gathering me to him, aligning every soft part of me with every very hard part of him.

I hid my smile in my pillow and tried not to nudge my ass into his hardness.

A growl tore through the silent room, and then his hand was coasting down my side, pebbling my skin as it pulled my leg back and over his to reach between. "You'll be my end, Audra." His breath heated my skin as he inhaled my scent and rubbed his lips over the back of my shoulder. When his fingers found me wet and wanting, I moaned.

He cursed, dipping one inside and removing it to stroke me until I saw nothing but bright sparks, and I could do nothing but mewl and whimper as he held me still. With his other arm beneath my head, he held me against him. Two fingers plunged back inside me.

My breathing grew ragged, sharp sounds as he tortured me in every way I'd needed since I left here last week. "Inside me," I panted. "Please."

"I know you're still hungry," he rasped to my ear, his teeth grazing the curve of my throat, "but I want you starving. So slick and swollen that I can barely fit my cock inside."

I moaned, louder than I'd have liked from his words and the way his thumb brushed over me. I came apart once more. "Lord," I said, my voice scraped raw and my body seeking his even as it tried to move away from the mess he was making between my legs. "Zad, please."

"You do not beg." He eased his fingers out and then pushed them back inside.

"For you," I whispered, high on his touch and his scent and his voice—all that he was and was not. "I would."

He stilled, his voice hoarse when he finally spoke. "You are a queen, Audra. Take what you want."

Shifting my leg higher, I reached between us, desperate and shaking as I wrapped my hand around his cock. It was throbbing, a pulsing beat against my hand.

He hissed through his teeth, then groaned when I directed him to where I needed him most. "Holy goddess of fuck," he said, breathless and seated deep, holding me against him so tight.

For long minutes, he fucked me hard and slow, and then his seed was coating my walls as his lips traveled over my clammy skin. "So fucking beautiful," he murmured to it.

I moved my hair above my head for his lips to roam farther over my neck and shoulder.

His fingers gripped my chin, turning it for his mouth to capture mine, but he didn't devour it. No, he licked every inch of my lips as his cock thickened again.

Then, he began to move, slower this time, as he kissed the puckered skin upon my lips. So soft it was barely a touch at all, yet I felt it reach the marrow of my bones, igniting something I'd long ignored.

My fingers floated over his jaw, the coarse hair that'd sprouted, and then to his nose, tracing the tiny bump in the center. His cheekbones to his thick brows, perfect auburn arches above two of the brightest eyes I'd ever seen. Not due to their color, but due to the unique soul behind them.

Our breaths mixed, his forehead resting aside mine as the wet sound of our pleasure and the enraged tempo of our hearts cocooned us in a tiny world where anything but us, but this, ceased to exist.

We trembled and cried out together, then laid there for long moments, tangled in new ruins.

And as the stars began to flicker out of the night sky, sleep pulling us into its unpredictable grasp, he rolled me to my back, spread my legs wide, and stretched over top of me with his arms braced by my head. "I want you filled with so much of my seed, you won't just feel me leaking out of your beautiful cunt for days, you'll feel me wherever you go, eternally." He pushed my hair away and sank inside as he whispered against my cheek, "So I'm far from done with you yet."

The wind howled through the mountain range, bending the blades of grass and wildflowers and curling my hair around my face.

I leaned back against Van and closed my eyes as flakes of snow began to fall. They dusted my lips and melted into the fabric of my burgundy coat, seeping through to the long sleeves of my gown beneath.

Home.

A place I'd lived all my life, yet as I'd seen it upon the horizon that evening, its cream turrets soaked in the last rays of daylight, blending into the white-capped mountains beyond, my heart hadn't warmed.

Every thunderous mile covered beneath our horses' hooves as Azela, Berron, and I raced away from Zad's manor felt as if I was running away from dry land to immerse myself in muck-filled waters.

I'd left him sound asleep, dressed in a gown that had been draped over the armchair with my sword, then I'd grabbed my boots, and had woken the others.

Duty could no longer wait, and I had a shit list the size of an entire kingdom that needed tending to.

The heart had no say when it came to responsibility. It would only get in the way.

Zad had a dead wife he refused to talk about, let alone allow himself to love that completely again. And I had a dead heart that I refused to let rule my decisions ever again.

No matter what it hungered for, it had to remain that way.

All thanks to the husband of mine who sat sick with mismatched memories in my dungeon.

A crazed laughter echoed across the landscape as my hands plucked at the damp grass. I had to wonder what I'd been thinking, really, when stealing him from his new life like that.

I'd believed I could handle the consequences, that I was equipped to deal with the repercussions.

A young female prone to tantrums indeed.

I opened my eyes and brushed away a rogue tear, smearing it into the cashmere and cotton of my skirts. There was no time for tears. There was never a time for tears. Time was a thief that would keep draining us dry if we didn't learn to stay afloat and swim above its paralyzing waters.

Van snickered and turned his head, his breath steaming the air beside my face.

Looking over at him, I found his eyes fixed on my ruined skin. The burns had healed, but the scars would remain.

I stroked his snout. "They will pay."

He blinked, impossibly huge eyes drinking in my face.

"Quit looking at me like that."

He huffed and bumped my hand with his nose, then returned to the grass, licking the frost from the blades before deciding to nibble at them.

We returned to his stables before the sun could reach the highest peak, and then I trudged back down the mountain. I'd wanted to give Wen a rest after his ordeal in the forest as well as our journey back home yesterday. Besides, I'd needed the crisp air on my face, its icy kiss brushing every strand of my hair, curling the ends.

The pathway down the mountain—little more than hollowed out soil between rocks—wound all the way to the rear gardens. I let my fingers traipse over gleaming petals. Plucking a rose, I dragged my finger over one of its thorns, watching the groundskeepers bob in and out of the maze-like gardens behind the castle.

Had they wished I'd perished when they heard news of what'd happened to me? Had some small part of them hoped that my husband would break out of the dungeon and save them all?

Paranoia was a beast planted by past transgressions and other people's own insecurities.

I would question, but I wouldn't falter from my own loathsome thoughts. No, I'd wrap them around me like an ice-layered blanket and let them reinforce my will.

My finger pricked the thorn, and I dragged it down the stem as I reached the keep.

Mintale came rushing outside, blathering about a healer who'd been waiting to see me for the past two hours.

I took in his pale, lined face, the tufts of gray hair I used to tug as a child just to hear his mock-screech.

"You're bleeding, my lady," Mintale said, his eyes on my finger.

I blinked and lifted it to my mouth, tasting the metallic tang as it coated my tongue. Releasing my finger with a pop, I said, "Have the prisoners chained in market square before dawn."

Mintale nodded.

"What of the others? The vanisher?"

"Nothing yet, but we have our spies and best soldiers searching the kingdom as we breathe."

"Bring the vanisher to me. I want the others killed on sight." Before he could scamper off, I called, "Oh, and have the girl shackled and fetched from the tavern." I smiled at his furrowed brows. "Let her have a taste of what awaits."

※

From the highest turret, I watched as dawn leaked across the horizon, inching over the sloping city and valleys below.

There, within the flat center of market square, two bodies were chained to thick, towering posts. I could almost see Corra's brown hair swirl around her face and felt the singe anew to my own when I gazed at Cid's tall form next to her.

Were they scared?

My nails, buffed and painted crimson to match my lips, scraped over the rough stone wall. *Tap, tap, tapping* to the sound of the executioner's bell that blared six times, loud enough for the entire kingdom to hear. Every resident knew what it meant.

There was a time, however brief, when the sound of the six haunting chimes would chase my dreams into nightmares as a child.

When my father had overheard my mother hushing me back to sleep one night, he'd plucked someone from the dungeon and dragged me out of bed at dawn the following morning.

"Listen," he'd said, walking me to the square. "They're a warning. A final beating of one's heart. A reminder. And one of your greatest weapons."

"A weapon?" I'd squeaked.

His hands had gripped my shoulders, his voice riddled with that crazed excitement that sometimes scared me. "Yes, yes. A weapon." Another squeeze, then he'd pointed at where a body was being lifted into the air. "The sound of the six bells are enough to send a stake of fear through any foe's heart. Believe me, they are your friend, your protector, and your enforcer, all wrapped in six deadly chimes."

I'd swallowed as we reached the thickest part of the crowd, and he'd moved me closer to the wooden dais that was smattered with speckles of brown stains.

The scent of excrement hung thick in the air. It made my stomach churn and my nose twitch. My eyes lifted, and my spine locked as a man with clay-colored eyes gazed down upon me, muttering, "Please, please, please…"

"Father," I'd started.

"Quiet," he snapped. "Watch. If I see your eyes leave the sentenced, I will pick another to hang. Perhaps one of the children who are still sleeping in their beds."

I'd have given anything to still be sleeping in my own bed. To be able to look away as a guard pulled a lever and the snap of the man's neck had ricocheted through the square.

His soul fled his eyes, and I swore I felt a cold breeze dust my right hand before the crowd began to part, and he was left there to hang.

"Good," my father had said, his hands so heavy on my shoulders, and my knees trembling so hard, I prayed to the goddesses' that I wouldn't fall. "Now, was that anything to be afraid of?" He shook my shoulders when I didn't answer.

But my stomach heaved. So violently I'd coughed, then swallowed the rising bile. "No, Father." I forced my eyes back to the dead man. Forced them to see it for what it was.

Flesh and bone and deceit.

And those who deceive the crown in any way, shape, or form must be dealt with accordingly.

"They're waiting for you," Azela said now.

I turned from the wall, my hands stiff and my nails ruined as though I'd dug them into the stone and mortar.

Azela looked from them to me, her eyes narrowing. "Are you okay?"

I tugged my white fur-lined black cloak tighter around me, brushing past her. "Just fine. Any news on Ainx?"

"Not yet, no."

We descended the stairs, around and around until we'd reached the ground entrance, then crossed through the throne room to the courtyard. "Why did you return with me?"

"You are my queen." It was said as if it should've been reason enough. And perhaps it should have been.

"He needs you, and you're clearly worried." I peered over at her as we met with the rest of my guards. They took their positions around us, and we moved to the gates. "You should go back."

Azela was slow to answer, her blond hair whispering over her cheeks as the wind groaned and swept through the side streets to greet us. "He and I..." She stopped, and I withheld a groan. "We're not—"

"I'm no fool." Guards philandering with other guards was not permitted during my father's reign. Frolicking off duty was fine, but relationships beyond that would have them exiled or hung. "I'm also not my father."

Azela's teeth clicked as she shut her mouth.

"But I am a queen, and I don't like false truths any more than he did."

The gathered city dwellers parted as we neared, and gradually,

Corra and Cid came into view. There were enough guards surrounding the dais on all sides, shields and weapons at the ready, to keep unwanted vigilantes at bay. Rare, but it sometimes happened. Though not often, seeing as it landed them in the same spot as those who were being executed.

Two guards dipped their heads and parted. I walked through them toward the dais and smiled at my two would-be captors and Casilla. The latter was tied to a chair behind the dais, a gag in her mouth and her face blank. "Good morning, friends."

Corra frowned.

Cid laughed. "Save the theatrics, you piece of evil—"

His words were drowned by his howl, the small blade that'd been tucked inside my sleeve now imbedded above his groin. Dangerously close to his genitals.

The crowd grew thicker, murmurs and gasps exploding.

Spittle dribbled from Cid's lips, and Corra moaned. "We gave you the merchant's name and t-the guard."

I tilted my head. "Did I just hear you stutter?"

Corra gritted her teeth, lifting her chin as much as her chained body would allow.

"Secure them," I told the guards standing behind the dais.

Four of them moved forward and bound their heads to the poles with metal chains strung through their teeth.

My magic groaned as I clenched and unclenched my fists. I'd woken it early and had it flex its limbs, readying for the task. The air changed, growing charged as the guards slashed open the soles of Corra's and Cid's feet, and the wind gathered speed.

Their muted screams barely registered as I told myself to wait, to hold on, until the guards had moved back into the crowd.

Then I entered, a slow crawling wind that slithered through their pores, the gashes in their feet, their noses, their eyes, their mouths, and their arteries. I pushed. Blood began to pool as their eyes fissured and rolled, falling in tiny splats to the wood of the dais, sliding between the cracks to the street below.

Casilla sat eerily still, her expression still unreadable as her eyes watched the blood vacate Corra's and Cid's bodies.

No one dared to so much as whisper during a draining. It was the most torturous and inhumane way to die for our kind. Not because it was the most painful—I'd heard and guessed it was most certainly horrific—but because whether you were human or royal or both, your soul was left to rot inside your empty corpse instead of reaching the ever. A kingdom of eternal peace, rest, and riches.

They would forever walk the in-between, forced to stay trapped within the unknown, accompanied by their boundless sins.

When the metal chains around their heads gleamed with froth from their mouths and slackened, I knew it was almost done. Any moment now, the thread that bound my magic to their bodies would snap, indicating an empty vessel. Nothing left to play with.

My body hummed a steady, content timbre as it pushed and coaxed and forced the life from their bodies through their feet. In my mind, their blood was once a rushing river, and I sent it all flowing downstream to meet a cliff to nowhere.

Then I blinked, my stiff limbs slowly relaxing.

The silence could have cut sharper than any blade. I ignored it and turned to Mintale when I saw the top halves of Cid's and Corra's bodies begin to deflate, bone crumbling and muscle eroding.

"See that they remain here until nightfall."

Mintale gave a brisk nod. "Of course, my queen."

Azela and the rest of my appointed guards escorted me back to the castle, where I returned to the highest turret to watch the ever-stunned, murmuring crowds dissipate.

EIGHTEEN

"Majesty," Mintale said, hurrying after me.

"What?" I asked, not slowing my stride as I bypassed the throne room and took the outer hallways to the farthest one in the castle.

"Where are you going?"

I couldn't keep the bite from my tone if I tried. "To finish this."

Mintale stopped. "Audra."

The use of my name, a rarity I hadn't heard from him in years, had me stopping too. I spun to face him.

Concern etched his features, deepening the lines on his forehead. "You don't really want to do that, though, do you?"

"What I want holds no weight in this situation." I steeled my spine and turned on my heel. "I've done what I wanted with him, and now it's time to keep my word."

He said nothing else as I walked on, but I could feel his worry seeping into my back and sinking beneath my cloak until I'd joined the connecting hall and disappeared from view.

I did have to keep my word. Not only that, but I couldn't see any other way to end this.

I'd let him go. I'd allowed him to live his new life, and it hadn't worked. Not for me.

And I wasn't sure if I could have Truin mess with his mind like that again without doing serious damage.

My chest hurt with every step taken down into the dark innards of the castle.

He'd betrayed me in many unforgivable ways, yet with every inch closer, it grew harder to draw breath.

Few guards were on duty in the dungeon now that the other two guests we'd had were husks in market square. I nodded to Didra and Alya, and ignored the curiosity lingering on their faces as they unlocked the gate and let me in.

My boots hit the ground with barely a sound as I took my time approaching his cell. He heard them anyway and looked up from where he was seated on the floor with his head leaning against the bars. Darkness pillowed his forest green eyes, and the stubble that'd coated his jawline was thicker, almost a beard.

His gaze dipped over me, then moved back to my mouth. "What happened?"

I propped myself against the torture table and fiddled with one of the cuffs. "Concerned now, are we?"

Raiden stood, gripping the bars. "Audra, look at me."

Refusing to, I instead stared at the tear running through his tunic. Scratches and dried blood marred his skin, and I wondered if maybe he'd been injuring himself during moments of abstract confusion. "Take a seat," I said and lifted myself to the table. "We have a story to finish."

"I know how it ends."

I clicked my tongue. "I don't believe you."

A clang sounded as he smacked the bars. "Damn it, Audra. Just look at me." I could hear his shallow breathing. "I've been asking for you for days. I remember it. *All of it*. Where have you been?" Those last words hinted at desperation, and desperate he would be.

"You're insane." I inspected my chipped nails, then dragged them over the table. "You flip flop between clarity, anger, and confusion."

"I've thought of nothing but who I am, who I really am, for days. But you haven't been here, and someone has clearly hurt you." A growl left him. "Shit, Audra. Just damn well tell me already."

Fine. "I was taken by some of your people."

"Our people?"

I laughed at that, studying the white lines my nails carved into the wood. "No, they will never be *our* people." I looked at him then, let him see the unrest that laid upon my soul and this kingdom. "They wish me dead, and it only grows worse."

Raiden's head was shaking. "It's because of Tyrelle. You need to let me out. Let me help you." I tore away from the vehemence in his eyes and ignored the way it deepened his voice. "You can kill me after if it still means so much to you."

I was beginning to believe that maybe he was of sound mind once more. That he was back.

But to believe was to hope, and hope was nothing but a wasted four letter word.

I licked at the scar running through the side of my lips. "The days of me trusting you were over long ago, Prince."

"King," he said. "I am a king. Your king."

I sneered. "And what of your betrothed?"

He bounced his head off the bars in my peripheral. "I don't know this Casilla. It's like there's this dream version of me, and every time I try to visit that place, I slip between the two again and grow confused. I can't..." He stopped and then began to pace, tugging at his thick dark hair. "Not yet, not until I've grasped enough control of my own mind."

"Very well," I said, uncaring. "Let's end this then. After Zadicus, the few surviving guards and myself returned to the kingdom, the hunt for you and your merry band of traitors began..."

"No."

Rearing back, I arched my brows. "No?"

He rubbed his chin, his laugh crisp and low. "It's my turn."

Raiden

I was happy. Quite possibly the happiest I'd ever been in my entire life.

Even with Tyrelle seated across from me, that malice-filled glint in his eyes as he stared upon us didn't bother me as it once had.

This had always been the plan. From the very start, we were to infiltrate the Moon Kingdom via marriage and then remove its black heart.

The games, the cruelty that had spread far and wide—it needed to stop. King Tyrelle's rule was unjust and wicked, and he only grew in strength and cruelty as the years sped by.

The first time I met my future wife, she was fucking another male in the fields. If that hadn't cemented what I was there to do, I wasn't sure what else could. But even then, mere minutes after he'd no doubt spilled his seed inside her, she'd managed to make me forget for a few breathless heartbeats.

They say she's the most beautiful creature in all the land.

To that I would say beauty meant nothing when they're rotten on the inside.

I quickly learned just how rotten she could be. A brat with too much unchecked power, unspent anger, and unshed grief. But oh, how I'd learned of other things too.

Nothing was ever as it seemed, and there were no truer words for Allureldin's princess.

Audra acted upon feelings, instinct, and instruction that laid buried deep. If you looked closely, she was surely flawed—perhaps more than most of us—but she was also a product of her upbringing, of the horrors she'd beheld when only a child.

She was wicked, yes, but she was also more. She was unshakably loyal to those she showed a glimmer of affection for and honest. It was that honesty that so often got the people talking.

Audra had this unapologetic way of saying what she meant, what she felt, and acting upon it while the majority of the rest of us harbored our hurts, our real urges and thoughts, and pretended they didn't exist.

She was cruel. She was caring. She was horrid. She was devoted. She was intimidating. She was confident.

The contradictions could be listed for days, and for those reasons, it was no surprise I became enamored with her. That my eyes became a slave to every move she made. That my heart changed its beat whenever I felt that violent magic of hers approach.

My parents couldn't know.

Not only did they think their son incapable of loving Audra, but they also wouldn't have listened to me if I'd told them she was different. That if I ruled alongside her, the fear and unrest created by Tyrelle's rule could and would be squashed.

Yet they found out, and it was all my fault. I'd given up caring if my affection, the way I was growing to adore the brute's daughter, would be realized for all that it was.

I was falling in love.

And by the time she welcomed me inside her body, I had already hit the ground hard enough to create fissures in the earth.

When they realized what had happened, I tried. Darkness be damned, did I try. They wouldn't listen when I explained why we should spare her. That only her father needed to die. They wouldn't listen, and then the plan, the assassination, was changed without my knowledge.

The last meeting before the night that ruined us was conducted without me.

We were supposed to act when we left the cabin in the Forest of Promise, when her father ventured back in the carriage to pick us up.

I'd planned to explain everything to Audra once we were secluded in those woods, away from the whispering walls and wind, in our own little version of paradise. I was to tell her we would leave. I would take her someplace safe until the king was dead and I could convince my parents that was all that was necessary.

They'd acted while I was still planning the speech, memorizing the route we'd take, and wondering what she'd say and do in my head.

Then our whole world was aflame.

A scarf wrapped in laced toad dust was stuffed into my mouth as soon as I was hauled from the carriage. I'd tried to pull it out as I struggled not to inhale the ginger mildewed fumes, but it was in vain. You only needed a whiff of the tampered dust, and you were screwed. Count the butt of a sword meeting my head as I removed my own, and the next thing I knew, I was staring up at the sky through a rooftop of trees, a group of guards and my advisor from back home sitting around a small fire.

As soon as they saw I was awake, everyone stood and bowed. "My king."

Disorientated, I searched the gathered faces for Audra. But that was pointless. They all detested her.

She wasn't there.

I kept searching anyway, getting to my feet and spitting the acrid taste from my mouth. "Where is she?"

"Who?" Meeda asked, braiding her hair.

I growled. "Audra."

She looked at the fire, and I felt my heart sink. "What happened? If she's dead..." No.

No. The thought alone sent searing pain right through me, threatening to cleave me in two.

I grabbed Serdin, the soldier closest to me, by the cuff of his armor, hauling him to his feet. "What has happened to her?"

"T-t-the carriage." His wide eyes shuttered. "She was still in the carriage last I saw, and it was falling t-to pieces, burning to the ground."

My fingers slid from the coarse material, and he fell to the grass.

"We defeated them, but we have suffered a grave loss in doing so." Patts, my father's advisor, stepped into my line of vision. Tears brimmed his eyes. "They slaughtered your parents."

Audra.

My parents.

A hollow laugh croaked from me. My hands gripped my head, and I stumbled back. "You weren't supposed to attack yet. You weren't supposed to change plans, *especially* without telling me…"

"We thought it best, considering how you'd grown to enjoy your time with the princess."

"You fucking thought wrong," I spat. "Now they're…" I couldn't even finish saying it. "How long have we been here?"

"We've journeyed a day south. We hope to reach the border tomorrow eve—"

I was off and running to the nearest horse. Untying it from the tree, I jumped on, spurring it into an all-out gallop.

"You cannot return! Their soldiers might be there or worse, hunting for you."

I didn't care, and I forbade them to follow. Three of them did anyway, but I lost them within the night.

It took me almost a day and many wrong turns to reach the site where it'd happened.

My heart threatened to disintegrate at the sight of the charcoal remains on the dirt road. Scraps of burned wood lay amongst the ash and debris. And then I saw them, tied to two sycamore trees with my sword between them.

My parents. Or what remained of them.

The growing thunder of hooves vaguely registered, but I was beyond caring or capable of hearing much over the struggling beat of my heart.

A band of Tyrelle's soldiers dismounted their horses and raced toward me.

My hands were bound, and a sack was flung over my head. "Traitorous filth." A glob of spit splattered against the flimsy material covering my face, some seeping through to my cheek.

"You're no king of ours," a rough voice said.

A whistle pierced the air as I was shoved, my bound hands

attached to a rope. It didn't bother me. I had a knife in my sleeve and the power to burn through anything.

"Don't even entertain the idea. I'll end you before you can summon enough fire to roast a leaf." I knew that voice, knew who had the power to kill instantly. "Let's move."

I dared ask, "Zadicus?"

He didn't answer, but I knew it was him. "I didn't kill her," I said to him. Though I had no idea where he was, I knew he'd hear. "I'd never…" Words failed me as the thought of not seeing those blue eyes again tripped my feet. The horses began to move, and I lurched forward, obviously tied to one as I was forced to keep up. "Zadicus, you know I wouldn't, that I could *never*, harm her."

"Hush, filth," the one with the rough voice said. "The queen lives."

Those words almost shattered me on the spot.

I stumbled, my arms tearing on rocks as I heaved myself up with my knees and elbows in relief. "She lives?"

Laughter rang out. "Your forced excitement is no longer needed. Your plan failed."

It didn't. The king was dead. That had been my only plan in the end, second to ensuring Audra's safety.

My steps quickened, and it was all I could do not to shove the guard off his horse and take it for myself—to race toward the kingdom and lay eyes upon her.

She lives.

I urged my magic to settle and simmer and allowed them to drag me to the castle like lost cattle overdue for slaughtering.

The queen lives.

When the sun reached the highest point in the sky, we arrived.

I hadn't known what I expected. Rotten fruit. Cussing insults. The city, normally abuzz with frantic life, felt vacant. I couldn't see much through the mesh covering my face, but I could feel it.

It was as though no one was even outside at all.

The soldiers dismounted, and I was led almost blind through

the castle halls, and then down, down, down to the bowels of the monstrosity that once housed the cruelest king this land had ever seen.

The sack was pulled off, and then I was shoved inside a cell and left there under the watch of at least twenty guards. "Try to burn your way out," Ainx said, unsheathing his sword. "I dare you."

I wasn't moving. I wasn't going anywhere. Audra was going to be brought to me, and once I explained… Her heels clicked over the ground in time with the booming of my heart.

And there she was, all silken ink-black hair, red painted lips, high curved cheekbones, and eyes as blue as the midsummer sky.

Her lithe frame carried her closer, but it was her empty eyes that rendered my mouth dry. Gone was the wonder she'd so often shine upon me, the unfettered, amused adoration that would send a charge of lightning striking through me.

There was nothing there.

"Did you send for her?" she asked.

Ainx nodded. "Mintale, General Rind, and Alya went as soon as we received word."

Audra nodded, then stepped back.

I wanted to ask who she was sending for and why. But it was all I could do to breathe as I let my eyes roam every inch of her body, checking for injury. "You're alive."

At that, her eyes simmered, her lip curling. "Disappointed?"

Shocked, I laughed. "What?" I shook my head and gripped the bars. "Audra, there's so much I need to explain."

"We know all about your family's botched plans to take my kingdom for their own." She turned and walked away. "To rid it of myself and my father, and the blight we supposedly put on this land."

Ainx sneered at me.

"I didn't want you dead," I said. "Never." She had to know that.

Her laughter was a broken, dusty chime. "Save it. We all know lies when we hear them."

Then she left, and I paced the confined space for hours until she returned. When she did, Truin was beside her, carrying a basket and what looked to be a pail.

"Audra," I begged.

"You know what I need to do." She wouldn't look at me as she said it. "I cannot have someone commit a betrayal of this magnitude in my hands and not trial you for all you have done."

"So trial me," I said, desperation growing. "I'll explain everything."

She smiled at the book Truin began riffling through. "You seem to have forgotten one important detail, husband." She might've been smiling, but her eyes were again vacant. "Only monsters reside here." Truin sat down, not with a pail, but with a small cauldron. She then dug inside the basket beside her, opening jars and tiny sacks. "We see wrong," Audra continued. "We act swiftly and accordingly."

She had to kill me.

I'd known it a possibility when they'd collected me from the outskirts of the forest, yet I never truly considered that she would.

And I had no idea how or if I could stop her.

"Leave us," she said to the guards.

They looked from her to me as though they'd protest, but they knew better and filed out.

Truin didn't so much as glance at me while she mixed something that smelled like vomit and poison in the dented cauldron.

Audra wouldn't look at me as she slowly paced behind Truin. "You have two choices, my prince."

"Your king."

She raised a brow. "As I was saying, you have two choices. To drain. Or be exiled."

I swallowed, wondering if I should fight her on this. If I should heat my hands enough to melt the bars and grab her by the nape to force her to listen to me.

As though she could hear my thoughts, her eyes collided with mine. And I knew, staring at the endless ice-veiled depths, that it would be futile.

Going against her would prove her right when I so desperately needed to prove her wrong.

"Did you or did you not plan to take my kingdom for your own, to assassinate me and my father, via the arrangement of marriage?"

She and Truin waited. "I did," I admitted, "but—"

Audra raised her hand, looking at the ground. "Choose and choose quickly, you have five heartbeats."

I couldn't. I had to. Two impossible choices… or perhaps not.

If I were to be sent to The Edges, then I could find a way back. I could find a way out of there or get a letter to her, explaining everything.

I could do none of that if I were dead, and the betrayal, what my family had done and tried to do, it was all too fresh for her to hear anything over the sound of her turbulent feelings.

But no one left The Edges. The only way out was by royal decree—which rarely happened—or death. It was akin to living imprisoned, but with some freedom, if you could ignore a lot of the scum that called it home.

I was now a king. She could strip me of my title but that didn't change what or who I was.

I'd find a way back. Only when the time was right.

"The Edges," I said.

Audra nodded. "Very well. Guards."

They filed back in and unlocked the gate to my cell. "Hold him down."

I frowned at them, then Audra. "What? Why?"

"Quiet before I decide to rid you of your tongue." She walked closer, and with a slight tremble in her hand, she tipped up my chin. Her mouth lowered to mine, and a sigh filled with relief so potent, I thought half my soul left my body to enter hers, coated her lips.

"I loved you," she whispered, her lips ghosting over mine.

I tried to reach for her, but my bound hands and the three guards on either side of me, pushing my arms and shoulders down, prevented that. "Silk—"

"Shhh," she crooned, and before I could fully open my eyes, that pungent aroma was gliding down my throat.

I choked and sputtered, trying to spit it free.

Her magic snapped my mouth shut and forced enough air inside my nostrils to push it down my throat. My eyes went wide, pleading, riddled with questions. *What have you done?*

She simply stood there, her expression now raw and open, exposing what I'd done to her for all of half a minute. Then everything went dark.

And I woke up in a different life.

Audra

Silence hollowed deep within the large, doom-stained expanse.

Not even the dripping of leaking pipes or stalactites could be heard above the thunder drowning my ears.

"So you see," Raiden said. "You see now that I never wanted any harm to befall you. Ever."

I unstuck my tongue from the roof of my mouth, unable to look at him as I croaked, "But you did. You did want me dead." I wasn't sure how I could move past that. He hadn't known me at the time, but how far into our relationship had we delved before he had that change of heart?

I was afraid of learning the answer. Afraid of it being too late to matter, or early enough to change everything.

"Silk," he said, voice rough and wet. "You need only look at me, and I mean really look at me, and you'll know. You'll know I love you. That I could never do that to you."

I stared at his boots. *You're no better than the scum beneath our nails, the shit stuck beneath the soles of our boots...*

"Love means nothing in the face of what is right and what is wrong." I hopped down and rounded the table. "And that which is gray can only be ignored for so long."

"You cannot kill me. You couldn't then, and you can't now." He didn't sound so sure of himself, though. "If you still love me, then we both know it's an impossible task."

I stopped and fluttered my lashes in his direction. "Then perhaps I do not love you."

Footsteps sounded out in the entry chamber. Guards began to argue before the gate was opened, and Mintale hurried inside.

A glance at me and Raiden, and he swallowed. "Majesty, you need to see this."

"See what?" I snapped.

Mintale's face paled further by the second. He stretched a hand to the exit. "Please."

I looked back at Raiden, whose brows were pinched as he watched Mintale go. When his eyes met mine, I looked away and lowered the gate behind us.

"What is it?" I hissed, moving up the stairs. "If this is an attempt to make me change my mind, you're wasting your time. I cannot make exceptions because of—"

"We've received word that an army bearing the Sun Kingdom's sigil marches northward."

My palm hit the wall to aid in keeping me upright. "How long do we have?"

"Three days." His jowls wobbled. "At most."

I followed him to the highest tower, where we stood on the turret and used the scope to search the horizon.

There, tiny specks in the far-off distance moved. I turned the scope, sending it down the line of specks, and felt my blood turn to ice. "How many?"

"Our scouts estimate seven hundred, maybe more."

NINETEEN

"And what of the city?" asked one of the generals. "We cannot have most of our soldiers gone and leave the people without protection."

I set my empty teacup down. "We have them leave."

"Where would they go?" Azela asked.

I pondered that for a moment. We couldn't bring every citizen of the city and the neighboring provinces behind the castle walls. It would trap them if we were defeated.

"The mountains," Didra suggested, pointing at them on the map. "We tell them to leave and head between the mountains, through the pass to the sea."

"The young and the elderly might not make it in the cold and over such treacherous terrain," I said.

Mintale brushed his fingers over his moustache. "We could have the furbanes fly them over."

"They don't take well to strangers," I reminded him.

He sighed, then sipped his tea as if it were a shot of liquor.

The wind roared against the windowpanes, rattling them. Snow flurries drifted through the air, floating toward the ground.

I wished Ainx was here. Practical, unflinching Ainx. I tapped my nails over the edge of the map where the Gray Sea sprawled. "So we bring the young and the elderly here. If trouble comes, we leave some soldiers to help them escape via the tunnels in the dungeon."

"They were sealed half a millennia ago," Mintale said.

"So we unseal them." I sat back and steepled my hands.

Nods and murmurs of agreement arose. Azela took notes on her parchment. "I'll have that underway by morning."

"If magic was used, come find me, and I'll see what Truin and"—I glanced at Truin to my left—"I can do."

More nods and still, my chest felt too tight.

"I say we take the long way around," Dervin, one of the younger generals, suggested. "Give us the element of surprise."

A smooth, deep voice entered the room. "This is war, not a game. You cannot have an army of at least six hundred soldiers surprise anyone at this late notice."

Dervin gaped at Zad, then stuck his nose in the air before looking back at the map.

General Rind failed to hide his smirk behind his tea.

A bouncing sensation shook my stomach, that tightness easing somewhat, as our eyes met. The lord drifted through the room in his crimson and black coat and removed his gloves. But it was the sight of the male who entered after him that had a smile blooming on my face. "Welcome home, soldier."

Ainx bent at the knees, smiling briefly. His neck was bandaged, and he moved as though he was worried his head would topple off his shoulders, but he was here.

Azela gasped, and I watched her struggle to contain her relief as a few people clapped.

I cleared my throat. "Azela, please show Ainx to his quarters. I'm sure it's been quite a journey for him."

Ainx's gaze slid to me, wary and guarded, but I said nothing and refocused on the map while she escorted him from the room.

"We march straight to them," I said, my finger following the steep slope of the city and the roads that wound through the villages and valleys and forests beyond. "No pretenses. Lord Allblood is right. This is war, and it's too late to try to outsmart them."

A hush descended over the room, sending shivers skating up my spine.

Zad stood to my right, over by the arched window, with his

arms crossed over his chest. I didn't look at him. I had no need to when I could feel his presence and those keen eyes upon me.

"My queen," a young male spoke up, so young I hadn't yet learned his name. "Do you think we will win?"

One of the soldiers seated by him tried to shush him. Raising my hand, I tilted my head at the pup. "Your name?"

His throat bobbed as he sat straighter, bony shoulders pulling back beneath dark curls. "Euwin."

"Euwin," I repeated. "Do you think we will win?"

"I-I don't know," he admitted, frowning.

I sighed and pushed my chair back. "Well, neither do we."

We adjourned until the morning, and I tried to escape the eyes I felt boring into the back of my head, the heat that encapsulated me with every step closer he gained.

I made it to the hallway that led to my rooms before he finally decided to act.

My waist was wrapped in his arm, and then I was against the freezing cold window, the sill digging into my rear as he loomed over me. "You dare to run from me?"

"Did you see me running?"

His lips tilted, fingers reaching out to tuck a tendril of hair behind my ear. I felt that touch like a feather drifting over every sensitive place. "I saw you hurrying."

I raised a brow. "Why not just ask me to wait?"

"Because," he said, his mouth moving over my cheek to skim above my jaw where the two jagged scars decorated it. "I rather like chasing you."

My pulse began to skitter, my hands reaching for his hard chest.

He licked the puckered skin, and my knees quaked. "I miss having you in my bed."

"I couldn't stay forever," I said, hating how soft the response was.

"You ran from me then, too."

"I had to leave," I reminded him.

"Without a goodbye?" His mouth found mine, and I pushed at his chest.

"Goodbyes aren't necessary when you know you'll eventually see whomever you're leaving."

He straightened, staring down at me with a crease between his brows. "Eventually."

I moved around him and headed for my rooms. "Thank you for coming."

"Audra." A quiet yet firm demand.

"What?" I turned to face him.

He took five long strides and gripped my cheeks within his hands, searching my eyes.

"Stop it." I shoved him away.

"You still have not killed him." His tone reeked of disbelief, his eyes shining with disappointment. "That is why they're coming. For him."

"I know," I growled. "You needn't remind me like I'm a child."

The smirk was back, only more cruel than I'd ever seen. "We both know you're most certainly not a child. But…" He backed me into the doors, voice laced with velvet soft aggression. "What are you then? A queen still in love with the asshole who conspired to destroy her?"

"What I am is none of your concern." I sent a wave of wind at the doors, stepping back and slamming them shut on his granite expression.

He banged on the wood. "You know that's not true."

Then he was gone, his footsteps fading down the hall.

※

With heavy limbs, I hauled myself from my bed, where I'd spent most of the night staring at the ceiling, wondering if Zad would let himself in.

He never did, and then I wondered where he was sleeping, for he surely planned to stay until we left.

Then I wondered if Raiden now had enough sense of self to access his magic. If he could summon enough to break out, get past the guards, and find his way to my rooms.

Then I wondered what would happen if he did.

Would he kill me once and for all? Or would he try to insist he loved me?

Either way, as I ate blueberry porridge alone in the dining room, I decided it was best to ignore him and the ever increasing problem he posed.

Zad too. I had bigger ones to worry over.

"Any word on their whereabouts?" I asked when Mintale entered, tugging at the lapels of his coat.

"It's estimated they will cross the border before noon tomorrow." He helped himself to some tea. I set my spoon in the bowl and pushed it away. "They don't seem to be stopping more than once a day to sleep, and even then, it's only for several hours at most."

Truin bobbed her head at the door. "Good morning, my queen."

I flicked a hand at the formality, and she smiled, crossing the room to take a seat beside me.

I sipped some tea as she rearranged her skirts and eyed the rows of now cold toast. "Have some."

She didn't need to be told twice and began slathering jam over two slices.

"If you'll excuse me, Majesty. I'm needed in the guest hall," Mintale said. "There was a skirmish with some staff this morning, and they broke your great-grandmother's vase."

My brows crinkled. "A skirmish?"

His lips wriggled as he tried to contain his smile. "Over catering to a certain male, I believe."

My chest caved with my next breath, and Mintale left the room.

Truin laughed and patted my hand.

I scowled. "What's so funny?"

She took her hand back to make some tea. "You. For someone incredibly hard to read, you wear every emotion possible when it comes to those two males."

"Excuse me?" I coughed and quickly drank some more tea.

Truin flicked her yellow-blond hair over her shoulder, then finished chewing a bite of toast before saying, "You know very well who I'm referring to."

I said nothing and stared daggers at my cooling tea.

She lowered her voice. "Though I do have to ask, what are you doing to yourself?"

"Isn't that obvious?" I asked over the lip of my cup.

Truin brushed some crumbs from her gray linen top as her eyes danced with amusement. "Perhaps, but tell me anyway."

"I'm torturing myself." I placed my empty cup down. "It's not much fun, so I cannot say I recommend it."

Truin laughed, and I dragged my finger around the rim of the porcelain. "He remembers."

"I heard."

I looked around the room, but there were no guards. They were busy readying for our journey and recruiting any city folk who could handle a weapon to protect the city. "He told me his version of events."

Truin swallowed, a harsh sound, then sipped some tea to wash down the bread. "He remembers that far back?"

"He hadn't told you?"

She shook her head. "No, but I haven't seen him in a few days. Gretelle has been checking on him while I tended to the influx of orders I'd abandoned."

"And what has she said?"

Truin stared down at her toast. "That he was growing less confused by the day, and he'd stopped throwing up." She looked at me then and leaned closer. "Granted, this type of thing doesn't occur very often, suppressing ones memories, but I didn't think…" She trailed off, but she didn't need to continue.

She'd thought my plan would wind up being nothing but wasted time and would only serve to unbandage damaged wounds.

"If I'm being honest, I didn't truly think it would work either."

"Love," she said. "It really is the strongest power of all."

I snorted. "That or I'm simply a determined bitch."

Truin laughed as I left her to her toast. "You're never simply anything. But what will you do now?"

"Nothing. We're off to war."

Before I could leave, she said, "Oh, and Zadicus slept alone. I heard the handmaids fighting over who got to tidy his room after he left for the training yard."

Steam tendrilled toward the ceiling, wafting off my skin as I unfolded the towel and swept it over my body.

I'd never experienced war. Never had I known what it was to battle for your very life until some weeks ago. Though I'd been trained for it, the unpredictable tide that rolled for us all had every one of my breaths counted.

Raiden. This had all started because of him. Though I'd be a fool to place the blame solely on his shoulders when really, it began with my father.

That didn't mean I trusted him. I could never trust him again. But I wondered if perhaps I could end him swiftly and soundlessly. Let it be done. Only, even if I did, I knew it wouldn't end there.

A howl wrenched the air, echoing off the mountains behind the castle.

Time jumped with unrecognizable speed when you were heading for what might just be your doom. Maybe I'd been heading toward it my entire life, and that was why I felt somewhat resigned to it. Not to die, but to ride into battle, to immerse myself amongst the flavor of hatred and death.

Peace could only last for so long without all-out resentment and long-buried feelings eventually clawing their way to the surface.

I'd contemplated going to the dungeon, but all day long, I was taking my time and doing everything else I could think of instead. And now, nightfall had arrived, bringing with it a shirtless lord on my bed.

I kept the towel around me as I sat before my dressing table and began brushing my hair.

Mint and cloves filled my lungs with every swipe of the bristles over the damp strands. "I believe we've been here before."

"A different time," Zad murmured.

A glance in the mirror to the left showed his eyes on me. "Is it, though?"

He lifted the pipe to his lips and wrapped them around it, his gaze probing.

I sighed and set the brush down, then pulled the lid off a pot of lavender and vanilla bean lotion to dab some over my face, neck, and arms. "Will you be returning to your room?"

"Do you want me to?"

I wasn't sure what I wanted. "We're not fucking if you choose to stay."

Zad huffed as I stood and draped the towel over the chair. He kept his eyes on mine as I traipsed over the soft rugs and patches of cold floor between them, then climbed inside the bedding. "You think me interested in only one thing?"

I turned to press half my face into the pillow. "We never speak of you. It's always me."

He was silent for a few minutes as he finished smoking his pipe. I watched the light from the night sky break through the window, robbing some of the shadows of their souls.

"Did you think I was too self-serving to notice?" I asked when he remained silent.

He set his pipe on the nightstand, then shifted to gaze down at me. "You've been to my home; you've met my family, my friends…"

I stared up at him. "Some of them. And as much as you probably love all those things, you never speak of her." I paused. "Of Nova."

He did not flinch at the sound of his dead wife's name, but he did draw a harsh breath. "What would you have me say? That was a different life."

"That may be so, but I'm no one's bandage or distraction, Zad." My stomach clenched. "Obtaining more power won't ease the longing."

Mirth, quick and gleaming, lit his eyes. I frowned, unsure what he found so amusing.

He sank down further until our faces were almost touching. "I do not speak of her because it does new love no good to speak of old love."

My frown morphed into a scowl, my eyes and heart burning.

Zad's mouth curved, and he reached out to ghost his thumb over my bottom lip. "If you want to know something, you need only ask." His eyes dropped to my mouth, following his thumb's caress, then moved back to mine with a softness that wasn't present before. "I have nothing to hide." Honesty rang clear in his voice, in his eyes, and in his touch.

A strong arm wound around my back and pulled me close, long fingers trailing the indent of my spine until his hand was buried in my hair. "The games end here." His words danced over my lips. "At this embrace, at this touch of my lips to yours, I swear to you"—he kissed me, hard, soft, and swift—"what is left of my heart is yours."

My next exhale faltered. I took his mouth and held his face tight to mine as something wet rolled over my cheek. He caught it with his thumb and groaned as my leg hitched over his hip to keep every part of him touching me.

When he tore away, his lips all over my breasts, hands feasting at my stomach and squeezing my hips, I panted, "I said no fucking."

His wicked laugh pounded through me, driving my need for him higher as he spread my legs. "I'm not going to fuck you." His tongue swiped through my center, and my head flew back. "I'm loving you. One delicious inch of skin at a time."

TWENTY

STILLNESS. IT ARRIVES IN THE HEART OF FEAR.

In the stampede of horse hooves galloping across memory-laden terrain. In the sweat gathering at the brow of my second in command. In the flexing groan of leather gloved hands. In the clanking of arrows tucked inside quivers, awaiting their prey. In the dragging beat of hundreds of hearts, wondering if they shall meet our makers or go home to live, to love, another day.

I felt plenty of those things, but what I did not feel was fear.

I had neared death more than many in my short life, and never, not once, had I encountered the trepidation of finality.

I would live another day.

Those with blackened souls did not perish. They continued forward, carrying their misdeeds and scars like that of overgrown shadows.

A curse for the blessed. The dark would never be granted true rest.

Allureldin and its neighboring provinces had been evacuated, save for a few traders, shop owners, and aging folk who refused to leave and instead, boarded up their windows and barricaded doors.

It wouldn't stop what was coming for us should we be defeated, but none of us had the heart to tell them that. Let them slather ointment over a gaping wound if it made them feel better.

I only hoped they knew how to run.

We headed south to try to meet them in the valleys of Densbow, where a better chance for victory on flatter terrain might be achieved.

On his stallion, Zad rode alongside me, and my thighs clenched at the sight of that sinful mouth. Bristling, I looked away when he smirked.

He'd asked me to stay behind. After shattering me three times, he thought I was spent enough to suggest such a thing. I'd ended up fucking the stupid right out of him—Raiden and my useless, conflicted heart be damned.

Mintale had stayed behind, as well as Ainx, who was not impressed but wasn't well enough to ride that far again. He'd been tasked with assisting the soldiers from the castle rooftops, overseeing the archers who were at the ready should we be tricked and anyone tried to invade.

We would soon discover we had not been tricked.

After camping in an abandoned village overnight, we woke to news that the Sun Kingdom's army was mere miles away. I suppose they'd heard word of our approach, so they hadn't stopped.

I trailed my finger over the doll with a missing eye, the small white bed with faded purple knitted afghans creaking beneath me.

The worn wooden floor protested as Zad's boots came into view.

"Perhaps we should've brought the furbanes."

"You would never forgive yourself if something happened to Van." Affixing the last of his armor, he crossed the room, slipped the doll from between my hands, and set it gently upon its home on the wicker dresser. "Come, my queen." He held out his hand. "We've a war to win."

I watched those long fingers enclose around mine. He pulled me to my feet and took my face in both hands. Capable hands, calloused hands, magical hands.

We'd curled together in this little girl's parents' bed. Too tired to play and too wired to sleep, he'd held me, his breath tickling the top of my head while I'd gripped his arm and listened to him tell me made-up stories about the family who lived in this tiny cottage.

My hands glided over his cheeks, and I rose onto my toes, my eyes closing as I rested my lips against his. "Thank you," I breathed.

"For what?"

Releasing him, I just smiled, and backing away, I began to braid my hair.

Outside, Zad was talking with two of his friends over a map as everyone mounted their horses and pulled down tents.

A blond male nodded at me. I remembered him as one of the lord's friends who helped rescue me and Berron. Landen. "Good morning, Majesty," he murmured.

My boots thudded down the two steps of the cottage. "That remains to be seen."

"Kash," the other said with a dramatic bow.

I inclined my head, taking in his blue-black hair and dark onyx eyes. Peering back at Landen, I noted the specks of silver in his bronze eyes. "Interesting."

Both of them watched me with a calm I knew was forced.

Zad took my things to Wen, fitting them in the satchel attached to his saddle.

The other two males ducked their heads, but I heard them snicker.

I didn't care. I moved between them and climbed onto Wen, then directed him through the ranks to the edge of the village, where Azela and Rind were waiting for everyone to fall in line. Displeasure crinkled Azela's features.

I tightened my hands around the reins. "Ask me to take the rear and I'll gut you."

She laughed, shaking her head as Rind whistled four times, indicating our departure.

Zad found me as we left the valley and entered the forest, riding hard to try to avoid having too many obstacles at our backs. "You need to stay back."

"Don't you dare," I said once the next village came into view beyond the trees.

But the army that awaited us just beyond the village had my breath quaking and my hands pulling at the reins, slowing Wen's pace.

"Goddesses' save us," someone said.

I'd have punched whoever it was, but it was all I could do to keep my eyes fixed on the horizon teeming with warriors.

As far as the eye could see, red and gold moved in a steady nearing wave.

The silence became a drumbeat in my chest, then Rind and Azela roared, swords raised, and the rest followed suit as we charged.

We collided in the middle of the valley between the forest and the village, no words exchanged, no acceptance of any demands or chance for surrender.

Grunts and screams and cussing filled the air as blood and oxygen mixed and tainted every inhale. Horses and soldiers fell, some hard enough to cleave the earth, as a royal of the Sun Kingdom jumped from his horse onto the ground and caused cracks to open.

I watched a soldier scream as he and his horse disappeared into the gaping crevice.

"Audra!" Zad was yelling at my right. "Shield yourself."

"They have no shield," I shouted back, meaning my own army. There was a time and place to be selfish, and this was not it.

"They're also not queens of an entire continent, nor can they be," he gritted. "Shield."

I did as he said, knowing he was right but loathing it. I could've sent a bubble of air around all six hundred of us, but that would leave me with little ability to do anything else and would empty my reserves within a few hours.

And for as inexperienced as I was, I wasn't so naïve as to think it would all be over in time for afternoon tea.

Blood trickled from a soldier's face as I fought him and his comrade, and then his head exploded.

I shot a glance at Zad, but he was busy fending off another royal jumper with a battle-axe.

And still they came, in groups of two to one, cutting our numbers down faster than we could've ever predicted.

My blood became pure thunder, rumbling against my skin with each confrontation. There were hundreds more than we'd estimated.

"We don't surrender," Zad growled, his sword arcing through the air to remove someone's head. "We don't give them what they want. Release it," he urged.

Exhaling, I nodded. I imagined filling heaping pails from a black well and tossing them high into the air. My fingers curled as my anger scorched hot and cold at the same time. The sky darkened, and lightning streaked across it.

And then it rained.

The few distracted warriors were easy kills, even more so as I beckoned the storm to leave as quick as it'd arrived. Swords and axes and daggers clanged, and when their arrows began to fly once more, I sent a burst of wind for them, turning them all around.

Our soldiers took advantage of some of the shocked and cut them down as I sent their arrows back and more than a dozen Sun Kingdom warriors fell.

Knowing better than to get carried away, I inhaled impossibly deep while knocking down a screaming warrior as the rain stopped and the clouds parted, giving view to the hiding sun.

As we fought on, the screams seemed to collide into a never-ending roar, fracturing the sky as the sun began to fade.

As though it wanted to leave early and not bear witness to such horrors.

I rode to the front, shield still in place, when I saw Azela tumble from her horse to the damp, blood-puddled grass. The beast raced through our front line and disappeared.

She fought her assailant off as she laid upon the ground, wincing, but another moved on her before she could get up. My sword pierced through his ribs, finding his heart, and I gritted my teeth as I forced it up through his shoulder. My hand and arm shook with the effort.

I swallowed, my throat dry, fearing how long it would take

before magic became useless—before most of its users were useless, too drained to even lift a weapon.

Grabbing my hand, Azela swung to the back of my horse, and we raced to the rear lines where more people were falling. She grabbed a thoroughbred before it could join her horse in the village and stuck a warrior in the jugular before he could take her head.

Again and again, I sent their arrows back every time they came for us, but only some of them found their mark, thanks to their gigantic golden shields.

I had to stop when we became so mingled, black and silver mixing with red and gold too much to be sure I was taking out the enemy. I wiped blood from my eye, spurring Wen over a crevice in the ground, and found Azela once more.

"We cannot win," she panted, her eyes, one of them swelling, taking in the overwhelming sea of red amongst us.

I was about to agree, to search for Zad, when a burst of light blinded.

Three male roars sounded, Zad and his friends slaughtering their way through stunned warriors.

"Who did that?" I asked no one.

Azela had gone, and even the warrior before me, who'd had his sword dancing toward my leg, hesitated at the flare of light. I took the opportunity to end him by emptying his lungs, and then I moved onto the next.

Soon after, Zad came into view, his arm bleeding and his friends fanning in different directions. "What was that?" I asked him.

"What?" He kicked a fallen warrior in the neck when he tried to get up.

I growled, slashing at a female whose dagger skimmed my arm. She folded as I drained her lungs too. "I'm not stupid. Was that their power, or one of ours?"

The way he refused to look at me, brushing sweat and blood from his brow, was answer enough.

But I remembered the stillness, their eyes, and I realized what it was and who it belonged to.

Faeries. His friends… not royal after all.

The Fae were thought to be nearly extinct after my father decreed they were a threat to our society. With the agreeance of the Sun Kingdom, no faerie were permitted to enter or reside in Rosinthe. Any that dared to remain were hunted and killed—or worse.

I didn't have the luxury of staying shocked for long as another wave of warriors crested the small knolls on either side of us.

Zad groaned. "Fuck."

"Uh-huh." We were surrounded.

I slit a soldier's throat, and gore splattered onto my cheek as Zad caused another head to explode.

He looked at me after, then at the battle crying warriors who were thundering toward us in the middle of the valley. "You need to go." His sword cleaved through someone's face, then he turned back, eyes pleading. "Please."

I shook my head, riding away from him before he could try to do something stupid, like save me.

I got as close to the front lines as I could when it happened.

Fire arced across the grass in two even lines, stopping soldiers in their tracks so fast that some of them fell into the flames. It roared and flared, licking toward the sky and jumping into the Sun Kingdom's paths when they tried to run around it.

My heart was a drum beating in my throat as I watched those golden flames dance and felt their heat creeping beneath my armor.

We were caged animals, penned in.

Everyone stopped. Even the injured who were capable squinted to the growing fire, looking for its owner.

Zad's gaze met mine from across the field, the gold of his eyes glowing with questions I couldn't answer.

A few wrangled breaths later, I didn't have to.

"The king," some of the Sun Kingdom's warriors cried.

They then began chanting as the male on the back of a gray dappled gelding galloped over the plain, right through his legion of loyal traitors, and through the flames.

They parted for him, closing before anyone could follow. An extension of their master, of the very male himself.

His skin gleamed with perspiration. His chest heaved as he slowed and raised his hands when my soldiers moved forward, swords bared and their eyes bouncing back and forth between us.

Raiden's throat bobbed, and those iridescent green eyes roamed over me, concern and relief etched upon his face and evident in his voice. "Even covered in gore, you rob me of breath."

PART TWO

UNCAGED LIES

TWENTY-ONE

I WASN'T SURE WHERE TO LOOK, WHAT TO DO, OR HOW TO even breathe properly.

Raiden's soldiers, blinking and dazed, while others crying, backed up, retreating and regrouping, leaving our lines separated once more.

Slowly, as if he knew, even with his army behind him, that he could still die, Raiden came forward.

"My queen." The words were not words, but breath with no sound.

I tore my eyes from his curving mouth, glaring. "Seize—"

"Now, now." Raiden tutted. "We both know what will happen if you finish that sentence."

A low snarl entered my ears.

Zadicus.

A glance at his tense frame, coiled tight and ready to explode, didn't offer any help.

"Stop," he said between gnashed teeth. "Any closer and I'll end you, your precious army be damned."

Taking in the sight of Raiden, free and smiling amidst the bloodshed, I reached out, my hand resting over Zad's arm.

Raiden's eyes fixed on the touch as he came to a stop, his nostrils flaring. "Been busy, my queen?"

I ignored that. "You need to surrender."

"Or what?" he said, the softness in his gaze replaced with dancing arrogance. "You cannot kill me without killing yourselves, and you know it."

Looking at Zad, I found his eyes on me, but I couldn't glean anything of use from them.

The male in him wanted Raiden dead, but he also wanted me alive. "We leave," Zad murmured through tight lips.

Raiden laughed, gruff and short. "Does he make all your decisions for you now?" I clenched my teeth. Raiden flicked his eyes to Zad, snarling, "It would seem you finally fucked, I mean slithered, your way to the very top, my lord."

Zad bristled, but I held up a hand, cutting off any retorts he might have made.

The soldiers and warriors around us began to grow restless, and I blinked at Azela when she approached.

Lips thinning, she nodded.

"Fall back," I said, staring straight at Raiden but speaking to my people. "Bury the dead and gather the wounded."

A low hum eased my fraying nerves as movement and voices filled the valley once again. Albeit much quieter than ten minutes before.

"Okay, I'll play."

Raiden's brows rose, as did his lips.

"What is it you want?" I asked of the traitorous king before me.

He swiped a hand over his bearded chin, huffing out another laugh. "Many things, my queen. You, back in my bed, my children filling your womb, and peace, of course"—he gestured around us to the soiled scenery, death still floating upon the stained air—"for all the land."

Zad growled, and I felt his rage smother like a protective, bristly blanket. "You forfeited the right to any such desires when you betrayed our queen."

Eyes trained on me, Raiden ignored him. "You and me, Audra. We fix this, as I'd always planned for us to."

I could scarcely breathe, trying to absorb all that was happening here. All that would now change, or go unchanged, thanks to his escape.

"Over my rotting body," Zad said.

"I'll take great pleasure in arranging that. But for now, I must take my leave." Raiden clutched the horse's reins, clucking his tongue, and they turned. With a heated look at me, he then swung his gaze to Zad. "All in good time, my lord. All in good time."

"Wait," I said, unsure why.

"Oh?" Raiden stopped his horse. "Are you to join me?"

A shocked laugh barked free. "No. I am to kill you."

He held out his hand. "Then by all means, you must accompany me to have that chance."

Staring into his eyes, I found he was being dead serious. "You really did lose your mind."

"You're worth insanity." With a sigh, he glanced at his army, who were awaiting orders, then grinned at me over his shoulder as he rode off. "I'll be in touch, *wife*."

We could do nothing more but watch him leave.

I did nothing as my soldiers and his own tended to their wounded and began to disband.

"Majesty," Azela said, startling me when she approached and touched my arm. "We're leaving."

Raiden and his people soon became blobs beneath the sinking sun, but he knew, he had to, that I was watching.

Turning Wen, we slowly joined the others. Zad was at the front, overseeing our route home, and he refused to look at me when I neared.

⚜

Exhausted and confused and a myriad of other things no one could aptly name, we rode through the night and set up camp the following afternoon in a small village a day's ride from the city.

The weather was that of spring given our distance from the capitol, but campfires were still lit to boil water, clean wounds, and cook skinned animals that'd been killed on the way in.

After seeing Wen to the stables outside a tavern, I left him with the guards, instructing they feed him and wipe him down with a tone that had them snapping into action immediately.

I'd have done so myself, but the lord's silence and inability to so much as look at me since we'd parted ways with the escaped king had irritated me to no end.

I found him inside, rummaging for liquor behind the wooden countertop with two of his Fae friends. When I should broach that I knew what they were, I wasn't sure. It was up to me to decide their fate, and I wasn't in the mood to bother with such matters right now.

I snatched a stool and tried to infuse some warmth into my voice. "My lord."

He poured himself a whiskey, then capped the bottle and returned it to its home.

As if sensing the brewing tension, the few other soldiers in the room made their way outside. His friends, however, just wandered to the farthest corner to take up a game of darts.

"Zad," I hissed, slapping a hand down beside his drink.

He picked it up, tipped the entire lot down his bobbing throat, and then shook his head. "What?"

I blinked, sitting back on the stool. "What do you mean, *what?* You're ignoring me."

"How lovely of you to notice." He poured another, throwing it back immediately.

"I didn't know he'd escape."

"Well, he has." He again placed the bottle of whiskey away, then finally, gave me his golden eyes. "And now we will all pay the price."

His tone hinted at more than one price. "We might have been dead if he hadn't shown up."

A gruff laugh barked from him. "Now you have gratitude for the bastard?"

I swallowed, unsure what I was feeling.

He seemed to notice that and sighed. "You should sleep. We all need to sleep."

Walking to a door at the end of the bar, he opened it and began marching up the stairs.

I followed, racing after him, and caught his hand before he could enter an empty room housing a single bed. "Stop it."

"Stop what?" A tremor wracked his hand, and he pulled it away.

"I will fix it, but for now, we count ourselves lucky the bloodshed seems to be over."

Staring down the slant of his nose, he licked his lips. "You're no fool, Audra."

My brows crinkled. "What do you mean by that?"

Stepping closer, he lowered his head, whispered words hitting my cheek as his eyes bored into mine. "It means you set this up. You have your husband back. And now"—he took a step back, his eyes never leaving mine—"we must all hold our breath while we await what comes next."

"Nothing is going to happen." Not at this point in time. "We might still be vowed, but I don't know what to believe. I don't trust him, but I do trust that if he wanted me dead, he had his chance and he didn't take it."

"You are still vowed," he repeated, and the way in which he'd uttered it, with such low vehemence, stilled my breath.

We were still vowed. So where did that leave me and Zad?

"I must not rank very high on your list of priorities," he said. "If this new problem has only just occurred to you."

"Don't," I said when he turned his back to me, about to leave.

His hand wrapped around the brass handle, his shoulders shaking as he exhaled. "I cannot do this with you right now."

Then he was gone, the door closing in my face.

For untold minutes, I stood there, staring at the dirtied door, wondering if I should use what little I had left to break it down and get to him.

I decided against it.

It had only just transpired. It wasn't fair he already acted like some snarling beast over the outcome of a situation that had so recently tied a noose around our necks.

I found some unused laundry water readied in the small room next to mine, which housed cloths and aprons and other miscellaneous items, hanging from lines hooked into either side of the walls. It was freezing, but that didn't matter. It was fresh, as though someone had prepared to wash the garments next to the three pails but was then told to leave.

In nothing but leggings and a silk camisole, I crept out of the room and found two guards stationed at the top of the stairs.

Garris, his arm in a sling, jerked his head, being sure to keep his eyes trained on my face. "There is a room for you to your left, Majesty."

I didn't bother saying I'd already guessed as much. "The horses?"

"All taken care of. A few had to be slaughtered due to injury."

"How many?"

"Three. Maybe four come morning."

I winced. "And our people?"

"We're not yet certain." He shifted, then cleared his throat. "We presume at least a hundred and sixty or more losses, and a few more are sure to follow."

I stared, then blinked and nodded, heading to the room he'd mentioned and closing the door.

Inside, there sat a twin bed by a window with filthy gauzy curtains, and a chipped dresser against the far wall. Other than that, it was bare of belongings. Whoever stayed here had wisely taken them with them when they'd fled.

The bed squeaked when I sat, and I listened as voices were slow to fade outside the window and downstairs.

One hundred and sixty gone. More to follow.

I'd known the loss would be grave, but to actually have it happen…

It was quite possibly one of the most stupid decisions I'd ever made, bringing Raiden out of exile.

And also one of the smartest, as I thought about what could've happened if he hadn't shown up and blown everyone's plans to the darkness. Perhaps we could've found victory, but at a cost that would make it unbearable to celebrate.

Still perched on the bed, I stared at some chalk drawings done by a child on the wall, when voices traveled up the stairwell outside the room. They filtered into the small hall outside and crept beneath the thin wood of the door.

"You cannot, she will kill her."

"He will only grow weaker as each hour passes. Do you have any other ideas?"

"Stop it," someone hissed. "Fuck what she wants. She won't even know if you hurry up and quit yapping."

"Now's not the time to let your hatred show."

"Whoever said anything about hatred?" a male said. "Her father has killed so many of us that it is not hatred I feel, but a bone-deep need to seek retribution."

"Enough," another voice said. "Cool your shit, Kash. The walls have ears."

"So let them hear."

I would've rolled my eyes if I weren't so tired. They stayed planted on the wall as they prattled on. "... bring her in already."

My head tilted, and then a feminine laugh echoed before they shushed her. "Will it hurt?" a woman asked. "I've heard it feels good."

"You heard right," one of Zad's friends said. I stiffened. Landen. "Don't moan too loud."

A door closed on her next bout of giggles, cutting them off.

I marched across the room, flinging open the door to find four sets of blinking eyes on me. "What are you doing?"

Kash's lip curled. "The same could be asked of you." Landen kicked him, and he cursed. "My queen."

With my eyes narrowed, I tried to read their closed-off, stiff postures. "Would someone be so kind as to tell me what is going on," I said. "Right now."

Kash licked his teeth, and Landen sighed. "The lord needs some… assistance."

"Assistance," I repeated, frowning. It dawned then, and I felt my stomach fill with cement as I turned for Zad's room.

Landen raced after me. "Majesty, please. I'm afraid we cannot allow you to interrupt…"

I rattled the door to no avail. It was locked. Then I started banging. "Zad," I shouted. "You open this door right now or darkness help you."

Silence, except for one of the faerie males at my back, who tried and failed to muffle his chuckles.

Well, I'd tried to do the respectful thing. As it so often happened, it got me nowhere.

With an enraged thought, the door splintered, collapsing into pieces on the beaten wood floor.

Utter silence.

No laughter now.

Seated on the side of his bed, the lord watched me, paler than usual, with an expression of patent boredom upon his etched features.

The girl stood beside him, her teeth sliding over her lip, looking uncertain, then quickly bowed when she realized who I was.

"Who are you?" I soaked in her petite frame, the golden curls spilling over her chest, and the pale blue summer dress that'd seen better days.

"Merrin, your majesty." My brow lifted, and she hurried on, "My family's camping in the woods nearby, and I was told the lord of the east needed—"

"Shut up and leave."

Without a moment's pause, she scampered out of the room. I followed, saying to my two guards and the asshole males who were biting their lips, "Leave us."

Garris protested, "But my queen, we still need to be—"

"Keep watch from downstairs and see that the lord's…" I trailed off on purpose, being sure to meet Kash and Landen's eyes, "*friends* stay outside."

Landen swallowed, but otherwise, the two just stared with blank expressions before finally heading downstairs.

"Was that really necessary?" Zad asked, though there was no humor, no inflection at all, in his tone.

I walked over and seated myself beside him on the bed, curling a leg under me, the other hanging to the floor. "You dare to bring another female to bed while I'm in the next room?" I reached out to grab his chin with a firm grip, my nails denting his skin as I turned his head to me. "You must take me for…" At the sight of his eyes, which were dulling to a buttery yellow, and the shadows pillowing them, I paused.

I paused, and I realized I was an idiot after remembering the violent, extreme ways he'd used his blood magic. "You were going to feed from her."

His hand folded around my wrist, swallowing it whole. "I wasn't—"

"You were." I found this new horror almost as bad as the one I'd thought was taking place moments ago.

"Darkness' sake, Audra." He dropped my hand to lay back on the bed, his eyes closing. "Do you ever let anyone finish their sentences?"

"When they have something useful to say, yes."

"You're a brat."

I blinked. "Oh, I'm the brat?"

"If you'd have let me finish," he said, eyes still closed. "You'd have heard me tell you I wasn't going to feed from her."

I felt my shoulders sag, and then I frowned. "Then who would you have fed from?"

"There are some females at home in the village who've offered should I ever need to." With a sigh, he continued, "Or I don't at all and just wait it out."

"Wait it out?" I made a mental note to make sure these females knew to never visit him. "How long does it take for you to…"

"Refill?" he offered. "A few weeks, depending on the severity of the exhaustion."

I sat with that a while, watching the harsh rise and fall of his chest.

He was still in his battle leather. Blood crusted it, as well as his hair, being that no one had the opportunity to bathe properly yet.

That didn't matter.

Crawling across the bed, I hovered over him until he opened his eyes. "Use me."

"No."

I balked. "Why not?"

Reaching up, he tucked some hair behind my ear. "You are a queen."

I nodded, my eyes fluttering at his whispering touch as words rolled off my tongue without warning. "Your queen."

He stilled. His brows lowered as he stared, eyes flickering between mine, gaging and assessing. "You will tire easily over the coming days, having spent a lot of your own power."

"I'll be fine." I lowered my head, brushing my lips across his.

A heated exhale fled him, and then his hand wrapped behind my head. He flipped us, his tongue sweeping into my mouth as I clutched at his cheeks.

Tearing away, he read my eyes once more, and I nodded. His lips returned to mine for a brief but toe-curling kiss, firm and then tender as they drifted to my chin, then my neck, his tongue leaving his mouth to skim the curve of my shoulder.

A muted scream faded into a gasp as he ran his hand down my side, and his canines pierced.

I struggled to breathe as he drew blood from my body into his, a soft groan heating my neck.

My eyes closed, and I grasped his hair, and then I moaned as his hand entered my pants.

His fingers were gentle in parting me and matched the slow stroking of his lips and tongue at my neck.

Within seconds, I grew dizzy with a growing ecstasy I'd never encountered before. The sound of my leggings and the lace beneath tearing snapped off the walls as cool air met my shifting legs. I lost track of time, of my own breathing, and of our whereabouts as he slowly suckled at my neck and brought me to orgasm, over and over again.

I had a fleeting thought, strong in potency, to destroy anyone else he'd given this to.

Just when I thought I couldn't stand anymore, he was rising above me with blood red lips and eyes alight with foreign hunger. "I have to."

I opened my thighs in response and welcomed him inside, wishing I hadn't wrecked the door after all.

But this was not the lord I was used to bedding.

He moved in hot, quick, fluid jerks, his groans a beastly rumble that echoed through the room. Beneath the haze he continued to envelop me in, I watched him, hypnotized by the bunching of sinew and muscle and the sheer animalistic power oozing from every inch of him as he ravished me.

His mouth dragged over my chest, teeth grazing my nipples. I moaned, long and loud, unable to help it as he gently bit one and planted himself deep. With a grumbled curse, he filled me again, his harsh breaths dampening my breasts.

My breathing had only half slowed when I thought we were done. And then I was face down in the bedding as he entered me from behind, delirious and shaking.

On and on it went until the sun began to trace the shadows in the room, and my fingers did the same to his muscular back as he lay over top of me, sweating and breathing heavily.

I was nearing sleep when he finally spoke, his voice rough and hoarse. "Are you okay?"

"Perfect," I yawned. For I was, though I knew it was likely I'd think differently some hours later. "Are you?"

"That depends."

My legs, still wound around his waist, tightened. "On?"

"Did you mean what you said?" He rose, his hair, freed from its tie, falling around his face. "My queen." He pushed some hair out of mine, studying me with bright eyes and flashing teeth. "Eternally my queen."

Wiggling beneath him as he thickened inside me, I smiled. "Yes."

Horses shifted and snorted, singing birds and quiet chatter drifting to the trees as I walked outside the tavern and made my way to the stables.

Eyes, too many of them, fell upon me before quickly darting away.

I frowned but continued, running into Azela as one of the soldiers brought me Wen.

Her lips were pinched; her eyes careful not to connect with mine as I took the reins from Markus. "Majesty," he said without looking at me, bowing low and then walking off.

I watched him go. Understanding slow to dawn, I turned to Azela. "Was it that obvious?"

She coughed, patting Wen. "Just… um, loud, Majesty."

Darkness swallow me.

I sighed. "Everyone heard?"

"I'd not be surprised if they did." She lifted her head, her uninjured eye laughing. "If I may be frank, some were making bets on whether the tavern would rock to pieces." She then added, "I heard it was raining dust."

Lovely.

My nose twitched with annoyance. With nothing to do for it, I stuck my boot in the stirrup and swung up onto Wen, determined to ignore any whispers and laughter.

Then I hissed, wincing as I tried to get comfortable in the saddle. "Oh, fuck."

Azela couldn't hold it in and burst into all-out giggles, waving her hand as she mumbled, "Sorry, I'm so sorry."

My lips curled, but I shook the smile away and headed for the growing crowd of people readying to leave. Zad was already there, his head thrown back as he laughed at something one of his stupid friends said.

When he saw me, his eyes turned feverish, but he only nodded. "Good morning, my queen."

Eternally my queen.

Words of the vow, yet they'd now taken on a whole new meaning. It took considerable effort to keep my tone aloof as I muttered, "So it is."

A snort from Landen had Zad reaching around to punch him, but the chuckling male was too quick, darting away to his horse.

I rolled my eyes and gave my attention to Garris while he filled me in on today's plans.

After a moment, I stopped him. "Where is General Rind?"

Zad cursed, and Azela looked over, her expression pained. "He was gravely injured."

"Answer the question," I snapped.

Even Landen's head lowered as a strangling silence descended upon our assembly.

If you let them see your heart, do not complain when they tear it apart.

I shoved my mother's voice away and steeled my shoulders. "Does he live?" I was glad the question was steady, almost flat.

Garris answered. "No, my queen. He requested we leave him."

On the battlefield where many noble idiots like himself wanted to die.

I nodded, and we started to file out.

The leather of my gloves creaked, my fingers clenching and unclenching the reins as I remembered the times Rind had snuck me sweets while on duty. The unflinching loyalty he had for my father and our family—when it was not deserved.

He'd had no other family, no partner, no offspring. He'd served us for his entire, long, tedious life. It shamed me to wonder if it had contained much in the way of joy at all.

Zad rode quietly beside me, shielding me from requests and questions, but somehow, his presence was all the comfort I needed. Words were often completely useless.

Zad's silence ended a few hours later when we'd stopped at a lake to wash and allow the horses to drink. "We need to talk."

"About?" I splashed water over my cheeks and rubbed.

He threw a glance around, but I'd chosen a nice cozy spot on the opposite bank, wanting to be alone. It was bad enough we'd had to travel for days, let alone having to endure so many people's company, their aches and scents and grief and exhaustion.

I needed to be alone.

I gave him my eyes when he didn't respond and found him staring at me. He searched my face, seeming to be waiting for something.

He'd be waiting a while. "What?"

His lashes dropped to my neck. You couldn't see the marks left from his canines, but I could feel them. I was willing to bet he could too, somehow. "I want you."

I fell to my ass. "You had me so many times I lost count."

Crouching beside me, he reached over to brush his fingers along my jaw. "I'll always need more."

His touch was feathers and velvet, but I pushed it away. "We need to get home." I'd heard, and had now seen firsthand, that the need for those with his magic to fuck after feeding was brutal. But it could last for days, depending on how drained he'd been. "Besides, I didn't even know Rind was dead. I was so caught up with you and your silent tantrum."

Zad grimaced. "I hadn't known either. The number of fallen are still being accounted for, Audra."

"That's beside the point," I said. He knew what I meant. It didn't matter we hadn't been extremely close, or that he was mixed; Rind was still family.

He nodded in understanding.

I looked at his pants, where he was tucked and hard against his leg, as a different worry infiltrated. "You won't seek another."

"I've no need. I can control myself."

"Did we... enough for that to be true?" My lashes fluttered as my eyes swam up his huge frame. "Or are you merely placating me?"

Before I could meet his eyes, his hands were gripping my face, tilting it up for his mouth to open mine and his tongue to enter. "I wouldn't dare lie to you," he said, gruff and terse, pulling back just enough for his words to sink between my cracked lips. "I'm fine. Just a little hungry."

"But you can wait."

In answer, he kissed me again, this time with his lips only, soft and sigh inducing. "I can wait."

"What did you need to talk about?" I asked when he moved to the water and rolled up his sleeves. "Or was that it?"

He stared down into the murky blue depths, then said, "I no longer wish to talk about it. What of the king?"

"I have no idea." He plunged his hand into the water, trying to catch a fish, I realized when he did it again. "All I know is that I need out of this marriage." Zad stilled at that. "Only, I'm not sure how." He knew what the rules were, what I was up against.

"He won't agree to it."

I knew that. "He committed treason. He has to."

"It's gone too far for it to be that simple anymore, and you both know it." His hand broke through the water again, and he cursed as he missed a darting black blob.

"What am I to do, then?" I hated saying the thought aloud, but I needed to do something.

Raiden had one-upped me, bested me, for the second time. I was no longer sure if I was merely an idiot who'd been tripped by love yet again, or if he was more cunning and calculated—more dangerous—than I ever could have known.

Zad's voice was soft as he said, "I'm honestly not sure, my queen." He plucked his hand out of the water a few seconds later and turned to me with a squirming clay fish within his fist. "But for now, we eat."

My nose crinkled, and I laughed as the fish flapped about and wiggled free, landing on the grass and bouncing.

Zad growled and raced after it, stomping on it before it could reach the water.

"I prefer my fish not squished, my lord."

Unamused eyes shot to me, and I laughed again.

TWENTY-TWO

Raiden

Mosquitos flitted and cicadas sang while I stood on the highest rock overtop the waterfall and inhaled. My shoulders quaked as I drew as much air as I could inside my lungs, then slowly let it leak out.

Home.

Only, it felt foreign. As though I wasn't supposed to be here but someplace else.

The oasis rimmed by treacherous desert called to me, settling something restless deep inside me, but it failed to soothe the abstract rhythm of my heart.

Palm trees, vines, and flowers in every color known to Rosinthe sprouted and crowded in any space and crevice available. Coupled with the copious ponds and pools and the river that raced underground, and the illusion of paradise was unparalleled.

But it was all magic.

None of this could exist here without magic. The binding of our essence that swam through our genetic bonds, our blood, and fed the land with its presence alone.

Questions. So many questions had been thrown at me.

For a kingdom who'd fought so tirelessly to retrieve their king and seek revenge, not one person seemed to care much about my well-being, rather only for what happened next.

"Will the queen rule with you?" my advisor had asked as we'd set up camp a day's ride from Merilda.

Lem, one of my warriors, had cursed. "She's a monster," he spat. "She drained Corra and Cid."

That had raised my brows.

I'd known Audra had drained someone while locked away in her dungeon, but I hadn't known who.

Cid was a miscreant anyway, but Corra… Before she was a soldier, she'd once served in my harem. She'd served me since I'd discovered I had pubic hair and a deeper voice.

That stung, but not as much as when I'd asked for the why.

"Why? Because they'd kidnapped her, of course," Spane, our healer, had said. "Corra, she always had been clever, that one."

"Oh, but don't worry, Majesty." Meeda had laughed and added, as if forgetting I had love, quite a large expanse of love, for the queen, "She and Cid burned the darkness out of her face, I heard."

Kidnapped. They'd kidnapped my queen.

She'd been mutilated by those I trusted.

I'd then shocked them all by stating, "Then isn't it lucky they're both already dead," before walking to my tent.

The sight of her on that battlefield had just about stopped my heart, blood speckled over her face, her eyes wild.

They wanted peace. She gave them ruin.

A monster indeed, though wrath had never looked quite so beautiful.

Arms wrapped around my waist from behind. I would've jumped had I not heard her approach. "My king."

I closed my eyes, knowing I shouldn't but unable to help myself.

For months, I'd gone without another's touch, but Eline wasn't just another.

Once upon a time, she'd been everything.

My hands slid over hers, squeezing before I turned around and took her bronzed, lightly freckled face within my hands.

Her dark green eyes welled as her lips wobbled, and she

gazed up at me as though she could scarcely believe I was standing before her, let alone touching her. "My Little Lion."

A nickname I'd given her when we were children that'd followed us into every adventure since.

There'd been many, too many, and shame filled me for losing them. For allowing them to leave my memory at all, let alone bury them as deep as I had.

A shame so much worse threatened to drown me when she rose onto her toes to press her lips to mine.

Nectarine and spearmint reached my taste buds, and I lost myself to it, to the taste of her, and kissed her back. Once then twice, groaning on the third as I wrenched myself away.

The waterfall at my back loomed, but I skirted around Eline as her hand gripped mine.

I stilled, knowing what was to come, but made no move to stop it.

Her other hand collided with my face, the ring she wore, a gift from me on her eighteenth birthday when I'd promised her more than I should have, ripping into my cheek.

I gritted my teeth, opening my eyes just in time for her to strike the other cheek.

"Fuck," I hissed, snatching her wrist. "Enough. I am still your king."

She spat at my feet, sneering up at me. "You're just a male who failed me. Who failed our kingdom."

"Little Lion," I started.

"Shut your filthy mouth." Her breasts heaved behind the golden wrap she wore underneath a shimmering silver kaftan. "You were supposed to kill her. Allureldin was supposed to be ours."

I opened my mouth, but I had nothing to say. I couldn't explain. Not when the explanation would hurt her beyond anything I could repair.

Tugging her hand, I pulled her close, infusing as much remorse into my voice as I could. "Eline, things happened…"

"You promised me." Her eyes grew wet again, her tone grittier. "You promised me it would be us, and then you fucked it all up." Her eyes traveled up and down my body, taking in the clean linen pants I'd donned after bathing in my private pools. "What in the darkness happened?"

Air whistled into my mouth, drying my throat as I dragged in a steadying breath. "The queen happened."

I waited, watching her golden brows crinkle. All too soon, understanding creased her beautiful features. The water cresting her eyes spilled over while she stood frozen, staring at me as if she couldn't believe any of this were real.

"Tell me you don't."

I feigned confusion. "Don't what?"

Her tone hardened. "You know exactly what I'm talking about."

My lips parted, a thousand apologies about to roll off my tongue, when she staggered back. "So not only did you fuck her, but you fell for her, too?" Those last words were almost screeched, her head shaking. "H-how? She's a monster. A cruel bitch who killed your parents." When I remained silent, she added, "And Corra and Cid and some of our best people too."

I knew whatever I said would do no help, only harm, but she wouldn't let me get away with saying nothing. "She did what she had to do to survive. She's not her father."

Her eyes raked me up and down, her words harsh and guttural. "Neither are you, *failure*."

She made sure to sway her hips as she traipsed barefoot into the throne room.

Patts cleared his throat, and I didn't care to know how long he'd been standing behind the swaying gauze covering the exit outside. "Not tonight."

"Very well, Majesty. Food awaits you in the kitchen should you desire more." With that, he bowed and disappeared.

Meal after meal had been forced my way since entering the kingdom, and I'd already eaten more than I could stomach.

Turning back to the waterfall and the small rainforest that surrounded it, I ran a hand over my too-long hair. I'd decided to sleep outside, climbing into a nearby hammock, but then I wondered if Eline would kill me in my sleep or if I even cared.

A stupid thought. Petulant, given all I'd done and been through to make it back here.

With that in mind, I dragged myself through the sand-sprinkled halls and up the sandstone steps of the highest tower to lock myself in my chambers. I'd hardly looked around the large, rotund space. It was all the same.

As though their precious prince had never really left. As though he'd never dare allow himself to fall for the wicked winter queen he'd been sent to kill and would journey back home the same male he'd been when he'd first left.

I had to wonder if I'd disappointed the lot of them, and perhaps myself, by not living up to their ideals.

I heated the locked doors to a scalding temperature should anyone have a key and then dropped to the monstrous-sized mattress dressed in fresh white linens in the center of the room.

TWENTY-THREE

Audra

Vanamar's nostrils blew a gust of hot wind onto my hands and wrists as I fussed with his reins to secure them. "Oh, stop it. Do you want them chafing?" Another huff, and I smiled. "Exactly."

Once his saddle was secure, I unlatched his enclosure and led him out into the cavernous hall of the stables.

"You always speak to him as if he were your friend."

I climbed up his back, throwing my leg over and situating myself comfortably in the saddle. "That's because he is."

Zad straightened from the stable door he'd been leaning against, then strolled toward Cook's enclosure, a black and silver temperamental female. A low snarl rippled through the cave, but the lord only smiled and procured a large turnip from his pocket.

Cook stilled, then crept forward. Her tail thrashed into the walls, causing dirt to rain as her excitement grew.

"You'll lose your hand if you don't throw it in," I warned. "She has little tolerance for strangers." Especially males, I didn't add.

"Sounds familiar," Zad murmured, and the affection in his voice mirrored that of his eyes when they flicked to me.

Something kicked inside my chest, then a stable hand rushed over. He blinked rapidly as he watched the lord of the east hold out his hand, balancing the turnip upon his flattened palm.

Cook lunged, and Zad pulled back, tutting.

Huffing, the beast shimmied closer, her long purple tongue sneaking out to lick the air.

Again, he moved his hand forward, and then with lightning speed, he plucked it back when she moved too fast. "Easy," he said, voice soft. "Gentle, or nothing."

I raised my brows at that but chose to keep my mouth shut.

I loathed to admit it, but I was a little nervous. I'd grown to like those hands of his a little too much.

Finally, Cook seemed to receive the message, and her handler and I both stared in stupefied amazement when she licked the turnip from Zad's outstretched hand, then backed up to chew it to pieces. "Good girl," Zad crooned.

If I thought he was done here, I was wrong. "What are you doing?"

"What does it look like?" Unhooking Cook's saddle from the wall, he walked inside her enclosure. The beast stood frighteningly still as he ran his hand down her flanks, then began to prepare her for flight.

I waited, knowing she was going to snap at him eventually, but it never happened.

The handler, still open-mouthed, turned to me as Zad led her out of her pen. "Uh, Majesty?"

I flicked my hand. "It's fine." Eyeing Zad, I said, "If the lord thinks he can best a beast, who are we to tell him not to?"

Zad's shoulders shook with silent laughter. Mine did too, when he tried to mount Cook and her head flung around, teeth snapping dangerously close to his knee.

After staring at him a moment, Cook relented, begrudgingly allowing him to climb onto the saddle.

"I was hoping to be alone," I said, moving Van to the cave's rear entrance.

"Sorry to ruin your plans."

Outside, on the lip of the cliff, the wind kicked back my hair, of which I'd forgotten to braid. "You are no such thing."

"You're right." He threw me a roguish smirk, then clicked his tongue, spurring Cook into a run.

My eyes widened as she raced toward the edge, rock crumbling beneath her clawed feet, and took flight.

They dipped, so low that my breathing halted, and then, with a laugh that thundered through the skies, a laugh that never failed to steal my attention, they rose and circled the mountain.

Smiling, I urged Vanamar to follow, remembering a time when I'd first heard that laughter.

※

"Momma," I whined, yanking on her soft dress. "I want to go."

Her hand landed upon my brow, gentle, protective, and reassuring. "We must stay for a little while longer, Audry. Remember what I told you?"

Her bright blue eyes peered down at me, and I sighed. "No talking. If I need to answer someone, do so carefully."

Her smile was more of a frown, but her fingers running through my hair put me at ease as the music started. People laughed and began to dance, moving about the room.

Father soon took her from me. He didn't so much as look at me as he hauled her to their thrones.

I looked around, finding Truin against the far wall talking with her grandmother.

Her funny eyes fell upon me, filling with the smile that arched her pink lips. Her fingers fluttered, and I frowned, unsure if I should wave back.

I decided against it and winced when someone trod on my foot, my silver slippers no match for giant grown-up feet.

Bristling, I snuck outside where it was quieter and rounded the courtyard until I found the moss-infested fountain that was never paid much attention due to it being out of sight.

The perfect place to hide.

Seated on the dusty ground, I leaned my elbows on the rough edge. My fingers skipped over the water, my eyes tracking two lonesome carp swimming through the murky little pool.

A croak echoed, and staring across the water, I saw a dark green toad seated upon a lily pad. It stared at me with bright yellow eyes. I stared back, willing it to go away.

It croaked again, then splashed into the water.

"The ground is no place for a princess."

I startled, glancing up at a huge male that knew my mother. I'd seen them talking sometimes at these fancy gatherings my father liked so much.

I couldn't remember his name even though I'd been introduced to him some months ago, only that he was a lord. He looked it, with his finery and that regal sparkle in his amber eyes.

"A princess can do whatever she wants." My eyes scrunched closed when I realized I'd already done the wrong thing. I'd opened my mouth when I shouldn't have.

The large lord only laughed. My eyes fluttered open at the throaty, deep sound, and I blinked up at him.

He looked behind him when a bunch of males stumbled past the walkway, pushing and shoving one another as they sang and hollered. I think he sighed, and then his long legs brought him closer until I had to crane my neck right back to see his face.

I couldn't see much from where I sat, and it wasn't comfortable, so I stopped and leaned back over the edge of the fountain to watch the fish.

I wasn't positive he wouldn't hurt me. Not when there was an odd energy to him that screamed I should run from and to him at the same time.

"You should be inside," the lord said, taking a seat near my hands on the lip of the fountain. "Where your mother can better keep an eye on you."

"She can't do that when the king is always taking her away."

"The king?" His voice rose a little with interest.

I almost cursed, my cheeks heating. I was such a fool. "My father, I mean."

The lord was silent for a long while, his hands clasped together between his bent knees. He smelled nice, like mint and sunny winter mornings.

"Why are you out here?" I asked, not caring that I'd broken another rule. If he were going to hurt me or take me to my father for punishment, it would have happened by now.

"It's stuffy in there."

I laid my head on my arm, watching his hands. They were quite large. I was willing to bet they'd be as large as my face. Then again, I was only ten summers old. "I like the cold, too."

I felt his eyes on me then, but I didn't want to meet them.

He was too big, too intimidating, and I was growing tired.

The noise emanating from the ballroom began to fade, my eyelids falling.

I awoke in someone's arms, my eyes fluttering open to find a bristly chin. It wasn't my father. He never carried me, and he always shaved.

The smell of winter sun and mint invaded. It was the lord. "My momma?"

A lumpy thing in his neck moved before he said, "She'll be in to see you when she's finished seeing guests." I yawned, struggling to keep my eyes open. "She asked me to make sure you found your way to bed."

Inside my rooms, he laid me on my bed, dragging my blankets up to my shoulders as I turned onto my side and mumbled, "What is your name, lord?"

"Zadicus," he said. He then took a seat in the chair by the fireplace.

I heard the sound of a book opening and pages turning, but I collapsed back into sleep.

※

We landed upon a large crag that overlooked the lower portion of the city, where cobblestoned streets faded into dirt lanes and dense woods.

With the furbanes tied to a thick tree, Cook looking unimpressed as Vanamar kept encroaching on her personal space, we took a seat on a lichen-speckled rock.

"How did you know my mother?"

If the random question bothered him, I didn't notice. Staring down at the kingdom, Zad took his time to answer. "I never bedded her, if that's what you're wondering."

I had wondered that on the odd occasion. It wouldn't exactly be uncommon. Royals were known not to give a shit when it came to lust and love. If they wanted something, they took it, regardless of who the person was to someone else.

The woman from The Edges, Raiden's betrothed, came to mind.

"She knew Kash."

That brought me up short. "Your friend Kash?"

He nodded.

Volatile, cruel smiling Kash. "In what way?"

With his lips twisting, he then smirked at me. "In every way a female and male can know one another."

I looked away, remembering what he'd said about me in the tavern. "He wishes me dead."

"He wouldn't dare." His voice was drenched in winter cold vehemence. "He knows what you…" He stopped.

I gazed back at him. "Knows of what?"

Zad's teeth grazed his lower lip, his eyes bright on mine. I withheld the shiver that tried to wrack my entire body. "He knows what you mean to me."

Swallowing, I ripped my eyes from his. "So they were together."

"Some think they linked, though I've never been able to get a straight answer from him."

"What?" I wheezed.

Zad plucked at some grass. "They'd known each other since she was a child. For a time, Kash lived in the village your grandparents attempted to raise your mother in. Before the king laid eyes on her and had her brought to the castle once her womanhood had arrived."

The wind gathered my hair, blowing it sideways and causing it to tickle my lips. I shoved it back, tucking the ends into the neck of my tunic, for all the good it would do. "She… so she loved him?"

His voice was rough. "Until the day she died."

I closed my eyes, feeling goose bumps rise upon my exposed skin, and breathed. I'd known my mother had suffered at the hands of my father for hundreds of years, that she had done her best not to procreate with him, and she'd been beaten half to death for it.

But I hated that I hadn't known this. The regret of never truly knowing her, not for all that she was. The female I knew was timid but strong with eyes that seemed to never close for fear of what might happen. She was song, and she was whispers, loud in ways that covered and smothered who she was. That enabled her to play my father's games and survive.

Until she didn't.

"My father hunted his kind."

Zad didn't curse or shift. He didn't seem to react at all as I opened my eyes. He simply asked, "What shall you do?"

"Nothing," I said, then added pointedly, "So long as they don't."

His eyes assessed. "You mean that."

"You know that, or else you wouldn't have dared to bring them within breathing distance of me."

His mouth curved, and he then reached for my hand to slide a small grass chain I hadn't noticed he'd been making around my wrist.

"You sicken me." And he knew I meant so in all the best ways as he lifted my hand to his sinful lips.

I laughed when his tongue snuck out, and then squeaked when he tugged me over to sit on his lap. His arms banded around me, lips warm upon my neck. "How long have you known them?" He knew I was referring to his friends.

"Most of my life. My mother knew theirs, and before she died, she asked that we look out for them."

"An exceptionally dangerous request."

"We'd grown up together, learned how to fight and fuck together—they're my brothers as much as I am theirs."

I crinkled my nose but sank into him even more. "So they won't touch me because of you."

"For as much as Kash might think he hates you, and the others are wary, I do not think they would."

It occurred to me then. "Perhaps it is not that my father hunted them and their kind, but because I am a reminder of something that was stolen from him." His arms tightened around me. "I was hers, but not his."

"I think you could be right."

"I usually am," I said and felt him shake with laughter. "How have they gone this long without someone figuring it out?"

"Many years of looking over their shoulders." Ever the storyteller, his tone held notes of affection, of a love as ancient as time itself. "They're cunning by nature, their senses more attuned to threats. It's been relatively easy since the king's men have stopped looking for them." Zad contemplated that a moment. "Which seemed to be around the time your nuptials to Raiden were being planned."

I chewed my lip, feeling the puckered smoothness of the scar cutting through the edge. "Was my father aware that many Fae parents had missing offspring?"

"Yes," he said. "Though he and his hunters weren't certain, they suspected and tortured a few good people trying to find them."

My eyes shuttered. "I do not foresee peace for me and your… brothers."

"You'll be fine," he whispered against my neck, his lips brushing back and forth over the curve.

I released the withheld shiver. "So confident."

He hummed, and I felt him hard beneath me.

Perhaps I'd ride him before we left. For now, I was content to have him hold me, something I once thought would irritate me forevermore.

My eyes wandered over the sprawling city to the hills on the other side, skirting the forests and racing rivers. Something clenched in my chest, and I tried to let it loose with an admission. "I was worried for a second there."

"Just a second?" Zad teased.

I ripped up a clump of grass, turning in his arms to shove it in his face. He ducked, of course. Cook lunged forward to eat it. "Fine. A couple of days."

"Why the reluctance to admit you love it?" He pushed ribbons of hair away from my face, clasping my cheeks within his warm palms. "It is your home."

"Because..." I paused. "Because although it's a land of great beauty, it has seen so much horror." I watched his lashes lower and rise as he stared at me. "Because of him."

His brows furrowed. "Your father."

"And now Raiden."

Zad continued to stare, the breeze curling pieces of his hair around his square jaw. I wanted to touch it, to brush it back.

Slowly, I did, and his eyelids fluttered as he sighed. "Just because something has experienced scarring horrors does not mean it is not worth loving."

My lungs cinched. "And what if it is the horror?"

His hand reached behind my head, weaving into my hair as it lowered, my lips expelling breath with his. "Then you love it anyway, and you love it twice as much."

Staring out the window of the third floor as night began to blanket the city, I pondered how to proceed with all the change that'd transpired.

I could contact Raiden and ask him to meet to discuss the future of this continent and our marriage. To see if there was a way he'd bow out without any trouble.

Remembering his parting words to me on the bloodied battlefield, I released a frustrated breath, even as my stomach quaked.

The cocky shit was probably seated in his sauna of a castle, eating grapes and drinking the finest wines while gloating about all the ways he'd duped me.

You rob me of breath.

My eyes closed as my hand reached out to meet the damp cold of the stained glass window.

I felt my blood hum and my core clench as the chill seeped inside my pores.

Was it all a lie? Or had he been telling the truth when he'd said he'd never wanted to harm me?

He had wanted to, though. From the start, the marriage had been more than a sham.

Our marriage was never more than an assassination in progress.

Hurried footsteps reached inside my dark thoughts, forcing open my eyes.

"My queen." Mintale came to a stop behind me, and I slowly turned to face him, ice now crusting the glass where my hand had rested.

He eyed it, then me, swallowing harshly. "I've some unfortunate news."

I contained a groan. "Spit it out, already."

"The girl," he said, his hands wringing. "We just received word that she's gone."

"How did she escape?" I asked again for the hundredth time.

No one seemed to have an answer.

"My queen," Zad said, closing in behind me to rub my upper arms. "It matters not right now, and only that she has."

I knew he was right. I knew it, and still, I couldn't believe it. She'd been locked in a cage. In a cage that was locked beneath the tavern. Behind a magic enhanced steel door.

Shrugging his hands off me, I moved to the table where a map was spread, pins locating all the places the guards were searching.

"It won't be enough." I lifted my gaze to Zad. "If she escaped the cellar, she will not be found."

His eyes said he agreed, but the thinning of his lips said he would scour every dwelling and forest until she was.

Turning to Azela, I asked, "Where's the bartender? Eli?"

Her head shook. "We don't know, your majesty."

I fought the urge to upend every chair in the room, the desire to tug at my hair until the sting overruled the frustration coursing through me. "Have him found and delivered to the dungeon immediately."

She left the room to inform the other guards on duty.

"If he indeed set her free..." Mintale trailed off.

"Then he knows he's in deep shit," I finished for him and turned for the door.

"Majesty," Mintale called, following me out into the hall. "We really must discuss a plan. If she is on the loose, I fear where she'll go next."

I stopped, turning back to glare at him. "Do you think me a child?"

His jowls wobbled with his shaking head. "N-no, of course not, but I have concerns for your safety." He looked at Zad for help, who was leaning against the doorway to the meeting room with his hands inside his pockets, watching us. "We all do."

Zad's stare was hard and impenetrable, but I knew he agreed.

With my eyes threatening to roll into the back of my head, I made haste for my rooms. "Notify me if you find the bartender or the girl."

"Of course, my queen."

Zad didn't follow, but he did eventually show as I was combing my hair, seated in a pale blue silk robe at my dressing table.

"You already washed."

"I couldn't relax." Not even a hot bath could soothe the annoyance festering inside me, so I'd cleaned myself and climbed out.

"We'll find her."

"And how?" I asked, dropping the comb with a clatter as I rose. "She won't be found until she wants to be, and I highly doubt that will ever be the case." My nails dented my palms. "I should've just killed her when I had the gaping chance."

Plucking up the comb, he grabbed my hand and pulled me to the bed.

I folded in front of him as he gently ran the comb through my wet strands, the silk of my robe sticking to my damp back.

I shucked it off, smirking when I heard his breathing stall, and whispered, "It just doesn't make sense. There are many who'd betray me, but Eli is not one of them. The people of this city are still here for a reason." Expelling an exasperated breath, I rasped, "The kingdom will think me a blithering fool for letting not one but two prisoners escape."

Zad said nothing for the longest time. My skin began to heat when he dragged the comb all the way down my back, stopping at the curve of my hip.

Dropping it to the bed, he shifted my hair over my shoulder and pulled, angling my head for his mouth to traverse the arch of my shoulder and throat. "I promise you, my queen, a fool is the last thing anyone would consider you." His lips pressed, his voice lowering. "We will find her, and we will ensure she meets her end."

"Together?" I asked, my thighs clenching. I opened them when his hands ghosted down my arms, wanting them between my legs.

Settling back into the apex of his thighs, I moaned as his fingers fluttered over my stomach, tickling with featherlight touches until he found me wet and desperate. "Together," he told my shoulder, his teeth scraping it.

He dunked a thick digit inside, the fingers on his other hand drifting down to my center to gently circle. "For now..." he murmured, and my head fell back, lips seeking his. His eyes were fire and ice, capable of melting me to the core with one cold, narrowed look. "You let me rid your mind of all the things polluting it, and then..." He kissed me—deep, hard, quick—and then pulled back, whispering to my lips, "You come home with me while I tend to some business."

"I'm fine here," I panted, and he stroked me, firm enough to make me jolt in his arms.

"Yes, but you're needed with me."

"Oh, am I?" I teased, seeing right through his words, his actions, and still, I tried to kiss him.

He bobbed back, grinning, and inserted a second finger. "Desperately so."

My lashes fluttered, my hips rocking over his hand. "Then shut up and convince me."

TWENTY-FOUR

I felt like a fool as I rode through the forest, headed for the lord's estate, but not enough to turn back.

In this rare case, I was happy to be one, even if it made me look as though I needed the red-haired devil's protection. I knew better, so I decided to let anyone who gave a damn think whatever they wished.

He'd stolen beneath my skin and opened festering wounds to plant himself inside as they'd healed. I was too afraid to wonder if there was a way to rid the need for him after something as unchangeable as that.

Even though I'd seen it a handful of times already, the sight of his glass-encased home still captured my breath. We thundered downhill, my braid bouncing behind me as rain began to spill from the bloated clouds above.

Stable hands and two guards rushed to the gates, opening them and leading our horses to shelter as soon as we'd dismounted.

Inside the foyer, I laughed, swatting droplets of water from Zad's sharpened cheeks. "Hold still," I said, my tone firm enough to make his mouth twitch as I reached up to brush beads of water from his curling lashes.

"It won't hurt me."

"I just like to touch them," I admitted without much thought at all. "To touch you." My cheeks filled with heat, and I turned my eyes to the water-streaked floor, marred with splotches of mud from our boots.

With a gentleness that threatened to bring water to my eyes, his fingers snuck beneath my chin, tilting it as he pressed close. His bright eyes locked with mine, messages I couldn't read trapped inside. "It's not like you to blush." I scowled, and he smirked, his free hand lifting for his fingers to smooth over my brow. "I should like to see it again."

I felt my expression blank as my limbs loosened. "A queen does not blush," I whispered.

"Mine does," he said, lowering his head. My eyes closed as I waited for his lips, but they skimmed my nose instead, the action emptying my lungs alongside his soft words. "And I fucking love it."

A throat cleared, and I pulled my head free of his grip, turning to the door where Landen stood. "Majesty." He gave an overly dramatic bow, then looked at Zad, trying and failing to conceal a smirk. "My lord. Welcome home."

Thunder cracked outside, lighting the doorway behind him enough for me to see he wasn't alone.

Zad cursed, so violently that even I startled, especially when he stumbled back over my feet, his face paling.

"Oh, yeah," Landen said, moving to the side. "You have another guest."

Casilla, clothed in a clean dress, stepped forward, and I watched in horror as her red hair changed to honey blond, and her nose and lips widened the tiniest amount.

No longer did she look like some peasant woman from The Edges. Her chin, narrowing to a slight point, tipped up, her eyes, now a vivid hazel, aglow.

She was a lord's wife.

Nova stepped forward, smiling tightly. "I do hope I'm not interrupting."

<hr>

Shouting and yelling and crashing ensued from the study as Landen and I sat in the kitchen.

Me, with my heart in my throat, speechless, and he, with that maddening crooked smirk.

"How long," I finally said, finding my voice. It was rough, but it was steady enough. "How long have you known?"

Landen leaned over the counter to snatch an apple. He inspected it, then brushed it on his cream loosely buttoned cotton shirt and took a bite, chewing loud. "Two days."

Out of all the fables and horror stories our continent had been brought up on containing faeries, one thing was true. They couldn't lie.

"She was dead."

He gave me a look that suggested I was daft.

I bristled, and he smirked again. I was tempted to shove that apple down his annoying throat and leave it lodged there. "A few pieces of clothing hanging strategically from branches upon a cliff does not make a dead lord's wife."

To that, I stood. "So you knew she was alive?"

Zad's other friend, Dace, entered then, his white hair standing in eye-drawing directions, and bowed. "Queen."

"You knew too?"

He looked at his brother, who shrugged, then back at me. "Two days ago."

I rolled my eyes, slumping back onto the stool.

Dace chuckled, snatching an egg from a bowl and cracking it open on the sink. I cringed as he held it above his head and let the raw yolk fall into his mouth.

Smacking his lips together, he tossed the shell into a small yellow pail on the countertop. "Oh, right." Swiping a hand over the back of his mouth, he grinned, his canines longer than mine but only slightly. "This would be rather inconvenient for you."

Landen scoffed, retying his long hair. "Being that you've finally decided to give our lord the time of day."

My teeth gritted. "Do not fuck with me. I'll forever not be in the mood."

Then my mouth fell open at the sound of Zad yelling, "You wanted out? Fine, but you should have just fucking said so."

Dace pursed his full lips, tapping long fingers upon the counter across from me.

"You wouldn't have let me."

"What?" Zad laughed the word, without humor.

Both males looked at me, lips pinched and brows high.

I sneered at them, and they laughed. Dace stabbed a finger at me. "You're funny."

I blinked, my tone dry. "So happy to be of service."

Nova's and Zad's voices lowered, and I gave up trying to eavesdrop

"Where's the other one?" I asked.

"Kash?" Dace asked.

"The other one," Landen repeated with a chuckle.

"The one who detests me then." I rolled my neck, unable to rid the prickling tension tightening every muscle. "Yes, Kash."

"Not sure," Landen mused. "You don't think we detest you?"

"How interesting," Dace murmured, his eyes gleaming with his smile, crawling all over my face.

I forced myself to remain still and sighed. "I don't particularly care."

Landen hummed, and I looked at him. "You don't remember?" I lifted a brow, and he went on, "The night of the burning apple."

"The night of the what?" I asked, growing more exasperated by the minute.

Dace cut in, voice low and growing deeper. "You saved him the night of your ceremony. Stepping in before Phane buried his sword in his back."

Landen shot Dace an irked look. "Save is a strong word for an…" He stopped there, lips bunching up to his straight nose, and swung his eyes to me. "But yes." His tone was more resigned than pleased. "You had no reason to do that, to stop him, yet you still did."

Stunned, I felt my eyes bounce back and forth between the two males. Of course, it was them who'd helped Zad rescue me. "Oh," was all I managed to say.

Landen angled his head, unblinking and unnerving. "You look like her."

"You have his hair, though, and his personality." Dace scrunched his shoulders, mock shivering. "Not your fault, we know, but it's still rather… unfortunate."

"You're fucking the queen?"

My gaze snapped to the hallway.

"You have no right to know or question any business of mine," Zad hollered back. "You're supposed to be dead."

"So sorry to interrupt," she spewed, sarcasm dripping. "It's only been sixteen years. You couldn't keep your vows for sixteen fucking years? We're practically immortal, you fucking asshole."

"I waited a long time before I bedded someone else even though I didn't have to," he snapped. "Because you were dead."

I looked at Dace, sighing. "You'd be wise to watch your tone."

"Oh?" His teeth and eyes flashed, and he bent forward, that sweet scent hitting my nostrils. "And why is that, queen?"

"Because," I said, leaning closer, my fingers brushing his. He flinched, and a low laugh left me before I sobered. "I'm not exactly like him." Landen cursed. "But catch me on the right day, and I can assure you, I'm far fucking worse."

Instead of being horrified, something that looked a lot like intrigue widened the faerie's eyes. His teeth took his lip, deep blue eyes dropping to mine. "Are we to fight, queen?"

Something crashed in the study. "You lying whore of a male!"

"Me? You never told me you were a changer."

"I didn't know until I reached breaking point, you ignorant ass."

I sat back. "I'm in no mood, faerie."

They both laughed and then settled onto stools as we waited for Zad and Nova to finish tearing themselves, and the study, apart.

After a time, their voices lowered, and we had to strain to hear what was being said.

Well, I had to, but I stopped bothering. Instead, I began to wonder if I should just leave.

What seemed like some cruel joke had now planted roots, and it was growing into something very real, tall, and impossibly imposing.

Queen or not, I wasn't sure I could scale it, but the thought of leaving like some wounded animal…

A door banged open. "She did, I swear to you." All three of us lifted our heads as Nova sped down the hall, a finger pointed at me. "Your precious queen is even worse than the whispers say."

Slowly, Zad followed, his hair a tousled mess, and his eyes aglow with anger. Yet weariness etched his frame, his face, his tone—as though the unexpected gift of his wife returning from the dead had aged him a thousand years.

Understandable, but seeing so still gnawed at me.

He wouldn't look at me, no matter how much I willed him to.

The Fae males stood when Nova hissed, "Zad? Are you even listening? She tortured me and made me drink my own urine. She's a fucking lunatic."

I wondered how much more I might have done had I known it was Zad she'd touched.

The thought triggered a hundred other questions, the most prominent involving Raiden, who had no idea he'd been about to commit himself to a female who was already married.

But finally, Zad gave me his attention. And the look he threw me, cold and unfamiliar, even though he already knew I'd tortured her, shattered something loose inside my chest.

Something that was too recently healed to identify.

Dace and Landen both glared at me, their eyes hot and

accusing, but I didn't remove mine from Zad. I stared back, keeping my expression blank, as he came to terms with what I'd done—and who I'd done it to.

I wasn't sorry—no matter how much anyone might want me to be—and he knew that.

After a long moment, he blinked, his jaw tight as he tore his eyes away. "Enough."

He left the room, and after a panicked glance at me, Nova wisely did the same.

Rising, I decided I'd had enough myself.

"Where are you going?" Dace asked.

I stopped in the doorway to the kitchen. "I don't know."

They said nothing as I walked upstairs and headed to the roof.

It was nightfall when all talk had ceased inside and a disheveled Zad climbed through the opening to join me.

"You won't touch me now?" I asked, when he sat upon the other end of the bench.

He didn't answer, just glared up at the moon as though it were responsible for fucking everything up.

A sickening feeling flooded my stomach, but I remained quiet, as patient as I could bear, while I waited for him to speak.

Though when he did, it was with words I'd rather not have heard him say. "You'll be escorted home at first light."

He was up and climbing down through the ceiling before I could even think to protest.

Rage, hotter than I'd felt since I'd discovered Raiden's transgressions, threatened to incinerate me. The tips of my fingers tingled. I clenched my hands in my lap, and the swaying plants in the numerous gardens around me slowly stilled.

I waited until it grew completely silent inside, assuming everyone was asleep, and then I scaled the vines over the side of the house, jumping to the grass below with a thud. My teeth clacked as a sharp pang shot up my legs. Shaking it off, I glanced around at the moon-glazed landscape, then continued. Horses huffed and whinnied as I entered the stables.

"Hey," a lone guard said, but I locked his next breath in his throat until I had my horse, suffocating him just enough to knock him out.

I did the same at the gates when two sentries appeared, but I should've known as I raced uphill and reached the trees that someone would find me.

Kash.

Spurring Wen into a gallop, we jumped fallen logs and weaved between tree trunks as thick as castle turrets. Hours passed, and still, the Fae male followed, never reaching me, but rather, keeping a short distance behind.

I knew better than to think he was worried for my well-being. No, he was stalking me for his own personal needs, whatever those would be. Revenge, perhaps. Though if he wanted me dead, he'd have surely attempted so by now.

The sun was crawling into the sky when I finally slowed at the lake skirting the exit of the woods. There would be little water until we neared the villages outside the city, and the last thing I felt was afraid.

Even though I should have been.

After hours of silence, he finally spoke. "You know what we are, yet you haven't done anything."

I hadn't heard him climb off his horse or even approach, but I stopped myself from letting any surprise show.

Taking my time to answer, I wrung out the hem of my skirts, which had fallen into the water when I'd led Wen to it. "Do you want me to?" I pressed, my emotions brimming just high enough to make me lose all sense of caution. "Do you want me to give you more of a reason to seek that bittersweet retribution?" Letting my dress fall back around my ankles, I pushed the hair that'd escaped my braid away from my face.

With a jaw harder than steel, he glanced away. "There is much you do not know, winter queen."

Kash's comment festered for stretched minutes, and when I snuck glances at him, his smirk told me he knew it. Seating himself upon a large, smooth rock, he plucked at some reeds.

I watched, mouth hanging open, as the looped stems shimmered, then grew wings and took flight.

His stare was goading, but as he watched the flying insect disappear, it turned contemplative.

I'd heard the magic of the Fae was like nothing we'd encountered before, but seeing it, even in such a seemingly small demonstration, raised the hair on my arms.

I lowered to the grass, staring at the gurgling stream of water. "My mother is gone, yet you remain here," I stated the obvious.

"We cannot go back, even if we wanted to." I flung my eyes his way and found him staring at his long fingers clasped between bent knees. "Beldine is an impenetrable, forbidden land."

"What?" I asked. "Why?"

A dry bark of laughter exited his flat lips, all the while his expression turned to stone. "Oh, how little you know, indeed."

I was beginning to tire of his presence, of this journey, and every damn thing.

I moved to get up, but Kash said, "You're a race of half Fae who've been led to believe they're descendants of two goddesses. Goddesses who never even existed."

My brows jumped, and I would've laughed if not for the serious edge to his tone and those hard dark eyes. "Excuse me?"

"I think you heard me just fine, half breed."

"I am no half breed, asshole." Getting to my feet, I stomped to Wen and hauled myself up into the saddle. I'd heard enough nonsense for a lifetime, and I hadn't the desire to hear anymore.

"You are." His tone might have been light—conversational, even—but the words were sharp. "You and all of your precious royals are half Fae who consider yourselves holier than thou. You're not of pure blood, else your ears would be more pointed for a start. You're a half breed. Half mortal, half Fae."

With only slight points, his own ears were just like any other royal.

And then they weren't.

Glamour.

Sweat coated my palms, my hold on Wen's reins slipping, as Kash let it fall.

With a gleam in his eye, he reclined back over the rock, his voice riddled with indifference. "A race who continues to sully themselves with humans, diluting your precious royal blood so that high royals can continue to hold their precious positions of power. Power you should not have. Power you abuse appallingly at that."

Still staring at the now unveiled, severe arch to his ears, I could hear myself swallow. "This cannot be true." But he could not lie. "We have our own history, and it has nothing to do with yours."

A history I'd never been sure I believed.

"It has everything to do with ours. We just wanted nothing to do with you," he said so plainly. "Think about it, I dare you."

My eyes thinned, my heartbeat a storm brewing in my ears. With a shake of my head, I readjusted my hold on the reins.

I froze when he kept talking, unable to help it. "No royal should possess the type of power you and Raiden do. That your lineage does. It was not a gift bestowed by some so-called goddess or two but an accident made by a long dead faerie queen who fell in love with a mortal."

"No…" But looking at his features, feeling his words resonate, I knew. I knew it was true. "You're saying our history is a lie?"

"What history?" he said, a little exasperated now. "You've been told minor fables about goddesses who do not exist. They never have. Rosinthe is but a sliver of land that used to belong to Faerie until there became too many of *you*, and the queen's brother soon ended our shared existence." He wore a grim tilt to his lips. "And also her existence. For when she intended to place her human plaything upon the throne beside her, our people fought back. A line was drawn, homes were lost to the ocean as Beldine cleaved a portion of the continent and forbade half breeds and humans from ever returning again."

"When?" I asked. Feeling my unease, Wen shuffled beneath me, huffing.

Kash rolled his eyes. "Some millennia ago." He came to his feet. "And without the pure source of magic given from the royal bloodline of Beldine, that they share with the land and the land with them, the many creatures, plants, and ancient trees of Rosinthe have perished. The ones that remain are all… replicas. Evolution, if you will."

I thought of the blithes, of the tisks, and of the furbanes. The fact that *we* were the half breeds, the mixed, was a startling point not lost on me.

Nor was the way Zad had not been entered into the equation of too much power. "What of Zad?"

With another smirk, he climbed his mount. "Death and life himself?" Noticing my frown, he continued. "Zadicus is many things, but he is not like us, and he is not like you and Raiden. And before you ask, of course, he is very much aware of all this." I was trying to make sense of that when he gripped the reins, and said, "So, half breed, what are you to do with this knowledge?"

"Nothing," I said, already imagining the possible ramifications, the upheaval, the fear, and the unrest. My words were too thin, too low, a croaked rasp. "Nothing at all."

Sitting straight, Kash regarded me with too dark eyes. "Very well. I suppose it would not behoove you royals," he said the word as though it shouldn't exist, and perhaps he'd be right, "to make yourselves seem… less than, now would it?"

I balked, uncaring as I blinked. "As opposed to?"

Kash laughed, and the sound was shocking in its sharp, musical quality. "Oh, you have no idea." He adjusted his tweed jacket and neck scarf, and clicked his tongue.

So many questions raced through my mind, and I found it

terrifying that I was able to match each one with the shocking explanations Kash had thrown at my feet.

My lips parted, then closed a dozen times. I bit them shut. I was burning with intrigue—with the need to know more, to ask more—but I couldn't. For now, I needed to leave this information where it belonged.

In the dark.

We rode in silence until the first village came into view, and the sun began to glow high in the sky.

"You have her face."

"My mother?" I asked, already knowing that was who he meant.

Instead of confirming, he brought his mare closer, riding almost neck and neck with Wen.

I slowed Wen's pace, and Kash pulled back, trotting beside me.

Glancing over at him, I found his eyes forward, his dark hair swept back from the wind, exposing a profile that would make any female, human or otherwise, weak in the knees.

The thought made me angry. "She was weak and stupid. You and I both know she should've left, but she never did."

"Because she didn't think she could, and then along came you," he said, bluntly. "She would never leave you."

I scoffed. "She couldn't take me with her?"

"You'd have been hunted."

I was painfully aware of that. "A shorter life spent with someone I loved might have been preferable."

"Your father would not have killed you."

To that, I snorted, uncaring how unladylike it was. "He'd have done far worse than kill me. But you're right. I'd be kept alive." I was his only heir. "Dead everywhere it counted, but alive."

Kash sat with that a minute, his eyes flicking to me a few times before he blew out a frustrated breath.

"Exactly," I said, quiet as I absorbed the sight of the castle looming far off in the distance.

"You really tortured Nova?" His tone, the question, seemed impassive.

I didn't much care if he cared. "I did." I sniffed, lifting my chin. "I've yet to figure out what her game is, but I can assure you, she is not what she seems."

Kash laughed, and I almost jerked at the dark, musical sound. "The same could be said of you." He paused. "I've known her for most of her life. You could say she's like a little sister to me." Another pause as I felt his gaze upon my profile. "Are you not afraid of the repercussions for hurting someone we care about? For abusing the female Zad loves?"

His use of present tense didn't slip by me.

If his aim was to upset me, it was working. My voice was too gentle for such vicious words. All the better to let him know I refused to be toyed with. "Darling faerie," I purred, smiling his way. "Haven't you heard?" His brows scrunched. "Monsters fear nothing. You'd do well to remember that." At my urging, Wen took off over the hills, and my hair came loose, flying behind me as his hooves sent dust-shrouded wind sailing back at Kash.

He didn't follow.

Between one village and the next, I tugged on the reins, my breathing harsh and my heartbeat erratic, booming in my ears.

I refused to cry.

I would never reduce myself to such a state over a male.

They were to be used. To be enjoyed. To be kept at a safe distance from the heart.

How many times would I need to remind myself of that before I finally fucking learned?

Sniffing, I closed my eyes, the iced breeze washing over my face as Wen trotted closer to home.

When I reopened them, I discovered we weren't alone, and I prepared to run.

"Uh, uh, uh." A gentleman with a wiry beard wearing camouflage green waggled his finger. "We have a message from your king."

I lifted my brows as his friends, a woman and a mixed male, stepped out from the gnarled cluster of brambles to join him.

"Well," I snapped, impatient and wary. "Tell me this message so I can be on my way."

The woman frowned, speaking low but still loud enough for me to hear. "What in the darkness is the queen doing out on her own?"

"Good question," the man with the beard said, stroking it as he eyed me. "We were to pass this message on to one of your village messengers." His head tilted as he no doubt took in my flushed cheeks, crumpled dress, and tangled hair. "You've saved us the trouble… but why?"

Of course, the messengers of the kingdoms loved their jobs; they not only did it for the coin it provided but for the gossip too.

"None of your business." I turned Wen to leave.

Before I could skirt around them, the woman said, "The king said to tell you he has your witch."

A ting sounded as I plucked my dagger from its sheath on my thigh.

The male and bearded man took a step back while the woman gulped, raising her hands. "Apparently, she's fine, M-Majesty. Perfect health."

"What does he want with her?" I asked through gritted teeth, alarm snaking through every nerve ending. My hand clenched around the hilt so hard, it would bruise.

"He wants a trade," the male said, rubbing the back of his neck. "You for her."

I wanted to scream. To bellow to the useless, nonexistent goddesses above.

I wanted to run from this stupid continent and never look back. But I couldn't.

The male watched me lift my dress and return my dagger to its home, his cheeks coloring when I raised my brows at him. "Send word that I'll be there by sundown tomorrow."

They all blinked, and I knew they were about to ask how. They'd soon find out.

"Run," I said to Wen, flicking grass and dirt in our wake, galloping to the castle.

We reached it within the hour, and I left him at the stables with Olin, the young stable hand blinking profusely as I ran off through the gardens and scaled the steps to the mountain paths.

Breathing hard, I soon walked inside the caves and smiled when Vanamar grumbled at me.

"I know." I shooed the handler who approached and opened his stall door. "I never bloody learn."

Van huffed in response.

"Enough of that now. I've a mission for you."

His tail wagged, and I felt the sad, dark corners of my heart pinch when his eyes shut at the touch of my hand upon his cheek.

TWENTY-FIVE

Zadicus

Entering the drawing room where my useless friends were sipping tea while listening to Nova regale them with tales from her time in The Edges, I snarled, "Where is she?"

I'd looked everywhere, had combed every corner of the estate and edge of the forest beyond.

She had to have left, but on her own? She wasn't that stupid.

But remembering the blank look upon her beautiful face the night before, I sighed.

Not stupid. Upset.

There was a time I'd thought myself incapable of ever meaning anything to her, let alone meaning enough for her to break down a door and all but throw an innocent woman out of my room.

For years, I'd been there. I'd watched, and I'd waited because darkness, she was young.

She was so incredibly young, and I struggled with that. Not with guilt since our kind did not harbor any such notions toward sex. If they'd bled and matured, and it was consensual, we did it, and we did it without a second's thought.

It wasn't that, but rather all she'd endured—all she'd been confined to and forced into being.

She needed room to breathe, to learn, and time to flourish into who she really was before she could look at me the way I'd looked at her. Before she was shackled to another commitment she might not want or be ready for.

But things had changed. Not only did she look at me, she wanted me, and such was my addiction to her, that full-bodied pull whenever she was near, that I'd hardly even hesitated. I'd selfishly thought that perhaps she could still grow, evolve, live, and I would help her.

I'd finally gotten all that my heart desired, but I couldn't figure out a way to keep it.

"Who cares?" Nova said.

None of the males in the room laughed. A wise move.

Nova stood, traipsing across the room to me. "She's a queen, Zad, and a mean one at that." Circling me, she said more delicately, "Let her return home to her dark castle. It's where she belongs." Her laughter, laughter that once lit up every face in this room, especially mine, grated. "A queen doesn't gallivant about the continent like some infatuated puppy." Her arm grasped mine as she stopped, her skirts swishing around her ankles. "You are mine, and she is Raiden's."

The mere idea of her and Raiden iced all the blood inside me.

Withholding a barrage of disgusting words, I shrugged her off. She gasped, and I left the room. I felt wretched, knowing how hard Nova had worked and all she'd been through to return home.

To return to me.

But I couldn't control how I felt to save my own life. I needed to hit something, drink something, or smoke something.

I cursed, backtracking to my study to light the pipe I kept in there, and closed the door.

Laughter broke outside the room, Nova no doubt telling another story from a time when she'd chosen to leave me.

I couldn't believe it. I didn't know what to believe.

All I knew was what I wanted, but what I wanted was gone.

She didn't know; the queen wasn't even aware just how much she'd been played.

I had to tell her… but my wife.

She was back. I'd thought her dead for years. I'd known her

since she was only seventeen summers old, and we'd vowed five years later. She was back, and I had no idea what to do with that. With her. With any of it.

Of course, I was overjoyed, riddled with relief that she was here. Alive.

But I was also sick with guilt over the fact that some large part of me, the one who'd been locked away, waiting for someone I couldn't have, hated that she was here.

Rubbing my eyes, I cursed, yanking the bottle of whiskey from the drawer and unscrewing the lid. I coughed, cursing again as I swallowed.

Inhaling deep from the pipe, I sat back in the chair, trying to relax as the scent of cloves filled the room. I needed to ease the tension long enough to fucking think.

Sleep had been a ghost until the early hours of the morning. Nova had knocked on the door of my rooms ceaselessly until I'd finally snapped at her to go away.

She wanted me to forgive her. To simply accept her return for what it was—a miracle—and be happy. She'd said she regretted her decision to leave from the moment she stepped foot in The Edges, but she couldn't find a way back.

It had been too dangerous, especially under Tyrelle's rule, and to mess around with the law during his reign was like dangling a sweet before a child.

I should know. I'd dodged his wrath for endless years, knowing that one day, if I wasn't careful, he'd peg me for more than I was. For more than a lord looking to climb the ranks into his daughter's bed.

Minutes crawled into hours, and still, she didn't know. My queen had no idea of all the ways she'd been duped. It ran so much deeper than she or I could've ever foreseen.

I'd locked the door, but such things were no match for Kash, who only had to touch something for it to break, if he so chose it.

The sun had long since set, and I was halfway through the bottle of whiskey, cloves littering the desktop as he opened the door, looking far worse than I probably did. Which was alarming. Not much rattled the male these days. "I followed her."

I straightened. My eyes narrowed, and my spine locked as I gritted, "Why?" I knew he wouldn't hurt her. Not only because of what she meant to me, but because of what she meant to the female he loved and missed with every breath he drew.

That didn't mean he would be a comforting presence to her. Far from it.

"If I could tell you, I would. It's not as though I wanted to."

I frowned. "Interesting."

He kicked an ankle behind the other, leaning against the doorjamb. "No, what's interesting is I saw her race up the far side of the city to the stables beyond the castle, then as I was riding back, I saw her again." His brows rose. "Flying over top of me."

I sat back, dread weighing every limb. "No."

Kash nodded, his eyes hardening. "Headed south. One guess as to where."

I was up and pacing the room in one fractured heartbeat, my hands scraping through my hair. A million reasons as to why she would do that filtered through my overwrought mind.

I tried and I tried, but I came up empty. Yes, she'd loved him, but that was before. "Was she with anyone?" Perhaps she'd been coerced. I wouldn't put it past Raiden to trick her into playing his games.

"She flew alone on the back of her beast."

With a growl, I stormed past Kash out into the hall, heading to the front of the house to pace some more. *Think, think.*

But I was stuck. I couldn't chase her, especially not now. She'd gone there of her own accord, so demanding for her return... I paused outside the sitting room, hearing that bird-song laugh.

"She cannot help herself, can she?" Nova kicked her feet up onto the table. "From one male to the next."

My eyes slammed closed, and my fists balled, ready to barrel through the walls.

It felt as if my chest was being set on fire. Over and over again.

I walked out, I had to, and headed straight for the trees. I didn't stop until I'd breached them. Until I was surrounded by nothing but shadows and alone with this never-ending ache that only seemed to grow.

Until I could howl and roar at the fucking moon.

TWENTY-SIX

Audra

AN ISLAND PARADISE SURROUNDED BY SAND-VEILED horrors.

As though he didn't want to land, Van circled above the clouds, giving me just tiny glimpses of the kingdom below. I let him for a time. Stepping foot in the Sun Kingdom was the last thing I wanted to do.

I wanted to go home, inhale a bottle or two of wine, and sleep. *Truin.*

I sighed. "We must."

Once on the ground, I feared he wouldn't leave me, but he'd been trained, brutally, to follow every command no matter what. "Home," I said, shielding my eyes as his wings continued to stir sand into the air. "Vanamar, go home."

With a growl that shook the sand, he rose, flapping his ginormous wings high into the sky.

He was nothing but a speck in the clouds by the time the kings sentinels crossed the sand, bows drawn, arrows nocked, and threatening to soar.

"Shoot him, I dare you."

One archer lowered his bow, his eyebrows furrowed.

My hand rose, a strong wind lifting the sand right over our heads, and the rest followed suit. Slack-jawed or scowling, they kept their weapons aimed at the ground until Van was out of sight. "Apparently, the king requests my company."

Wordlessly, we crossed the sand, the sun a ball of bright torture, causing sweat to break out over every inch of my skin.

My escorts seemed unfazed, acclimatized to the brutality.

My boots were filled with sand, its rough grains wedging between my toes. I gritted my teeth against the urge to pluck them off, knowing beneath the sand lived things that would enjoy nothing more than a fleshy snack. Even if it were a sweaty foot.

Moving swiftly, I shielded my eyes, feeling the gazes of two soldiers at my back.

The female was in front, throwing glances at me over her shoulder every few minutes.

I didn't bother telling her to quit, but I made a face next time she did, and that did the trick.

Sweeping blotches of cacti stood before the road that was covered in a thin layer of sand, aiding in marking its presence. My ankles almost sighed in relief at the feeling of flat ground beneath the soles of my feet.

We walked between bamboo huts on towering steel stands that served as lookout towers. Six of them circled the sprawling desert oasis, and at least three sentinels occupied each one, watching our every move.

Soft music and the sound of traders offering their wares soon reached my ears as the road wound into the outskirts of the rock lined city.

Lime green trees, foreign but beautiful, dotted the sandstone and brick-filled quarter, providing much-needed shade and a slight breeze.

It took longer than I'd have thought, but when people eventually realized who was within their walls, some bowed. Others sneered, and one woman even spat a wad of phlegm at me.

It landed on my boot, and I halted, my breath freezing as I stared down at it, then glared at her.

Unperturbed, she stood there with beautiful gray eyes and a hard jaw, her freckled arms crossed over her ample chest.

Before I could mutter a word, the female escorting me backtracked and whispered harshly, "Leave her. It would not behoove you to attempt to make an example of someone in a city filled with resistance."

"Attempt?" I questioned, blinking at the female with eyes so dark they were almost black. They matched her hair, which curtained her shoulders like a gleaming layer of silk. Her pink lips parted as her face paled, and I smiled. "Have no fear. I'll just be a moment."

I marched over to the woman's stall, snatched the pail of water from beside it, and washed the muck from my hands and face.

The number of eyes watching began to multiply, and I rose, perusing her cart. Selecting a stunning woven purple scarf, I dipped it in the pail, then used it to clean the filth she'd lobbed onto the toe of my boot.

Staring down at it, I nodded. "That'll do." I then tossed her soiled scarf back onto the cart, and grinned. "Good day."

Gaping, she glared as my escorts and I moved on. Dipping through the bystanders in front of me, I could've sworn the black-eyed beauty's shoulders shook with laughter.

The crowds grew thicker the closer we drew to the looming sandstone castle. Circular globs perched atop each squat but thick turret. Large rooms, I guessed, eyeing the swishing white material fluttering over the circular windows. There was no glass, no doors, I discovered, as the hill grew steeper and the courtyard, a flat expanse of rock with few gurgling fountains, came into view.

At least he didn't keep me waiting.

Within moments, he arrived, strolling out of the shadows to the top of the circular stairs of his home in nothing but a pair of linen pants and a crown.

I withheld a laugh. I couldn't remember the last time I'd donned my own crown.

A crown was typically worn at formal festivities and select life-changing events. How precious of Raiden to skip half-naked around his castle wearing the heavy metal as he saw fit.

Upon closer inspection, I noticed the gold contained inset rubies connecting with branches and snakes. The sun caught the jewels, flashing, and then my eyes caught his smile.

I reached the bottom of the stairs, and his lips tilted higher as if he knew where my thoughts traveled.

"You rob me of breath," he mouthed, then dipped and held out his hand. "My queen, welcome."

"Save it," I said and heard a few gasps from behind me.

The townsfolk weren't permitted to follow into the royal courtyard unless by invitation, but enough guards and nobility were loitering about to catch our interaction.

Raiden cocked his head, withdrawing the offer of his hand. "Come inside then, freshen up and eat."

"I'd rather not. Where's Truin?"

He nodded at the sentinels beside me. "Thank you, Meeda, Alix, Serdin."

With a low bow, they left.

"Your witch is fine." Raiden gestured to the doorway behind him, then stepped to the side, waiting. "Come."

It was on the tip of my tongue to tell him I was no pet.

Sucking in a breath, I inhaled the citrus and dirt and spiced scents surrounding me, then remembered why I was here. I'd need to keep my boiling emotions under lock and key if I wanted to leave with my witch and wits about me as soon as possible.

I climbed the steps, breezing by the smiling king, but paused inside the giant entryway.

Portraits of royals lined the walls, and baskets of fruit sat in almost every doorway where red and gold woven rugs lined the hard floor.

A man with silver hair and a flat smile bowed. "Your majesty. I am Patts, advisor to the king."

"That's nice." I crossed to a basket to snatch a glowing red apple. I sniffed it, then bit a chunk, almost moaning when its juicy fluff melted inside my mouth.

Raiden's hand fell upon my lower back, and I threw annoyed eyes at him before stepping away, farther into the enemy's territory.

I followed the rugs to a giant throne room bedecked in more red and gold with hints of silver thrown about in the form of sconces and the braided upholstery of the red-padded thrones.

"We have much to talk about."

"We really don't," I said. "You rule this side of the continent, and I the other. We meet when we have to and not otherwise."

His laughter was an insidious thing, scraping down my sweat-misted skin as he kicked his legs out before him and stepped closer. With his eyes roaming my body, he snatched the apple from me and took a bite.

It was kind of hard to avoid it. I'd done well, but eventually, my gaze lowered to the gloriousness that was his torso. Twitching muscle threatened to dry my mouth, his abs falling into a sculpted arch that gave way to the hardness tenting his pants.

Shaking my head, I lifted my eyes to his.

He tipped a shoulder, tossing the apple behind him. It splattered to the floor as he grinned. "Can't help it. Happens whenever I see you."

"Truin," I said.

He nodded. "Not yet. Allow me to show you to your rooms."

"Raiden, I mean it," I said as he turned, his bronzed back drawing my eyes. "Give her back to me. This is not a game."

With a lilt to his voice that raised the hair on my nape, he countered, "Oh, but it is, and I rather like winning."

He left, and I gaped at the space he'd occupied, my hands balling.

With no other choices available, I reluctantly hurried after him out of the room and down maze-like hallways. Up a curling set of stairs that never seemed to end, we arrived at a large circular room. I'd guessed right in my assumption of the turrets.

Only, it was evidently his room and not my own. I backed up. "Not happening."

"It is," he said with a calm I wanted to punch in the face.

My head began to swim. I needed sleep. I needed a bath. I needed a proper meal. But I needed my friend first. "What do you want?"

Walking to one of the three windows, its white gauze fluttering into the room, he tucked his hands into the pockets of his pants, staring through it. "I thought that would be obvious."

"Nothing is obvious with you."

Turning to me, he smiled, but it dropped quickly. "I want your time. A chance to explain." He leveled me with a blank expression and toneless words. "And being the beautiful, oh, so stubborn creature that you are, I knew you wouldn't give me that unless I took matters into my own hands."

"So you kidnap my friend."

"Kidnap is a bit harsh." He moved to the bed which sat in the center of the room, white linens rumpled and tossed around as though he'd had a fitful sleep or a tumble with a lover. "I did what was necessary to get your attention."

"Well," I said, drifting into the room, "you have it. Hurry up."

Raiden watched me for an unnerving moment, green eyes bobbing over my face. "You seem… more irritated than usual."

"Insults are a waste of our time."

Crossing the room, he stopped a foot from me, his scent clouding my head. "No," he said, eyes soft. "What happened? Word has it you were found riding alone toward the castle."

It shouldn't surprise me that word of that reached him faster than I had, flying across the kingdom. Gossiping miscreants. "A queen can ride alone if she so wishes."

"Not in times like these," he murmured, reaching out to skim his fingers over my cheek.

I stepped back. "Truin."

He tutted. "All in good time."

"Now," I said, throwing daggers at him with my eyes as he waded to the door.

"Bathe, rest. A meal is being prepared as we speak."

I blinked when he left, tempted to run after him out the door in search of my friend and a way out.

I looked at the arched hole in the wall, steam wafting from it, and sighed.

The bathing room was a small but luxurious space, filled with musky aromas and an array of washcloths to choose from.

I didn't trust I'd remain alone for long, so I washed quickly, cursing when I realized I had nothing clean to wear. With a towel draped around me, I padded back into the room, only to discover a female sprawled over the bed.

Golden hair draped over the gold, tasseled pillows, her white chiffon dress failing to hide much of the curving, ripe body beneath. "Majesty," she purred, rolling to her stomach. The glint in her eye was unsettling, but not as much as her next words. "Our king has asked that I provide you with something to wear."

Perusing the barely there clothing she wore herself, I decided I'd rather wear my soiled dress. "And who might you be?"

"Eline. Or..." She sat up, her eyes emerald jewels surrounded by brown lashes. "His majesty's Little Lion."

My teeth clacked, and I blew out a shaken breath. "That explains the purring."

Her brows drew in. "I beg your pardon."

"No need to beg." I saw the paltry excuse for a dress she'd brought with her and walked over to pick it up from the divan she'd tossed it on. It was lavender, quite beautiful, but I doubted it would cover much. I didn't peg Raiden as the type to want his queen's body on display.

Looking back at the little lion, who was staring at me with an expression that screamed of her desire to rake those long, gold-painted nails down my face, I smiled. "Thank you."

Again, she frowned. "You are... quite odd."

"Odd?" I said, dropping the towel and forgoing the wrap that was provided for my breasts. "Cold, cruel bitch, wicked queen, horror child, monster… I would go on, but I'm sure you've undoubtedly heard them all." I slipped the dress over my head, tugging it into place. "You, however, are the first to call me odd."

She was silent a moment, then said, "You're supposed to wear the wrap underneath."

I pulled my damp tresses over my shoulders, feeling them soak into the light fabric, then gazed down at myself. You could see the outline of my nipples and the hint of my mound. I hated it. But I hated that I'd been tricked into coming here more, so I'd do what I had to.

I feigned confusion. "Oh." Then I hurried out of the room.

The lioness was hot on my tail. "You cannot go down there dressed like that."

"Why not?" I brushed a hand against the rough sand-hewn wall as we circled down the steps.

"You know why. Your tits are on display for the entire kingdom."

"You're the one who supplied me with the dress."

To that, she said nothing, but I could feel the anxiety rolling off her like a rancid breeze as we wound through halls and eventually, found ourselves entering the dining hall.

Raiden, his advisor, and at least several members from his guard were in the large but slim room.

Eline stopped in the entryway, and I moved to the opposite end of the marble table, taking a seat.

"Um," Raiden said, clearing his throat and straightening. "My queen…"

"Is that chicken? Or pigeon?" I pulled the tray of steaming meat closer to inspect it. "Sometimes it's hard to tell the difference between the real thing and that which is fake."

Eline coughed to hide a curse behind me, and I grabbed a fork, stabbing the bird none too gently and dropping a huge breast onto my plate.

Setting my fork down, I looked up into the narrowed eyes of the king, licking my fingers. "Chicken."

A tic jolted his hardened jaw. "Are you done?"

"Whatever do you mean? I haven't even started," I said through a laugh, then yanked the bowl of roasted potatoes closer, selecting two. "I'm positively starving."

With a sigh, he looked at his guard. "Leave us."

"Majesty..." his advisor started.

"You too."

I plucked some plump tomato and bright lettuce from the salad bowl and began to eat as everyone save for the king and Eline vacated the room. "Not bad," I said, swallowing and sipping some wine from the golden goblet before me.

"Raiden," Eline said. "I offered the wrap, but she—"

"*She* is seated right here and can inform him herself," I said. "Thank you and goodbye."

Eline didn't move. Raiden gave her a look that spoke of years of silent communication. "I'll catch up with you later."

"Oh?" I said. "Are you siblings or something?"

"I'm his consort."

I laughed, patting wine from my chin with a cloth napkin. "I understand the need to make yourself feel better, but there's no such thing, little lion."

I felt her advance on my back and lifted a finger, ice encasing her feet to the ground.

Raiden rested his chin upon his hand, unamused.

I didn't care. He could rot in the darkness for all eternity.

"Unhand her," he said.

"I'm not touching her." I speared some more chicken, chewing as he glared.

"Raid," she whined. "It's starting to burn."

I wrinkled my nose but released her.

Raid. So he had a lover after all. I'd heard he had more than one, but I was guessing she was the favorite.

"Eline and I have been friends since childhood," he explained.

"We are more than friends," she snapped, then he silenced her with a flick of his hand.

"You'll find I care not." It was just another reminder of all the ways males could not be trusted.

"No?" Raiden's lip curled. "How intriguing."

I ignored him and ate my food, my growling stomach beginning to settle.

He watched me for a time, ignoring the food upon his own plate, and sipping from a tankard. Ale, I guessed.

"Leave," he said at last to Eline.

She did not.

His eyes lifted to her, a fury I'd not yet seen saturating them. "*Eline.*"

After a moment of tense staring between the two, her footsteps soon faded out in the hall.

"I do hope you're not too fond of her."

"And why is that?"

"Because," I said. "When she tries to kill me in my sleep, it's highly likely I'll end her." I waggled my fork. "Self-defense."

His laughter bounced off the walls and caused the food in my stomach to vibrate.

How different he seemed, I mused, gazing at him. How unfiltered he was in his own home.

I couldn't say I liked it, but old feelings do die hard.

"She knows to stay away."

Tutting, I said, "She's too far gone to care about what she knows." I drained my wine. "And you…" I set the goblet down. "Lying to me about who she is to you is honestly not only a waste of time, but it does nothing for me."

His eyes drifted down my chest, staying planted on my half exposed breasts as he said, "She is no longer that same person to me."

"She doesn't seem to agree."

He rubbed his chin, then sighed, his hands joining over his stomach. "We were to rule together."

I raised my brows, surprised he so freely gave that truth up. "Go on."

"Before I'd met you, the plan was to kill you and your father, so one day we'd rule Rosinthe."

"Together."

He nodded. "Together."

"You and your lover."

He huffed, smiling. "Correct."

"Sorry to have botched your plans." I forced a smile, flashing all my teeth. "No, wait. I'm not." I pushed my plate forward to lean my arms on the table, and sneered, "You're still a traitor. End this marriage. Rule the Sun Kingdom with your little lion. You can keep your stupid waste of life, just give me my witch."

His expression slackened into nothing. "You truly want to end it?"

He'd asked as if he were surprised. "You know I do."

His chair legs screeched over the rough floor. He stood, pacing the length of the long table. "Let me get this straight," he said. "You steal me away from my betrothed in The Edges, lock me in your dungeon, then retell our most intimate encounters in hopes I'd remember." He dragged a finger across his brow, then pointed it at me. "You succeeded…" He stopped, tilting his head. "Now, you've gotten what you want, and you no longer want it?"

It was hanging there, dangling like tempting, poisonous fruit before me, to tell him who exactly it was he'd been about to marry in The Edges. Instead, I said, "I never wanted you back."

"Liar," he said, in front of me now.

I refused to crane my neck back to look at him.

His fingers reached under my chin, and my teeth snapped together as he lifted it. "A female such as yourself does not go to such extremes for someone she cares nothing for."

"I did care." I wrapped my hand around his wrist, removing it from my chin, and knocked it away. "Things change."

"I don't believe you."

I pushed my chair back. "I don't care about what you believe." Rising, I said, "Now, where is my friend?"

"In my dungeon." My eyes widened, and he chuckled. "A little tit for tat never hurt anyone."

"Let her out, immediately."

He hummed, pursing his lips. "We both know that's not how a good bargain works, silk."

The nickname caressed and suffocated. "Raiden," I said, my voice gentle, earnest. "Please."

He shifted to face me. "Oh, how I love it when you change color for me." He retook his seat, lifting his leg to lay it over the other. "But until I get what I want, the answer will forever be no."

Cold heat burned through every vein as I realized what he was referring to. "I will not fuck you in exchange for my friend."

He laughed but sobered quickly. "I do not take. You will ride my cock of your own volition." He plucked a grape from the table, popping it into his mouth. "It's now my turn to make you remember."

I'd slept for all of an hour before I was woken by the unfamiliarity of my surroundings and then the sound of screaming.

A harsh crack echoed through the air, followed by another scream.

I sat up, wondering what in the darkness was going on, when a garbled moan sounded.

With a horror I hadn't realized I was still capable of feeling, I discovered the noise was coming from the room below mine.

From below Raiden's.

Eline's screams and cries of pleasure drifted through the windows to sail through the ones surrounding me. His name a hoarse plea driving another stake into my chest.

The fabric curtaining the windows swayed violently, the room seeming both too large and too small as I dropped back down to the bed.

With dry eyes and a pounding heart, I stared up at the ceiling until the noise abated shortly before the sun rose, wishing it were a different one.

TWENTY-SEVEN

"Sleep well?" Raiden asked, taking a seat at the other end of the table. He was at least wearing a shirt today, loose and gold with red thread.

My hands clenched my mug of tea. I said through a practiced smile, "Like a babe."

After draping a napkin over his pants, he glanced at me, reaching for some toast. "You look as though you didn't."

"You're too kind," I drawled.

He chuckled. "You're well aware of your beauty, tired or no."

"Whips?" I couldn't help but finally blurt. "How... brutish of you."

Aloof, he bit into his toast, watching me as he chewed. I wouldn't give him the satisfaction of allowing my feelings, whatever they might be, to grace my face.

Finally, he spoke. "You both needed punishing."

"Oh?"

"It needs no explaining, really," he said. "Why I had to punish you. But Eline disobeyed me. She wasn't supposed to enter my rooms. She's not allowed in there unless invited, especially while you're visiting."

"And when I return home?"

His teeth gnashed into a serpentine smile. "If you return home, then I suppose what happens then is up to you."

"I will not remain here."

He leaned forward to pour coffee from the carafe. "You might find you like it here, after some time."

"If last night was anything to go by, then I can assure you, I will never acclimate."

Stirring a sugar cube into his cup, he yawned. "You're jealous." He dropped the spoon with a clatter to the saucer, sitting back. His eyes swirled. "You needn't worry. I did not fuck her."

An incredulous laugh burst free. "Do you take me for a fool?"

"That is the last thing I'd ever take you for." He smirked. "All I did was make her come, over and over again." His shoulder tilted. "She likes pain."

Unbelievable. "And that's better than fucking her, how?"

"My cock never entered her body." He lifted his coffee to his curled lips. "It stayed in my hand."

My stomach dipped and churned at the same time, as images of him holding it, and images I'd rather never imagine, infiltrated. "For a male with the sun running through his very veins, you truly are a cold-blooded creature."

"Says the cruelest queen this land has ever seen."

"Quit with the flattery already, you might just make me blush."

He barked out a loud laugh. "I'd pay good coin to see that."

A queen does not blush.

Mine does, and I fucking love it.

A tightening sensation wracked my chest and closed my throat. I cleared it.

"Save your coin." I peered around the drab dining room. "This place needs it."

Again with a smug smile I wanted to cut from his face. "You can redecorate however you'd like."

"This will go nowhere," I said, frustrated. "I want this marriage ended. Until you admit that you want the same, we're stuck."

Placing his cup down, he shook his head, his thick brows lowering. "I am still in love with you, and I fail to see a future where that will change."

My heart liquefied. "I cannot say the same." But my voice was meek. It was true; I wasn't sure what I felt for the sly king seated across from me, but I knew it was no longer what it once was.

"The lord." Two biting words.

I hid what they did to me, stomped on any thoughts of the yellow-eyed devil who'd kicked me out of his home like a stolen toy he could no longer keep.

Humming, I murmured nonchalantly, "He's at his estate."

"Oh, I've heard." Raiden twisted his lips. "With his long-thought-dead wife."

The way he'd said it… nausea attacked. "Casilla is Nova."

"I know." Pulling his shoulders back, he prepared a steaming bowl of oats, sprinkling raspberries and raisins over top. "There is much you don't know, which is another reason you're here. I thought it best you find out from me this time."

"This time," I said with a huff, and then it crystalized. "Wait." Back straightening, I looked at the few guards in the room, then at Raiden. "You knew, all along, that she was Zadicus's wife?"

"Not at first." He spooned some oats into his mouth and kept me waiting while he swallowed. "I thought her just another woman trying to weasel her way out of The Edges."

Air moved swiftly out of my lungs, causing my head to spin. "What?" I backtracked. "So you…"

His eyes said it all, and I stood so fast, my chair fell behind me, clattering to the floor.

He caught me in the hall, an arm around my waist. "Do not run from me. Not after all I've done to return to you."

I pushed at his chest, but then I stopped.

I feared I was going to faint. The lack of sleep, the lack of honesty, all the lies undoing themselves in too quick a succession to keep up. "You remembered," I said, breathless with disbelief. "All that time I was telling you stupid stories, and you had already remembered."

"Your witch fucked up," he said, cruel and soft at the same time. "It didn't work, but I knew I had to pretend it did if I stood a chance at fixing all the wrongs I'd made and making it home."

"She wouldn't have," I hissed.

"I didn't swallow enough. Just enough to wander around like a headless chicken for a few days, trying to figure out who I was and where I was, and then she found me."

"Nova."

He nodded, brushing hair from my face and holding it still for his eyes to bore down into mine. "She allowed me to stay with her and filled in the gaps enough for them to eventually refill themselves. She's a changer, but changers can only stay in a changed form for so long before they need to become their true selves."

"Changers are thought to be nothing but fable. So rare, they're more rumor than flesh." But even as I spoke, images of her face, her hair, and darkness knew what else, changing in the foyer of Zad's home snuck in.

You never told me you were a changer.

I didn't know until I reached breaking point, you ignorant ass.

"Nothing in this goddesses' forsaken continent is ever merely a rumor," Raiden said vehemently. "You should know that by now. Six or seven months after I'd arrived, I accidentally saw her true form, but instead of bailing, I hung around, curious. Eventually, I told her I knew who she was, and we worked together."

"The marriage." My eyes flitted between his. "A setup."

"It worked," he said, dropping his lips to my forehead. "It worked."

I closed my eyes, dizzy from the revelations, the regret and embarrassment and alarm. That I'd been fooled in this way, and he'd so easily called my bluff… "I hate you."

"I love you."

"You had sex with her too?"

"I've been with no one else since meeting you. Only you." His lips rubbed across my skin, the sound of his deep inhale flattening my resolve as he groaned, quiet and rough. "Nova just wanted her old life back, and I wanted my new one."

A throat cleared, but Raiden tipped my head back, his lips brushing over mine before he turned to Eline. "Yes?"

She stared at me as she said, "The prisoner is asking for you."

I shoved Raiden off, marching to Eline. "Where is she?"

She hummed, eyes laughing. "Being prepared for the party in her pretty little cage."

Raiden cursed. "Eline, fuck off."

Hurt danced through her eyes, but I ignored him and snatched her wrist when she made to leave. "Party?"

She shrugged me off, a lone tear leaving her jeweled eye. "You didn't hear?" She smiled at Raiden over my shoulder. "So your precious queen doesn't know about your penchant for parties?"

She walked away before he could reach her, and Raiden raked his hands over his freshly cropped hair.

I wasn't sure I could handle any more surprises. I wasn't even sure how I managed the energy to ask, "Care to tell me what she was talking about?"

His teeth grazed his lip. "The harem, as well as some high royals of my court… they celebrate every full moon with a party. To aid in feeding the land."

That was but a folly faerie tradition, but I refrained from informing him so. The chances of him already knowing were high, and he likely didn't care. Sex was sex, and many people, both his and mine, had their fetishes.

But Truin would be there. That was all I needed to know, all the incentive I needed. "Have a proper dress brought to me," I said, and then I returned to his rooms.

After all he'd just dumped on me, I needed more than a minute to digest.

🌹

Zad knew. He had to have known by now that his wife had been in cahoots with Raiden.

Yet he'd sent me away without telling me the debilitating truth. My chest squeezed, each expelled breath colder than the last the longer I thought about the lord and the king.

"And they call me the monster," I said beneath my breath, dragging a wide-toothed comb through my tangled hair.

Raiden had sent handmaidens to help ready me for tonight, but I'd sent them away. I might've been embarrassingly blind when it came to matters of the heart, but I knew better than to trust anyone in this foreign, hostile land. One of them might have the urge and mettle to gouge a hidden dagger through my back, straight into my heart. Decapitation via a sharp, spelled necklace, perhaps. The hewn handle of a brush through the eye.

No, thank you.

For as miserable as I might've been, I rather liked being alive. Not to mention, I'd loathe to give anyone the satisfaction of seeing me bested or dead.

I'd been humiliated enough. If I was to enter the darkness, it would be at my own choosing, and I'd see it coming, or not at all.

Female laughter began to flood the stairwell outside Raiden's rooms. I wasn't sure where the king had been, but it hadn't involved his own bed chamber. I'd been in here all day. Alone and stewing on every betrayal and best kept secret.

"Majesty," a little voice said from the doorway.

Braiding the front of my hair, I knocked my eyes that way briefly. A little girl, no older than ten or twelve, curtsied in a cream tunic dress.

"Yes?" I said. My fingers were busy, but I still kept one eye on the golden-haired girl in the mirror.

She might've been just a child, but I was once a child capable of great destruction.

Packaging meant nothing.

Her voice shook a little, but she took one step forward. "His royal highness requests your presence in the ballroom."

I finished braiding my hair, inspecting the way it crossed from ear to ear, the rest of my hair a flowing river of black waves. Turning on the stool, I gave the girl my attention. "And who are you?"

"My name is Denae."

"Your affiliation to the king?" I stood, my deep blue gown of glittering silk flowing from the tops of my breasts to the tips of my toes.

My feet were bare, but no one in this wretched place seemed to wear shoes inside, and my boots would ruin the dress. It wasn't what I would have picked, given the choice, but it wasn't the worst thing I'd ever worn either.

Denae chewed on her lip, her large blue eyes rounding as they traveled over my dress and gazed up into my face. "My mother works for him."

He was a conniving, despicable, sneak of a male, yet I couldn't keep my next heartbeat from dropping. "He's your father then?"

She giggled. "I wish." Dragging a dirty toe across the sandstone floor, she said, "My father works in the stables."

I snuffed the relief that threatened to quake my knees. He could sire as many illegitimate heirs as he pleased. I'd need to get over it, just as I was getting over him.

"Very well then, Denae." My dress scraped behind me over the floor as I met her in the doorway. "Would you care to show me where to go?" I could find it just fine on my own, but I found myself enjoying the way her eyes sparkled when she looked at me.

A little awe in a kingdom riddled with people trying to stare you dead went a long way.

"Yes, my queen." She bobbed out of the way, curtsying toward the stairs outside.

I led the way, and she skipped behind me, racing in front once we'd reached the bottom.

"That dress sure is beautiful."

"It's not hideous, I'll give your king that much." She giggled again, stubbing her toe when I said, "I'll have it taken to you when I'm finished with it if you'd like."

Wincing, she glanced down at the graze on her big toe, then up at me. "Really?"

My lips wriggled. "Really."

Her lashes fluttered, her freckle-lined mouth opening and closing. "But I won't fit it."

"It will not be long before you do."

Dimples dented her cheeks as she grinned, displaying a crooked front tooth.

"Denae?" a brown-haired female called, coming around the corner. "Where have you been? It's time for you to join the other children in the pool hut." When she saw me, she raced over, coming to an abrupt stop. With a curtsy she shouldn't have even bothered with, she muttered, "Majesty."

I flicked my hand, then crouched down before Denae. "I shall leave it at the top of the stairwell."

The brunette frowned at me as I rose and left them both behind, following the sound of laughter and the haunting strain of violins to the ballroom.

I wasn't sure what I'd been expecting. Champagne, ale, merriment, couples pairing off. There was all that, but there was also so much more.

Feeding the land indeed, and to the extreme those old stories suggested.

Naked males and females and men and women were lounging, dancing, eating, and fucking.

Some in groups of three, others in clusters with any given number.

The musky scent of sex permeated, and I backed up, positive I had the wrong room. Raiden couldn't mean to meet me here in what seemed to be the thick of this... celebration.

A strong set of hands landed upon my shoulders, my hair moved aside for Raiden's lips to meet the skin of my cheek. "Not the party you were expecting?"

I struggled to remove my gaze from a group of males taking

turns with a woman, and when I did, it fell on three females who were laughing and feasting on one another. "It's fine," I croaked.

"If you leave now, they'll think you don't approve of our customs." Of course, they would.

His teeth nipped at my earlobe, his breath too hot. "Come. Sit with me. We don't have to take part."

Left with little choice, I placed my hand in his, and allowed him to escort me across the room to an empty chaise. A chaise that had probably seen a variety of bare backsides and its share of bodily fluids. I tried not to cringe as the dress I'd promised Denae separated my ass from it.

Raiden lounged back, pulling me with him. "Try to at least appear relaxed," he said through a crack in his lips, his eyes soaking in all the sights before him.

"Sure," I said as though it were the easiest thing to do in a room filled with people fucking like insatiable beasts.

My breath quaked when I remembered the experience I'd had with my own. Perhaps I couldn't judge much after all. That didn't mean I wanted to take part.

Raiden smiled at a passing server, taking an ale from a gilded tray. "You disapprove?"

I shook my head when the server lowered the tray to me, and he moved on to another couple who were watching. Watching with their hands in each other's undergarments.

Swallowing, I turned away. "I wouldn't say that." I settled deeper into the seat, into the curve of his muscular arm and side. "I simply prefer privacy when having my holes filled."

Raiden coughed on his ale, beating at his chest. Setting it down, he turned to me, his eyes dancing.

"What?"

"You." He gripped my face, bringing it to his. "I should like to fill them."

"It's too late for that," I said, my voice all breath, my lips hovering too close to his.

"It's not, and you know it." His mouth met mine, the barest hint of a touch. "I'm so hard for you."

"You're in a room filled with sex," I murmured. "You'd need to be dead not to be hard."

His chuckle tickled my lips. "But I want you."

Remembering my friend, and all the green-eyed asshole had done, the lies and the deception, I turned away and searched the room. "I thought Truin would be here." Though I'd hate to think of how she'd react. She was only ten summers older than I was, but I was certain she was still a virgin.

"Later," Raiden said, his fingers skipping across my bare arm. "I thought it best to wait until it… calmed down."

A woman screamed as two men impaled her, her head thrown back as one licked the column of her throat. One was beneath her on a red rug, the other behind, and it was impossible to keep my expression neutral when I glimpsed the size of them.

We sat in silence, the tension between us burning hotter than the sun that scorched this kingdom with each minute that passed.

"Walk with me," Raiden finally said, standing and taking my hand.

I wasn't sure we'd stayed long enough to leave, but I didn't care. Grateful to escape the moans and grunts and scents, I followed Raiden out of the room and onto a balcony.

People were out here, too. All males, judging from the quick glance I gave them as they fooled around in the shadows.

"Have you ever been with a male?"

"Once," Raiden said, tugging me around the corner onto another balcony, and around and around we went until we eventually reached a set of stairs.

We climbed them, and I shouldn't have, but I kept trying to picture it. "When?"

"I was seventeen summers, drunk, and it just kind of happened. It wasn't bad, but I find I prefer females."

"At one of those parties?"

"Yes."

"Did your parents ever take part?" I couldn't imagine that.

He laughed. "No."

I didn't understand how it was custom then. Surely, it would've been something I'd heard of long before now if so. "How did this become some type of tradition?"

Scratching the back of his neck, Raiden sighed when we reached a balcony. The balcony to his rooms, I realized belatedly. "Me. Eline and I were… rebellious teens, and I guess it just stuck."

At the mention of her, I remembered. "She wasn't there."

"She no longer participates." His voice was firm. Firmer than I'd have liked.

With a tug, I found myself plastered to his bare chest, my hands spreading over it. "My queen."

Those words coming from his mouth sounded wrong.

But his hands crawling up my back, undoing the ties of my dress, felt deliriously right.

After a dragging moment of staring, his head lowered, and our mouths collided.

With a groan I thought I might never hear again, he walked me backward inside, my dress falling in a puddle near the doorway, and we fell over his bed.

He climbed over top of me, his lips greedy on my neck. A moment later, he paused, a low grumble leaving him as his head lifted. Eyes aglow with disgust, he rasped, "He's marked you."

They would've been faint, Zad's puncture marks from when he'd fed from me, if they'd remained at all. Still, I'd known he could scent it, and I'd forgotten. I hadn't planned to let him get this close. At all.

"You can waste time complaining, or you can do what you brought me in here to do," I said, my voice breathy.

His jaw gritted. He stared down at me, his brows low and his eyes hard. "How many times?"

"Enough to make you a distant memory."

His brows jumped, his grin menacing as he reached between my thighs. It soon fell, his lips slack as he ran his fingers through me. "You're extremely aroused."

"Just because I do not wish to be passed around like a good pipe does not mean it didn't affect me." I licked my teeth, rocking onto the finger he inserted inside me. "Your plan worked."

He stopped moving. "It was not a plan."

"I don't care for your lies right now." I wriggled my hips. "Let's go already."

He removed his finger, his eyes sinking into mine. "I'm trying, I really am, but these…" He touched the skin where Zad's canines had pierced. "Why?"

"He needed…" I stopped. "No. I don't need to explain anything to you."

Raiden's nostrils flared. "He fed from you then? After the battle?"

I didn't answer, couldn't. The haze had broken, and in the aftermath, every bruised part of me awoke, screaming.

His eyes softened a little. "Are you okay?"

I swallowed thickly. "Perfect." But my lungs emptied as I remembered how it felt to be encased in his arms.

Cherished, protected, vital, and loved.

I pushed Raiden off me, drawing in breath after breath. My hands tore into my hair, ripping at the braid.

Zad's continued and increased presence in the city. In the castle. All these years, all this time, I'd ignored that primal, magnetic force. I'd accepted him with careful distance, thinking he was just another sly royal in search of more.

I'd thought so very wrong. He hadn't been searching.

He'd been waiting.

"Audra? What is it?" Raiden's hand touched the small of my back, and I launched off the mattress, stumbling into the bathing chamber.

Eternally my queen.

His.

To him, I'd been his, and darkness only knew how long he'd been waiting for me to make him mine.

Staring at the pale face in the mirror, I counted each breath, willing my heart to beat properly. To slow down. It couldn't, not while accepting what I shouldn't. Like a steaming poker had been shoved inside my chest, everything burned and swelled and threatened to incinerate.

Painted paler from fear and sorrow, the face that stared back at me was one I failed to recognize.

I knew what I had to do. I knew, and still, it felt impossible—unfair that what I needed wasn't easily attained or kept.

And how I'd even so much as allowed Raiden to touch me filled me with a shame so hot, I wanted to scream. The lies built upon more lies, the black tunnel of confusion he continuously swept me into with just the right look, a caress of his fingers… I'd never loathed myself or the male more.

Walking back into the room, resolved to end this charade already, I found Raiden sprawled on the bed, hands tucked behind his head, brows drawn as he watched me near. "What was that?"

"Me," I said. "Remembering."

"Remembering what?" he asked, impatient.

"That I shouldn't be here." I kicked the dress out into the doorway, then slipped into my own, which had been laundered and folded neatly on the wicker bureau.

"Audra, stop."

A bloodcurdling scream, followed by another and another, clawed at my ears, my soul, and I grabbed my boots, racing down the stairs and through the winding halls.

Each twist of a corner stole my breath, my feet unable to move as fast as I willed them, as I needed them to.

Another scream, fainter this time, coming from the ballroom. I turned back, skidding and shoving past people into the room. "Truin?" I panted out, my eyes frantic as they searched.

Some mating couples stopped, confused, and others didn't bother.

She screamed again, the sound cut off as I turned and backtracked, my hands shaking so hard I dropped my boots.

Raiden was already there with six of his guards when I finally found her on one of the balconies outside the ballroom. Bound and gagged, Truin laid upon the sandstone, and my heart turned to ash at what surrounded her.

Five males and blood. So much blood, she wasn't even conscious.

I blocked the nightmare that tried to force its way in. One of a similar scene with a different female. I had to, or I'd be of no help to her, just as I hadn't been then.

Seeming in shock, Raiden just stood there, his eyes vacant and his fists clenching and unclenching at his sides.

"Seize them," I told the blinking guards, who snapped into action and grabbed four of the five males.

One jumped over the ledge, landing on a trellis, and then leaped to the ground.

I sucked the air from his lungs, and he toppled over.

Then I crouched down beside Truin as Raiden yelled for a healer. Shifting some of her damp hair from her face, I found a swollen eye. "Truin." I gingerly patted her cheek and growled when Raiden approached, attempting to roll her over.

He raised his hands, his expression filled with apprehension. "I will not harm her, I swear."

I had no choice other than to believe him, my heart beating in my throat as he picked her up.

Like a tree folding in the wind, Truin flopped within his arms. He shifted her, moving inside the rapidly emptying room to lay her on the same chaise we'd sat upon hours earlier.

Her eyes fluttered, and two spellcasters entered the room, their faces grim as they studied her.

With a gasp, Truin tried to sit up, and the healer removed her hands from her thighs, waiting for her to gather her bearings.

"It's okay," I told her. It wasn't. I highly doubted much would be okay for her from this nightmare night forward. My hands gripped her shoulders, gently easing her back, her head falling to my lap. "They're trying to help."

One eye blinked up at me, and a bomb of every fury imaginable detonated when a lone tear slid down her cheek into her vivid curls. "Audra." My name was a rasp, choked, barely a breath.

I smoothed her hair from her face, nodding at the healer who was waiting between Truin's legs. Truin screamed, but I refused to let her head move. "Do you remember when I was twelve, and you found me out in the gardens, trying to capture bees?"

Truin's eye was overflowing with pain and horror, her lips muttering fast, "Stop, please, stop."

My tone firmed. "Do you remember?"

She gulped, a quaked exhale fleeing her cracked lips, and nodded.

"You asked why I was trying to capture them." I waited, and her legs shifted, wanting to close. "Why, Truin?"

"You," she croaked, coughing. "You said you wanted to bake them into a cake."

I nodded. "And to give it to Regineld." Regineld had been my father's favored guard, his right hand in many disgusting ways.

He was a brute, an asshole, and evil right down to his very core.

"It took you a minute," I said with a wet laugh. "You watched me throw walls of air throughout the garden, the stunned bees falling." The memory of the thawing rose petals, the scent of jasmine and new grass, carried us both to a different time, a better place. "Then I picked them up, one by one with my gloved hands, and dropped them into a box."

The murmurs from the healers weren't quiet enough for my liking, but I refused to take my eyes or my attention from Truin. "I was c-confused."

Blinking fast, I could barely hear myself talk, the roaring inside my ears growing too loud. "You were, and it amused me."

"You wanted him to eat it," she said after a moment of staring at me, at nothing. "The cake."

"I wanted him to taste what it was like to feel your body die a thousand deaths on the inside while still remaining perfectly fine on the outside." I licked my drying lips. "And you said…"

"Vengeance will cost you your soul."

I nodded again. "And I said—"

"That you cared not, for your soul was already black."

"Yes," I whispered, and her hand, bloodied and trembling, rose to mine on her cheek. Her fingers wrapped around my own, her grip almost painful as her lips wobbled.

Leaning down, I allowed my whispered words and lips to caress her forehead. "I will destroy them with my bare fucking hands, this I swear."

It was not like Truin to encourage me, but lying below me, broken and terrified, she just nodded, and closed her eye.

The witches stayed with Truin, muttering incantations I didn't understand, and lulled her into a deep sleep.

When I was certain she wouldn't stir, I gently laid her head on the chaise and crossed the empty room to Raiden.

He'd been leaning by the far wall, his expression void. "Unless you want a war, I'd have transport provided. Your most trusted driver. Only one. Now."

"Audra, you have to know I never—"

"Now."

"I gave my word she wouldn't be harmed, and I meant it. I left her under supervision of my best guards. She was not treated as a prisoner."

"She was kept in your dungeon, was she not?"

His teeth clamped together, and he sighed at the ground. "Yes."

"Then how were you to know what was happening to her, or

that she wasn't treated as a prisoner? You were too busy worrying about your ego and cock to do as I requested countless times and take me to her."

When his head rose, I almost flinched at what I saw in his eyes. "I failed you. I have failed you more than I can bear, and I am sorry."

Unsure what to say, only certain that I wanted to remove Truin from the place that'd surely marked her pure soul, I looked back over at her sleeping, bruised form. "I wish to leave. I must leave. Do not make this any worse than it already is."

His fingers skimmed my hand, and I did flinch then, watching as he left the ballroom.

I traipsed back over to Truin, standing beside her, every sense heightened as I watched the healers pack away their kits and bow.

"How," I said, stopping to clear my throat. "How bad is it?"

The young one with violent orange hair looked at the woman next to her, who, after running her somber eyes over me, nodded.

"She needed to be stitched several times," she said. "We put her to sleep first so she didn't feel it. She will remain asleep for most of your journey home."

She knew, or guessed, that we'd be leaving. I was thankful they'd done that for her.

The older witch with gray seeping into her burnt orange hair, stepped forward, her voice low. "She will heal just fine." Her gaze drifted over Truin, returning to mine with knowing gray eyes. "On the outside."

My own closed briefly, a breath shaken from my lungs, but I nodded. "Thank you," I said.

They stopped on their way to the door, turning back to curtsy, deep and with their heads dipped. "We are honored to be of help."

Raiden returned a minute later. "A carriage is ready and waiting in the courtyard."

I didn't care that it was dark and therefore more dangerous. I was getting us home as soon as possible.

With a gentle ease, he maneuvered Truin into his arms, and I followed him out, flicking my eyes everywhere, looking for threats.

I climbed in first so he could lay her over the soft leather seat with her head upon my thigh. "Let me come with you."

I almost laughed. "Not a chance, King."

"Audra," he said. "It is not safe to be journeying across the border, across the continent, with just a driver."

"We will manage."

"At least let me have some of my best warriors—"

I held up a hand at that. "And what if she wakes? What if the sight of them alone is enough to have her screaming and alerting every danger in the dark to our presence? No," I said. "Your warriors have done enough."

"They're not all savages," he said.

"I do not care what they are. I care only that you brought her here when it was unnecessary, and now, she will forever pay the price for your childish behavior." And my own.

For if I had been more forceful and less inclined to humor the rubble that was once my heart... I gritted my teeth and sat back in the seat.

Raiden's eyes darkened, his throat bobbing as he backed out of the doorway. "You're right."

I faced forward, telling the driver to go.

"Let me know if there is anything I can do."

"Yes." I pulled the shutter on the window. "Leave me alone."

TWENTY-EIGHT

Zadicus

THE QUEEN STUMBLED THROUGH THE COURTYARD WITH A bottle of wine in hand.

Standing in the shadows against the rough wall, I watched as she righted herself, glared at the glass bottle, and then took another sip.

It'd been two weeks since the king's passing. Ten days since she'd exiled her own husband.

Raiden had been sent to The Edges, where he'd live out his days wholly unaware he was a king, a husband, and a waste of fucking flesh who never deserved to so much as look at Audra, let alone find a way inside the fortress she'd erected around her heart.

She'd delayed it as much as possible, and Mintale, forever loyal Mintale, had done all he could to postpone it for the heartbroken princess.

But the princess could remain a princess no more. This evening was her coronation.

Only twenty summers old, and now, Audra was the queen of the entire continent.

During the whole silent and tense ordeal, not once had she smiled or seemed to appreciate that which had been bestowed on her.

Not that many could blame her. Her entire world had been reduced to a wave of rubble that kept on rolling.

She wouldn't let me in. I knew that, and still, I gave her all she'd let me—my presence.

"Stupid, ghastly thing," she muttered, plucking the crown from her head.

I bit my lips, then winced as she tossed the precious heirloom into the rose bushes and walked up the damp, leaf-strewn path.

Her gown, creamy white silk with skirts that would make most topple, ate half of the bench seat, the silver-beaded roses and jewels of the bodice glinting beneath the moon.

She sat alone, as she so often did, with the bottle hanging from her hand. It plonked to the grass, wine spilling beneath her bare feet, but she did not seem to notice. Or perhaps she just did not care.

Plucking a rose from the small cluster behind her, she cupped it within her snowy hands and gazed down at it as though it would answer all her misery-laden questions.

Purposely treading on a stick, I made my presence known as I walked up the path.

She didn't look up; she didn't move at all. Reaching between thorn-shrouded branches, I retrieved the crown, staring down at the heavy silver as I approached its owner.

"I do not need a companion," she stated, cold and sharp.

I ignored her and sat upon the other end of the bench, careful not to crush her gown. "A good thing then," I said. "For I am not interested in being one."

At that, her blue eyes, lined in smudged kohl, swung to me.

I let her assess, remaining perfectly still while they roamed over my body. She paused on the crown in my hands and looked back at the rose in hers. "They're all gone."

I did not need to ask who they were. There was not a soul on this continent who needed to. "Yes," I said, simply but not unkind. "They are."

For long minutes, we sat in silence, the celebration of a new queen continuing on without the queen herself.

Her thumb brushed over the largest petal of the rose, and it seemed to curl in response. "If there is beauty in breaking, I've yet to find it," she said, surprising me.

"I'm looking right at it," I responded, shifting my eyes to her face.

Her red lips parted, long lashes rising as she studied me. Then she scowled. "You wish to bed me? Is that why you're here?"

I withheld the urge to laugh. If only it were as simple as sleeping with her. "You're too drunk, so I think I shall pass."

Her scowl deepened, and she stood, unsteady on her feet. "I'm almost positive that has never stopped you before."

"Then you do not know me very well, my queen."

Her expression eased at that while she considered me, but then she swayed.

The crown looped around my wrist as I grabbed her arm, keeping her upright. "Let's get you to bed."

"Forever putting me to bed but never bedding me," she grumbled but allowed me to lead her back down the path to the doors of the drawing room. Pausing, she turned back. "My wine."

"You do not need it," I said, turning her back to the doors. "Besides, you accidentally fed it to the grass."

She sighed, leaning into me. "Lucky grass."

I smiled, nodding at Ainx who had been standing in the gardens, out of sight, and headed the opposite way once we entered the hall.

We reached the bottom of the stairs when her weight became more obvious, and she stumbled.

Bending, I picked her up, and her hand, the one not holding the rose, fluttered to my cheek. "Do you miss your wife?"

I missed her, most definitely, but not in the way she probably assumed I did. Nodding, I opened one of the doors to her rooms, then kicked it closed behind me.

Setting her on her feet, I unfastened her gown and then helped her out of it. Clad only in her undergarments, she crawled onto the bed while I set her crown upon her dressing table.

"Is she the reason you won't fuck me?" she asked, yawning.

Crossing the room, I pulled a book from her shelves and took a seat in the armchair near the fire. "No," I said, hoping she'd leave it alone. I could feel myself growing weaker, my pants tenting. I opened the book and began to read in hopes of avoiding any more talk of sex.

"The tale of two goddesses," I said, my brows rising. "Once upon a time, there lived two queens..."

Reciting the lie that'd been told all throughout the land was surprisingly easier when written well. By the time I'd reached the part where the two queens found themselves falling in love with mortal men, one a farmer and the other a knight in the mortal queen's army, Audra was asleep.

I closed the book, staring at its finely crafted cover for a moment, wondering over the story; the seeds of truth planted inside a fictional tale many had fallen asleep to each night.

Gazing at Audra, something melted and froze inside my chest. She was lying on her back, the bedding pulled over her stomach, and her hands atop it, still clutching the rose.

For minutes that raced into hours, I stared, and I felt not a lick of shame for doing so.

I hadn't known I'd been sleeping myself until my pants were tugged to my ankles, and I opened my eyes to see fissures of dawn leaking in through the windows.

Before I could ask what she thought she was doing, Audra, her beautiful hair a mess and her lips still stained crimson, had her mouth around my cock.

"If I'm to be a lonely queen," she whispered, voice thick with sleep and need. "Then I shall need a new lover." Her tongue licked up my shaft, and I groaned. "One who is loyal, discreet, and means what he says and does what I say." Her head bobbed, and I fisted the armrests of the chair, my eyes squeezing closed as she drew me so far into her mouth, I hit the back of her throat.

"So, my dear lord, what say you?"

I could scarcely breathe, not only because of the magic that was her silken mouth, but because I'd been handed what I'd so desperately tried to avoid and seek.

Her.

Swallowing hard, I forced indifference, lifting a brow and tucking my arm behind my head. "And what's in it for me?" Because there had to be something, surely. Even before her heart had been crushed, Audra did not believe in good and pure intentions.

Games and deceit were not only all she knew, but they had become a comfort.

"What is it you seek?" she asked, purring. Her hand clutched me and squeezed, forcing another groan from me. "Is the privilege of entering my body not enough for you?"

Pulling her up and over me, I gripped the back of her head, our mouths close, so close I thought I might perish from anticipation. "That is but a wonderful bonus, my queen, but I should like a more..." My eyes fluttered as our lips skimmed, her breath sweet and warm. "Permanent arrangement."

"Oh?" She exhaled.

"I am a lord, after all," I needlessly reminded her.

Her lip curled, her eyes brighter than I'd seen in weeks, as she took my bottom lip and dragged it with her whispered words. "So you are."

🌹

"How long must you ignore me?"

I looked up from the documents before me and sat back in the chair.

Nova, leaning against the doorframe, twisted her dress in one hand. "I don't know how many times I can say I'm sorry."

"There are some actions too grave for apologies."

Her chest heaved as she expelled a loud breath and floated into the room to my desk.

With narrowed eyes, I watched as she slid some paperwork out of the way, then sat in the cleared space, her legs shifting.

I didn't move, unsure what she was playing at. But I wouldn't be cowed. I couldn't run away from her at every turn.

She was right. I could only ignore her for so long.

"Then perhaps," she murmured, her bare foot sliding up my leg, taking my pants with it, "I can make it up to you in other ways."

"That won't be necessary." I tossed my quill to the desk and scratched at my cheek, wondering what the fuck I was going to do with this entire situation.

Her eyes narrowed. "You know, before I left, it wasn't necessary then either."

I raised my brows.

She went on. "For months after we lost the baby, I tried, and you wanted nothing to do with me."

That wasn't true. I'd been grieving myself, but mostly, I'd been walking on eggshells, worried that anything I did might only further worsen her own grief. Deep down, Nova knew that. "So you left."

She bent forward, her eyes sparkling with unshed tears. "I did what I thought I had to. We'd just lost a baby, and all you wanted to do was work and pretend it never happened while I slowly lost my damn mind."

Losing that babe had been one of the most horrific things I'd ever experienced. Watching the female I'd known for most of her life scream at the ceiling, the sun, the moon, for weeks as she grieved—indescribable.

"You speak as if I did not care." My tone was carefully gentle, but the manner in which she'd passively accused me could not be ignored. "You couldn't be more wrong."

Sitting back, she sucked her lips, eyeing her twisting fingers in her lap. "I sometimes wonder if you'd have loved me had she survived."

"I will always love you."

Her head snapped up. "Not how you used to. Not in the way I need you to." When I failed to respond, she snapped, "Why? Why, Zad? What did I do?"

"We need to drop this."

She laughed, dry and disbelieving. "You drop everything. Everything that doesn't involve the queen."

"She is our queen," I said as though she were daft. "There is no ignoring her."

"Did she request you visit her castle of nightmares all these years?" She laughed. "Yes, I heard that you spent a great deal of time there, especially after she'd matured." Her eyes flicked back and forth between mine, and I dropped my gaze to the desk. "Of course," she said, jumping down and snatching the pipe.

I watched, my spine pulling taut as she sniffed it. "Cloves."

There was nothing I could do, or think to say, as Nova paced before the desk, the pipe clenched in her fist.

"I learned a lot during my time in The Edges."

"Did you now?" My question was a warning.

She didn't heed it. "Yes," she said, her eyes beginning to overflow as she stopped and threw the pipe at me. I lifted a hand, catching it before it smacked into my face. "I learned the scent of cloves can mask just about any trace of magic you wish it to."

"It's also calming," I said, knowing where this was going but unable to stop it.

She slapped her hands onto the desk, face scrunched with rage as she hissed, "It hides the scent of a link."

The doors outside opened, and I pleaded, warned, begged, with my eyes for her to remain quiet.

Thankfully, it was only Kash, and he knew. Being that his sense of smell was a thousand times better than that of a royal, he and my other friends had known for years.

Nova stepped back, running her hands over her wet cheeks.

"Nova," I called.

"Fuck you, Zad."

Kash, his dark brows arching high, watched her go, then tilted his head at me. "So she finally figured out your deep, dark secret."

Groaning, I loosened my tunic. "Afraid so."

"Well, I hate to worsen your mood, but I've just received news from my friends of the forest."

His friends being wolves. Two giant beasts who blended with any shadow.

They were not only beasts but also human and could change forms when they wanted to.

They didn't want to. They were a species of Fae, and they'd rather roam the continent in wolf form than risk death.

At the unreadable look in his black eyes, I rose from the chair. "What is it?"

"The queen. She was seen being escorted home by carriage of the Sun Kingdom." He chose his next words carefully. "With her witch. Cross said he detected injury."

TWENTY-NINE

Audra

"Listen," my mother said. "For if you can, the beat of your heart and the whisper of the wind will tell you what you need to know."

Standing upon the highest turret of the castle, I could hear nothing. Nothing save for the howl of the wind and my heart in my ears. They weren't speaking, not in any language I could understand.

My hair twirled around my face, my fingers rubbing the puckered flesh upon the corner of my lips. Truin was home and resting. I was home, but I hadn't so much as glanced at my bed.

Cussing and scuffing came from behind, and I shifted to find my guards dragging a dark-haired bartender out onto the circular patch of concrete.

Azela and Ainx, the latter with a scar far thicker than my own, halted when I lifted my hand.

"The bartender, Majesty," Ainx said, kicking him in the back. The bartender lurched forward with a grimace, his split lip seeping as he dared to gape up at me. "Cursed Pints. The one who let the girl roam free."

"She wasn't her," the bartender, Eli, cried. "I swear it. She was a different woman. I-I-I opened t-the door to the cellar, and she was just standing there as though she'd been waiting for someone to help her."

My eyes, so dry they ached, protested when I blinked slowly.

Azela snarled, then gripped his hair, wrenching his head back. "You dare to speak to the queen without being addressed?"

"Release him," I said.

Confused, Azela did as I said, eyeing me skeptically.

Folding my hands before me, I crept closer to the shivering male. "Go on."

Swallowing hard, he did. "S-she said she walked in there thinking it was the ladies' room, earlier in the night, but before she realized she'd taken a wrong turn, the door locked behind her." With a helpless tilt of his shoulders, he whispered, "So I just let her leave. I didn't know until I'd walked down the stairs that I'd been fooled. I'm s-so so sorry."

"Get up," I said.

His eyes darted everywhere, his head shaking.

"She said get up, fool." Ainx kicked him again.

Eli stumbled forward, his bound hands unable to keep him upright, and his cheek scraped over the ground.

I sighed, looking at Azela, who grabbed him and hauled him to his feet.

Walking close, so close he could feel my breath upon the bleeding cut on his lip, upon the graze being stung by the wind, I whispered, "Return to your tavern, and should I hear of you running from ownership of your transgressions again, I will empty every bottle of liquor down your cowardly throat while sipping your best wine as you drown."

His gulp was loud enough to be heard above the whistle of the wind, and with a surprised nod, he smiled, his lip splitting even more. "Yes, yes, of c-course, your majesty. It will never happen again."

Azela pulled him back, cutting him loose of the rope binding his wrists and ankles.

Eli scampered to the doorway, but then paused, turning back to grace me with curious eyes. "Thank you, my queen."

I snarled, and he darted into the shadows, likely leaping down the steps as if he feared I'd change my mind.

"Audra," Azela said.

I angled my head, and she caught herself. "My queen." Confusion wrung her brows. "What… why?"

"He betrayed you," Ainx said, his face scrunched with outrage. "Risked your safety and countless others too."

"The changer was not interested in me."

Azela ran a hand over her forehead. "What do you mean?"

I turned back to the wall, splaying my hands over it as I gazed at the woods in the distance to the east. "She is the lord's wife, and if anyone should be trialed for treason, it is her for making a mockery of the law and tricking us all."

"Nova?" Ainx questioned. "But she is dead."

"She is very much alive." My nails scored into the mortar, breaking. "Unfortunately."

"A token of good faith," read the tag attached to the gagged male's neck.

I eyed him, the stubborn glint in his dark eyes, and then I moved onto the next. He wore the same tag, his face busted and bruised.

"Put up a fight, did you?"

He couldn't answer me, and I grinned. "I'll bet you did." My smile dropped as I circled him, scenting the fear in the air, inhaling it deep into my lungs to feed my soul.

Mintale watched on, shifting on his feet, while my personal guard stood in tense silence.

"What a lovely surprise to be gifted first thing this fine, drizzly morning." My tone was sickly sweet, my footsteps whisper soft as I continued to circle the huge males, my black nightgown dragging behind me on the rug bedecked floor.

A band of warriors from the Sun Kingdom had delivered the barbarians right to my doorstep, then bowed and retreated as soon as my guards had taken the mixed males inside our gates. I'd barely seated myself in the dining room for breakfast, not that I'd been interested in eating, when word had been delivered.

One of them groaned behind the gag in his mouth.

"Oh, yes." I tapped my chin. "That would be excruciatingly uncomfortable. Why, I'm sure your poor jaw is just aching relentlessly."

Nobody seemed to breathe, not even my guards, as I came to a stop before the lineup of filth.

Then Mintale scurried forward. "Should we escort them to the dungeon, Majesty?"

"No," I said, throwing a smile his way. His bushy brows swept up when I said, "The city square."

The guards snapped into action, and no one stopped me as I returned to my rooms.

Inside, I paused in the doorway, scenting him.

Seated in the armchair with his chin propped upon a fist, Zadicus waited for me to enter.

"I didn't know you were here."

"I was told you were busy." He stood, assessing me from head to toe. "I heard what happened."

The six bells rang. I licked my teeth, finding it hard to stomach his presence, especially on an empty stomach. So I stayed on task and headed to my armory in the next room.

"Audra," he said, right on my heels.

"Not now."

Trailing my finger over the glass, I paused on a serrated dagger with a wooden hilt encrusted with emeralds. Much the same as Raiden's Little Lion's eyes.

I opened the cabinet and plucked it out, tucking it inside my sleeve as I skirted the hovering male behind me, and hurried from my rooms. Slowing my pace at the bottom of the stairs, I heard his footsteps behind me.

Let him follow, I thought. I gave not a single shit.

Ainx and Azela were waiting for me outside and fell in step beside me as we walked to the gates.

On the other side, the crowds grew thicker by the minute, and down the hill in the square, five males were displayed on the bloodstained platform, their hands bound to a bar above their heads, and their ankles bound and bolted to the wood beneath them.

Mintale joined us outside the gates. "Have all those under the age of sixteen summers leave the square." I couldn't stop them from seeing it, but I could try to stop them from seeing it up close.

The screams would be enough to haunt them for the coming days.

He nodded, racing off to inform the guards stationed on each side of the street and outside every third business.

"What do you plan to do with them?" a smooth voice sounded.

"We're going to have some fun," I sang, keeping my attention fixed on the dais.

He couldn't rattle me. Not now. Not when my very blood was burning with the need for vengeance.

Zad wisely said nothing but stayed with us until we'd reached where the crowd could hardly breathe, and I waited. They parted, many ashen faces staring back at me as well as a lot of curious ones.

I slipped the dagger from my sleeve and climbed the steps, tracing it along the bare stomachs of those who'd abused my friend.

Murmurs and whispers began to abate, a silence that could only be in preparation for certain death settling over the entire city.

Turning to the city dwellers, the townsfolk, the sailors, and the farmers and occupants of nearby villages, I clasped my hands in front of me. Meeting the eyes of a few young men in the front row, I felt my tongue grow thick and looked away.

"A message, if you will," I said, loud and rough. "For those who touch what does not want touching. For those who take from those who request to be left alone." I pulled my shoulders back, my chin rising. "A message for those who think a female, of any form, is without enough power to harm you." I wasted no more time. "Remove their cloth."

Two guards rushed onto the dais, doing as I said, while the gagged males looked anywhere and everywhere.

I started with the one who'd tried to run away, and bent down, gazing up at him over the mound of his stomach. He whimpered, and I smiled, and then I struck.

Screams erupted from the crowd, almost loud enough to smother that of the castrated male, as the scent of blood and fecal matter drowned the air.

Slowly, and with steady hands, I removed every last piece of him.

By the time I stood, he was dead. "Pity," I clucked.

Then, I moved on to the next, and the next, each one fueling the inferno inside me, throwing fire onto flames that already raged, wanting more, needing more.

My hands were covered in gore, blood running down my arms and inside the gossamer sleeves of my nightgown, but I didn't care. I smeared it over my cheek as I stood before the last male and watched tears race down his cheeks.

Keeping my eyes on his, I leaned forward, and whispered to his lips, "Think of me in the darkness while your ass is raped by vermin just like you for all eternity."

His scream was silent, filling his eyes, blood vessels bursting as I reached between us and began to saw.

When the light left his eyes, I turned to find only two of them still alive and rubbed my blood-smeared lips together. "Weak, but we already knew that." I turned to the silent, gaping, horrified crowd. "Didn't we?"

Nods and shouted yeses were received, and with a glance at

Zad, whose expression hinted at nothing but steel calm, I shouted, "You may disperse."

Many left, and surprisingly, many stayed.

I stepped down from the dais but slowed my feet when I saw the line of human women and females approach it.

I didn't stop them. I wouldn't dare.

One by one, they spat at the deceased and barely breathing males. Well, what had been males.

When they caught my eye, they did so with a nod or a smile.

Azela, observing the gore I was covered in, approached with a wet cloth, but I waved her off. "Have their genitals impaled on the spires of the gates." The remainder of the crowd parted as I left the square and began climbing the hill.

Saying nothing, Zad walked beside me, but as if knowing I was in no mood for him, he left me outside my rooms.

Sometime later, my eyes fluttered open to find a bristle-covered neck and jaw, the scent of mint and cloves lulling my eyes closed as I was carried from the bath to my bed.

Zad dried me as best he could and then crawled into bed behind me, pulling the bedding up over our shoulders.

🌹

The streets were damp, the lights above struggling to shine through the fog that pressed heavy hands upon the city.

Outside her apartment stood two guards, one of them Berron, who had returned to service in my absence despite being told he may do as he wished.

"My queen," he said, a sad smile lifting his cheeks.

The female bobbed her head. "Quite a show, your majesty."

That pricked. "Enjoy it, did you?"

Her eyes widened, but her smile was genuine. "I did, yes."

I held her gaze for a moment, then nodded, shifting my focus to Berron. "I thought you'd be sipping wine in the trees by now."

"Too cold," he said, eyes dancing.

With a shake of my head, I squeezed his arm. "Has she been out?"

His lashes lowered. "No, but she also hasn't any need to leave." His gaze bounced up to the dark window above. "Not with all the meals you've had the cooks send her."

"Her coven?"

"Her grandmother has visited, but she does not wish to see anyone else."

I hated that yet I understood, as best I could without having the horrors she'd experienced wrought upon myself. I'd wanted to visit with her, but I'd been single-mindedly focused on dealing with the filth who'd assaulted her, being that they'd arrived shortly after we'd gotten home.

About to open the door, I turned to Berron. "When does your shift end?"

"Two hours." His smile was teasing, his face not as gaunt as it had been some weeks ago. "Why? Fancy a frolic in the frosted fields?"

The female next to him coughed.

"No more of that. Your male is not impressed."

His eyes darkened, his expression turning to stone. Such change was unexpected on the typically jovial face. "I heard. You should've had his head."

I knew he didn't mean those words, not entirely. "Then what good would he be to you?"

His bark of shocked laughter followed me up the stairs, the door creaking closed behind me, leaving me in dusty black.

My hand skimmed the scratched railing, the other lifting my skirts, and once I'd reached the landing, I found I could go no farther without taking a moment.

Steeling my shoulders, I pulled them back and drew a fortifying breath.

Then I knocked.

She didn't answer, and I frowned. About to twist the doorknob, I flinched when she finally opened the door, her hair a mess but her tiny smile genuine. "Well, if it isn't the scariest queen this land will ever see."

"Jokes, very good."

A laugh bubbled out, filling my chest with a cupful of relief. "Oh, it's no joke." Her eyes filled, mouth trembling as she said, "But I, for one, am grateful to know her."

My nose crinkled, my eyes stinging. "Shut up and let me in. It's disgustingly dusty out here."

With another merciful bout of laughter, she did, closing and locking the door behind me.

I noticed the action but did not deign to remind her that no one would dare touch her.

She needed to do what she needed to.

"Tea?" she offered, heading to the small stove.

I made for my usual seat before the fire. "No." She'd moved her mattress closer to it, and I bounced a little, lowering and shifting knitted blankets and fluffy pillows out of the way.

She joined me without a tea for herself. Folding her skirts over her knees, she rested her chin upon them. "Ask me how I'm feeling and I fear I'll scream, queen or not."

"Fine," I said. "Lovely weather."

She laughed, her bare toes scrunching as she watched the flames crackle. "I heard them," she said a sodden minute later, so very quiet.

I said nothing and gazed down at my hands. It'd taken many washes, but the blood no longer lingered in my cuticles.

"I find it a relief," she said after another minute had passed. "That instead of hearing their laughter, their merriment over my suffering in my sleep, I'll now hear their own pain."

"It isn't enough."

She plucked one of my hands, her fingers small and linking with mine between us on the bed. "It still helps."

I squeezed her hand, hating that she could never get back that which was stolen. That there would always be a stain upon her heart and soul she could not wipe clean.

"What will we do now?" I asked.

Tears were running down her cheeks as she looked over at me, her brows low and her right eye open but still bruised. "I try to move on."

"I should like to castrate them again," I said, my voice hoarse. "And again and again, each time worse than the last."

Her eyes widened, her hands rising to my cheeks as she scooted closer. "Audra." Her thumbs came away wet, and I glared down at them, then at her. "It's okay. I'm okay."

"Fuck," I wheezed, my chest rising and falling with a speed too fast to slow.

I couldn't breathe as understanding lit her pale brown eyes. She pulled me close, tucking my head to her shoulder. "She would be so proud of you." Her lips rested upon my forehead, her fingers combing through my hair while my heart capsized, drenching her lemon-scented neck and chest in tears. "So proud."

※

I stirred as I was lifted into the air, Zadicus murmuring, "I have her."

Truin tucked something in my pocket, and then I was being carried away from her.

Out on the street, I let the fact I was awake be known. Not that it was something he didn't already know. "You have this habit of carrying me places."

"Do not complain."

"Oh, I'm not." I yawned, then rubbed my eyes, frowning when I realized they were crusted and puffy. "But you should be."

He huffed, and I burrowed my nose into his throat, my arms tightening around his neck. "Why?"

"Because the walk to the castle is uphill, and I'm not exactly dainty."

His chuckle warmed my nose, my eyes fluttering. "You're perfect, and if I want to carry you uphill, downhill, or all around the city, then I will."

"Touchy this evening."

"I've been waiting for my queen, and I did not like what I heard when I found her."

My heart stilled. "How long were you outside her door?"

"Long enough. Berron kindly suggested I wait."

Great, so he'd heard too, then. I sighed. "It was fun while it lasted."

"While what lasted?"

"My reign of being feared."

Another chuckle, this one warmer. "You needn't worry about your friends sharing news of you."

"Because I'm so wicked I might dismember them?"

"No," he said, gruff. "Because they're your friends."

I absorbed that for a few minutes and then wiggled in his arms when the castle came into view. Reluctantly, he set me down but clasped my hand in his as the guards opened the gates, and we headed inside.

The halls were quiet, sconces lit and throwing shadows over the tapestry and gray walls.

"What of Nova?" I finally dared to ask what I couldn't bring myself to before now.

Perhaps it was the unexpected outpour I'd unleashed in Truin's apartment that had me resigned to it. Perhaps I'd decided I didn't care, and I'd take him for myself regardless.

"There's much you don't know, but I believe you know why I'm here with you."

I hummed, climbing the steps to my rooms, my hand still in his. "Raiden filled me in."

Zad's silence was telling—that and the hatred rolling off him.

"So their crazy plan worked." The doors to my rooms opened. "But at many costs."

"We need to talk about those."

"We do indeed." I locked us inside, removing my hand from his and crossing the room. Tucking it inside my pocket, I pulled out a dried bumble bee and smiled, setting it upon the shelves housing my books.

I removed my shoes. "I was with him."

The lord's gaze was a furnace, heating every place his eyes touched. "I know."

Seated in the middle of the bed, I crossed my legs, nodding. "It didn't… We didn't end up…"

Expelling a pained breath, he kicked off his boots. "I know."

I swallowed, the sound audible. "How?"

He pulled the tie from his hair, freeing it to fall around his sharp cheeks, the hard set of his jaw more pronounced as he joined me on the bed. "You really need to ask me that?" Something in his eyes screamed, a plea-filled fear.

Such torment. In those eyes, in his words, in the rigid bones of his beautiful face, in the clenched set of his broad shoulders. I'd always thought it just him. The quiet, intense, sullen lord who'd lost his wife and was in search of something to fill that void.

He did seek something, but perhaps it wasn't power at all.

It was me. I'd been tormenting him. Possibly for years, and I hadn't known, hadn't truly felt it, until that darkness-filled night, right before Truin screamed.

I didn't need to ask him, and we both knew why. Instead, I asked the more important question. "Since when?"

"The moment you entered maturity."

My head snapped up, my eyes bouncing between his. "I was fourteen."

"It matters not, it just happens." He scrubbed a hand over his mouth, his smile rueful. "You think I wanted to? In my mind, I was, and I technically still am, married." Reaching for the nightstand, he opened it and plucked out the pipe he kept inside. "So I hid it. For years."

My head was shaking, as was my heart.

The cloves.

Truin had known, or at least suspected. She'd once commented on it in the gardens when the lord had been visiting, presumably to discuss business with my father.

"Cloves," she'd said, whimsical. "Such a helpful spice."

I'd thought her weird—as I so often had when listening to her nonsensical ramblings—but nothing else.

He'd squashed the scent of it. It was undetectable to humans, but other males, even mixed males, could smell it should they get close enough to a linked pair.

My chest filled with fire, burning and yearning, screaming at the implications—the danger. "All these years, you put yourself in this castle, you risked yourself… for me." When his teeth flashed, his eyes yellow orbs of affection, I snapped. "You fucking fool." My chest heaved, and I slapped at his, once then twice, then grabbed fistfuls of his shirt, yanking as I growled into his face, "Stupid, moronic, blithering idiot."

His smile remained, softened, and I sagged against him, my forehead upon his. "And I want you. I want only you, but you know that means nothing."

His hands coasted up my back, one delving into my hair. Skimming my lips with his, he murmured, "It means everything."

I shivered, my heart a thrashing caged beast. "I can never be yours." I sucked in a scalding breath, willing away the sting in my chest and eyes, that ceaseless tugging pit of need I felt whenever he was near. A pit that had deepened over time until I'd realized what it was.

Something I could not accept.

"You know I cannot accept it."

"You already did. I felt it happen," he said, grabbing my hand when I tried to crawl away. "While you were gone. Audra, stop."

"You stop," I growled, glaring at him. "To keep this up now is insanity. It will only harm us both as well as the kingdom."

"The kingdom?" he said, the words a soft snarl. "We have linked, I with you many years ago. It's too fucking late. The time for ignoring it is over."

"Watch me."

He smirked, all predator with no mercy in sight. "I don't plan on going anywhere."

My teeth ground together as I sat before him, waiting for him to see how useless this all was. "You are married, as am I."

He could say nothing to that, and I huffed out a laugh.

The glint in his eyes was the only warning I had, and then I was on his lap with my legs around his back and his arms tight around me.

He cupped my face with one hand, his expression one of utter focus, trained on my mouth, his thumb rubbing my scars. "A marriage on paper cannot erase a bond forged by souls."

"It doesn't erase it, but it complicates everything. And complications like this have dire implications." My tone was gentle steel, willing him to understand. "We'll all go down, and I refuse to lose myself, or anyone else, again."

"It will not come to that. I would never let it." His eyes searched mine. "You convince Raiden to break the vow, and I do the same with Nova."

"He won't," I cried, low and breathless. "He will never, especially if he knows you're the reason."

The sweep of his long lashes captivated, and he groaned when I rocked over him. "I've waited years for this, wondering and worrying that it might never happen."

You could link with someone, feel that torturous pull toward them, the mind-bending need, but that didn't always mean they would link with you. Or if they were young, like I was, even figure it out. Swallowed within the iron-infused grip of revenge and heartache, the idea of Zad feeling this fire for me never even crossed my mind, not until some days ago.

"It won't happen. It can't." I took his chin, leaning in to lay my lips upon his.

"Such tasty lies," he said, his teeth taking my lip as his hands lifted my skirts.

Tilting my head, I kissed him, moaning. With a stinging snap of elastic, he freed me of my undergarments, and I freed him of his pants. "I am not myself when I'm with you, especially not now, and I so desperately need to be me."

He shuddered beneath me as I sank down on his length, and I swallowed his curses, my arms tight around his neck.

Slow and urgent, I rode him with the help of his encouraging arm around my waist. My skirts fanned around us, his hand fisting my hair. His tongue stroked mine with every rise of my hips, fingers rubbing my scalp when my harsh breaths morphed into fluttering moans, and my body began to shake.

I made to pull away, climaxing so violently I could scarcely breathe, but he held me still, his hips jutting up, eyes alight on mine as his teeth held my bottom lip.

"You are mine," he said, hoarse and deep, moving me over him slowly until goose bumps pebbled my skin and I was completely filled with his seed. "Eternally my queen."

"Zad," I started, my voice scratching.

When he laid me down, I hissed, but he only grinned. Then, thick and hard, he began moving inside me again.

I could do nothing but stare up at him with mixed feelings of awe and fear. Moving my thigh higher up his back, his grin slipped away. His nostrils flared, eyes gleaming with untouched hunger.

I trailed my fingers over the bulging muscles of his arms, felt them twitch and quiver, his breath washing over my cheek when his mouth lowered to mine.

That stirring, unnatural beat inside my chest spread its wings, the sensation tickling every breath I gathered. And when our eyes met, his lips and nose resting upon my own, those wings grew and took flight, and there was nothing I could do to stop it.

Breathing hard, I fell, and Zad rumbled, "Yes, fuck." His hand left my thigh to slide behind my head, his demand abrasive. "Look at me."

Trembling beneath him, I did and watched a shaking smile light his entire face.

Beautiful. In the way he looked, yes, he was unrivaled, but it was in the way he loved that truly ruined. He was the most beautiful creature I'd ever know. I felt tears crest my eyes.

He kissed me, so heavy in its softness that I feared I'd disintegrate. "Perfect. My perfect storm."

Swallowing knives, I grabbed his cheeks, fusing our lips as we rolled and started all over again. Again, I straddled him, and he pushed up on his elbows to hold me, as if he couldn't bear to not have as much of him touching me as possible.

Resting my forehead against his, I surrendered to the ever-climbing desperation to take as much of him as I could get—to satiate that which could never be satiated.

We were attempting to douse something that would burn until our dying breaths, and we'd happily die trying. It couldn't be tamed. Not now, not ever now that I'd done more than acknowledge what this thirst had been. Now that I'd accepted it, wanted it, and had taken it for myself.

With a growl, Zad tore my gown from my body, and I pulled at his shirt, my hands feasting as his mouth did the same with my breasts.

He was right. It was too fucking late.

Hours later, I dragged myself to the bathing room, my legs quivering like pudding as Zad chuckled behind me, sprawled naked on my bed. Mercifully, he left me alone to wash.

When I returned, that lazy, feline glint was present in the glowing eyes that tracked each step, traveling up my body. "Your hair always looks so much better after my hands have been in it."

I tossed my brush at him, and he almost dropped the pipe he was smoking to catch it and set it upon the bed. He tutted, inspecting the engraved wood of the brush as he exhaled a cloud of smoke.

"You've little need to smoke it now."

Through the dissipating tendrils, he squinted at me. I clenched my thighs, bit my tongue, determined to ignore that burning want I still felt. "You and I both know that's not true."

A brow arched as I slumped to the edge of the bed. "Does that mean you now understand?"

He eyed where I was seated, and the space I'd left between us. "Oh, I understand just fine." Another lungful of smoke vacated his lips, clouding his dark expression. "The question is, do you?"

I half rolled my eyes. "Now is not the time for riddles."

"We are no riddle." He straightened, emptying the pipe. Standing, he circled the bed, his bare feet eating up the cold floor in unhurried strides. "We are certainty mapped out by the stars."

I blinked, my lips parting.

He snatched me around the waist, a large hand climbing my back to hug my nape. "We are linked, and there's not a lick of anything you or anyone else can do about it."

Dreams, distant and fading, passed between his eyes, flooding my mind. What it would be like to give in wholly to these violent feelings and let whatever happened happen…

The memory of Truin on the balcony seared, setting fire to every thought and erasing them.

I stepped back. "This kingdom needs Audra, the queen. Not Audra, the easily tricked, besotted fool who wants only to fuck every time she so much as scents you."

Zad's lips twitched.

"Really? You think it's funny?" I marched to the doors, throwing one open.

"Audra," he warned, sobering.

He could warn and growl and glare at me all he liked, but it wouldn't change anything.

"You need to leave. You need to go home and stay there unless we have business to discuss."

With russet brows hovering low over his bright eyes, he prowled closer. "You can't do that. Now that the connection has been made, you can't last longer than a few weeks. Less, being that it's fresh, and you being so young."

I sent a look at Ainx, who was stationed at the end of the hall outside my rooms. "You have no idea what I can and can't do."

His smile was sad with glimpses of affection. "I'm very much aware of all that you're capable of. The entire continent is, but no one more than I."

Crumbling while internally screaming, I licked my lips, staring down at the ground while he tugged on his pants and collected his shirt.

His toes came into view, fingers tipping up my chin. "You can kick me out, but it changes nothing, and you know it."

Ainx stepped into the room, and without removing his eyes from mine, Zad huffed, his head shaking. I pushed his fingers away, stepping back. "Leave or be escorted out."

"I've already told you I'm not going anywhere," he said, finally moving into the doorway.

Curling my fingers, I swept his boots into the air and out into the hall. "Goodbye, Zad. Enjoy your wife." I watched as he shrugged Ainx off. "If she's half as crazy as I am, then I'm sure you will."

Then I closed the door.

THIRTY

Zadicus

I KNOCKED AND BANGED AND THREATENED TO DRAIN THE blood of any guard who so much as neared me to no avail.

I woke on the ice-cold floor, my nostrils flaring at the scent of lavender and crisp wind, as Audra stepped over me and continued down the hall.

My back spasmed as I launched to my feet and raced after her. Outside the dining room, I caught her delicate wrist.

She tugged it free and called, "Ainx, have the lord removed from the castle grounds." When Ainx paused, uncertain, she snapped, "Now."

The doors boomed to a close in my face, almost catching the tip of my nose between them.

"Come on," Ainx said, remorse lining the words.

With a sigh, I turned to him. "We will fight if I do not leave, correct?" While my very bones groaned at the idea of going, and my hands curled, readying to strike, I knew it would be futile.

I might win, but I'd lose in other unspeakable ways.

Azela rounded the corner, braiding her hair. "Yes." Her lips were pinched as she tied off her braid, then gestured down the hall.

I nodded, staring back at the dining room doors. Knowing that this wasn't what she truly wanted made walking away that much harder to do.

The streets were bathed in sunlight, but the breeze was iced, the wind gathering speed as we neared the castle gates.

On black spires, high above our heads, loomed the rotting genitalia of the scum Audra had ended. "Are they all dead now?" I asked, the guards opening the gates.

Ainx yawned. "The last one died in the early hours of this morning."

I withheld the wince, barely able to imagine the horrific pain that would've followed him to his dying breath. It was nothing more than he deserved. "Good."

With flat smiles, my queen's favored guards saw me out of the gates to my waiting horse. They then returned inside, leaving me atop the highest hill of the city with my heart locked in the fortress behind me.

The laces of my boots slapped at the ground, my feet reluctant as they carried me downhill.

Some merchants tipped their hats or offered food, but I kept my attention fixed forward, River's reins in hand as he kept stride beside me.

A flash of yellow snatched my attention. Truin stood outside her apartment between the two guards at her door.

I slowed, and she rushed over, her lips pressed tight. "You're leaving? You only just got here."

I rolled my lips, deciding with, "The queen needs a minute."

Truin's shoulders slumped. She knew exactly what had likely happened. "Just... don't give up on her."

That evoked a laugh. "I've been here, not giving up, for seven years. I'm not, but I know what she needs, and unfortunately, right now, that is to be alone."

"She was raised to live that way." The bruise around her eye was almost healed, but I knew the one residing inside, dulling her once bright eyes, would take far longer. "Alone and distrustful."

"I know."

"She might need it for now, but don't leave it too long." Looking up at the castle, she murmured, "When it continues to rain, the roof will eventually leak if not properly tended to."

My lips wriggled, though she was right. "You look good."

A short nod, and then she stepped back, bowing slightly. "I find I am a little more myself each time the sun rises, my lord."

I held her eyes. "I'm glad to hear it."

Berron walked uphill, strapping his uniform in place and holding a steaming cup of coffee. He slowed when he saw me and bobbed his head. "My lord."

I knew the mixed blood held a little too much affection for the queen, had known it since I'd first met him, but I also knew he was no threat. "Nice hair."

Frowning, he rubbed a hand over the sleep-rustled mess standing every which way above his head. Then he smirked. "Why, thank you."

"It wasn't a compliment."

Truin laughed, and that somehow made it easier to walk River to the bottom of the city and ride home.

❦

Landen and Kash were perched upon the divan and armchair in the sitting room, the former reading a book, and the latter staring into space. "Good to see you making good use of your eternal lives."

Kash blinked as though he'd been asleep with his eyes wide open. It wouldn't shock me. "He returns."

"Don't act as though you're surprised."

Landen tossed the book onto the side table, stretching his arms above his head. "I heard our queen made quite a mockery of the male species."

I tore off my sweat-damp shirt, using it to wipe the journey's dust from my face. A mistake, I realized belatedly as I waded into the kitchen. Her scent was all over it, now burning my skin. "No, she made an example of what happens when you not only cross her but also take advantage of any female."

Landen stood in the doorway, watching me chug from a jug of

milk while I prayed the erection that'd arrived from her scent died. "You are back far earlier than we predicted."

"What he means to say is, we were pondering whether to package half your things and have them sent to the castle." Kash couldn't wipe the smile off his face as he waited for me to explain.

"No need." I dragged my hand over my mouth. "Yet."

Landen scented the air. "She's all over you."

"That doesn't always mean good things with her majesty," Kash drawled.

I was tempted to throw the milk jug at his head but refrained. Just. "Mind your tongue."

"Or what?"

"Or I'll cut it out and have it sent to her as a token of my affection."

His laughter was louder than any I'd heard from him in the last decade.

I blinked, smiling as I turned for the pantry. "Something wrong with your home?" I rummaged through it, grabbed a loaf of bread and some cheese and closed the door.

They shared a cottage in the forest, behind the fat trunk of the largest tree.

It had belonged to Dace and Landen's mother. After she'd been captured and killed, the three males had stayed with me until the patrols lessened, and it was safe for them to return.

"It's not half as interesting as yours." Landen stole half the loaf, splitting it and passing some to Kash.

We ate in silence for long minutes. I drained a jug of water to wash down the bread and cheese. "What of the wolves? Any news?"

"Nothing," Kash said, chewing a clump of bread. "Last I heard, the Sun Kingdom delivered those warriors. They were seen heading south again straight after."

Nova chose then to enter the kitchen, and with a glance at the males, they sighed and left.

She was well aware of what they were. For although I had lost my affections for her, I still trusted her to a certain degree. She'd have sold them out long ago if she wanted to.

But they were her friends, too. She didn't have many of those left.

"You're back early."

If I received another comment like that, I was going to snap. Keeping my tone aloof, I said, "So I am."

"I heard what happened," she said. "To the queen's personal witch."

She was more than the queen's witch, and we both knew it. Diminishing their relationship kept her across the line, though. Firmly and forever in the wrong, as many would likely think.

I didn't bother defending her. I felt no need. She was who she was, and only those close enough to her would be fortunate enough to see all she was for themselves.

I found I preferred less people knowing her in that way. Selfish, maybe. But I didn't much care.

"She fares as well as can be expected."

"I heard she was a virgin."

I shook my head. "Nova."

"Sorry." With a sigh, she flopped onto a stool. "I just… it's horrible."

I hummed in agreement. "They met the end they deserved, though it won't remove the damage entirely."

Running a finger over the wooden countertop, Nova glanced up at me beneath her lashes. "When is my turn?"

Confused, I stared at her for a beat until it dawned on me what she meant.

A memory of us hiding in fields of wildflowers outside the forest warmed my mind. I hated that I'd been hurting her. I hated that she'd played me for a fool. But most of all, I was determined to make all this right, as best I could anyway.

"You won't be trialed," I said, knowing Audra would not think it. "But we need to terminate the marriage."

"Blackmail." Nova released a quiet, humorless laugh. Seeing that I was serious, her smile slipped.

After a heavy moment, she stood from the stool and snatched the bread from in front of me. "Don't worry, after careful consideration, I've decided there's no way in darkness I'd want to remain in a marriage with someone who's linked to someone else, let alone that of a psychopath queen."

"I am sorry," I said, meaning it.

"Yeah," she said, sniffing. "Me too, for even if I hadn't left, this still would've happened. You, finding yourself chained to a queen that will never make you her king." At that, her lip curled as she eyed me up and down, and turned to leave.

I didn't stop her.

THIRTY-ONE

Audra

The sun and moon rotated, dragging days and nights with them.

Zad had been right. The ceaseless pit of yearning only grew. A hunger unlike anything I'd ever felt before.

And nothing, no amount of wine or food or time could sate it. Each minute without him, it worsened, driving my mind into a frenzy that distracted me at every turn even as I sought to busy myself to keep from feeling the torment.

Interest in Berron, in any other male, evaporated. No one else would do. Nothing else would suffice. Not even taking care of myself every night to thoughts of him.

Only him.

Only he would do.

His own hunger was akin to a shadow that loomed at my back, inside my chest, and reflected my own feelings back at me.

"You wanted to see me?" Truin asked.

Turning away from the roaring fire, I motioned for her to close the door. Watching as she crossed the room and folded herself into a red velvet armchair, I took note of her hair, which was back atop her head, the golden strands curled into a large braided bun.

"I'm okay." She pressed her hands into her lap, her pale yellow skirts swallowing them.

"Your lies offer no comfort," I said, walking to the small table where a fresh vase of red roses sat.

Truin said nothing as I plucked three from the water, ripping the stems off and tossing them to the ground.

She tipped her chin up when I stood over her, watching with inquisitive eyes as I wove them into the mess she'd made atop her head. "How do I stop this?"

"What is it you wish to stop?"

I felt my nostrils flare. "Don't play when you know exactly what I mean."

"Your linking with the lord." I stepped back, inspecting the flowers' positions, then stepped forward to fuss with one. "I've heard it can gnaw deep. Their absence. After a time."

"It is no wonder that some who lose a linked one end themselves." For the briefest moment, I wondered whether my father had linked, and if that could be the reason for his unstable mind.

As if knowing, Truin said in a gentle voice, "He never linked, my queen. Not that I've heard of."

"Stop that." She smirked when I moved back again. "Better."

Her smirk crept into a smile. "Thank you. And I don't know what to tell you, other than you cannot remove a link once it's been forged by both parties."

"I do not wish to remove it." The very idea made me ill. "I wish to smother the..." My nose crinkled, and I turned to the snow-dusted windows. "The intensity."

"It is rather early for snow," she said, knowing why it'd arrived sooner.

"Exactly." The last thing I needed was for anyone to assume I couldn't get a handle on my powers, my feelings. To assume I was still unfit to rule.

"I'll talk to Gretelle. I'm sure there must be something, though it is bound to have side effects."

"A relief, in comparison."

A bang on the doors had us both looking that way as Mintale entered. "Apologies, Majesty." He bowed. "I came as quick as I could."

I scowled at his ruddy cheeks. "So tell me already."

"The king," he said, and I felt my next breath disintegrate in my throat. "The king is on his way."

Truin made a noise that threatened to shatter my teeth, they clenched so hard. "Alone?"

"He journeys with three of his most trusted guards." Mintale offered a grim smile Truin's way. "They will reach the city in but a few hours."

Truin was already leaving, and I cursed, rushing after her. "Stop."

She did, her eyes tear soaked as she faced me. "I am sorry, my queen, but I must."

I searched her features, the pale hue to her skin, and felt my shoulders sag with defeat. With a glance over my shoulder at Azela, I nodded, and she immediately followed the witch to see her home.

"Stay with her until further notice."

She turned to bow quickly, then turned back, rushing to keep up with Truin's hurried pace.

To Mintale, I said, "Fetch me some cloves as quick as possible."

He didn't need to ask why. He'd been walking on eggshells all my life, but it was even worse these past few weeks. "Right away, my queen."

※

In a golden cloak that swung snowflakes to the ground, he sauntered into the entry chamber with his personal guard at his back. "Quite an entrance," I murmured.

"Quite the reception," he said, eyeing the few people standing by me. Mintale, Ainx, and Berron. "Or lack thereof."

"Next time, send more warning." I moved forward, my hands folded before me. "Or better yet, wait for an invitation."

His smile was knives and poison. "I've a feeling I'd have been waiting forever."

He wasn't wrong, and the way his smile flattened said he knew it.

Mintale shifted, then scurried forward to take the king's cloak. "Refreshments await in the sitting room, my king."

With a bow, Mintale stepped back, but the king's gaze stayed fixed on me.

I gave him nothing but my blandest expression, and then trailed him to the sitting room.

Our guards waited outside, as per both our instruction, and I took the seat across from Raiden. Crossing my legs, I tapped my nails on the arm of the chair. "Care to tell me what this visit is about?"

Slouching back, he expelled a breath, running a hand over his hair. "Lovely weather." I didn't so much as breathe when he said, "A little early for snow, isn't it?"

"I asked you a question."

After studying me for a moment that never seemed to end, he leaned forward, hands clasped between his knees. "I thought it time we finally try this marriage on for size."

"We have," I said, tone crisp. "Twice. It doesn't fit."

"A valiant effort on your part." He paused for emphasis. "The first time."

"You get no second chances with me."

He dragged his tongue over his plump upper lip. "Is that so?" I didn't bother answering, and he huffed. "Well, I don't surrender easily."

"Stubborn beasts never do."

His laughter echoed throughout the room, and he sat back, grinning. "So, am I to take the right side of the bed? Or the left?"

My upper lip curled, and I sneered.

❀

My fingers curved around the frosted petals of the rose, and I exhaled, throwing warm air over it to help it thaw. Blood red softened in my hand, and I moved on to the next.

The king had made himself at home, and in doing so, it no

longer felt like my own. Another entry to add to the rather long list of reasons I loathed him.

How I'd loved him, I wasn't entirely sure. Though if I looked closely at what I felt for the lord of the east, then I had to wonder if what I'd once felt for Raiden was even love at all.

True love was the coupling of souls, and Raiden couldn't offer his even if he tried.

I highly doubted he knew enough of his own in order to do so.

"You cannot avoid me forever."

"I can if I so please," I muttered, heading to the rear courtyard, my black cloak curling around me.

Raiden's footsteps crunched in the snow behind me. "How is your friend?"

"Her name is Truin." And I hadn't seen her since the king's arrival. I wouldn't go to her even though I wanted to, knowing that she would fear the king might follow. "And she is as well as can be expected."

It'd been two days of the same thing. I continued to live my life as though he wasn't a pest I couldn't be rid of as he ignored my attempts by planting himself within my line of vision every few hours.

Inside, I handed my cloak to Mintale, who nodded at both of us, and then closed the door on the cold.

"Would it help if I paid her a visit?" he asked, hesitant. "I would like to apologize, profusely, and to explain that I never would've permitted such vulgarity."

At the base of the steps leading to my rooms, I spun to glare at him. "You stay away. The last thing she needs right now are any reminders of what happened."

Raiden's lips pursed, but he nodded. "I understand."

Searching his grass green eyes, I saw he was trying to, and that maybe, he really did feel wretched about what'd happened to her.

"What will it take?" he called as I began to climb the steps. "For you to at least give me your company. To give me a chance."

I couldn't give him an answer because there wasn't one.

Inside my rooms, I sat upon the windowsill, my lips wrapped around Zad's pipe.

Cloves were not the only thing I had to smoke. Truin had sent a leafy plant with her grandmother that weakened the desire to run through the city, through the villages beyond, and into the woods to the estate on the other side.

Though it mellowed the urge, it still remained. It was just easier to kick away.

Snuffing the pipe, I laid it down and dragged my finger over the damp glass of the window. Through the line, I saw treetops sway in the distance.

This was what needed to happen. Raiden as king, my husband, and Zad at his manor with his own wife.

It was the reason I'd sent him away, yet I couldn't bring myself to do what I'd so desperately insisted I needed to and move on as our continent needed.

A knock on the doors lifted my head, and I waved my hand, opening one for Raiden to walk inside. "I brought you some soup," he said, the door closing behind him as he crossed the fur rugs to the small table between my dressing chamber and the door. "You didn't come to dinner," he said. "Again."

I looked over at him, offering a brief smile. "Not hungry."

"You're beginning to give me a complex." He'd said it in jest, but I could tell that my inability to show him the time of day was beginning to wear thin.

Things could be worse. He could keep me contained in this marriage and make my life utterly miserable at the same time. He could tire of my antics and arrange to have me assassinated as he had first planned to before meeting me. He could end the marriage and ruin the fragile peace we'd managed to find with his return.

There were many ways in which this could be worse, but he was doing none of them.

Instead, he was offering an olive branch. A unified front. He was trying to make this work.

And I needed to quit behaving like a child and remember who I damn well was.

With a sigh, I shifted my leg down from the sill, my nightgown falling to the floor as I stood and walked over to the table, taking a seat.

Raiden busied himself with my books, flipping through the pages while I tipped the bowl to my lips and drained half of it.

Setting it down, I looked up to find Raiden watching me. "You can leave at any moment."

"Why do I feel as though you don't mean that?" Stepping closer, he dragged a finger over the table through a drop of soup, then lifted it to his mouth to suck. "Not entirely."

"What is it you hope to achieve here?"

"Forgiveness. Peace." I ignored the curving of his lips, the way his voice dropped lower as he finished his sentence. "Among other things."

I ignored it even though I knew I shouldn't. "You've played a lot of games with me, King. So you'll have to excuse me if I find myself exhausted and wary."

"The first one was necessary."

The words he'd said to me in the dungeon and the vehemence behind them had eaten at my mind for hours on end during the long trip home from his kingdom, with nothing to do but store my anger as Truin laid asleep upon my lap. "Have you ever taken theatre lessons?"

A confused laugh left him as he said, "Have I what?"

I gazed up at him, reminding him, "The things you said in my dungeon. The things you called me. The cold, callous attitude you harbored so well." I smiled, flashing my teeth. "So believable, so…" I pursed my lips, remembering, *you're one of the coldest bitches I've ever encountered.* "Heartfelt."

His lips rolled, and he began to pace the floor around one of the rugs as he no doubt chose his words carefully. "I had to."

"You had to," I repeated, trying to keep my temper in check.

He stopped, his attention on his chestnut boots. "You needed to believe I didn't remember you at all, therefore, that the stranger I was detested you. You needed to spend enough time with me, with who we'd been, if I stood a chance at being given another chance." His eyes affixed themselves to mine, a plea within. "Just as you do now."

My tone was whisper soft and full of incredulity. "I can assure you, I do not need to do a damn thing." I withheld the wince, the knocking on my gut.

It would seem I couldn't play nice after all. Still, knowing was useless. I had to try.

"We entered into this marriage for a reason," he said after a few cooling moments had passed.

"Peace," I said.

"Love," he said at the same time.

I crossed my legs, slinging my arm over the back of the chair as he growled and began to pace again. "You are infuriatingly stubborn."

"You're just plain infuriating."

He laughed, sobering quickly as he halted and stared at me. "Audra." My name was a silent breath. Coming closer, he lowered to his knees, startling me. "Audra, not only do I want peace. I want, no, I *need* you."

Reaching out, I brushed my finger over his hairline, then down his cheek, my nail skimming the hair prickling his jaw. His eyes shuttered, his throat dipping. "We are born alone, and we die alone," I whispered, sweet and matter-of-factly. "We need no one but ourselves." I knew the words were a harsh lie, but I'd already believed plenty, so why not another.

"You know that's not true." His hand gently wrapped around my wrist when my finger moved away from his chin. "You need time, and I can give that to you."

I needed more than time. "The one thing we have is time, King."

"I can be patient."

"Does patience involve whipping and bringing another female to climax?"

"I was desperate," he rasped. "A fool."

I was beginning to think I'd been the only foolish one for ever giving him a piece of me.

A piece that now belonged to someone else.

Someone I could not have.

This, I thought, peering down into somber green eyes. I had this. This was the bed I'd made for myself, and there was little point in acting like a brat about it anymore.

Standing, Raiden gently tugged at my wrist, and after drawing in a deep breath, I released it, allowing him to pull me up and into his arms.

Upon the bed, he tugged at the fabric of my nightgown. I heard it rip, the sound similar to the odd fissuring inside my chest. His boots clomped to the floor, the whistling sweep of his pants following.

Crawling between my legs, he dragged his lips up my thigh to my stomach, and then my breasts, his tongue and teeth tender as he teased and tugged.

His hands roamed my sides, one sneaking between my legs. I was wet but not enough.

It didn't matter. When he murmured, "You rob me of breath," I clasped both sides of his lying face and brought his mouth to mine.

My entire body pulled taut as he entered me, the discomfort sharp enough to have my back arching.

He took it for a sign of pleasure, growling with satisfaction as his lips trailed up my chest and over my neck. When they reached the curve of my shoulder, the same place I'd been marked by both males before, the world turned an array of gray and black.

Dizzy with panic, I shoved him off me and scrambled off the bed.

"Audra."

Grabbing my robe, I looped it around me, plunging my hand into my hair.

"Silk, come here."

My chest was heaving, harsh waves of air leaving me, and not enough entering to fill my lungs. "No."

The drapes swirled, the fire almost burning out, as the room became gusty and the sconces dimmed.

"Hey." Arms came around me, stilling me, his voice low. "Hey, settle. It's okay."

"It's not," I wheezed, burning.

He held me until I gathered my static emotions and finally managed to lock them back in their cage. "What happened there?" he asked, carefully.

"I'm…" I stopped, twisting in his arms and stepping back to find his brow furrowed, and his shoulders tense. He was preparing himself for the worst to leave my mouth. "I'm just… not ready," I lied.

Raiden licked his lips, nodding, then snatched his pants and tugged them on. "It's too soon. I knew it was."

Blinking, I stood there as he finished dressing and stomped into his boots.

Before he left, he asked, "May I at least stay with you?"

I should let him, I thought. But I shook my head, my eyes closing.

I waited for his footsteps to near the doors, but nothing happened.

Then, quiet and urgent, he grabbed the back of my head and pressed his lips to my temple. "If you think I'll give in, then you never really knew me at all."

When I could no longer sense him, I hurried to the doors, locked them, and slid to the cold ground.

Darkness and silence were two things I'd learned to make friends with many years ago.

So it was to no one's surprise when I scarcely left my rooms for days at a time, choosing to sit at the window or lay in my bathing tub for hours.

Mintale supplied me with any urgent documents to sign, minor problems to solve, and approvals that needed granting. Truin remained at home. And Raiden… last I'd heard, he was inserting himself in the city at local taverns, the theater, and darkness knows where else, with his guards.

"To get people used to his presence," Mintale had explained when I'd asked why.

I'd wanted to snap that he had his half of the continent, and I had mine, and there was no need for anyone to get comfortable with anything.

But that wasn't true.

We had made an alliance, and he was doing his part to make that clear. Which was far more than I could say for myself.

Mintale entered, studying the dark room as he did. "Majesty," he said, bowing.

I blinked, a slow sweep of my heavy lashes, and yawned.

"The king has made plans."

Shifting away from the cold window, my feet hit the even colder floor, the skirts of my dress swaying around my ankles. "What plans?"

His lips flattened in that way they did when he knew he was about to piss me off. "A ball. For any and all residents of Rosinthe to attend. On the next full moon."

I felt my brows scrunch, and then I laughed. "I am in no mood for jokes."

Mintale nodded. "I'm afraid it's, ah, no joke, your majesty. King Raiden is preparing to make the formal announcement as we speak. He merely awaits your approval."

My lips smacked closed, and I turned back to the window, snow flurries dancing on the other side.

He was insane. To invite the entire continent, not that everyone would show... "There won't be enough room." Castle or not, we'd have people spilling into every hall, every available room, every garden, the courtyards, and the city streets beyond.

"He has said that when the castle has reached close to full capacity, we could stop allowing people entry until other guests leave."

Of course. For every question, he'd forever find an answer.

Looking back at my advisor, I asked, "And what do you think of this ludicrous idea?"

Mintale's cheeks billowed as he scratched at his hairy jaw. "I think it's dangerous, but I can see the merit in taking the risk. He wants it to be known, far and wide, that there is peace and unity, and that any acts of treason taken against the crown are now an act of treason against the entire continent."

"And by merit you mean we hope to show the people of this perilous land that I am, in fact, not a monster, not my father, and that we see them as equals?"

Mintale's brows sank to meet his eyes. "Well, equals is perhaps putting a bit of a gold spin on it."

"To have commoners," I said, standing now, "humans and darkness knows what other creatures, enter royal ground is not only taking an asinine risk but it also shows them where they can hurt us most, should anyone else be planning to."

"And this is why you are queen, my lady," Mintale said with a hint of a smile. "I will pass this information on and tell him it is out of the question." He dipped and hustled to the doors, and I stared at the space where he'd been standing, wondering what the hell Raiden was thinking.

A unified front.

A front indeed.

"Mintale," I called.

He turned back, waiting in the doorway.

It almost hurt to say it, the words burning as they rode along my next breath. "Tell our king he can have his ball." With something tapping within my chest, faster and faster as the thought grew wings, I said, "Be sure the lord of the east is in attendance, as well as the king's favored lover, Eline."

Clearing his throat, Mintale murmured, "Of course, my queen."

"Oh, one more thing." Traipsing to the bed, I folded onto it as Mintale waited, his head tilted. "It will be masquerade, or there shall be no ball at all."

With a confused smile, he dipped once more, then scuttled from the room.

The latch of the meeting doors echoed through my silent sanctuary.

Snatching the dagger from my nightstand, I dragged its roughly hewn side over my jagged nails. "If the scheming king wants a ball, then a ball he shall have."

THIRTY-TWO

THE GARDENS WERE DROWNING IN SILVER AND GOLD.
My hands itched with the urge to pluck the garland and wreaths and baubles from the roses and tulips and send them flying at the heads of those who'd strung them over their thorns and leaves. Instead, I gently removed anything that would damage the stems and slipped the décor into the leafy bushes behind them.

Footsteps crunched, followed by a throat being cleared. I took my time straightening, finding Klaud when I turned.

His gold hair shone beneath the waning sun trying to poke through the heavy clouds.

With the ball set to take place tonight, I'd managed to wrestle my emotions into compliance. That prickly needy sensation inside me simmered low, knowing the lord would soon be within touching distance.

Snow sat in fat chunks against the castle walls and gardens, cleared from pathways and steps and the city streets. Still, the frost remained, an added shimmering extravagance I doubted many besides myself would appreciate.

Klaud bowed, deep and graceful, his brown eyes struggling to maintain contact. They flickered around the empty gardens. "Your majesty."

I dragged my tongue over the bottom of my teeth, tucking my hands before me. The belled sleeves of my dress joined to cover them. "Come to spit more filth at me? I cannot be sure you will walk away unscathed this time." My nose twitched. "In fact, I can guarantee you won't, as I'm in no mood for such disrespect."

His gaze shifted to the gardens, as if he knew the way they'd been trussed up was partly the reason, then back to me. With a wry smile, he said, "Actually, I came to apologize. I was out of line and terribly frightened."

I hummed, eyeing him down the bridge of my nose. "You were indeed out of line."

"He won't..." He stopped, retreating a step.

I moved on to a group of tulips, freeing them of the garland choking their necks, and loosened it. "Talk to you? I'm afraid that problem is not mine."

"I know," he said. "But he cares for you." He said the words as though the fact he had to annoyed him worse than the truth of them. "He cares for you, and so after the way I reacted, he refuses to acknowledge my existence."

Moving to a rose, I dragged my thumb over a thorn, blood popping through the skin. Turning to the young soldier, I placed the digit in my mouth and sucked.

His eyes narrowed as my tongue smeared blood around my lips, and then he swallowed.

"My mother used to say that those baring claws are not always so sharp." I circled him, my boots barely making a sound, my voice low. "Tell me, Klaud. Do you consider your claws sharp?"

Confusion swept his brows together, his head turning this way and that to keep sight of me. "My queen...?"

I stopped, staring him dead in the eye. "Berron is sharp, and he need not show that he is sharper than most. So quit sniveling about like a wounded mutt and go back to your quarters to sharpen your mind rather than those useless claws." Backing up a step, I watched understanding light his boyish features. "And next time you deem it necessary to bother me with troubles that do not concern me, remember I can do so much worse than take your favored male for myself."

My cloak billowed behind me, the wind catching it within its grasp before I entered the courtyard and passed waiting guards to the drawing room.

The halls were teeming with wreaths of roses, and I winced, finding that most had been dyed gold and silver, the colors of our kingdoms, of which we'd chosen to represent our unity.

Kitchen staff and maids fluttered past, bopping their heads quickly before hurrying to their next task.

At the foot of the stairs, Raiden waited, eating a peach and licking the juice from his lips. "Silk."

"Liar."

With a chuckle, he joined me, heading upstairs. "I must say, I am glad to see you outside your rooms."

"My home is about to be put on display for the entire continent to see," I snapped. "Naturally, I need to keep tabs on the preparations."

"Naturally," he said.

At the top of the stairs, I whirled on him. "Dare I ask what it is you want?"

"Oh, you should know better than that." His teeth sank into the juicy fruit, his strong jaw working as he chewed. "Are you nervous?"

Annoyed, I shook my head. "You came to ask me if I am nervous?"

He tipped a shoulder. "It's a valid question. As you said, a great deal of people will soon be arriving."

"Then I'll need a great deal of time to get ready," I said, walking away. "So if you'll excuse me."

His eyes tracked me until I was out of sight.

***

"Enter," I called, affixing the second braid to the top of my head.

"Beautiful, my queen."

The pin fell from my fingers into the overflow of silk in my lap as I gazed at the reflection behind mine in the mirror.

Truin smiled, closing the doors. In a gown of pale blue, her hair out and pressing heavy over her thin shoulders, she walked across the room.

"You came."

Plucking another pin from the table, she clasped the braid that'd fallen from my head and carefully spiraled it into a loop that met the other. The pin gently dug into the strands, holding it in place, and then her hands fell upon my shoulders.

Brown eyes shined. "You cannot throw a party this big and expect me not to attend."

That was precisely why I'd thought she wouldn't.

Knowing that, her eyes dropped, and the scent of citrus wafted as she rounded where I sat to the jeweled crown of thorns perched upon a pillow inside the glass cabinet. "I miss my friends, I miss noise, and I miss being unafraid." Pulling her shoulders back, she said with steel, "So I am ready to stop missing those things. To try harder."

Her fingers pried the glass into the air, and she set it down on the bureau before picking up the crown. The silver glinted in the shadowed light of the room. Truin turned to me. "Are you ready?"

Staring at the thorns, the twisting branches that weaved together amongst emerald jeweled leaves to make a heavy piece of metal seem more than, I found I could not answer.

I didn't want to wear it. The crown. The same one that'd been worn by my father, my grandfather, and my great-grandmother, and countless royals before me.

It was riddled with ghosts, their transgressions, their greed, their failures, and their bloodstained success.

I had no room, no desire, to drape the souls of those before me upon my head for all to see.

"A queen does not need a crown for all the land to know who she is."

Truin's lips twitched, pursing. "Be that as it may, you must wear it for the tedious welcome at least. Oh, and the speeches."

"I've a mask." My fingers swept out to stroke the black feathers that would shield half my face. "It will clash horribly."

Truin laughed, and the sound ignited a smile.

My cheeks tingled, and I huffed. "Fine."

I watched in the mirror as she carefully situated the crown around my braided one, and then reached for the mask. It slid into place with pins that caught my hair behind my ears, shielding everything but the tip of my nose, my lower cheeks and chin, the blood red of my lips, and my eyes. They appeared brighter, a sky blue, my dark lashes cresting the confines of the mask to curl against it.

"There," Truin said, barely a whisper.

When I stood, my gown fell to the floor in a waterfall of black feathers, the tight bodice inlaid with silver beads catching the light and spraying it outward.

I offered my arm, and Truin's pale pink lips parted, her eyes bouncing to mine.

Then she looped hers through it and slid her own mask, blue with butterfly wings sprouting from either side, into place.

Together, we left my rooms, the doors closing and locking with an echoing thud and clang as we slowly walked downstairs.

The halls were already shaking with noise—laughter, chatter, and singing—causing my heart to pound. We meandered through them, and a few cooks, maids, and servers stopped to bow and gape as we strode past.

Raiden was waiting at the top of the stairs leading to the ballroom in a gold jacket and gray pants that shimmered when the light caught them.

I snorted when I saw his mask. A fox.

He held out his hand, and a flame danced before our eyes, igniting his alluring smile and causing a few onlookers below to gasp.

Before my hand touched his, the flame disappeared, though its stifling heat could still be felt on his skin.

Truin curtsied, and then waded down the steps into the rapidly swelling crowd below.

A part of me wanted to call for her to come back. When I finally gave my attention to Raiden, I found his own crown of curling gold snakes and branches, ruby leaves glinting atop his head.

"I've yet to see you wear it before now," he said, his voice soft, but his eyes hard on the silver crowning my head.

"I'm not fond of it," I admitted, then gestured with my eyes to the crowd.

"A crow?" he asked, studying my dress and mask.

My smile bit into my cheeks. "A midnight eagle."

Our guards moved closer, flanking us on all sides.

"Ah, but of course," he said. "Dark and deadly."

In answer, my chin tipped up.

Raiden's eyes danced, and then he nodded, tucking my arm within his as we began to descend the stairs.

The guests, most of them wearing masks, fell silent. The entire room, large enough to fit a small army, filled with nothing but the roaring of my heart in my ears.

They parted, though it was no easy thing with so many people, and we crossed the room to the two thrones upon the dais on the other side.

Caterpillars, moths, another butterfly, and even a jester caught my eye, but it wasn't until we'd reached the dais, our guards settling below and behind it, and stood before our thrones, that I finally saw him.

Dripping from head to toe in black was a wolf.

His mask was fur, whiskers sprouting in silver lines either side of his crooked nose, the soft black crawling into shape around his golden eyes.

My chest deflated, my steel-infused shoulders drooping, but those eyes, glow as they might, were not shining in the way I'd thought they would.

His lips thin, and his jaw flexed into an immovable square, he stared, and I stared back, fearing the kaleidoscope of feelings inside me was on display for all to see.

Raiden's arm squeezed mine as he began to talk, and I gave my attention to the sea of faces below us, my shoulders and chin rising.

"Welcome," Raiden said, his deep voice carrying over the room built for such things. "We are thrilled to have you all here to help celebrate such an important time for us all." He paused, on purpose, and finished, "To celebrate peace. A unity that will lead to a prosperous, magical future for everyone."

I smiled, hoping it appeared warmer than it felt, as clapping ensued and even some whistling.

A tankard was handed to Raiden, likely planned, and he held the ale in the air. "Drink, eat, dance. Get to know your neighbors, and enjoy one another." Then, he tipped it back to more shouting and clapping and whistling before we took our waiting seats.

One by one, each guest was allowed to come before the dais and wish us well, but when the merriment grew too loud, the room reaching capacity within the hour, we were forced to put an end to that and left the dais to do the rounds instead.

To his credit, Raiden could charm even the surliest of storeowners and nobility alike, leaving them all in better spirits than what they'd been when we'd approached them.

"You are an expert," I said through my teeth, smiling at a group of young girls in homespun dresses with strips of satin tied around their foreheads. It was all they could afford, I knew, and they were quick to turn beet red upon meeting my eyes, before turning to one another to gasp and gossip.

"You're doing well," Raiden said in return.

I scoffed. "A few smiles and waves here and there. Why, I'm practically your show pony."

"I doubt there's a soul in this room who doesn't quake to their core should your eyes befall them." He'd said it in jest, but I still took it for the compliment I wanted it to be.

A peacock curtsied as we passed, draped head to toe in greens and blues, her blond hair falling over her half displayed chest. "My lieges."

Raiden froze on the spot. His arm tensing around mine, he gritted, "Eline."

Straightening, she displayed her teeth in a smile that could only be described as threatening, though not to me. "I do hope your stay has served you well, my king."

"Indeed," Raiden said, "it has."

Her eyes darted to me, her nose tilting up.

I only smiled and found doing so easier than the last time I'd laid eyes on Raiden's preferred lover. "We are taking excellent care of him, Little Lion," I told Eline. "I can assure you."

Raiden stilled, then coughed.

Eline's eyes narrowed on him. "Oh, I'm sure you are."

We walked on, and I couldn't help but notice how long it took the king beside me to unclench his muscles and offer a genuine smile.

"Does her presence bother you?" I asked, all innocence.

"Let me guess," he said. "You invited her?"

I tutted. "It was an open event, my dear."

Raiden sighed. "You torment me to no end."

"I do nothing of the sort."

"Your mere existence is enough," he whispered, bending to drag the words over my cheek.

My eyes flicked to the shadows beneath the stairs where the lord was standing, sipping champagne, his wife nowhere to be seen. "I need a drink."

Raiden clicked his fingers as we neared the stairs, but the server was headed in the other direction, and he grumbled before following him.

I bit my smile, and knowing Azela was trailing, as were the eyes of all our guards, but not caring, I slipped into the shadows and felt my breath plume out of me in a frost-bitten exhale.

Zad bowed, those sharp eyes on mine as he straightened. "Resplendent, even dressed dark as night."

His words, though they were crisp and short, evoked a pattering within me, light and restless. Needing to, I stepped closer.

To my confusion and dismay, he retreated.

I nodded, understanding. "Not here."

His response was a blunt knife. "Or anywhere."

Before I could voice my confusion, Nova appeared at his side, her arm slinging behind his back as her knees bent. "Majesty." She gazed around the room. "Quite a party."

I could feel my upper lip curl but set them both into a flat line as her eyes smiled knowingly at me.

Raiden returned, his mouth lowering to my ear. "Let us take a walk. Get some fresh air."

I didn't want fresh air.

I wanted my lord away from his wife.

I wanted him to look at me the way he usually did, to rid that cold detachment from his crystalline features.

My stomach swirled, my mind searching, but it found nothing.

I could feel nothing from him, save for the bitter trace of ire.

Shocked, I was easily led away from the pair and delivered outside into a hall filled with masked guests and servers carrying steaming trays of food to and from the ballroom.

Raiden kept walking until we'd reached a verandah, but I didn't stop.

I continued until the noise was swallowed by the silence found closer to the stairs leading to my rooms. Guards stood at the bottom to keep guests from finding their way to the higher levels, but they stepped aside when they saw me heading for them.

"Audra," Raiden said. "You cannot mean to sulk in your rooms when our enjoyment, our presence, on this night means so much."

"I need a moment," I said, opening the doors to my rooms.

Before I could enter, my wrist was grabbed, and I was spun into a hard chest. "Why?"

He tried to search my eyes, my expression, but the mask and the dipping of my head didn't allow for it. "Silk," he said, grasping my chin. "I've been patient. I've been here, waiting for this grudge of yours to pass, but even if you do not wish to share what upsets you, you must. You must share it with me, not only because I care, but because for better or worse, we are now a team."

My eyes lifted, stinging pools of water, and his grip loosened at the sight. "I might share this continent with you, but I do not need to share anything else."

"There was a time I'd have you spilling the inner workings of that beautiful brain," he murmured. "I miss it. I want it back."

With nothing to say to that, I just stood there.

And then the air turned malevolent, as if it'd grown a heartbeat born from fury, and Zad appeared behind Raiden.

Sensing it too, Raiden slowly stepped back, his gaze bouncing between us for a stalling exhale. "You're lost, Lord." He grinned, menace rolling from the hardness of it. "Turn back."

Zad grinned in kind. "I've spent far too much time in these halls to ever find myself lost, King."

Raiden's hands curled, his entire frame swelling.

"Give us a minute," I said, and when Raiden threw incredulous eyes at me, I added, "Please."

He stared for a long moment, and then sighed, his shoulder smacking Zad's on his way past.

Zadicus didn't move, not from the intended jostling and not after Raiden's footsteps faded at the bottom of the stairs.

"Well," I said, my hands spreading. "You corner me and then you fail to talk?"

"You were with him. Again." Such quick, heart-stopping words wrapped thick in disgust.

There was little point in denying it. He knew, as I'd guessed and feared he might. "I was."

Dragging a hand over his mouth, he shook his head at the ground, a low laugh preceding his next words. "I knew," he said. "I knew I was doomed the moment I linked to you."

"Well, we tried, but it didn't…" My teeth grazed my lip as I struggled to conjure the best words to use. "It didn't work."

At that, his head tilted, and he prowled closer. "It didn't work?" His tone was accusing, filled with disbelief. "You let a male inside your body, and it didn't fucking work?" He cut me wide open with his wrathful gaze. "You cannot lie to me, Audra."

"I am not lying. I found it too…" I paused, releasing words with a rough exhale. "I kicked him out. Not long after we started, I stopped it," I said, tonelessly. I wouldn't allow him to make me feel less than. "You knew, you know very well," I went on. "What I'll have to do."

Raiden was my husband. He was the future I was saddled with. It was pointless to plead forgiveness for something I had to, and would likely have to, do again.

"There are many things you have to do, but I fail to see why that is one of them." After staring at me for breath-faltering moments, Zad cursed, auburn hair falling to curtain his sharp cheek as he turned to the window. "This is a fucking nightmare."

I wanted to say so many things.

I wanted to ask him to stay. To make sure the king only entered my rooms, my body, when the time came to produce an heir.

But most of all, I just wanted him—his arms around me, his scent smothering me, and his obnoxious heartbeat dancing with mine.

"Zadicus," I said when he began to walk away. "Zad," I said again when he took to the stairs.

I followed, but still, he didn't stop.

In the hall below, Raiden stepped out from the shadows, his teeth bared as he launched himself at Zad, and they toppled to the ground.

A scream stretched my throat, trapped there, as Raiden's fist smacked into Zad's cheek, and then Zad flipped him, elbowing him across the nose.

Blood sprayed, and guards rushed into the hallway, but I halted everyone with the rising of my hands. "Stop."

With a wind that rattled the sconces on the walls, leaving us in near darkness, I forced Zad off Raiden, knowing what would happen if we didn't settle this.

One of them would die, and the result of that would be catastrophic, no matter who it was.

To me, and to Allureldin.

"I said stop," I ground out, looking at Ainx to seize the lord, who shoved him off. "Again?" Zad spat at the ground by Raiden's head. "You have me here again, only to have me dragged out like unwanted cattle?"

I nodded at Ainx, and he released the lord.

Adjusting his blood-splattered mask, Raiden rose from the ground, the rage in his eyes biting into my skin.

Looking at the guards, I said, "Leave us."

They did, but only far enough to give the illusion of privacy.

"You link to my queen?" The words rolled out of Raiden's mouth like hot flames escaping a fire. Moving closer to Zad, he sneered. "My wife? I will have your head—"

"You will not," I said. "For I have linked with him too."

As though he'd turned to stone, Raiden stood deathly still, his gaze on Zad, who just stood there with hard, expressionless eyes. Finally, he turned, and I wished he hadn't.

I'd never feared the male, nor had I feared any male except my father, until that moment. With his eyes burning, his gait slow and focused, Raiden stopped before me and spat, "You hid it from me? You link with a male other than myself, and you think to hide it from me?"

"It was only recent," I said, simply, struggling to keep my words steady, my very breath, under a gaze harsher than that of his desert sun. "On my part."

"On your part," he repeated, bland and unblinking.

I swallowed, choosing silence. I was not prone to driveling apologies, and I wasn't about to start with him. I owed him nothing, especially after all he'd done.

He had only himself to blame for any upset he felt. He'd changed the trajectory of all our lives with his lies and cunning nature.

I'd half expected the lord to walk away, but I should've known better. He wasn't going anywhere with the rage unfurling from

Raiden, especially when he was looming over me like a curling tree about to snap during a storm.

Looking back at Zad, he asked, "When?"

"It matters not," Zad said, words cutting like sharp shards of ice. "Now, back up."

"Oh, but I think it does matter a great deal." Raiden turned to him. "Considering you linked with someone who wasn't yours. She is mine." He jabbed a finger at his chest. "My wife. My queen. My future. *Mine.*"

As though he thought he'd glean some satisfaction from admitting it, Zad shrugged. "She was only fourteen, so it happened long before your painful existence was to become even a thought in her head. A stain thrust upon any of our lives."

That gave Raiden pause.

You couldn't trial someone for linking. It was about as natural as the sun and moon changing shifts in the sky. But when you were a royal, a high royal who sat on a throne no less, you could very well get away with doing whatever you pleased—within reason.

And it was within reason to have your wife or husband's linked one suddenly vanish, fall irreversibly ill, or be struck in the chest with a weapon of someone who'd been hired.

The mere thought of Raiden trying to break something that could not be severed ignited a black hole of wariness inside me, the likes of which had me saying, "You needn't worry yourself on the matter. He is but a lover. One I have chosen not to bed or entertain anymore."

Raiden continued to stare at Zad, and then, with a glance at me, he murmured, "We'll see." Then he was stalking down the hall, startling a server so much so that when he grabbed two ales from her tray, the rest toppled to the floor.

A few passersby stopped to help her clean up the broken glass and beverages.

Dragging my stinging eyes off them, I gave them to Zad.

"Just a lover?" he purred, though there was no softness behind the question.

"I will say and do whatever is necessary," I said. "You know that, and you know better."

"Do I?" he said, drawing closer, so close, I stepped back into the wall, its dusty tapestry trapped behind me. "You lay with him, you allow him free rein of your home, and for him, you ignore what it is you truly want."

"It is not for him, and it is only for the time being. I promise."

His brows lowered, his jostled mask shifting over his marble encased cheeks. "You promise?"

I nodded. I would make it work. I had to, for my own survival as well as his.

His hands trembled as he cupped my jaw, and I felt my eyes flutter closed at the touch. A caress and a burn, his smooth mouth whispered over mine. "You accept me only to turn me away. You care for me only to do so when you see fit. And you wound me at every turn."

My own hands reached up, gripping his. I opened my eyes, a plea within them. "You cannot think I meant for all this to happen. You know it's not what I want."

"You do nothing to stop it. To make it right. You're not even trying. You are not Audra; you are a puppet of your own making."

"I am no one's puppet," I seethed. "I am yours. My heart is yours. My soul is yours."

"My queen." His breath coasted over my lips, searing. "Your heart is about as good as the existence of your soul—a rotten fucking lie." He released me, his long strides carrying him down the hall and out of sight as I struggled to breathe.

The anger and hostility behind his lethal, silken words echoed throughout my spinning mind, clanging against my skull.

I swallowed repeatedly and blinked the wetness from my eyes, making sure they were dry. Then I reaffixed my crown and forced my feet into action.

Heading back into the ballroom, I snatched a glass of champagne and drained half of it in one swallow. I looked everywhere while trying to appear as if I were merely taking in the festivities, but I couldn't see him.

"You have not trialed me."

I stilled, glancing to my left.

Nova's smile was brief, her posture riddled with arrogance. "I do not care to be in your presence long enough to bother." She snorted. "Some queen you are."

"Some wife you are."

Her eyes widened, a shocked laugh erupting. "Touché."

Over the lip of my glass, I watched her curtsy and disappear into the thick crowd.

I needn't have worried over the possibility of Zad welcoming her back into his bed. I knew him, and I knew he was not the type to go marching around one's castle in a jealous rage if that were the case.

The lord was many things, but a hypocrite was not one of them.

Raiden was by the dais, in conversation with my cousin. Curling my shoulders back, I walked over, interrupting their chatter.

"Cousin," Adran drawled. "Please do throw more lavish events such as these." He swallowed his champagne, then gestured to the brunette beside him. "You do remember Amelda, yes?"

I gave her my attention for all of a beat, nodding as she dipped low, her gold dress far too bright. "Majesty."

"Engaged, right?" I remembered, sipping more wine.

Amelda glanced at the ground, and my cousin loosened the collar of his dark silver dress shirt. "Well, not exactly."

"He stepped out on me with a village child minder." My cousin coughed, tossing a quizzical glare her way. "What?" she said, looking away. "It's true."

I cared not if it were true and looked at Raiden, who was studying the pair with keen eyes.

"Needless to say," Adran continued. "We've put the nuptials on pause for now."

"Or indefinitely," Amelda murmured. "Time will tell."

"Not always," Raiden said, throwing his ale down his throat with a harsh shake of his head. Heavy, narrowed greens fell upon me, but I maintained eye contact.

If he was waiting for an apology or some type of groveling, he'd be waiting for all eternity.

I felt eyes upon my back, and I didn't need to turn around to know who they belonged to.

Zad stopped by our small circle, leaning in to say, none too quietly, "Be sure to touch her asshole when you're inside her cunt." He clapped Raiden's shoulder. Hard. "Maybe then she'll let you finish the job."

My glass fell from my hand, shattering over the mosaic tile.

My cousin's barely there brows shot up. "Juicy." His eyes danced as he watched Zad prowl to the eastern doors. "Nothing like a scorned lover," he sang, studying me over the lip of his goblet.

A large male wearing a furbane mask stood by one of the exits. Kash.

While a server fussed below me on the floor with the broken glass, I watched Zad reach him, and the both of them walk out into the courtyard.

He was leaving. I'd known he wouldn't linger long. Not after what he'd said.

Not after what I'd done.

Still, panic caught every breath, my empty fingers curling at the feathers of my dress to keep from shaking.

"Cousin, you're looking positively pale."

"Excuse me," Amelda said, ducking out of our circle. She weaved between the guests surrounding us, and the crowd swallowed her within seconds.

"I'm always pale," I said, shifting back as the server collected the shards into a pan.

Adran laughed, his head bobbing. "True. So, your majesties…" His brows waggled. "How does it feel, reunited at long last?"

I frowned at him, as did Raiden, and then we both walked off in different directions, leaving Adran to finish his champagne on his own.

Out on the city streets, I felt Azela at my back, struggling to keep pace with me as I ducked and weaved between guests, searching for something I knew was no longer here.

A rotten fucking lie.

Stopping at one of the fountains housing wine that gurgled like purple water, I spun in a useless circle, growing dizzy as masked faces stared at me, laughter and talking and singing all blurring into a cloud of thunder that threatened to send me to the cobblestone street.

"Come," Azela said, her hand wrapping around my arm.

"But…" I sniffed, stumbling a little.

"He is gone, Audra." Rarely had I heard her use my name and never with such finality.

It did the job, and I whirled on Azela, taking in her somber expression.

After a moment, I nodded, and she led me back inside through hallways that'd been blocked off to the public, taking the long way to my rooms.

A moan stopped us in our tracks, and Azela cautiously rounded the corner.

I needed my own space, the silence to think and the chance to breathe without failing every time, so I rounded the corner and continued.

My feet tripped. I caught myself, slowing to take in Raiden and Eline.

He had her up against the wall in an alcove right beside the stairwell leading to my rooms, her legs wrapped tight around his waist.

Her cries were muffled as his mouth swept over hers, his hand gripping her thigh as he fucked her with hurried juts of his hips.

"Lovely," I muttered, even as the remains of the wasteland he'd made for himself inside my chest panged. Yet as I headed upstairs, Azela accompanying me, I realized that pang lessened with each step.

Azela closed the doors but did not leave. I knew she was readying herself to say something about what we'd seen downstairs, but I hadn't the energy to stop her. "He was fucking her. In the hallway."

"Yes," I said, removing my crown. I set it upon the pillow inside its glass home, then pulled off my mask. "A rather prime spot to do so."

Azela cussed so violently, I almost laughed. "That filthy animal. He is your husband. And tonight of all nights." She cussed again. "He should be setting an example."

"He sure is setting one," I said, moving my hair aside and motioning for help with undoing my corset.

Her hands were gentle as she unclasped each hook, and my shoulders drooped as I was able to finally draw my first deep breath for the evening. "What of the lord?" she asked carefully.

"The lord is the reason the king is currently inside another female and making a show of it." That was all I'd give her, and she knew it.

"The marriage is a sham?"

"It is now." I stepped out of my dress, leaving it behind in a mountain of feathers on the rug, and unclipped my undergarments on the way to the bathing chamber. "Good night, Azela."

"My queen…"

"I said good night." After plugging the tub, I turned the faucet and straightened as Azela reached the doors. "Oh, and please tell our king that I am unwell and to express my apologies to our guests."

Azela's smirk caused my lips to wriggle. She nodded, leaving.

I climbed inside the tub, waiting for the heating water to fill around me, and stared at the wall. After a time, my dry eyes began to close, but I shook myself awake.

There'd be no lord to carry me to bed.

There'd be no lord awaiting me in my bed.

There was a good chance there would never be a lord in these rooms of mine ever again.

The regret caught fire, spreading to my eyes. I squeezed them shut.

Rotten souls did not cry.

THIRTY-THREE

Pushing my tea aside, I paused on one of the documents before me, and reread it.

A request for the termination of marriage, signed by Nova and Zad Allblood.

Cupping my mouth, I read it again and again, double-checking, needing to after what had happened two nights prior in this very castle.

After what had been said.

Then I was up and crossing the study, my ears ringing with my increasing heartbeat.

Mintale, on his way in, sandwiched himself into the doorway. "Majesty?"

"Zad. Lord Allblood. Is he still in the city?"

"At the Rosaleen, I believe, awaiting the approved termination."

Fisting my skirts, I hurried down the hall. "I'll be back later."

"Wait," Mintale rushed after me. "Your guard."

I ignored him. The city was the safest it'd been since well before my father's death.

Even so, Garris snapped into action when he saw me heading for the exit, keeping hot on my heels. I lost him within the crowd of an auction being held near market square.

The Rosaleen was a high-class bed and breakfast that most royals preferred during their stay or after a night of too much debauchery. Some for more sinister and secretive things.

The narrow pale blue three-story structure was wedged between a bar and a café along the harbor, providing a view of the glistening water and mountains beyond.

Inside, a bell tinkled, the concierge glancing up from the book he'd been reading with a start. "M-majesty." He cussed when he bowed and bumped his elbow on his ruby red desk.

Glancing around the red and pink trussed-up establishment, I searched for the stairs.

I found them behind the desk to the left, white and twirling through the ceiling.

Mirrors of every size and frame bedecked the pale pink walls. The concierge sang after me while I scaled the squeaking metal stairs.

He gave up after a moment, his high-pitched voice fading beneath the loud thump of my heart and boots over the plush gray carpets lining the halls.

He was on the third floor, I realized, climbing the stairs again and catching a whiff of that blood-bubbling scent of his.

I knocked and waited. Then I knocked again before deciding I was through with waiting. "Open the door or I'll force it open."

Kash walked out of the neighboring room, and with a lingering look my way, he took the stairs down.

The hinges squeaked as Zad, clad in an undershirt and loose pants, his hair falling out of its tie to shield half his agitated face, finally opened the door.

"Are you ready to apologize and plead forgiveness?" That was apparently the wrong thing to say as he made to close the door, annoyance rolling off him like a thunderstorm. "Wait."

"Audra, I've no desire to do this right now, and surely, you've better things to do."

"Excuse me?" I blinked.

He rubbed his forehead, sighing. "You don't seem to understand."

"Understand what?" I checked the room behind him, making sure there were no females in there. There was only a lavishly dressed large bed, an armoire, a kitchen nook, and a desk with inkpots and quills.

"Satisfied?" he said, brows high.

I lifted my chin. "What do you mean?"

With a half roll of his eyes, he stepped back. "This." Waving a hand, he said, "Exactly this. You chase me, but it's futile because you're not willing to actually do anything."

"And what would you have me do? Have you stay with me, make a life with me anyway?" I shook my head, laughing at how ridiculous it sounded. "What life would you have? How would you fare with the constant reminder that he is my husband, and therefore you will always remain my lover?"

His brows and tone knitted with impatience. "That is a question you should've asked weeks ago."

I almost growled, my temper burning. "What difference does it make?"

"Because weeks ago, I'd have told you I'd be happy to sleep on the floor of your rooms. I need no title. I already have one I don't particularly want. I only wanted you."

My roiling anger fled in the face of fear. Still, I was no coward. Even when confronted with questions I had a feeling I might not like the answer to. "And now?"

His cold eyes traveled my body, his top lip lifting. "Now, I'd be happy to never see you again."

I pushed the door open before he could close it in my face. "You terminated your marriage."

"You assume that is all your doing?" His eyes twinkled with incredulity. "I'm not sorry to inform you that not everything revolves around you." When I gaped at him, he reached for a strand of my hair, looping it around his finger, his thumb stroking. "She did not wish to remain married to a male who'd linked with someone else, and I do not blame her."

Balance was hard to maintain as I tried to absorb what he wasn't saying, not that I had room to argue. I couldn't help myself. "But you would've remained married."

He released my hair, his eyes roaming mine in that way they did when he was waiting for me to figure something out. Turning away from me, he walked to the window that overlooked the harbor. "You can leave now."

I wanted to stomp my foot, then march over and demand he look at me. "I don't want to."

Slipping his hands inside his pockets, he said in a tone that reeked of indifference, "It was not a request."

"But I am your queen."

"No." He threw a wolfish smile at me over his shoulder. "You may be a queen, but you are not mine."

"You do not mean that," I said, voice quaking.

"I do," he said, too firm. "You once told me a queen can do whatever she damn well pleases. So if it were me you truly wanted, you would have taken me already." Unhurried, his bare feet ate the space between us. "You chose not to, and not for the sake of the continent, but for the sake of your dark heart." He leaned closer, his scent and voice dizzying, as he said low, "You prefer it black. You prefer it hurt rather than feel good because then you needn't worry about someone destroying it again. So this game of push and pull that makes you feel safe?" he said. "I will play it no more."

With that, he slammed the door, and I couldn't even bring myself to knock or force it open. A dagger was cutting through my insides as I bit my lip, tasting copper on the way out.

※

Hope. It was hope that carried the most buoyant type of joy.

It was hope that was the most addictive feeling of all—that sense of such euphoric happiness lying just out of reach.

You can smell it. Taste it. Imagine it. Long for it.

And that is why hope is the most dangerous foe of all.

For when that glimmer of happiness falls away, slips from reach and from sight, you don't just fall. You plummet.

And many do not survive the impact.

A ship filled with trading goods was entering the harbor.

I watched its captain at the helm, and the way he slowly grew into a more detailed man the closer he brought the vessel to the docks.

He was hairy. His face and his long hair gray. A human covered in tattoos we'd often hear about in neighboring countries. Countries that would trade with us but nothing else.

To them, we were a land of monsters. Tyrants with too much power within our midst.

Certain beings were better left inside the pages of a book in order to sleep well each night. It would do us and the rest of the world no good to acknowledge our existence too closely. Someone might get a bright idea. Or a dark one.

And there were some wars you couldn't win, no matter how much power you possessed.

A blue tail peeked through the waves created by the long ship, then a glimpse of gray.

A mermaid.

So many said they rarely saw them, the creatures of Beldine who roamed its bordering seas.

They were the very reason I stopped to stare at the water, even at the expense of gawkers and mothers asking me to wish their babes well.

I saw them often. Though never up close. I wasn't sure I wanted to, for I wasn't sure what it was I'd see.

Some said they were beautiful; true sirens who would draw many men to their deaths.

Some said they looked like regular human women. Some pretty, some not so much, and some in between.

Some said they were the true monsters of the sea, not the serpents or the sharks or sea dragons, but the women with bodies who lured and faces that would chase a child into nightmares for the rest of their existence.

Some said they had no souls and would forever search for them in the still beating hearts of mortals.

Your heart is about as good as the existence of your soul—a rotten fucking lie.

Had he meant such cruelty? I should've known better than to

even wonder. The lord was born with a tongue that could so casually cut through any adversary, no matter how he felt for them. He could be cold and indifferent, but never in this way.

"They like the ships," Truin said, appearing next to me.

I didn't look over at her. I kept my chin on my arms, which were folded over the wooden railing used to shield the residents of the city from the sharp rocks fringing the ice-flecked waters below.

"You see them, too."

"All my life."

"Have you ever met one?"

She laughed. "No. Most likely, no one has. Or they haven't lived to tell the tale."

"What tale do you think that would be?"

She was quiet a moment, as if thinking about it. "I've no idea. When I was a girl, I'd sometimes wonder if they could meet a handsome prince, kiss him, and then grow legs. And if that was why they called them sirens."

"Did you think they'd kill the prince after getting what they wanted?"

"Horrid," she said, smiling wide. "No, I did not."

"I bet they would," I said, smiling a little myself as another tail flapped through the water behind the slowing ship, this one orange. "I would."

"You know," she said, "I don't know if you would."

My eyes snapped to hers, and she grinned, as if that were her plan. Gradually, her smile sank, and a tiny crease formed between her bending brows. "I'm sorry I left last night."

I gazed back at the water, sighing as I straightened. "It's fine. I'm just glad you attended at all."

She joined me heading up the slow incline that bordered the city, wrapping around it like a noose toward the mountains where the castle sat, waiting. "Did Ainx escort you home?"

"And Berron."

I nodded, dodging a puddle of sludge that had once been snow.

"You look as though you did not sleep." Truin pulled her fur coat tighter around her shoulders against the winter breeze. "I heard some things in the market this morning."

"Such as?"

She waved her hand. "Oh, just that the king and the lord fought to the death for ownership of your heart."

We both laughed, and then I informed her of what truly happened.

"He's frustrated, by the sounds of it," she said.

"I know." I just didn't know what to do to fix it.

We rounded the corner, then cut through an alleyway to a shorter one, the breeze whistling through the buildings either side of it. "Perhaps I need to show up at his manor naked."

Truin snorted. "You could, or you could just tell him how you—"

She screamed, but it was cut off as she fell.

I hadn't the chance to remove the blade from my thigh. Before Truin had even hit the ground, something heavy slammed into the side of my head, and then I was falling into black nothing.

THIRTY-FOUR

If rainbows had a scent, I imagined that this place I'd awoken in, teeming with trees that curled together in faceless shapes against a bright cloudless sky, was it.

Blinking up at it, I struggled to keep my eyes open as hushed and hurried voices began to crawl inside my ears.

My head pounded, and when I glimpsed to my left, I saw why.

Vadella. I'd requested the stone be destroyed after being stuck in the ground what felt like many moons ago with Berron, yet I wasn't naïve enough to believe those were the only ones that existed, and that we'd find them all.

This one was smaller, the glittering demon no bigger than my head. Reaching for it, I found it wasn't just pounding because of the stones' proximity. My hand came away wet, and my eyes struggled to focus on my fingers when I brought them to my face to inspect them.

But I could smell it as well as feel it. Blood. So they—whoever brought me to this rainbow-scented place—hadn't relied solely on the rock's effects to render me incapable. I'd been struck over the head. I wanted to sit up, the urge to was so strong, but I feared how much worse my head would feel if I did.

The voices became clearer, closer, and I closed my eyes.

"Bring the witch."

Truin. The harbor and then the alleyways came back to me in fogged patches.

My eyes flung open of their own accord, anger funneling through me like a building cyclone ready to unfurl. But it couldn't.

Thanks to the rock, it could go nowhere, snuffed out like a cinder hitting damp brick.

"Good," a female voice said. "She's awake."

I was yanked by the shoulders, but I wrenched away. My hands sank into sand so soft, it felt like liquid, as I sat up, groaning behind clenched teeth.

But it wasn't just any female, I discovered when my vision cleared enough to focus. "Amelda?"

She kicked at my ankle. "Quiet."

"What is the meaning of this?" I tried to stand, but I was knocked down, my teeth clacking with the impact.

Amelda swiftly tied my wrists behind me. "You'll soon see."

Squelching sounded as a young male who I didn't recognize dragged Truin over the sand.

Glancing behind me, I noticed the harsh brightness of water, the way the sand darkened to a creamy gold to greet it.

And I noticed the trees and coastline across it in the far-off distance. My home, the mountains of which I'd so often climbed and sat upon, were nothing but specks on the haze-dusted horizon. Which could only mean one thing.

I was in the long lost west.

A land that had been cut away from our own many millennia ago. Beldine.

But of course, this was only a small slice of a forbidden land. A small island that wouldn't exist if the tide swept in, of which I knew, it wouldn't. Not even the tide could smother land as ancient as this. And where its mother was, the landscape I'd only heard of in whispers and folklore throughout my younger years, I didn't know. I couldn't see it.

Shimmering blue was all that existed on either side of us.

Upon the shore, some ways down, was a boat that had seen far better days. "You brought us here in a boat that small?" I couldn't help but blurt. "Have you no mind for what lurks beneath the waters of this place?"

Amelda tutted. "You did not arrive here by boat. I vanished you here."

So she was the vanisher.

Her eyes gleamed at whatever she saw in my own. "That's right. Those idiots who captured you were supposed to hand you over to me, but despite all the coin I'd paid them, I was duped."

"The king…" I started, trying and failing to string the pieces together.

"Oh, fear not. For though your dear husband, upon finding out what I could do, hired me to play spy on the useless noble snobs in your court, he was not, and is still not, aware of all the ways I used the position he'd given me to my own advantage." Amelda cackled, this rich and tinkering sound I'd not heard before. Or perhaps where we were brought its real sound to life. "But you needn't bother worrying over this or your safety, queen. We have plans for you."

Truin collapsed to the sand at least ten feet from me, and I quickly looked her over, finding a huge bruise, crusted with blood, upon her temple.

Her lips wriggled even as her eyes glowed with unshed tears—her way of trying to tell me she was all right.

We were so far from all right it wasn't even remotely funny.

Sighing, I decided to play. It wasn't as if I had any choice in the matter. My powers, my hands, were tied. Literally. "And pray tell, what are these plans, oh, deceptive one?"

Amelda was unpacking what appeared to be a small cauldron, jars of insects, and sand and dirt and leaves beside it. "You may as well know," she said with a resigned tone, unscrewing a jar and tipping what looked to be large beetles inside the cauldron.

The male made a sound of warning. She disregarded him and picked up a pail from behind her, trudging to the small, lapping waves to scoop up both sand and water inside it. "A decade ago, a queen was brought here by request of the king."

Truin's eyes tracked Amelda's every move as she poured the contents of the pail into the cauldron.

"You see, the foolish queen had not only betrayed her husband by associating with creatures of Beldine but she had also gone and fallen in love with one."

My stomach dropped, and I looked over my shoulder to the kingdom behind me, to the barely there glimpse of a home I wondered if I'd ever see again.

"Many believe the Fae to be cruel creatures who were therefore hunted and unwelcome in Rosinthe." She paused, a lick of a smile curving her lips as she glanced at me. "And while that may be true, it is not the entire truth."

The male cut in, "Amelda, we are running out of time."

Tilting my head back, I tried to make out his features, muted by the burning sun and unbearable glow of the vast blue water and sky. "Who are you?"

He shifted, not looking at me as he scoffed. "Of course, you would not know of who I am."

"He made it so," Amelda said. "I am muddied, my father was Fae and my mother a royal."

"And you?" I asked the male.

"Pinn. Fae." He crouched down, baring his teeth for me to see his longer canines, and when he removed his spectacles, tossing them over his shoulder to splash into the water, black eyes replaced brown. I knew Fae ears were hiding beneath his long white blond curls. "I've lived with a kind nursemaid in the village for a decade, just waiting for this day."

"More than waiting," I said. "A lot of planning must have gone into whatever this is."

"I've heard you're not one for mindless chatter. I've even witnessed it myself. Tell me," Amelda said, her turquoise eyes glittering, "when you are afraid, does that cold tongue come unglued?"

"And why would I have need to be afraid?" I knew it was stupid to goad her, but old habits die hard.

"Because today is the day you meet your end. The same way your mother did."

She was insane. "I see. And what of Adran? Does he know of this?"

Her non-answer intrigued, but I couldn't ask much else. The male, Pinn, trudged over, and then I was gagged, and Truin finally spoke up. "What is it you hope to do with the contents of that cauldron?"

"I'm merely preparing it for you, witch. Don't worry." Amelda shot her an unconvincing smile. "You'll be free to leave once you've done your part."

Pinn chuckled. "If you can make it across the Whispering Sea, that is. Might want to give that old boat a try. Darkness knows how long it's been here for, but it's bound to be better than swimming."

Truin's eyes jumped to mine, filled with fear. She knew then. She'd figured out what nasty things would transpire on this little patch of magical land.

A dagger, rusted around the hilt but sharp as the sun hit its edge, was plucked from the sand.

I dug deep, as deep as I could, filling my head with thoughts of burning threads of revenge, but all that rewarded me with was a headache that threatened to explode my skull.

Truin screamed as she was dragged before the cauldron, which was now gurgling with a faint steam rising into the air.

Amelda lowered to her knees beside me, the hem of her skirts wet and covered in sand. "A heart for a heart will keep them apart, but the heart of that heart will eradicate the dark."

I felt my heart race within the throb of my skull as all Amelda had said became clear.

They planned to drain me.

My mother wasn't torn apart by savages. At least, that wasn't how she'd died.

She been brought here to drain for her uncontrollable heart. As punishment to both her and Kash for committing treason.

"Yes," Amelda said, watching me. "Your father was wicked in so many ways, but this one takes the cake. Beldine is blocked, no one can enter and no one can leave. All because of his bloodthirsty need for revenge."

"You will die today, but not without good cause. We just want to go home, and there is no other way," Pinn said, then to Amelda, "Let us begin."

I refused to beg for mercy. For years, I'd told myself that when my time came, there would be no pleading, no bargaining, only dismal acceptance of my fate.

I was a queen, and I would die as one should. With grace and dignity.

I leaped to my feet, kicking Amelda in the cheek, then raced for the rock. My foot panged, my head screaming, as I kicked it as hard as I could to the water.

It rolled to its edge, the frothy blue trying to swallow it, but though Truin tried to stop him, Pinn backhanded her, and got there quicker.

I backed up to the water, unsure what I'd do once I reached it, but not really caring.

Unshed tears shone in Truin's eyes, and her chest began to heave. "You can't do this. She is our queen. There will be war."

To that, both creatures just smiled, Amelda wincing as she rubbed her cheek. "No one has ever dared to start a war they could never win."

She was right. To wage war against Beldine was a death sentence.

The ruler of their continent, I'd heard, was not only cunning but also lazy. Which was the reason we'd been able to co-exist alongside them for so many years.

Until now.

Darkness only knew what they'd decide to do should the block be removed, and they learn who was responsible for it.

"This is dark magic," Truin said. "The darkest there is. There will be a cost."

"We've already decided, naturally, that the queen's life is of little importance to us." Amelda snarled as I reached the water. "You will kneel before the waters of those you have trapped, and you will bleed."

I shook the gag loose, pushed at it with my tongue, and spat it on the ground. A lemon printed kerchief. "I'd rather not."

"You think to swim with your hands bound? We'd catch you."

She was right, but I wasn't about to admit it. I turned for the water, about to throw myself in, when the male grabbed me around the waist and carried me to the other side of our little island.

I kicked and writhed, but it was no use.

I was set down next to the cauldron, the water taunting my knees as it lapped over the sand. With a yank harsh enough to tear hair from my scalp, the male glowered in my face. "Try to move again, and I'll bludgeon you. We don't need you conscious."

"Such a kindness," I said, sarcasm heavy.

Amelda's bare foot collided with my back, knocking the wind from me.

I coughed, bent over the water, as Truin began to cry. "No, no. I won't. I refuse."

Staring up through my lashes to the endless sea beyond, I tried to imagine a continent there. An ever-stretching land my father had shut off from the rest of the world through his own greed and hatred.

It wasn't right. That did not mean I would ever agree to forfeit my life for their freedom if given the option, but I had no option. So I supposed there were worse things to die for.

I wondered if my mother thought the same thing when they'd drained her life from her body. If it had been worth it.

"Truin," I said, glancing at her over my shoulder.

She was sobbing, tears lacing her cheeks in wet ribbons, as Pinn and Amelda struggled to keep her before the cauldron. Slowly, she calmed, and I nodded.

She shook her head, but whatever she saw in my face had her conceding, her shoulders falling heavily as Amelda told her what she needed to say and do.

"A heart for a heart will keep them apart, but the heart of that heart will eradicate the dark."

Turning my face back to the water, I closed my eyes, but reopened them when eyes of glowing amber filled the back of my lids.

Truin stuttered over the incantation a few times, but as I was shoved to the sand, the ends of my hair falling into the cool water, and a blade sliced open my wrist and foot, she began to say it right.

I hardly felt the sting thanks to the two limbs being submerged in the sea.

But I did feel regret.

Insurmountable, it began to build behind my open eyes—created the urge to scream at them to stop. To give me a little more time to fix all that was still broken before I left.

In the darkness, I told myself, his smile coming forth, the affection that brimmed his eyes and re-sculpted his face from something bored and sinister to a priceless artifact you longed to stare at day in and day out. The years I'd spent darting away from him as though he'd ruin all my fun before I was ready. The countless months he'd been by my side, providing counsel I'd consistently snarled at while trying to staunch my bleeding heart. The many weeks he refused to leave when I gave him every reason to.

The times he'd saved me, not just from danger but from myself.

He couldn't save me now, so I'd carry him with me.

Find me in the darkness, I whispered to the gathering wind, hoping he'd hear it somehow.

It was strange, feeling your life leave your body. I hadn't known what to expect when I'd done the same to those who'd betrayed me and their kingdom, but it wasn't this.

A peaceful swaying while lying perfectly still.

The sound of the water and Truin's voice were beginning to fade as I realized with a gradually moving sadness that I'd never bear a child.

I had no heir, but that part didn't bother me as much as

knowing I'd never get the chance to grow a babe inside my womb and birth him or her into their father's strong and gentle hands.

The lord would make a wonderful father.

Turning my head slightly, my stuttered exhale stirring grains of sand, I saw a world of red colliding with blue. A brilliant purple, the likes of which I doubted any had seen before, unfurled, rolling with unnatural speed into the depths beyond.

Each breath grew loud, too loud, in my ears, and I fought to keep my eyes open.

With her long brown hair falling over her shoulder, glossy and almost as vibrant as the blue of her eyes, she swept her fingers across my brow. "Wait," she said. A tear slid down my cheek and her finger collected it. "Just a little longer."

"I'm…" It hurt to swallow, to even rasp, "I'm scared."

Her angelic face creased, eyes filling with tears that would never fall. "Brave girl, let me sing you a song."

Suddenly, she was no longer touching me, but seated atop the water clouded with my blood, with two babes in either arm.

My brothers.

One had inky black hair and bright, forest green eyes that didn't smile, but rather, seemed to look through you. Rahn. Jonnis was smiling, his dimpled cheeks smooshing his deep blue eyes as he sucked on his fist.

My mother bounced them a little, humming as she did.

I wanted to touch them, tried to, but I could no longer lift my arm. It was as if it did not exist even though I could see it, drifting just below the surface of the purple-colored ocean.

"Little princess, little princess don't you sigh, these stars will want your every smile. Little princess, little princess don't you weep, it's past time you went to sleep. Little princess, little princess it's all right, Mommy's love will see you through the night…"

The male, I'd already forgotten what his name was, began to shout, and I heard Truin pause, but not before I saw shadows begin to take shape.

A clang sounded, faint, and so was the scream that followed.

My lips parted, shallow bursts of air moving between them. My mother looked up, then down at me, her eyes still glistening. "He comes."

Then she and my brothers were gone. I screamed for her to come back, but I couldn't hear it leave my tight throat.

Trees faded in and out of view, taller than any trees I'd ever seen before, and among them, I swore I saw huts and homes.

A tail flicked. Blue or green, I wasn't sure. Everything became a muted, duller shade of its true color. It made sense the darkness would steal it all. It made sense and... Two red eyes peered at me from beneath the water, pink lips shaping around words I couldn't hear or make out. Her bronzed skin shimmered, her green hair clouding around her oval face as she repeated herself. "Hold on," I think she said.

A waste of time, I thought, smiling slightly. A mermaid.

Then my wrist was in her cool, long-fingered hand. My eyelids flickered as I wondered if she'd tear my limb from my body or perhaps take a bite of my flesh, but the green-haired creature only covered my wound with her hand.

I would've flinched had I the energy as I felt another hand wrap around my foot and watched the merwoman exchange a look with something I could not see.

My eyelids continued to flutter, and my chest ached with the urge to breathe when I couldn't. I tried, but it burned, and I coughed.

My sight began to thin even more, everything turning a muted shade of gray. I coughed again and began to heave, and that angry part of me tried to contain what little life remained inside me.

And then I was pulled away from the water, from the mermaids, the scent of mint and sun soaked winter mornings registering inside my fractured mind.

"She needs tending to," I heard Truin say. "She won't make it."

"We need to leave, now," someone said. It sounded like Kash, and then everything was black once more.

I woke alone, feeling as though I'd taken an axe to the back of my head, and immediately shut my eyes.

Dreams of a land far off the coastline held me captive. Its giant trees and soft as butter sand and its rainbow scent carrying me on a phantom breeze, high above in the cloudless sky. Of mermaids with evil eyes but kind mouths and hands that saved.

I woke five more times before I was finally able to keep my eyes open, and when I could, I found the lord seated beside my bed, reading.

For a time, I just listened, relieved to hear his velvet smooth voice. "…And her grandmother said, 'those who wake wanting will forever roam unsatisfied.' The child peered up at her, unsure what the old crone meant, and not so sure she cared…" He paused, his eyes lifting from the page.

"Did it work?"

Zadicus closed the book, the leg that had been resting over his knee dropping to the floor. Somber eyes, riddled with concern, fell on me. "Yes."

I nodded, knowing the implications of that could be vast, but also knowing I was in no state to worry right now. "Do I resemble a corpse?"

He laughed, a dry, tired sound, and rubbed his hand over his whiskered chin. "You've never looked more beautiful."

"Liar," I croaked.

"I would never lie to you." Rising, he dropped the book to the chair, then came to the bed. "You're alive, and that makes you the most wondrous, stunning thing I've ever seen."

My throat felt tight, words unable to form. His smile was soft as he reached for the pitcher and poured me some water.

He helped me sit up, and my hand shook when I tried to grab the goblet, so he held it to my lips and carefully tipped until I'd drunk it all.

Falling back to my pillows, I felt my eyes flutter. "Don't leave."

He didn't respond, but he stayed.

When I woke again, I watched him for a time. His eyes were shut, his hands clasped over his stomach, but I knew he was not sleeping. "You knew of Beldine, and of what happened to my mother?"

His eyes opened, and he stared at me for a long minute before finally saying, "I knew of Beldine's fate, but I was not aware of how it had happened. Not until the night of the ball when Kash finally decoded your father's journal."

Traces of memory raced in. "The one you had at your estate?"

He nodded once. "After seeing him with it, just the once, and how confused he'd looked as he'd stared at it in his study, I'd never forgotten. So I took it after he died. It wasn't full of admissions so much as nonsensical ramblings. As though he'd tried to take up the pastime of journaling to aid in keeping his mind longer." He brushed his thumb over his bottom lip. "As his thoughts grew more erratic, so did the entries. Some were nothing more than scribbled, unrecognizable drawings."

"What," I started, gathering scrambled thoughts. "What was it that made you realize?"

"A picture of a heart, large in size, and a smaller one beneath it. It was his last entry."

I wasn't sure what to make of that. Why he'd left behind evidence, however poor, of what he'd done.

As if knowing so, Zad murmured, "Perhaps some tiny entity inside him, a fragment of who he once was and could have been, resurfaced. It would make sense," he said. "For there were not many entries after you were born."

Numb, I absorbed that for some moments, staring down at my bedsheets. "So you finally figured it out." Remembering how he'd left the ball around the same time Amelda had, I shot accusing eyes at him. "You also knew what Amelda was planning, and you did not deign to warn me."

Seeming unaffected by my tone, he stated blandly, "No."

"Then what?" I snapped, tired of his carefully said truths. "How?"

"We knew she was up to something, but we lost her that evening. Landen discovered her whereabouts the following morning." Sighing, he straightened in the chair, leaning forward to clasp his hands between his knees as he looked at me. "Kash and I followed you when you left the Rosaleen, but we lost you when you headed back to the castle with Truin. By the time we found the alleyway you'd been taken from, you were gone. They were quick, too quick."

"She's a vanisher," I supplied.

His brows lifted, and he continued. "And so it took far longer than I'd have liked to find you." A hand dragged down his face as he said those last words, as though he were reliving the moments all over again.

"How did you figure it out?"

He smiled down at his hands. "Fae senses are rather... extraordinary. We assumed it would need to be in proximity to Beldine, and once we'd hit the water, I could feel you."

I stared at him as he crossed to the bed and fed me water, and I stared some more as he smoothed the hair back from my forehead. "Sleep."

"We need to—"

"Sleep, Audra. There will be time for that later."

"Promise?" I asked, my eyelids closing when his fingers swept down my cheek.

He did not answer me.

The following morning, Truin and Azela were trying to force food into me, and I knew without asking that he was gone.

THIRTY-FIVE

A MONTH CRAWLED BY, AND I SLOWLY REGAINED MY strength, but the lord of the east did not return.

After a week, I wrote him and received no response.

I wrote him one more time before I made myself stop, fearing the messengers might sneak a look at what I'd written—even though I'd been careful to word it plainly—and have themselves a good laugh at my expense.

I would have rode there myself, but I was quick to tire while my body tried to regenerate all that it'd lost to the Whispering Sea, and the land it had helped uncover. And the thought of going all that way only to have him reject me yet again… I preferred to tend to the battered remains of my heart in private, and such a thing would not happen with my guard accompanying me.

I was alive, a miracle I often caught myself marveling over. I was alive and angry and at a loss for what it was the stubborn lord wanted from me.

As it turned out, my cousin was aware that Amelda had less than desirable plans for me, but he had thought she was all talk, and he enjoyed her in his bed too much to come to me. With an honesty I respected, he'd stated simply that he and his mother had never much cared for me. That did not mean he wished me dead, he'd said. It meant he did not care to stop it.

As punishment, I'd sent him over to Beldine with a boatload of goods as a token of apology, and then I'd made sure the ship left without him.

He could stay, or he could swim. I didn't much care, just as he hadn't when he'd decided to sleep with someone who needed me dead.

Whether the token had been received well, or received at all, I wasn't sure. The captain of the ship had returned and informed us it was done, the packages and my cousin left upon their shores.

As for Amelda... I'd given her to Raiden, being that she was supposed to be working for him, and not for her own nefarious cause. It wasn't long before he gave me the gift of her hand, stating the rest of her had been incinerated.

I leaned back against my throne, yawning as Mintale delivered the past month's mail.

Raiden had said he'd sort through it with me to help get the tedious task out of the way as fast as possible.

After the lord had left my bed chamber, the king had taken his place. He'd been silent, a guard I wasn't sure whether I could trust, seated in the shadows beside my bed.

As the days passed, I'd decided he probably could be trusted, even after all he'd done. For if he wanted me dead, he had many hours in which he could've carried out the task with little to no fight from me.

He returned to the Sun Kingdom the following week and arrived here again just yesterday.

"An issue with an irrigation system," Raiden said, his nose crinkling as he no doubt struggled to understand the contents of the letter.

"Riveting," I muttered, sorting the read from the unread.

"What in the darkness do they think we can do about such matters? I've no idea what he's even blathering on about."

"Pass it on to Mintale." That was what I did with most of them anyway.

"Oh, look, another love letter." With a loathsome amount of glee to his movements, Raiden unfolded it, then frowned. "Damn, this one's for you, and it's... quite long." His brows jumped. "Detailed."

I snatched it from him, growling when I read who it was from, and balled it up to throw it across the room.

"So it's not from your lord?"

"Shut up."

He chuckled.

Inkerbine, the first one since the kings return, was the following week, so we had agreed he'd return to oversee the preparations with me.

Raiden watched Mintale scurry out of the throne room, then looked at me. "We should talk."

"About?" Judging by his cautious tone, I would much prefer we didn't.

"Your linkage to the lord."

I lowered the letter I'd been reading to my lap. "There is naught to be done about it."

Raiden's lips rolled, and he nodded. "I know, and I'm making peace with that." His tone brooked sincerity. "Trying to."

"I do not wish to remain married to you, and you know it." I drew in a quick breath. "If you refuse to agree out of it, then you must deal with what I do within it."

His eyes stayed on the ground between his splayed legs. After a moment, he lifted them to me, a brow arching. "Then you must deal as well."

Our eyes stayed locked, a silent battle of wills that would never end, until finally, I conceded, "Why won't you just agree to terminate it?" The very thought alone excited me to no end. To have my castle, my land, and my prickly lord back...

"Because," Raiden murmured, giving his eyes back to the pages before him. "Not only does the continent need this marriage, but as we both know, I do not walk away from things I want."

"You cannot possibly want me anymore."

Without looking at me, he shrugged. "I do, but most importantly, I want to remain king of Rosinthe."

Of course, he did.

From behind the podium, I watched as the sun began to set. People, young and old and magical and everything in between, spread all the way to the horizon.

A scent I'd remember until my dying breath, of sweets and rainbows and pine and many things I could no longer name, clouded.

Kash clasped his hands behind him, staring straight ahead.

After observing his unreadable, sharp profile, I did the same. "How?"

"I'd been watching the female for a few weeks after she tried to bed me. Mainly due to the vague way she'd spoken, as if she wanted to share something she couldn't."

I nodded. "Was I bait then? A way for you to go home?"

His tone carried humor. "I am still here, am I not?"

"Does your king frighten you that much?"

Kash chuckled, and I stiffened at the rare, heavily deep sound. "That is not why I remain."

I absorbed that for a moment, watching as Mintale berated a scowling local squire. "I saw her." I cleared my throat. "I saw them."

Kash stilled, and when I felt his eyes on me, I gave him mine. "She seemed… happy. At peace," I said, unsure if it was true, but hoping it was. "With her babes."

His lips parted, his eyes began to shimmer, and I felt mine well. He studied me as though weighing what it meant for me to see her. Knowing it meant everything and nothing. His Adam's apple shifted, and then he faced forward again. "I am glad."

Zadicus, accompanied by his two other friends, sifted through the crowd to the side of the podium that had been erected upon the border.

The soft swaths of my dress, a deep dark blue, tickled my arms as a cool breeze arrived. Between the land of winter and summer, it was perpetually spring, and I couldn't say it wasn't growing on me as I watched the golden-orange leaves flutter and twirl to the ground.

The array of pink cast over the large clearing between two villages livened the gold and silver ribbons that danced from tall maypoles. Vendors were preparing feasts from carts, saturating the air with the scents of sizzling pork and spiced chicken.

A night of dancing, eating, and getting to know thy neighbor in various ways was underway, as it had been in the center of each year for centuries.

Regardless of the rumors of what'd happened to my mother, any violence on Inkerbine was not tolerated, and people stopped trying and learned to cool their tempers and hostilities many years ago. To act out in any way was to die by the crown's hand the following day.

I had hope that, like the ball, everyone behaved, and this alliance I couldn't escape was not for nothing.

Kash bristled as Raiden and his advisor, Patts, approached. Patts joined Mintale on the podium where they fussed over the thrones that were used each Inkerbine and erected the megaphone upon a stand of steel.

"You look delicious," Raiden whispered, and Kash shifted beside me.

I smoothed a hand over my hair, which I'd left down, and straightened my crown. "Are you ready?" I didn't wait for his answer. I held my hand in the air, and slowly, he dragged his eyes from me and laid his arm out for it to rest upon.

Mintale and Patts joined Kash behind the podium, Zad choosing to remain at the side.

I didn't allow myself the treat of gazing at him, for it was no treat. It was staring an addiction in the face, knowing you could no longer have it. It was allowing the festering ache inside to throb in harsh, breath-stealing waves.

Silence greeted us as the crowd settled, and Raiden approached the megaphone, his smile large. "Welcome to Inkerbine, a celebration of peace and love." Clapping and whistles and shouts ensued, and he waited for them to quiet before continuing. "It is our great pleasure to introduce this year's Inkerbine as not two halves of a country celebrating peace but as a unified whole." More shouts and clapping as arms holding candles lifted into the air.

I stared at our people, then at the king wearing his giant grin and crown beside me, and I knew he'd prattle on, speaking for the both of us.

Too bad what he had to say was of little importance compared to what I'd planned, and in any case, I was done letting him take the lead in this partnership.

I lifted my chin, and with as little movement as possible, I nudged him out of the way.

I didn't look at him, but I could feel him frowning as he grudgingly stepped aside, making room for me to talk.

"Before we begin," I said, my voice carrying over the faces before me, to the trees surrounding us, to the foothills in the distance. "There are some amendments to the law that must be made known at once."

As though a faucet had been shut off, the excitement in the air evaporated, and murmuring began. "Almost eleven years ago, a law came into place regarding who is believed by some to be the ancestors of royals." I gave them a moment, then said, "The Fae were hunted, chased from this land that had always welcomed them, and that had been home to them before our existence was even a speck on the growing horizon."

More and more were coming out of hiding, but their presence was stirring unrest, and it needed to be dealt with swiftly. "From this evening forward, should any harm befall a creature of any sex, of any age, by the hands of a human, mixed blood, or royal, the punishment shall be instantaneous and unmerciful." I paused for effect and then gazed back at the stunned faces before me. "Death."

I waited for that to sink in, expecting outrage or distress, yet there was only silence, and as I peered at some of the faces in the first rows surrounding the podium, even some smiles.

Drawing in a quick breath, I went on. "As you all know, any royal and human who mate and give birth to a healthy mixed blood must surrender their offspring to the king and queen when that offspring comes of age." I paused. "From this evening forward, all mixed bloods will remain with their rightful parents or guardians until they so wish to leave of their own accord, and they may take up whatever job or education they desire."

Screams cleaved the burgeoning night, and my heart kicked forcefully as thunderous clapping sounded.

Lifting a hand, I motioned for quiet. "However, due to their magical abilities, no matter how little, they must attend training within the castle grounds as soon as they come of age. Failure to enroll your offspring into the training program will mean they forfeit their right for a free life. Should they be discovered"—I glanced around—"and we all know they will be, they will serve under the crown's command until their dying breaths."

A deathly still moment saturated my lungs, and then more clapping took place.

Looking over the miles of people spread toward the forest and foothills, I discovered some were weeping.

Weeping with gratitude.

I frowned, then hovered over the megaphone once more. "You will find the punishments for breaking any law during my reign harsh. You will also find archaic and barbaric laws crushed over the following months as we revise and amend them, and new ones are put in place." I raised my chin. "You will soon find there is a difference between good and evil." Everyone quietened, grew completely silent, as I finished with, "That difference is me."

I stepped back from the megaphone, then placed my hand in Raiden's.

Crickets chirped as the updated law was passed around, whispers growing louder into chatter that eventually ceased when

Raiden and I walked toward the two awaiting torches either side of the stage.

Patts handed Raiden sticks, and Raiden set the tips aflame, Mintale bringing one to me. Together, we lit the torches at the same time, then stepped back to watch sparks of silver and gold fly high into the sky.

Joining hands again, we walked to the steps, when the rumbles and crying and screaming formed a sentence that paused Raiden's feet, and then my own.

My eyes swam as their chanting became clear, but I couldn't turn around. I could hardly breathe as I registered what they were saying.

"Long live the queen, long live the queen!"

Amused, Raiden's eyes met mine, and then he turned back, raising my arm into the air as their ear-shredding cries rose higher than the trees surrounding all of us.

I could've killed him, but I stood still, staring unseeing to the dark sky atop our heads while I tried to keep my eyes dry.

Once we were safely down the steps, Truin hurried over, stealing me from Raiden in a breathless hug. "You are magic, my queen."

I hugged her back, overwhelmed with gratitude that I could, and then joined Raiden in the tent set up a ways back from the roaring celebration and protected by a thick circle of guards.

Inside, he spun to clasp my cheeks, staring at me with an intensity that, once upon a time, would've lit my chest on fire. Now, I only felt a flickering ember of affection.

"Wicked and cold and fair and unforgettable," he said in a rush, his hands tightening. "Audra, the unforgettable, we, *you*, have made history."

I grabbed his hands, removing them from my face. "There is still more to be done."

"And I cannot be more thankful that it is happening, and that I get to be right by your side as we erase all that rots this land together."

With a genuine smile tugging at my lips, I nodded but took a step back. "I must go."

Raiden's brows gathered as he poured himself a goblet of wine. "You will not stay and celebrate with our people?"

"Do not guilt me," I said. "My job is done, and I am tired." It took a lot for me to admit as much, but I had to, else I fall prey to dizziness in front of the wrong people.

For as much as I'd hopefully swayed those who once wished me ill, I wasn't a fool. Many would still see me as they wanted to forevermore.

Raiden paused in lifting his drink to his mouth and nodded. With a soft smile, he approached and laid a kiss upon my brow. "Fair enough, my queen. I'll see you in one moon."

He would be returning home at first light, and I would see him again in a month's time to resume the work of amending the other barbaric laws and begin work on brokering new trade opportunities with neighboring countries who'd rather ignore our existence.

The time for ignoring us was over. Especially when there was more to gain from doing business with us than ever before.

"Enjoy the festivities," I murmured, smirking.

Raiden only winked, lifting his goblet into the air before tipping its contents down his throat.

I opened the tent flaps and waded past dipping guards to the awaiting carriage.

Rounding the other side, I found my drivers over by the trees, and the reason as to why leaning against the carriage door, half cast in shadow. "Quite a speech."

I hadn't lied to Raiden about being tired, but even so, I was not in the mood for Zad's torturous presence. With a blank look at him, I gathered my skirts and opened the carriage door, forcing him back.

"Find me in the darkness."

My lungs and heart seized, and I turned to him.

His eyes shined as he straightened from the carriage. "I heard you."

"How?" The word was stolen by the breeze, though it was barely a sound to carry.

He'd heard it anyway. "The wind is the fastest messenger, and I must say…" Stopping before me, he curled his fingers around my cheek, and my knees quaked. "Never have I thought I'd end myself to be with someone. Not until that frightful day."

"You have a strange way of showing such devotion." I made myself climb inside, lowering to the velvet black seat. "Good evening and happy Inkerbine, my lord."

Zad grabbed the door, closing it when he'd leaped inside.

"Oh, really?" I dragged out, incredulous.

He smirked, taking a seat beside me. "Really."

Rage unfurled, one born of sheer, mind-bending frustration. "What is it you want? I've thrown myself at you, begged you, lowered myself to ridiculous standards all because I fucking love you, and you don't care. You just toy with me."

As if I'd stated the sky was blue, he said with too much calm, "You never said it."

"Said what?"

"That you love me."

"You already know I do."

"Maybe. Sometimes, I feel what you feel, but closing parts of yourself off to me is not an option. I've crept inside every dark space of yours. I've seen it all. I love it all. Yet you slam the doors after and expect me to knock every single time I seek entrance."

"I love you." It was all I could think to say. Then desperate, I asked, "Do you want me to risk war for you? Our very lives? Because I will. I'll get out of this marriage before a judge. I have enough to be released, and we'll see what happens."

"No."

"No?" I shook my head. "What do you mean no?" I was tempted to scream, unable to figure out what he needed. "It might not come to any of that, but should it happen, I wouldn't care—"

"Stop." He grabbed my face, his eyes boring into mine. "I just want you. Just Audra. So stop closing doors. Stop playing with me only when you see fit. Stop running from me and just be with me."

Relieved, I nodded, knowing he was right. I could do that. For him, for what I'd almost lost, I would try with all I had to do that. My lips wobbled, the command leaving me on a shaken breath. "Then you must never deceive me, and you must stay. You must stay and never leave."

"Audra," he said, throaty and heated. "When are you going to see that is all I've ever wanted? That *you* are all I need." Tears escaped, slipping down my cheeks. His hands tightened. "Better yet, when are you going to finally believe it?"

"When it happens," I said, for there was no mistaking what he felt, what I felt, but I couldn't lie, and I didn't want to. "When I see it with my own two eyes. When it becomes so normal it's bothersome and magical and tedious and all consuming."

His expression gentled, a laugh coating his exhale. "Okay," he said, lips grazing mine as he repeated himself. "Okay, my queen."

The carriage rocked as the drivers climbed into their seats outside, and we began to roll forward, dipping over tree roots and crevices until we reached the road. But his lips never parted from mine.

They refused to as he accompanied me home, where he remained all winter long.

THIRTY-SIX

Zadicus
Three months later

ACROSS A FIELD OF FROSTED WILDFLOWERS, THE QUEEN of winter twirled, her fingers dragging over ice-crusted petals and sweeping them up into the wind.

It followed her command and sent them high above her head. They fluttered to her awaiting beast, and he tensed in anticipation, his large claws digging giant trenches into the soil beneath us.

Vanamar's eyelids drooped as he caught them and swallowed, the steam from his nostrils clouding the air before us. Then he gazed back at his queen, content to watch, but hoping he'd be fortunate enough to receive more than just the sight of her.

I knew exactly how he felt, and with a sigh, I handed him the apple I'd been eating.

He licked it from my palm, teeth far larger than my hand appearing and gently grazing my skin.

I ran my hand over his soft coat, watching Audra weave a chain of wildflowers on her walk back to us.

"Can we sleep up here?"

I bit back a smile. "We would turn to ice. Besides," I said with a heaping dose of reluctance. "The king arrives tomorrow."

Much to his eternal annoyance, the king and queen continued to live separate lives. He would visit when needed, and she refused to step foot in the Sun Kingdom unless necessary, of which, thankfully, it hadn't been. At least, not yet.

I preferred her where I could see her, and not because I did not trust her or because I doubted her ability to fend for herself. There wasn't a creature in this land unaware of her prowess. But because a love like this necessitated closeness.

The king could have her in small increments, but never in the ways that I could.

I was happy to be nothing, so long as she was mine and mine alone. Besides, I would never be nothing to her, and that was all that mattered.

I was hers, and she was mine, and not even her rightful husband across the border could change that.

Approaching Van, Audra held the chain above his head, pouting. "He better leave when hinted at this time." She tutted when Van made to lunge for the flowers, and he huffed, plonking his rear to the ground once more. She gave them to him, and he carefully slurped them from her palm.

I doubted the king would take the many hints sent his way. His extended stays were mostly out of spite, empty minutes spent in endless stare downs with me over the dining table.

"What is this visit for?" I was beginning to think he'd make whatever excuses necessary to situate himself before the queen.

Audra scratched the underside of Van's chin. "To finalize the new trade route deals we've brokered."

I refrained from growling and rolling my eyes, knowing that could've been done without his presence.

Sensing my annoyance, Audra slunk toward me, a gleam in her sapphire eyes that never failed to make my heart stomp like a wanting, eager child.

She fell into my lap sideways, her arms draping around my neck as mine looped around the perfect curves of her waist, holding tight. With her lips whispering across my jaw, she said, "If you behave, I might let you ride Van."

I stilled, blinking. No one, not even his trainer, rode the beast.

Van, seemingly disinterested, snuffed at the grass in search of more flowers.

I took that as a good sign. "You mean it?" I asked, feeling my brows rise.

Her laughter was rain dancing over ice, quiet but beautiful all the same. "No playing, Lord. Remember?"

Swallowing, I nodded. "Now?"

She laughed again, pressing her lips to the corner of mine. "I'm no fool."

"And I'm always on my best behavior," I stated, meaning it. The struggle of being in the king's presence was unbelievable.

She pulled back to give me a bland look. "Death glares over dinner? Muttered insults veiled behind a cough? And let's not forget how you had me in the hall above his rooms…"

All perfectly reasonable things to do, I thought. Not too bad either, considering.

Clearly, she thought otherwise. "Okay." Scowling, I pursed my lips. "That doesn't mean I agree, but fine."

Brushing strands of hair that had escaped their tie from my cheek, her eyes searched mine, sobering. "Mintale says we are to discuss Beldine."

I failed to keep from stiffening beneath her, quickly saying, "What of it?"

Her eyes scrutinized momentarily. "Of the consequences that might befall us all."

Our home—an extricated limb of Beldine—Rosinthe, was a continent of peace once more.

The king of Beldine had never sought to reclaim their land. Of course, that was before Tyrelle had locked their continent away from the rest of the world for years, while many were none the wiser.

We had paid gravely for Tyrelle's sins, especially his daughter, but the creatures of Beldine did not care for trivial matters of who, when, and why.

They hadn't yet, but that did not mean they wouldn't come asking for who was responsible.

Or perhaps, they wouldn't bother asking.

My arms tightened around her. "If it happens, we'll face it, and we'll do what we can to make it right." Hollow words, even to my own ears, but there was little else I could say.

Eyeing me a moment, Audra nodded, then took in the view of Allureldin, the waters to the west that skirted The Edges. "Together," she murmured, barely audible above the whistling wind.

Grasping her cheek, I brought her mouth to mine, and promised, "Together, my eternal queen."

THE END

... for now

STAY IN TOUCH!

Instagram
www.instagram.com/ellafieldsauthor

Facebook page
facebook.com/authorellafields

Website
www.ellafields.net

ALSO BY ELLA FIELDS

STANDALONES:

Bloodstained Beauty
Serenading Heartbreak
Frayed Silk
Cyanide
Corrode

MAGNOLIA COVE:

Kiss and Break Up
Forever and Never
Hearts and Thorns

GRAY SPRINGS UNIVERSITY:

Suddenly Forbidden
Bittersweet Always
Pretty Venom

Printed in Great Britain
by Amazon